The Book of Dreams

CRAIG NOVA

THE
BOOK
OF
DREAMS

TICKNOR & FIELDS
NEW YORK 1994

For information about permission to reproduce selections
from this book, write to Permissions, Ticknor & Fields,
215 Park Avenue South, New York, New York 10003.

Library of Congress Cataloging-in-Publication Data
Nova, Craig.
The book of dreams / Craig Nova.
p.   cm.
ISBN 0-395-63650-7
1. Motion picture producers and directors — California
— Los Angeles — Fiction.   2. Man-woman relationships
— California — Los Angeles — Fiction.   3. Extortion —
California — Los Angeles — Fiction.   4. Hollywood
(Los Angeles, Calif.) — Fiction.   I. Title.
PS3564.086B66 1994
813'.54 — dc20   93-23343
CIP

Printed in the United States of America

AGM 10 9 8 7 6 5 4 3 2 1

This book is dedicated to
Christina Barnes Nova

As Solly Violinsky once remarked about Hollywood,
"No matter how warm it is in the daytime,
there's no place to go at night."
—*Groucho Marx*

*

But motives were mysterious,
fates unpredictable.
—*Tacitus*

BOOK
1

Warren Hodges

FOR A WHILE Warren Hodges *was* Hollywood. He went about his life in long, dark cars, the lights of the city showing on the hood and fenders as streaks of gold and silver, the colors somehow filled with all the promise of illusion. Sometimes a photograph would appear in the paper, taken in front of a club in the hills above Sunset, at Chez Pierre, say, of a long car with a young woman getting into it, her slender hands holding a small handbag while on the taut silk that covered her thighs there was a sheen of light, and as she slid over the leather seat, she looked as though she trailed a scent of flowers that grew in Eden. And there, in the darkness of the car (which was lighted by the sudden illumination of a flashbulb), Hodges sat, dressed in evening clothes, his shoulders broad, his hair combed straight back and gleaming, his white teeth visible. Then, with what must have been a swish of Dior stockings, the woman moved across the seat, her eyes filled, as she looked at Hodges, with something like devotion.

Hodges always said he liked to see a problem with his own eyes. For instance, a few years before, he had been responsible for a picture that was being made in the equatorial Pacific, on an atoll in an out-of-the-way part of Micronesia. The budget had been enormous, perhaps the most money ever spent on a picture, at least up till then. The crew built a castle, painted all the palms green (so as to suggest what paradise really looks like), flew in meals from Paris, made a fleet of authentic Polynesian canoes . . . What did it all cost? Who knows. The accountants, years later, are still trying to come to terms with it. The picture made money, but the question is, how much?

It is hard to believe such places as this island in Micronesia exist, especially if you are living in Los Angeles or Detroit or New York, but they do, and there is something in the sky — the white puffs of clouds, the shaggy palm trees, the white beaches, the graying huts, the canoes cut from jungle hardwoods — some beguiling thing that exists all the more definitively if you have just been in some American city where in the smoke and the dust, in the atmosphere of making money, there isn't time to imagine a beach over which blows the constant, hot pressure of the trades.

Communications aren't the best between a Micronesian atoll and Los Angeles, and the stories that did make it back were somehow inconclusive . . . an actor, Sean York, had done something offensive. You probably don't remember Sean York, but he was all the rage for a while. It wasn't clear, though, what he had done on the atoll. All Hodges heard was that there was some trouble to be worked out, nothing serious really, although things were being delayed. Bad news usually came with a contradictory disclaimer, but this time there was a little more desperation than usual. There was even a mention of Micronesian men armed with Winchesters (.30-30s, the kind usually seen in cowboy movies), and Japanese bolt-action rifles that had been left behind at the end of World War II. The islanders, of course, were peaceful. This was one reason why the director had decided to make the picture there, yet . . . there was something a little unyielding about those men with the .30-30s and their bolt-action rifles held together with wire and fishing line.

Hodges flew out there. West of Honolulu the jet stopped at a number of atolls, and at one of them, Majuro or some such place, Hodges got out of the plane and stood on the airstrip. Above him there was that sky, and there were the palms moving in the unbelievably hot wind. He stood, away from the shadow of the wing of the jet, his arms crossed, facing the wind. There, in that stance, he seemed defiant, but in fact it was probably something else, a kind of recognition of the place, if not as something he had seen before, why, then, as the site of dreams, the substance of which he had always been attracted to as though illusion were a kind of weapon, something that kept the sense of being alone just beyond his apprehension of things. He was drawn toward illusion like a migrating bird, not giving a second thought to anything else. Or perhaps, as he stood there, his arms crossed and facing the trades, he was just thinking how far he had come, not in distance measured in miles, but from the places in Hollywood where he had grown up. He always said a studio biography should fit like a good suit, which is to say, it should cover all the right places.

The trouble was beyond Majuro. The atoll was just one of those spits of sand and greenery you see from the air, the surf breaking around it, the sea scaled like something made out of silver plates where the sun lies on it. The islands were isolated even in this age, or so it seemed.

Hodges had to change planes in the eastern Carolines. There he got into a single-engine Cessna on floats to fly to the island where the trouble was. There was a lagoon, which from the air looked like the turquoise in Indian jewelry, and after the plane glided up to a wooden jetty, which was dark and frail, Hodges got out and stood in the slash of sunlight and felt the constant, hot, moist pressure of the trade winds.

The island was a kind of kingdom. That's as close as you could get in English. It might be best to describe it as medieval, in that there were a number of "counts" or "dukes," who were devoted to an overlord. And he was not, by any means, what you'd expect — not a fat man in a grass skirt who presided over barbecues held among flowers and bare-breasted girls. He was a man of less than medium height, bare-chested, dark, a little heavy, gray-haired. His eyes were red, as though with fury, and not just over the fact that Sean York had gotten two girls pregnant, and had got them, too, in all their innocence, to pose for some Polaroid photographs that were, through York's own, unique sensibility, patently obscene, no matter how forgiving one tried to be about them. Sean York had a knack, or even a genius, as compensation for his lack of talent, for reducing people to a kind of nightmare version of themselves. He could do it even to someone as innocent and smiling as a Micronesian woman, reducing her to . . . well, you can imagine. Anyway, it wasn't just the photographs or the pregnancies but what they represented that had made the king send his warriors, armed not with spears but with lever-action .30-30s and rusty shotguns, to drive the movie company into the air-conditioned house trailers where they were living. The king had sent the men with the cheap Winchesters as though, if he could stop the movie company, he could stop the furious advancement of the modern world, the symptoms of which included both the fishing boats from Japan and the infants born blind because their mothers had been infected with syphilis.

The king stood on land, at the end of the jetty. Hodges waited, listening to the hush of the wind over the wing of the airplane and watching the chaotic movement of the tops of the palm trees. Then he walked up to the beach.

The king stared for a moment, not contemptuous exactly, obviously interrogatory, angry. Then he said through an interpreter, "You. Are you the one who is going to answer for the trouble here?"

"Yes," said Hodges.

The king pointed to the house trailers, about five hundred yards away, where the film company was now sequestered.

"Over there," said the king. "They tell lies."

"I understand," said Hodges.

"Do you?" said the king. "Good. Because if I hear one more lie, I'll kill them all."

The king's eyes were red, his chest seeming to make no movement, even when he breathed. A man from the movie company came down the beach, walking quickly in the heat, his footprints marking the sand like exhaust that came in discrete puffs. Both the king and Hodges watched him approach, neither of them saying a thing. Then the man walked up to them, already speaking into the wind. "You see, it's all a kind of mistake, really —"

"Why don't you go roll a hoop around?" said Hodges.

The translator explained this to the king, who looked at the man from the movie company. Then he looked at Hodges and said, "All right. You. Come on."

So they went out along the beach, walking away from the

house trailers where the members of the movie company had been confined for weeks. The king did not look back at Hodges, and the two went along, the king short and dark, and Hodges tall and fair, both of them with their eyes on the distance. They came to a thatched shelter where they went in and sat down on mats, a matter of a few feet between them. They stared at each other, neither saying a thing, although Hodges was thinking, "Well, so, here is a decent man."

They sat that way for an hour, each looking at the other's face, Hodges seeing the scars along the king's side, which had been made by a spear. The king's teeth were white and perfect, and there was a quiet, frank, unambiguous definition to him: he made you think twice about even the smallest falsehood, about anything that wasn't as precise and as good as one could possibly make it.

"Do you like to go fishing?" asked Hodges.

"Yes," said the king.

"At home, we catch trout on a hook wrapped with feathers," said Hodges.

"We use bait," said the king. "I'd like to try feathers. I am named for a bird."

The king spoke to one of his men, who turned and went out, carrying a lever-action .30-30, to get the fishing boat ready. It was a fiberglass boat with an outboard engine, the sound of which the king endured, his attitude toward it coming as an ongoing accusation, as if it were the sound of syphilis. A man took a long knife and prepared the bait, which he put on a hook and then tossed overboard. When he was done, he didn't put the knife in its sheath. He stood next to Hodges, the blade curved in the sunlight. The man looked at the king, who was holding a line, thinking it over. The boat rocked in a swell, the knife staying next to Hodges's neck, the blade of it so sharp Hodges imagined he could feel the itch of the edge even though it hadn't touched him. Birds flew around the boat, their shadows flitting over the deck, their dark shapes sweeping over Hodges with all the insubstantial pressure of a phantom. Hodges held a hand line, although there was no bait on it. He glanced down at the bare, blue hook, seeing the shadow of the knife swing back and forth over the fiberglass deck. Then he said to the king, "Would you put yourself in my hands as I have in yours?"

The whites of the king's eyes seemed more bloodshot than before.

"That is an honorable thing to do," said Hodges. "We'll go fishing together in the mountains. Well?"

The king looked back at the island behind them, the waves breaking over the reef into a white mist.

"You know," said Hodges, "you need a hospital here."

"Who are you to tell me what I need?" said the king.

"Just a man," said Hodges. "You could use one of those house trailers. I could contribute something toward having a doctor fly in twice a month."

The king sat for a moment, his shadow rocking back and forth beneath him. After a while he said, "Now, when someone is sick, he takes the plane to Honolulu. There they have the god of death. It is a big machine. Many people who have been there have told me about it."

Hodges nodded. "I never liked Honolulu," he said.

"Well," said the king, his eyes more angry than before, "does this offer of a doctor come as a bribe?"

"No," said Hodges. "I may try that yet. But it won't be with a hospital. No, I offer it as an honorable man who thinks the people here could use some help."

A fish struck, a long silver one that looked like a barracuda, and when the king pulled it in, he looked at Hodges, who sat, head down, neck still exposed to the knife, the blade steady, moving in time to the swaying of the boat.

"Do you have responsibilities?" asked the king.

"Yes," said Hodges.

"Then you understand," said the king. "I owe something to the gods. I must protect my people. Have you seen the children here, born with no noses?"

"No," said Hodges.

The king nodded. "I want you to look at them. Then you will understand my problem. I can do two things. The first is I can kill you and throw you in the lagoon. Then maybe your tribe who lives in metal huts will go away." The king stared at Hodges. "Do you think they will?"

"No," said Hodges. "Not for long."

"That's what I think," said the king. "So the other thing is that you and I can go fishing in the mountains. So, see about the hospital in the trailer. Finish the movie."

"I understand," said Hodges.

"Do you?" said the king. He turned to the ocean, the blue chop of which sparkled in the sunlight. "OK," said the king. "Are we fishing or are we talking?"

There is a photograph of Hodges and the king in the Sierras, both of them standing before a pond beyond which peaks rise above the tree line. The king is holding two rainbow trout, not smiling, his face set in an expression of severe friendship. Anyway, as soon as the movie crew came back to the States, Hodges fired every one of them, for good. It was the end of Sean York. He has a lawn mowing service in Encino now.

The Scandal Sheet

Scandal Sheet Classifieds, Screen Actors Guild Members (SAG) ten cents a word, all others fifteen cents a word, cash on placing ad. Our credit manager is Helene Wait. If you want credit, go to Helene Wait.

CLASSIFIEDS

ZIMBA, Asian Elephant, can count, nice disposition, seen in *Elephant Walk,* other films, available birthday parties, celebrations, corporate occasions, TV ads, what have you. Call Raj, anytime, 398-1289. Encino.

CHILD STAR, waiting to happen, seeks part major production. Violin, tap-dancing, sings, impressions (killer Jackie Gleason). 421-7860. Beach City.

NEW IN TOWN? Want to give your child a birthday party but don't know any kids? Call us. Kids For Hire. Boys or girls. We'll show you how to put on the dog. 421-7860. Beach City.

AGENT, seeking talent. Travel. Vegas, Philippines. All acts. Leave message at 679-3214. Downtown Hollywood.

IDEAS for scriptwriters. Fifty foolproof story lines. Just fill them out and collect top dollar. Box 391, Hollywood Station.

GERMAN SHEPHERD, can sing, available advertising, birthday parties, you name it. First song free with this ad. Silverlake. Nights. 347-8713.

Sure-fire tips for SANTA ANITA. Make a bet for me, I'll give you two winners. Valley. Anytime. 561-4589.

TROMBONE PLAYER. Good. Temporarily out of work. 340-1256. Keep trying.

CASTING for Intimate Videos. Men, Women, send snaps in Natural State, cash paid every day. Box 1968, Van Nuys Station. Strictly Legitimate Operation.

JACK HAWK'S AROUND TOWN, *Scandal a la Mode.*

First, the Police Blotter. The Malibu Sheriff's station reported that **Marianne Kiltner,** involved in messy divorce from Academy Award-winning producer **Jack Kiltner,** was arrested at 2 A.M. on the Pacific Coast Highway for public intoxication. Marianne reportedly was going to walk to the Rose Bowl as a warmup for New Year's Day. Arresting officer informed her it was July. **Sarah Palmer,** currently appearing in *The Trigger,* alleges in court custody papers that husband Mickey had a two-year affair with eighteen-year-old Manuela Ortega, an au pair from Hermosillo. Narcotics paraphernalia was found in the car of **Jack Berry, first husband of Beverly Mason,** late of *Summer Heat* and of the Topanga Murder Scandal a few years back.

Well, gang, that ought to hold you until next week's paper (every Wednesday, $2.00 at your Newsstand or by subscription). If you hear anything good, call it in to *The Scandal Sheet*'s Office (818-378-8790, leave message on machine). No story too shocking to print. If you have anything good on **Warren Hodges,** new studio head at Gemini Productions, don't hesitate to call collect.

* * *

Gourmet-On-The-Run Tip: Pinks on La Brea has a gorgeous chili dog on a steamed bun for a buck and a half. You can't go wrong, and the view is absolutely horrible.

* * *

Star-Gazers: You can catch the film crowd at the Kitchen, downtown L.A. Go late.

The Party

OUT OF THE DARKNESS a line of cars turned off Malibu Canyon Road onto a private dirt road, and as the dust streamed away from their tires and as they rocked this way and that, the accumulation of automobiles had the aspect of a genie that had just been let out of a bottle. The dust added to this notion, since it rose in billows, and in the headlights it appeared to be silver faceted and shimmering, like the wings of a million insects.

The cars were headed for a party in a large house at the end of the drive, and of all of the guests there was one who stood out. She was a slender woman of about twenty-five who wore a pair of blue jeans and a white shirt. Her hair was blond and short, and she got out of a car driven by a man who wore black leather pants, a transparent shirt, and a gold chain. There was another man in the car, too, whose name was Victor Shaw, and he got out and stood in the dust, looking up at the house with a kind of amazement, as though the place had been made out of vanilla ice cream. Then he turned to the woman. "Won't take but a minute, Marta. Then you can go home."

"All right," she said, her voice a little tired. "Let's get it over with."

The other man, the one in the black leather pants, said, "Didn't I tell you? It's a real Hollywood party. Didn't I? This is Warren Hodges's house."

Victor Shaw looked up at the house again.

"How did you get invited?" he asked.

"Oh," said the man in the leather pants, "one way and another. One way and another."

"Looks like they're going to have a bathtub full of shrimp," said Victor.

"Naw," said the man in leather pants. His name was Nicky White. "That's the kind of thing an advertising agency does. Warren Hodges runs a studio, for Christ's sake. He's got a champagne fountain. You hold your glass into a stream and fill it up."

"No kidding," said Victor. "Mostly champagne doesn't agree with me. Gives me a headache."

"That's because it's cheap stuff. There isn't any of that here," said Nicky. "It's interesting what money can buy. I heard a lot of interesting stuff here."

"Like what?" asked Victor.

"The last time I was here a woman told me what a bag of frozen peas is good for."

"I don't like peas. They're hard to get on the fork," said Victor.

"Naw," said Nicky. "She wasn't talking about *eating* them. A bag of frozen peas is good when you have a face-lift. You put it on your eyes to keep the swelling down."

Marta waited. There was nothing specific about her posture or the movement of her hands, yet in every gesture, in the way she faced the house, she had a taut remoteness usually associated with fear or a profound uneasiness. It was so definite and palpable as to make her appear not fully engaged here: she looked like a tall, attractive woman distracted by a bad hangover, only somehow you were convinced she hadn't been drunk. She seemed to be standing up to whatever the turmoil was, facing it with defiance, and this added to the overall effect of tautness.

"Well, you hear that, Marta?" asked Victor. "About keeping the swelling down?"

She turned back to look at him, but after just glancing at him, she looked away again.

"Let's get it over with," she said.

"You're too pretty to need a face-lift," said Victor.

"Thanks," she said, looking at the house.

"You know where it bleeds the most?" said Nicky. "Around the ears."

"No kidding?" said Victor.

"But, hey," said Nicky, "there's big bucks in looking good. You can't knock money."

Marta sighed.

"Let's go in," said Victor. "Marta wants to get home early."

Behind them more cars approached the house, their shapes barely discernible through the dust, some long, low sports cars in the front, mostly brightly colored ones, reds and yellows, their tires black and shiny. A Ferrari emerged from the dust, one of its headlights newly smashed and hanging by a wire so as to suggest an eye hanging by an optical nerve. There was a streak of creosote along the side of the car, too. Then the cars pulled up and the passengers got out, women mostly, who looked up at the house, their figures marked here or there by a facet of light from a diamond bracelet or an earring or from light in an eye, the accumulation of the diminutive flashes giving a twinkling aura to the evening, as though a few fireflies were out.

The house looked European. It was made of stone, was three stories high, and had about it the severity, or perhaps just the fortresslike quality, of houses in Normandy. There were tall windows, small terraces, and the scent of stone. Inside, through the windows, chandeliers were visible, their lights forming large upside-down beehives. The doors were made of heavy wood and had black iron hinges, and to one side there was a formal garden with a reflecting pool.

From the terrace on the second story, it was possible to see the monument to the Dead Trooper on Malibu Canyon Road. Warren Hodges stood on the terrace now, watching the cars approach. He was in his forties and was wearing evening clothes. His hair was blond, streaked around the ears with a little gray. He was just over six feet tall. His features were regular and clean with a straight nose and full lips, and his complexion was a little rough, as though he had had an experience with frostbite somewhere along the line. He did not seem arrogant, but certainly as he watched the cars approach he was alert. The voices on the warm summer air, the scent of eucalyptus mingling with the fragrance of the Pacific and the perfume of the arriving guests, the shouts here and there all had the first brittle edge of a kind of hilarity. Hodges seemed to hover over it, mildly expectant, curious, engaged. It was this moment he would remember when, the party over, he stood in the dining room downstairs or in the ballroom, his polished shoes crunching the broken glass that had been left behind, that sound and the stink of the room always leaving him with the realization that, against all odds, the evening had come to an end after all.

Standing next to Hodges was Charles Houston, a man who was a little shorter, and who had dark, slicked-back hair and very blue eyes. He had been born in the Midwest, in Saint Louis, into a family of surgeons. His great-grandfather had been a pioneer of surgical technique, and Houston's father was known for his precision and his speed. Charles had four brothers, all of whom had become doctors and who, even when they were still at home, had sat at the dining room table in the evening as if they were already in medical school, the house around them dark with old wood, gloomy with a million perfect incisions. Charles went east to good schools, to St. Paul's and Yale, although when Charles didn't go on to medical school, he more or less ceased to exist for his father.

When Charles announced he was going to California, to Hollywood, he was standing on the apron in front of the St. Louis airport. Charles's father stood up straight as he listened to the words, his shoulders squared, hands behind his back, as though he had just seen a botched piece of surgery. Then he said to Charles, "Don't be an ass. If you want to go to Hollywood, go as a plastic surgeon," and then he turned away, shaking his head, his fingers moving as if tying a final surgeon's knot.

Hodges had hired Charles for his manners. Manners were important to Hodges, if only as an antidote to his business. There were times when formality, even a little gallantry, seemed to take some of the tawdriness out of his ordinary life. There were times when Hodges believed manners were what told people the difference between right and wrong. Or, this is what they had in the absence of other things. When Hodges was growing up, he had assumed there was a world of polite and elegant people, and he desperately wanted to be part of it, but when he had made enough money to get close to this world, he found it was mostly an illusion. Then manners became for him an argument with an all-pervasive grimness.

Charles's job was to take people out on the town — visiting directors, actors, financial people — and if they needed some more elaborate . . . entertainment, well, that could be arranged, too. Charles lived in a small house in Beechwood Canyon, read Seneca and Caesar, and saw, three times a week, in the afternoon, a woman he knew from the East who was married to a banker here. They had a good time together, and never thought about divorce. That was not the kind of thing either one of them even considered. Mostly, Charles kept his mouth shut, although there were times when, late at night, he found himself trying to determine the difference between right and wrong and realizing that most of the world, if not nearly all of it, didn't live by the tidy rules in a gloomy, Midwestern surgeon's house.

Now, as the cars came up the drive, Charles said, "It looks like a good crowd."

Hodges turned and looked at Charles, thinking this comment over.

"That's one way of putting it," he said.

"You've included some people from town," said Charles. This is the way he referred to the hustlers, car thieves, sometime prostitutes, waitresses, bookies, rainmakers, cowboys, and street Indians who somehow, through a process Charles never really understood, would arrive at this house on certain evenings.

"Yes," said Hodges.

"I've always wanted to ask you why you invite people like that."

Hodges shrugged. "What's it to you?" he asked.

"Nothing," said Charles. "Not really. Some people say you do it as a kind of slumming."

"*Slumming*," said Hodges. He turned and looked at Charles.

"That's what I heard," said Charles.

Hodges nodded, looking down at the arriving guests, the more usual actors and directors, hairstylists and set designers, the dust from their cars rising into the air and disappearing like smoke. The sun had set completely now.

"Charley," said Hodges, still looking away. "I grew up here. I even spent time on the streets. And you know something? It's not a bad thing to remember where you came from. Anyway, a lot of these guys are interesting. You'd be surprised."

"Uh-huh," said Charles. "I know. Like a month ago someone offered to sell me a Mercedes, not 'hot, just a little warm,' for fifteen thousand dollars. The guy said it had 'full documentation.' In fact, that's him right there."

He pointed at the man in the leather pants who was with Marta and Victor Shaw. All three of them had emerged from the darkness, Marta's short hair taking on a golden cast from the lights in front of the house.

"Well, you could use a new car," said Hodges. "Who's the woman with him?"

"I don't know," said Charles.

Now, as Marta approached the house, she stepped into the pool of light just beneath the terrace where Hodges stood, and as she did so, she looked up. Above her she saw a man in evening clothes, his arms on the terrace wall, his hair gleaming in the light from the room behind him, and above him, through the misty, faintly salty air of the coast, there were smears of stars. She stopped, one hand to her lips, her lack of motion sudden and absolute, her gaze so strong that Hodges seemed to feel it on his face as a physical sensation. She did not look ashamed, or curious, or anything other than frank. It was as if she had looked up to see if there was hope, and that while she was intrigued, she was by no means convinced of anything. Hodges smiled, and she looked away, as though a smile were the last thing in the world she wanted. Then she turned and walked into the house, leaving Hodges with a strangely numb, buzzing sensation on his face.

"She's scared," said Hodges.

"Is she?" asked Charles. "Well, I wouldn't know. I'm not an expert about that."

A car came up the drive, going fast. The driver honked his horn a couple of times and then swerved into the dust, the clouds of which hid a eucalyptus tree. There was a *thwack,* a tinkling of broken glass, and a deeper *boom* as the hood of the car sprang open. The hood bounced up and down, the movement suggesting the mouth of an animal, an alligator, say, that was gnawing on something. The driver got out and looked at the sprung hood and the rising ghost of steam, which mixed with the dust. Then he dropped down on all fours and stared at the leaking radiator.

Another driver, a young woman, got out of her car and knelt, too. She said, "You're Danny Myers, aren't you?"

"What of it?" said Myers.

"I always thought you were very funny," she said. "I've seen all your movies."

"How about a kiss then?" he said. "How about taking a chance on a blanket, and I'm not talking about a raffle ticket."

The woman ignored him and stared at the car. Danny Myers waited for a moment and then looked at the car, too, where water was dripping out.

"You see that?" said Myers.

"What?" said the woman.

"It's green," he said. "The water is green."

"That's antifreeze," said the woman. "Antifreeze is green."

"You're pulling my leg."

"No," said the woman. She shook her head earnestly.

Danny Myers took another look. Then he stood up and said to a man and a woman who were walking through the dust of the road, "Hey, did you know that antifreeze is green?"

The man, a film director, was wearing a jacket and tan pants and a blue work shirt. His wife looked up at the house ahead and said, "Well, so it's true. I bet the place really was brought a stone at a time from Normandy. It sure is big enough."

"Don't believe everything you hear," said the director. Then he turned back to Danny Myers and said, "Well, Danny, come up to the house and have a drink. Forget about the antifreeze." The director looked at the house now, too. "Jesus, look at the woodwork around the windows. You see how it's all mitered?"

"Well, I always say," said Myers, "one man's meat is another man's miter."

The film director turned and looked at Danny Myers. "Is that a joke, Danny?"

"No," Myers said. "When I make a joke I'll tell you in advance. I'm going to write a book for guys like you. *Thirty Days to a Sense of Humor*. First step: Recognizing a Joke . . ."

"I think I need a drink," said the director's wife. "I told you I didn't want to come."

The director shrugged.

"You know," said Danny Myers, "the president of the United States had dinner here. Can you believe it?"

"Not with this crowd, I'll bet," said the director's wife.

"Last Tuesday he was here," said Danny. "One of the Secret Service guys ate some abalone and got sick. He was throwing up like . . . everywhere."

"Let's go in," said the director's wife.

"Hey, listen," said Danny. "You want to buy a Mercedes, low mileage . . . hey, there's a guy here who can get you one . . ."

All of them went up to the door, where people waited as at a crowded restaurant, and then more guests materialized out of the dusty air — a man in a leather jacket who had a small tattoo on his face, a star on one cheek; two women with frizzed hair, one in a silver dress and high-heeled shoes and the other in a pair of red, shiny pants and a white T-shirt. The T-shirt was almost transparent, and her nipples appeared as shadows against the thin cloth. The guests emerged into the light at the front of the house, and after waiting impatiently for a minute or so, they disappeared inside.

*   *   *

As a few more cars pulled up to the house, Hodges contemplated a tree that stood about a hundred yards from the house. It was a large sycamore, the kind that has splotchy bark. Supposedly it was still possible to see the indelible stains left by the blood of a Spaniard who had been hanged here for stealing horses in the days of the Spanish possession of California. Hodges crossed his arms and faced the tree with an expression of such severity that you could almost imagine the Spaniard hanging there at the end of a good California hemp rope.

Downstairs, the party progressed.

An elephant now stood in front of the house. It was a large one, its head lumpy, its trunk segmented where it curved up toward the mouth, its ears making a slight sound, like someone folding up a cardboard box, when they were twitched. In the end of its trunk, where it was curled tightly, the elephant carried a large bouquet, and as the animal stood there, it appeared to be about to eat a collection of red, white, and yellow flowers which were surrounded by a spray of ferns and wrapped in green florist's paper. A red blanket, trimmed in gold and with the word "Zimba" stitched onto it in gold sequins, lay across its back. There were lights in front of the house, and the elephant stood in them, the sequins on its blanket flashing.

Next to Zimba stood a man in white, billowy pants, a flowing shirt, and a white turban, in the middle of which a piece of red glass about the size of a pocket watch was suspended by a gold chain. Whenever a woman or a man emerged from the darkness of the drive and approached the house, the man in the turban said to Zimba, "Is she pretty?" or "Is he handsome?" and the elephant would nod its head, the flowers swinging a little at the end of its trunk. The flowers were fresh and bright in the light against the elephant's side.

"Hey, Billy," a woman said to her husband. "Hey, look at the elephant, will ya?"

"So what?" said her husband. "You've seen one before haven't you?"

"This one says I'm pretty," said the woman.

"He's paid to do that," said her husband.

"Oh, yeah?" said the woman. She was holding a glass of fruit juice, ice, and vodka, which she had brought with her out of the car she had arrived in.

Her husband shrugged.

"You know what?" said the woman. "I think we should get the elephant to come to a birthday party for Mike. What ten-year-old boy wouldn't want an elephant at a birthday party?"

"Mike doesn't know anyone to invite to the party," said the husband. "He didn't even know that many kids back in New Jersey."

"Oh, come on. You can hire some kids, can't you?" said the woman. Then she turned to the man in the turban. "Do you do birthday parties?"

"Of course," he said, producing a card. It was printed on thick paper with the picture of an elephant in an ink that was rough, like letters on a Christmas card. The woman took it and then went inside, her husband saying, "The thing stinks. Can't you smell it, for Christ's sake? Kids don't like things that stink."

Inside the house, in the living room, sitting on a long white curved sofa, there was an actress who was referred to in the gossip magazines as the most beautiful woman in the world. The actress was tall and had slender arms and legs, broad shoulders, and a long neck. There was in her features, in her grayish eyes and full lips, in her slender nose, in the hair which was thick and a little unruly, an indication of some quality that was as ephemeral as the light that glinted off the Pacific at dusk. It was hard to say what it was precisely, and the maddening thing was that it came and went as she turned her head, as she smiled, or as she put out her long fingers and accepted a delicious tidbit, a little slice of bread with caviar flown in that day from Moscow, but in that moment when one got a glance at it, when the quality lasted for a few seconds, it seemed to be an assurance of some sultry warmth, of an absolute fearlessness at contemplating any abyss. Mixed with this there was a quality of milky cleanliness. She smiled and glanced around the room. You could tell she was in the room as soon as you walked into it, without even seeing her. There is no other way of putting it, aside from saying the air itself seemed filled with some essence, like a fragrance, that made everything it permeated brighter and a little raw.

Some young men, a woman, and an astronaut who had been to the moon were sitting around her. The astronaut said he drank Tang out of a tube like the ones toothpaste comes in. She said that with the pollution being what it was, she'd like to have a space suit to wear when she drove on the freeway. They talked about how you put a space suit on. She listened, smiling, winking once at him, and then with an almost unbearable promise, she put her hand on the astronaut's when he blushed. Her name was

Sharon Dyer. She gave the impression she maintained her identity by main strength, as though if she wasn't careful her personality would simply flutter away, like an insect on anxious wings. She was pleased by her effect, which was less profound in person than on film, yet she was a little shy, too, as though the entire thing had become an embarrassment, or a piece of gaucherie she wished she could drop.

Hodges came into the room. Sharon Dyer glanced up, the brightness that surrounded her, or that appeared to emanate from her, seeming more pronounced as she extended her hand. He reached down to take it and to give her a kiss on the cheek (the slight lingering of it making the gossip columnist on the other side of the room take a note for her column). Sharon Dyer said, putting her lips close to his ear, the words coming in warm, moist puffs, "I took your advice. I shorted IBM and I'm making a bundle."

"Maybe we'll deduct it from what you make on your next picture," said Hodges.

She smiled at him, keeping her eyes on his.

"We won't even joke about that," she said.

"Well," said Hodges. "No. I guess not. But after we work out the details, I'll tell you about a company I have some money in . . . a biotech outfit that is about to get a permit to test a cure for cancer on human beings. Would that interest you?"

"Of course," she said.

Then they separated, their heads rising, her eyes settling on his, her aspect one of thinking things over.

The housekeeper came into the room. She was a middle-aged woman wearing the white skirt and shirt of a nurse and holding a towel. "Mr. Hodges," she said, "the governor is on the phone," and then she waited for a moment, until Hodges had walked back into the hall where the telephone was.

The room was full now. At one side of it, next to the window, stood a man who wore a leather jacket, a tie-dyed shirt, and a pair of blue jeans. He was balding and had a tattoo of a shark on the back of his right hand. Earlier that day he had stolen a TV set from a house in Laurel Canyon, and even though he wanted to appear as a "class guy," he still couldn't help thinking there were a few things here he'd really like to boost. Next to him there was a man wearing a sport coat, one made in Scotland, the colors of it suggesting the blue-granite of heather. The man in the sport coat wore a turtleneck, a pair of beige pants, and handmade shoes. He was drunk.

"What a fucking place," said the man in the coat, looking around.

"Lot of nice stuff here," said the second-story man.

"This?" said the man in the sport coat. "This is just a bunch of nouveau trash. Look . . . Early American antiques."

"I was thinking about the Sony," said the second-story man.

They stood silently for a moment.

"Those bastards," said the drunk man. "Those bastards."

"Which ones?" said the second-story man.

"Why the ones at Mid-Atlantic Pictures," said the drunk. "You know what they did?"

The second-story man shook his head.

"No," he said.

"They didn't renew my contract. I produced more hits for them than you can shake a stick at. You know that? You're talking to Sidney Green, you know that?"

"No," said the second-story man.

"Well, that's right," said Sidney Green. "And you know what they gave me after ten years of making money for them? You want to see?"

"Yes," said the second-story man.

"Here," said Sidney Green. He took out his wallet and removed a check, which he threw onto an end table with a furious, unsteady motion, saying, "Look. Jesus, that's what they gave me. After the money I made them."

The second-story man looked at it for a moment. It was more money than he and his father and four or five other people he knew would make in their entire lives.

"I'm going to have to sell a goddamned Matisse to keep going, for Christ's sake. A *Matisse!* And look at the art market these days. Just look at it."

"Say," said the second-story man. "Where do you live?"

"Ah," said Sidney Green. "You don't understand. I was at the top of my game. At the top."

Then Sidney Green went outside, picking up his check and sticking it into the side pocket of his jacket from Scotland. He went into the shadows beyond the lighted part of the terrace, and for a moment he could be seen, facing the darkness of the Pacific. He looked up at the terrace above the one where he stood, and then he walked out of sight.

In a few minutes someone said, "He's on the balcony rail. Up above." An electric murmur went through the room, an accumulation of voices asking, "What? What is that," which were mixed with "Oh, my God. Oh, Jesus." Then it was silent.

"Is someone on the balcony?"

"Sid Green," said a man by the door to the terrace.

"Sid?" said another man. "Jesus, I thought he was dead."

"No, sir," said the man by the door. "Look."

He pointed to the upper balcony. There was a little pushing at the door, people craning their necks to see as they emerged in a group on the stone terrace. Against the sky, which was now filled with stars like silver paper on a black sheet, stood Sidney Green. He was about fifty, gray-haired, and a little heavy. He stood with his heels in the air, his toes on the balcony rail. He also held a bottle of vodka, poised just in front of his lips.

The people below simply stared, although one said, "Oh, my God. Oh, my God."

Inside there was the sound of music from Brazil, high and light, and then someone outside said, "Can't you turn that down. There's someone on the balcony. For Christ's sake."

Hodges came out on the terrace, too. Then he said, "Pssst. Hey. Sid."

Sidney stood, just his toes on the railing. The vodka in the bottle washed back and forth, the silvery splash of it the same color as the stars. He was sweating, too, the streaks of moisture running from beads on his forehead. His hands were shaking a little.

One of the young women down below looked up and said, "No one understands him. His wife is just a bitch."

"A saint is more like it," said someone else.

"His father was a drunk," said the young woman. "No one understands. Oh, God."

"Sid," said Hodges.

"Yes?" said Sidney.

"What are you doing up there?" said Hodges.

"Drinking vodka," he said.

"Well," said Hodges. "I'm going to give you a little advice."

"I don't want your advice," said Sidney.

"Yes, you do. Here it is. Drink your vodka and get the hell down from there."

"Why should I want to come down?"

"Because I got a deal for you," said Hodges.

"What's that?"

"I got a script by Jack Mather," said Hodges.

Sidney looked over his shoulder, staring.

"I got Billy Petersen to direct it," said Hodges.

"No shit?" said Sidney. "Billy agreed to do it?"

"Are you interested?"

Sidney Green swayed back and forth, his slow movement peculiar to a mixture of tranquillizers and alcohol.

"If you're interested," said Hodges, "you'd better get down."

Then Hodges turned and went into the house. Marta was sitting at the end of one of the sofas, looking out the window at the Pacific beyond the crowd of people who waited on the balcony. She had her hands together, and sat quite still. Hodges came over and said, "Hello. Can I get you a drink?"

She shook her head.

"No," she said. "Thanks."

"Maybe a little champagne?" he said. "It's a beautiful evening. Champagne's nice on a beautiful evening."

"Beautiful?" she said. Then she looked down and shook her head. "OK. I'll have a glass of champagne."

"Good," he said. "My name is Warren. Warren Hodges."

She looked at him and nodded.

"Hello," she said. "Nice to meet you. My name is Marta Brooks."

Outside, in the group of people with their necks craned back as though a flying saucer was hovering over the house, someone said, "Jesus, does anyone know the name of a good therapist?"

"How about August St. James?" said a woman at the front of the crowd.

"Sure," said a man with a New York accent. "St. James. That's the guy. He treated my daughter's very serious eating disorder."

Up above, Sidney Green held the bottle.

"Sid?" said a woman from below. "Everything's going to be fine."

"Billy Petersen," said Sidney.

"No, no," said a woman. "August St. James."

"He's delusional," said another woman.

"No," said a film director. "He's just figuring the deal. No one was ever faster than Sid Green."

Hodges took a glass of champagne from a tray and handed it to Marta, saying, "Come on outside for a moment. Out front."

"What about that?" said Marta, gesturing toward the balcony outside.

"What?" said Hodges. "Oh, that. That's all fixed."

They went through the room, passing Sharon Dyer, who sat with the astronaut. Marta and Hodges went downstairs and out into the air scented by orange grove and eucalyptus trees.

Victor Shaw stood by the door. In the lighted room his black jacket, jeans, and basketball shoes seemed to cover him like a shadow, and his face, which was white to begin with, seemed even more so against the dark clothes: the entire effect of the man was suggestive of the cold patience of creatures that hunt by waiting. Yet, in addition to the dark clothes and his steady, remote gaze, there was something else, too, which revealed itself as a kind of dread. He watched Marta come up to the door, searching her face a little, looking for a sign he could trust, and as she began to go out, he said, "Are you going to be gone long?"

She looked at him and then dropped her eyes.

"No," she said.

"Are you sure?"

"I told you," she said. "I won't be gone long."

Hodges stood at the door, holding it open, looking outside, although now he glanced back at Victor Shaw.

"I'm just going to get a little air," said Marta.

Victor shrugged.

"You know," Victor said, "you and I have got to be able to trust one another. You understand?"

She looked down.

"Yes," she said.

"Make sure that you do," he said.

"What are you?" asked Hodges. "A cop?"

Victor looked at Hodges for a moment and then said to Marta, "I think you'd better tell him he doesn't want to start causing trouble."

"That's right," said Marta. She took Hodges's arm. "Come on."

"*Trouble?*" said Hodges. "Are you threatening me?"

"Not yet," said Victor. Then he turned to Marta. "Don't be long."

"Listen —" said Hodges, but Marta pulled him outside, saying, "Please. There's nothing wrong."

She gave him another tug, and then they stood in the open space in front of the house. As they passed the windows, light played across Marta's hair, the side of her face; she walked with a straight carriage, as though there were an abyss on either side of her. She sipped the champagne and held it to her nose for a second, feeling the bubbles there, as though the sensation of them came from a great distance.

From the darkness beyond the hills the sound of a small airplane could be heard, the drone of it rising and falling and seeming a little ominous, but in a romantic way, like the sound of a train heard late at night or in the middle of a rainstorm. On the balcony a man and a woman argued over whether or not a vegetarian diet was a condition of enlightenment. Marta looked at Hodges and said, "Thanks for bringing me outside."

"At your service," said Hodges.

"Now you're mocking me," she said.

He shook his head.

"No," he said.

She glanced back at the house.

"What's the trouble?" he asked. "Maybe I can help."

She stood and looked at the house, keeping her eyes away from him. There were some lawn chairs on the grass and Marta sat in one, simply letting go, just giving in to the desire to sit down. She drank the champagne in one draught and put the empty glass down. Then she looked up at him, not smiling exactly, and said, "There's no trouble."

"Of course," he said. "I didn't mean to pry."

The sound of the airplane came closer; it seemed to be flying a little low. Marta sat with her head in her hands, her elbows on her knees. Hodges stood next to her, both of his hands touching his glass of champagne, his shoulders square, the light from the house playing across his hair. The airplane passed overhead, and as it did so, it released tens of thousands of small, glowing stars, each one of which had printed on the back the logo of Hodges's studio. They simply appeared in the sky as a silent explosion behind the now disappearing sound of the airplane. They were so constructed as to wink on and off as they turned end over end, filling the yard, the house, the hills, the orchard with an infinity of stars, and as Marta looked up, she saw the man in front of her defined in a slowly settling glitter, the individual points looking like fast-winking fireflies. From the house there came a kind of sigh. Someone said, "Lookit that, wouldja?"

"This is all a little too hilarious for me," said Marta.

She turned and looked at the house, behind which light slanted into the air in long, distinctly lined rays. Victor Shaw waited in the doorway, his figure taut, one hand on the stone wall of the front of the house. Marta turned away, back into the warm scent of the orange trees and eucalyptus.

Hodges and Marta walked down to the garage, which was a hundred yards or so from the house, through the sharp throb of the crickets in the grass. Marta put a hand to the side of her face and rubbed it across her cheek and down to her lips. She bumped against him, and as he reached out for her arm, he could feel that she was trembling. She turned back and looked at the lights of the house, her face streaked with shadows, her hair, here and there, filled with filaments of its sheen. Her lips were full and dark here against her pale skin, as though she were wearing black lipstick.

Behind them there were the dark bays of the garage. Hodges reached inside and turned on the light, the garage immediately revealing itself as a large building holding four cars, each under a cone of light like those in movies where a man is being interrogated in a basement or a police station. The cars were long and dark, shiny, streaked with discreet lines of chrome. At the end, though, there was a low red sports car, the top down, the hood long and narrow, the shape alone suggesting four or five hundred horsepower. The interior smelled of good, soft pigskin, the stitching so small as to be almost invisible. There were aviation-grade instruments on the dashboard, and a wooden steering wheel. They both got in, and Hodges started the engine, the gentle, constant throb almost liquid as they turned and headed out to the main road.

From time to time, as they drove toward the beach, they passed under a street lamp, the purple light falling into the car in a cold slash. Marta's short hair blew around her head and exposed her smooth skin, her long neck. "I grew up in Hollywood," he said. "And you know what we wanted when I was a kid? We always wanted to get to the beach."

She looked out through the windshield. The Pacific was in the distance, dark, scaled with light.

"I grew up in Hollywood, too," she said.

"Did you?"

"Beechwood Canyon."

"Really?" he said. "You hardly meet anyone these days who actually came from here."

"I went to Hollywood High," she said.

"Me too."

"Were you in one of the gangs?"

"Yes," he said.

"Which one?"

"Mohicans," he said.

She looked over at him.

"Well, at least it wasn't the Spartans. They were the worst."

At the beach Hodges parked in a driveway.

"I always park here," he said. "It's all right."

There was a street lamp at the entrance to the driveway, and they both sat in the irregular purplish sheets of light that lay across their legs and their laps. The scent of the Pacific was strong, a salty odor mixed with the smell of seaweed, and along with this there was the ripping sound of the waves, and a hissing, too, as the water washed up and then ebbed on the sand.

Marta glanced over, her eyes in the shadows, her skin pale in the light. She raised her hand and put it to her face, sniffling once, and then there appeared on the purple-white legs of her blue jeans a round, dark spot, and then another, and when Hodges looked at her face, he saw that between the fingers of her hand there were dark, almost oil-like lines of blood. There was a slight *tick tick tick* as the drops of it fell to her lap, the marks there dark in the light of the street lamp.

"Oh, God," she said.

"Here," said Hodges. He took a handkerchief from his pocket and passed it over. "Here."

She took it and put it against her face.

"I hate nosebleeds," she said. "I'm sorry."

"Whatever for?" he asked.

"I hope it stops soon," she said. "Why won't it stop?"

"Just sit for a minute."

"No," she said. "I want to get out."

She wiped her face with the handkerchief, at first leaving a smear over her lips and the side of her cheek. Hodges reached into the glove box, but it held only the registration for the car in a plastic pouch. She looked down at her hands for a moment, seeing the dark smears, and then started shaking her head as if she were appalled or frightened. The drops immediately fell from her face into her palms and fingers and then onto her lap, the drops appearing on her legs almost as if by magic. She looked down at the drops and started shaking her head again.

"I just wish this bleeding would stop. I hope I didn't get it on your car. It's such a beautiful car."

Marta got out, holding the handkerchief to her face.

"I must look pretty stupid."

"You look like you're having a nosebleed," he said. "So what?"

They took off their shoes and began to walk across the sand, which in the light from the road looked like a snowy field that has been walked on a lot. It was easier going where the sand was a little damp, and beyond it, closer to the water, the sand was wet and shiny, mirrorlike. There were yellow streaks on it from the windows of houses on the Pacific Coast Highway, and a blur, too, of red light from a signal, the ruby of it turning to emerald as the signal changed from red to green. Marta looked down at the stains on her pants. The dark spots had a mesmerizing effect on her, as though the marks were evidence of some malice.

"I'm going to take a swim," she said.

"OK," he said. "I've got a blanket in the car. You can dry off with it."

"You don't mind?"

"No," he said.

"I want to get the stains off my pants." She looked up at him now, her face still a little dirty, her eyes fierce.

"Sure," he said. "I'll get the blanket."

He walked up to the car, and Marta stepped into the water, wetting her thighs, where she scrubbed at the spots on her pants, slowly at first, and then harder, more quickly, and finally she stepped out of them altogether, standing in her blouse and underwear, scrubbing. Then, leaving them on the sand, she dropped her blouse and underwear and waded into the edge of the surf, the white, phosphorescent water breaking over her with the color of bones in an x-ray. She splashed the foam and water onto her face with both hands with the repetitive insistence of someone working at a task that has to be done thoroughly and without much time. Then she stepped out and stood on the sand, shivering.

"That's better," she said.

"Here," said Hodges. He held out the blanket, which she took and put around her shoulders, holding it together with one hand, reaching out from underneath. Her teeth chattered.

"I just felt . . . sullied," she said.

"Because of a nosebleed?"

"Because of what?" she asked, looking at him. "Oh, that. No, not because of that."

Hodges gathered up her clothes, and they walked back to the car, the two of them silent, his shape tall, dark, hers ill-defined, the blanket hanging from her shoulders like an oversize towel.

"I'll turn the heater on," he said.

Her skin smelled of salt and the harsh scent of iodine and seaweed. She touched her face now, as though making sure it was clean. Hodges started the engine and turned on the heater and then drove along the Pacific Coast Highway, up toward Trancas, where there was an all-night gas station and sporting goods store, and after he pulled in, under the lights, he said, "They sell jeans here. What size do you wear? You can't wear yours. They're wet."

Hodges went inside and walked along the tables stacked with T-shirts that had "Malibu" and "California" printed on them, and in among the fishing rods and below a wall on which there were brightly feathered lures, he found some blue jeans. He bought a pair and a shirt and brought them out, and Marta went into the bathroom to get dressed. While she was gone, Hodges waited, thinking of her phosphorescent shape against the darkness of the ocean, her back and shoulders covered with foam like strands of pearls, and her shivering in the car, too. Then she came out and got back into the car, her hair wet and stringy around her face, her lips clean, her face fresh. Now, in addition to the scent of the Pacific on her skin, there was the practical scent of sizing.

"I'll send you the money for the jeans," she said.

"Why send it?" he said. "Why don't we meet tomorrow and you can give it to me?"

"No," she said. "I don't think that's a good idea."

"Why not?"

She shrugged.

"Take my word for it," she said.

"I can be pretty good company," he said.

"Can you?" she asked. "That's nice."

Her skin was very white, and he thought she was going to start shivering again.

"Have you taken anything?" he said. "A drug or something?"

"I wish I had," she said. "Wouldn't that be nice? No, I didn't get it in a pill."

"Get what?" he asked.

She glanced over at him and shook her head.

"I don't want to cause you any trouble," she said. "Let's leave it at that."

He drove for a while.

"Listen," he said. "It's still early."

"Not for me," she said. "I've got to get back."

He turned into the drive of his house, the scent of eucalyptus and orange trees strong around the car.

"I'll call you tomorrow," he said. "All right?"

She shook her head.

"Come on," he said.

"No," she said. Then she turned to look at him. "Take it from me. I'm doing you a favor."

They drove up to the house, its shape defined in a kind of furious illumination, and even from the orange grove they could hear the hilarious voices. Hodges let Marta off at the house.

"Well, good night," he said.

"Good night. I'll send the money for the pants to you in Malibu. I guess the post office knows you."

"Yes," he said. "I guess that's right."

Then he drove down to the garage.

*   *   *

The elephant was still near the front door, his feet as big around as an umbrella stand, his side like a gray wall over which someone had thrown a red and gold blanket. Zimba looked up at the house or at the cars that lined the drive, his skin twitching and his trunk moving as if he were surrounded by flies. When Marta came up to the house, he offered her the flowers he still held in his trunk.

"Take them," said the man in the turban.

Marta looked at the flowers. Zimba brushed them against her, the touch of his trunk like a shove.

"Take the flowers," said the man with the turban. "We're going home now. I want to get rid of them."

"Take the goddamned flowers," said Victor Shaw, as he stepped out from the shadows at the front of the house. "Jesus, where have you been? Had me worried."

Marta took the flowers.

"Did I?" she said.

"Yeah," he said. "Where did you get the clothes?"

"He bought them for me," said Marta.

Victor had a drink in his hand, and he rattled the ice in it now.

"Say, that was Hodges who took you out, you know that?"

She shrugged.

"He's interested in you," said Shaw. "I can tell."

"So what?" said Marta. "I just want to go home."

"What did you tell him?" asked Shaw. "Honor bright, now."

"Nothing," she said. "I told him he couldn't see me tomorrow."

"I wouldn't be so hasty," said Victor.

"I don't want him to get mixed up in anything," she said.

"Oh?" said Victor. "Is it like that already. Well, well."

"I told you," she said. "I just want to go home."

"The party's just getting started," he said.

"I'm tired," she said. "Please."

"We'll stay for a little," he said. "Won't take but a minute."

"Then can I go home?"

"What?" he said. "Oh, that. Sure. You know something? A band's going to play soon . . . some funny-looking kids with purple hair. One of them's dressed up like a woman, but you know something? I think it's a guy."

Marta Brooks

ON THE DAY of the party at Warren Hodges's house, Marta ran an errand that took her to the beach. Even in the morning, when she was only half awake, she thought about the house she had to go to. She had never seen the place, but it occupied a part of her mind usually reserved for fears that were only half realized. But even in the warmth of the August morning and in the delicious sense of going back to sleep, which was a kind of surrender, too, in that she was already late, she imagined the house she had never seen: it had a view of the Pacific, and it sat in a small valley at the end of a private road. She imagined a gull or two, gray, soaring creatures, which were waiting for something to die. Then Marta felt the sun coming into the room.

She slept on one side, a sheet wrapped around her hips and waist, and, from between the blinds, slats of light, which were yellow and about the width of a yardstick, fell across her bare back. There were no blankets on the bed, just the sheets and two pillows, and as Marta breathed, her ribs became more defined. The sheet was pulled tight over her hips, and the shape of them under the taut white cotton seemed cast in plaster of Paris. Then she woke. She swallowed and put an arm over her eyes, as though she could shield herself from the fact that she was late. The discomfort of being late and the fear of losing her new job somehow mixed with the lingering image of the house in Malibu. A police car passed, its siren blaring, and the expression in Marta's eyes changed to one of complete alertness.

She sat up, putting both feet on the floor, a corner of the sheet in her lap, her head in her hands, her short hair falling around her face, the slats of light across her back where the bones in her spine made a series of diminutive mounds. Then the hangover caught up with her, and she put her elbows on her naked knees. The best thing was not to move too quickly. She stood, her legs moving through the slats of light, her tall figure absorbed by the gloom of the hall, her hips marked by the shadow of a bathing suit, which fit her like a pair of skin-colored briefs. She stopped and put the back of one hand to her forehead, the other hand aimlessly examining her ribs, as though expecting to find some mark that hadn't been there the day before. She'd been bringing strange men home recently, each one a little rougher than the previous one, and if nothing else, she told herself, this was positively the last time.

Then she turned on the shower and got in, adjusting the water until it was icy, and as she panted, she thought it would make her clear-headed. That was the important thing. She drank from the shower head, her mouth open, the tinsel-like strands filling her mouth until the water overflowed and ran down her cheeks. With her mouth full, she made a sound which was a collection of words spoken against the sensation of cold water in her mouth. It sounded as though she was drowning.

She thought it would take an hour to get to Malibu. At least the traffic wasn't bad at this hour. She could go out the freeway and then take the canyon. That was probably the best way.

She dressed quickly, brushing her short hair and feeling the tug in the slick, heavy mass. She looked in the mirror once, staring at herself now with disbelief that she had overslept, knowing in her heart she had done so in spite of her best intentions, and in the glance there was a frank acknowledgment that she was being asked to do something new today. It hadn't been part of the original arrangement, and in the fact that she had agreed to go to Malibu, she felt she had crossed a threshold. Something had changed. She didn't like the idea she had somehow gotten into it without really thinking, or that it had somehow been sprung on her in a way that had left her unprepared. Would she run down to Malibu to pick up a box? Sure. How could she say no? The demand that she go to Malibu had its own, unmistakable tendrils of . . . well, it was better not to put a word on what it was. Then she dressed, putting on a pair of blue jeans and a cotton shirt and taking a sweater with her in case it was cold at the beach.

Western Avenue, south of Santa Monica, had a lassitude that comes to California streets at about ten o'clock in the morning. The first uneasiness of rush hour had gone, and now the avenue was filled with a stream of less insistent cars, no longer changing from lane to lane or jumping across an intersection at the first glimmer of a green light. The traffic moved with all the languid grace of anxiety that has been carefully submerged by the morning's first tranquillizer. The light was yellow and the sky a layer of red and gray dust and smoke, which hung like an island in the air. By afternoon the sunlight would have changed the air into something even more irritating than it was now. The haze made Marta glad she was going to the beach, although she wished it was on some other errand.

She got into her car, a white Dodge two-door with a stick shift, for which she had traded a Chevrolet and a hundred dollars. There was a man at the gas station, a place called the World on Western, who had made the trade. He had come from Ohio and spoke with an accent which she had difficulty understanding, and now, each time she put the key into the ignition, she thought about the look in the man's eyes when he had taken the hundred dollars and said, "Well, I guess you got the best of me on this deal. Yeah, but you have to take what comes your way," the money, five twenty-dollar bills, disappearing into the man's shirt pocket. "Here's the pink slip."

She put the key into the ignition, turning it with that same small thrill of anticipation of the thing's not starting which she had each morning, and which she guessed if she didn't have, she might actually have missed.

On Santa Monica she passed a church, the interior of which, seen through the maw of the open door, seemed cool and dark. Marta looked at it through the California sunlight, which in the late summer angled only slightly into the street. The shadows of the buildings lay on the north side in dull sections, all of which were about two feet wide and looked like gray paper that had been laid on the ground. It was an Episcopal church, its stones gray and the spaces between them lined with mortar, the entire place having a quality that suggested a quiet village in England, or in the eastern United States, rather than a block that was three hundred yards from the Hollywood Freeway.

Marta wanted to stop and go in, just the way she used to do. She even pulled over and looked into the gloom, already imagining the odor of old hymnbooks and the polish on the pews, but then she pulled back into traffic, feeling somehow cheated that she didn't have the time. She thought briefly of her mother, with whom she used to go to church, and then the image of Malibu from her half-wakeful reveries came back. It was strange that this made her want to go into the church more than ever.

Anyway, the light was too strong to walk through. If she had stopped, she'd have gotten out of her car and stood in the yellow slash of sunlight, feeling her hands tremble. She put a hand to her head, just thinking about it, feeling the hangover's slow, steady sway, as though she had been at sea. She drove on, looking at the directions she had on the seat next to her and then getting on the freeway, hearing the car's engine, which seemed to compensate for lack of power by making noise, as though if the car couldn't make the speed, why then at least it could call attention to itself in some other way. Marta went through the Caheunga Pass into the valley, which appeared as a sheet of cluttered rubble, marked here and there by the sun glinting off the window of a car or a house. In the distance there were bluish mountains.

Malibu Canyon came as a relief. She took the canyon road all the way down to the Pacific Coast Highway, and from there she turned back into the hills, passing stands of eucalyptus trees through which she saw the Pacific. It was just as she had imagined it this morning. She glanced at the ocean from time to time, telling herself it was just the hangover that made the ocean look as though it was a substance that existed only to make things disappear into a blue, cold oblivion. Then, as she saw the sun on it, and the glint on the water, the silver and white chop appeared with a cool, beguiling hope. She took a deep breath, telling herself everything was all right, that she had just gotten the willies somehow and that there was nothing to worry about. Maybe she'd get lucky. She felt better then and rolled down the window so she could smell the salty reek of the ocean.

To the north, the hills curved gently down to the sea, and between the ridges of them, there were isolated beaches. The froth of the breaking waves was a platinum color that dissolved into glare. Further out on the ocean there was one black freighter, the smoke from it trailing away in a languid wisp. The scent of the ocean and the wake of the freighter, which formed a white V on the water, and the odor of the exhaust from the ship's diesel engine, which Marta could only imagine, all combined to evoke a romantic impulse, a longing for . . . well, she didn't want to be too precise about it. Something exciting, mysterious, and yet dependable, too. Marta let the salty air, on which there was the bouquet of eucalyptus, blow into the car and through her hair, the sensation seeming to cut right into the hangover. The first thing that came to mind, in the momentary sense of having her head clear, was an admission that she was afraid, not just of having to go to the house, but of her seeming inability to pierce that loneliness which crept up on her at 3 A.M.

The house came into view. Marta stopped at the side of the road and looked at the mailbox, which was at the beginning of a drive that seemed to disappear over a cliff. The mailbox tilted, and it looked as if it would actually move in the wind. Then Marta got closer to the drive and saw it went down the side of a small canyon, at the back of which, with a view of the ocean, there was the house.

The sight of the place made Marta stop. The dust from the shoulder slowly blew by, although Marta scarcely noticed it. She couldn't even say what it was precisely about the place that made her think something was wrong. The road went down the steep hillside and then turned back onto the flat of the small canyon floor, which was brown and dusty. There was a little grass, but it was the color of hemp rope and had a sheen to it from the sun. The house itself was light green, a one-story place built in two sections at right angles to each other. There was a gravel drive and a parking space in front of the house. A grove of citrus trees had been planted at the side of the drive, and the bright oranges, which were the color of coals in a wood stove, pierced the otherwise dung- and money-colored hillside. A breeze blew, and Marta concentrated on the erratic movement of the leaves in the grove and on the slight undulation of the dry grass. Then her eyes came back to the house, which in its silence, in the lack of movement around it, suggested not so much a place that was deserted as a silent, windblown desolation.

Marta's eyes moved from window to window, finally stopping at the front door, which stood open a little, as if someone had left in a hurry and hadn't had time to pull it completely shut. Marta wished another car would come along the road, not because she wanted any help but because the steady, ordinary puttering of a car on some ordinary business would bring a kind of relief, like a glass of cold water.

She started down the drive, the car pitching forward as it crossed the shoulder. The drive was narrow, with the hillside going straight up on one side and straight down on the other, and as Marta drove along, hearing the car creaking on its springs and the loud popping of the engine, she had the sensation of somehow penetrating an otherwise profound silence. The drive passed through the small grove of orange trees and then came to the front of the house. Marta stopped here, the dust catching up to her like a ghost, its languid movement, in the stillness of the yard, making her more cautious than ever, if only because the dust, in its slow progression, implied the stillness of everything else. The slash of shadow in the partially open doorway, the glass in the window frames, the empty porch seemed to have been standing here, untouched, for years.

Marta concentrated now, thinking there was something obvious here, but when she tried to put a name on it (beginning to describe the house as a mixture of the mundane and the ominous), she had an almost irresistible desire to turn and look at the road she had come on. She thought of the freighter and the V-shaped wake cutting through the sparkles on the surface of the Pacific. Then she told herself she was just overwrought, tired from the night before, that she'd been drinking too much and that it had to stop. She'd get healthy again. She'd go back to running. She'd eat yogurt and wheat germ for breakfast and put sprouts on her salads, but it all seemed like thin stuff as she looked at the front of the house from her car, wishing, more than anything else, that the place didn't have the atmosphere of her heated, sweaty dreams.

Marta got out of the car, leaving the door open a little, instinctively thinking it would be easier to get back into it this way. No fumbling with the handle. She stepped out, a tall, slender woman, her lips the color of raspberries, her eyes green, squinting a little in the noon sunlight, her hair filled with sun-colored highlights.

She walked from the house to the orange grove, where she could smell a citrusy, acrid odor. She reached up and pulled down a leaf, which she held up to her nose, glad for the scent, which seemed to come from some other place, eons away from the thing that the house seemed to imply. The odor made her think of the Mediterranean. She'd never been there, but she had always wanted to go.

She had grown up in California, but even so, there was a lot about the place she had avoided, or simply looked the other way about. But now she found she was facing one of those things she had always told herself she just didn't need to know about. More and more, in a way she didn't really understand, a lot of the things she thought she had been successful in avoiding revealed themselves to have been disguising themselves, or just waiting for the right moment.

She came back to the porch, which was covered by a shingled roof and which had a poured cement floor. Marta reached out and pressed her fingers against the wall of the house, reminding herself that it was just wood and paint. There were no curtains over the windows, and inside she saw the sheen of a polished hardwood floor, which didn't seem to have, as nearly as she could make out, any rug or carpet. Then she looked over and saw the space that was defined by the open door, the six- or eight-inch slash of darkness.

Marta knocked on the door frame, tapping lightly as though

not wanting to disturb anything inside, but then, after hearing nothing and becoming exasperated, she rapped harder, listening to the hollow reverberation inside the house. There was no reason why a deserted house should give her pause, yet she hesitated at the prospect of the empty rooms, not wanting to feel the occasional sway of her hangover in an anonymous place.

"Is anybody home?" said Marta.

She waited, turning to glance up the hillside, where the drive was a dry road in the dry grass of the hillside.

"I said, is anybody home?"

She felt the resonance of her voice in the door frame, and then she reached out with one finger, touching the door and giving it a small shove. Then she waited as it swung open with a steady, soundless invitation. The sheen on the floor of the dim room inside seemed bright, as though a bottle of wax had recently been spilled on it. There was an odor, too, one that stirred an old memory, a mixture of soap and something like perfume and sweat and a low-tide funk. Marta was unable to determine, as she stood in that slight, almost pleasant odor, whether she was filled with anxiety or was just keenly alert.

She stepped inside. She was tentative now, since if anyone surprised her, she didn't want to appear as though she was arrogantly walking into the place. It was all a mistake, right? She'd just walk out and forget the entire thing. That's what she felt like saying, even though she was supposed to ask for a man by the name of Earl Graves.

"I said, is anyone home?"

The sound echoed, the reverberation carrying some hint, some clue Marta tried to understand, as though animosity came with its own vibrant tone. She finally let go of the door and entered a short hall which stretched to the living room. Only part of the living room could be seen, but it had a sliding door that faced a deck, and the room was brighter than the hall. Marta decided that the house gave her the creeps because in its peculiar emptiness it implied a kind of cynicism, she guessed, or a lack of interest in other human beings apart from the most brutal and mercenary concerns. Then she dismissed her fears through sheer will. It didn't seem right to be so jumpy, as she stood in a stranger's house.

The living room didn't make her feel any better. It had the same shiny hardwood floor, marked here and there where furniture had been dragged out of the room, the scuff marks suggesting that the things had been taken with a jerk, as though they had been repossessed.

The room wasn't completely empty, though. It had a white sofa with a white shag rug in front of it. A floor lamp stood in the corner, and along the wall there were some wrappers from candy bars and an ashtray, too. The ashtray was made from an aluminum film can that had had its sides pinched in. Something about the angle of the sofa, perhaps that it was not lined up with any wall, left the impression of having been given a violent shove. Marta wanted to sit down, but she didn't. She looked at the sofa and then walked around the shag rug. In among the candy bar wrappers there were some empty Kodak film boxes, each of which had held four hundred feet of Kodachrome, and on the wall someone had stuck a piece of white adhesive tape that had been around a can of new film. A photographer's light stand stood against the wall, and its feet reminded Marta of some piece of equipment that astronauts had taken to the moon. The sliding glass door was closed, and the room was warm, although the heat had an oppressive quality that reminded Marta of the apprehension she had felt when she had first come in, as if nothing here was other than rankly practical.

She went down the hall and into the bedroom, where the windows were closed and the air was hot and stuffy. The room had a bed in it, in the middle, pulled away from the wall. There were more candy bar wrappers on the floor and a tube of lubricant, too, which was half used up. The hot air smelled of sweat and powder. One lacy stocking, made into a slip noose and having a run in it, lay on the floor next to a small, corrugated wrapper, the kind photographers' light bulbs come in.

Marta stood in the doorway a moment, looking out through the window at the Pacific, the glitter of it impossibly distant, about as far away from the atmosphere of the room as anyone could get. There was in the tawdriness of the place a kind of anonymous excess, or perhaps just a kind of license, suggesting that almost anything could be done. Marta understood it as a feeling of being alone, the sensation mingling with the scent of the Pacific and the fragrance of the citrus trees.

Now there came into the room a steady, repeated sound, as if it were being made by someone chipping away at cement with a tool that wasn't meant for the job, like a screwdriver. The sound had a kind of fierce resignation to it. Marta wasn't sure where it was coming from. She reached out and touched the wall and then moved her fingers to the window, where she could feel the slight, repeated throb of the sound, which was something like a heartbeat. Then she turned away, out of the room, more certain than before that it was not a good idea to be caught here, not surprised in the least that she was even using the word "caught" to herself, since she knew now that she wanted to get away.

She stood in the hall. The door of the room she had just been in wasn't shut, and the light from it cut into the hall. Here the sound was not as loud as in the room, although its remoteness, its lack of definition, was all the more maddening since, as Marta stood there, her head cocked to one side, it seemed to her the sound was so slight as to be almost imagined, the cardiac-like cadence reminding her of the pulse, enhanced by the hangover, which she felt in the side of her face and in her arms.

The hall was dark and hot. Marta's eyes were filled with specks from the room where the sun had streamed in. She put her hand out, the specks forming and disappearing like small, silent explosions. She already knew the house was empty, and yet she didn't turn and walk out. She even stopped, impatient that she couldn't get hold of things sufficiently to just turn away, out of the darkened hall. So she stood there, fingers reaching out, the small explosions of light diminishing now, finally admitting to herself that she was compelled by the house, if only because it seemed to suggest those fears of hers that had always been just beyond her line of sight. The terror of the anonymous, at which everyone in California politely looked the other way, seemed to be close here, and Marta contemplated it with something like a salacious anticipation, as though she was finally going to get a good look after all.

She put out her hand in the dimness ahead of her as if she were walking at night along a path where wires were strung. The fingers of her other hand touched the wall, the constant plane of it making Marta feel better, if only because she took comfort in one hard, identifiable object. Then she touched the doorknob of the next bedroom. It was warm, and Marta could feel the heat of the room in the metal of the knob. But there was something else there, too, a vibration which seemed to mesh with the taut buzzing in her own nerves.

The vibration got stronger as she opened the door, the sound becoming as loud as a beehive where a swarm is forming. There were a couple of hundred flies in the bedroom. Marta pushed the door open. The mass of flies rose in a blue-green shimmer from a stain on the wall and on the floor. The shimmer of the insects, like peacock herl, moved into the sunlight, the flies spreading through the room, their entire movement suggesting the various paths of chaos. The buzzing seemed to increase, and Marta now wanted to turn and go back into the hall, but instead, with the same fascination as before, she decided to wait for a minute.

The room had a view of the Pacific, which seemed cool and distant. There was no furniture here, and sunshine lay in nearly identical parallelograms on the floor. Marta looked from the ocean to the sunlight on the floor, and then turned to look at the stains on the wall and on the floor. The flies went on buzzing.

The stains on the wall were long and thin, dark now, the color of coal oil, although on the floor the stuff had been half cleaned up, wiped with a towel or a rag so that there were swirls, not quite so dark, a little brownish, over the hardwood floor. The flies moved back and forth, and through the buzzing there was that steady ticking or pecking sound, the cadence of it constant, not machinelike so much as just dedicated. Marta took one good look, facing the details that so clearly indicated violence. She blinked, thinking things over. Obviously someone had been hurt and had stumbled against the wall, resting against it and then moving again, trying to get to the window. The stains on the wall, like an enormous electrocardiogram, showed the place where someone had rested. Then the shimmer of the flies crossed the room again.

Marta stepped back into the hall, closing the door behind her, not wanting the flies to come into the hall, but this was unnecessary: they instinctively avoided the darkness beyond the door of the room.

She looked into the other bedroom for a moment, hearing that steady tapping sound, a kind of *swick swick swick*. She didn't know whether the sound was an indication of danger or not, and as she listened, she tried to make sense of the room, her eyes going over the used tube of lubricant, the candy bar wrappers, the stocking, a pair of net underwear thrown into a corner, the used sheets of paper towels that had been rolled up and tossed along the wall, the sheets on the bed, which looked rumpled.

She went out to the living room and through the sliding glass doors onto a deck. Down below there was a Japanese gardener, dressed in a khaki shirt and khaki trousers and dark boots, using garden shears to trim a hedge in a long, neat box. The hedge went around a flower garden, the reds and blues of the blooms, the filaments of orange like sparks, the yellows and purples all stood out against the sere landscape.

"Excuse me," said Marta.

The man looked up, the jaws of the shears open, the sharp edges glinting in the sunlight. The khaki shirt he wore had been cut off at the elbows, and the edge of the cloth had been frayed to a kind of fringe. The entire effect of the man, as he stood with his arms emerging from the lopped-off shirt, his forearms thick with years of work, suggested a keen sense of the Orient, as if he were working his way across a glassy rice paddy planted with orderly rows of green stalks. He looked at Marta, his eyes the color of black marbles.

"I'm looking for someone," she said.

He went on staring at her.

"Have you seen anyone here?" she asked.

"I look after the garden," he said. Then the sound of the shears started again.

"Wait a minute," she said. "I'm looking for Earl Graves."

"Don't know him," said the man.

"Then you haven't seen anybody?"

"I didn't say that," he said. "Yesterday I was working on the oranges. They don't grow so good. Salt air no good for oranges."

"Oh?" asked Marta.

"Yes," said the man. "The place to grow oranges is in the valley. But they cut down all the orange groves and built houses."

The man looked at her, holding the shears, their sharp edges flashing a little in a steady rhythm, as though the beating of his heart were responsible for their movement in the sunlight.

"Are you with them?" he asked.

"Who?" she said. "With who?"

"The people who were here."

"No," she said. "No. I was just supposed to pick something up. From Earl Graves. He has blond hair."

"Don't know," he said. "I know the landlord. He rents to people. I don't know them. Sometimes they throw things on the plants. It kills them."

She nodded, putting a hand on the rail, which was weathered a little, the edges of the grain turning. She glanced out at the ocean.

"There's no one here?" she asked.

"No," he said. "They were here before. Some young women. Some men. Pretty women. They came in a van and took off their clothes. You know, like nudists. Then they went inside with some movie cameras."

Marta nodded. The man looked at her and said, "You know, they were . . ." He made a gesture, his arm emerging from the fringe of the cut-off sleeve, the fingers slowly undulant. It was a gesture of extreme economy, the fingers moving with the cadence of kelp swaying in the tide, but somehow, in their stubbiness, in the tanned skin and the beauty of the color of the fingernails, like the pink of a conch shell, there was a hint of something salacious. He made the gesture for only a second or so, glancing at Marta until he was certain she understood. Then he looked away, at the neat, square shape of the hedge that ran down into the garden.

"They were making dirty movies," he said. "You know?"

She nodded.

"Were they all here yesterday?" she asked.

"In the morning and afternoon," he said. "In the evening there were two men. One had blond hair. I left before they did."

"Have you been inside?" she asked.

"No. When I have to . . ." he made another gesture, as descriptive as the other, "I go into the bushes."

Then he turned and went back to his work, the shears making a *swick swick swick,* although there was something hesitant in his movements now, a question or uneasiness, as though he were trying to decide, as he went about his work, if he had said too much.

Marta turned and went back into the house, seeing that now there were flies in the living room, too, their emerald, quivering movement suggesting to her the reflection of light off the surface of a swimming pool. For a moment she thought about this imprecise association, the fact of which made her pause. That flickering, undulant light from a pool had always seemed somehow filled with all the most vulgar promise of California, as though people here could finally escape into pure romance. But there was something else about it, too, and when Marta saw that reflection on the underside of a veranda around a pool, or on the wall of a house, the aquamarine shimmer always seemed to suggest a kind of natural, momentary hint of pleasure and desire.

She left the front door of the house as she had found it, open about eight inches, the darkness of the doorway having the air of an invention that was at once malicious and indifferent.

As she opened the door of her car, a van came down the drive from the road, two long streaks of dust rising behind it. The dust carried with it the dry scent of the hills at this time of the year, a kind of bitterness distilled out of the short spring. The cloud swept over the van and up to the front door of the house like a curse.

A man opened the door on the driver's side and got out. He was short but compact, long in the torso but short in the legs. He reached around and took a mop and a bucket and some paper towels and cleaning solutions out of the back of the van, and then began to carry them to the house. Then he stopped, the last of the dust from the drive blowing around him.

"Who are you?" he said to Marta.

Marta swallowed.

"I'm lost," she said. "I just stopped to get directions."

"Is that right?" said the man, looking at her.

"Yes," she said.

He was still bent over, carrying the bucket which held the plastic bottles of cleaner.

"I was just going," said Marta.

"Have you been inside?" He straightened up now.

"Me?" said Marta.

"Yeah," said the man. "You."

"No," said Marta. "I just put my head in the door. No one here. So I guess I'll just be going."

"Where are you trying to get to?" he asked.

She just looked at him.

"What directions did you have?"

"It's OK," she said. "I'll get there."

"I asked you a question."

"Don't get so pushy," she said.

"Have you been inside?"

"I told you," she said. "I'm going now."

She walked into the last of the dust, which now had the quality of a thin, almost burned-off fog, and as she went, she was sure the man was still watching her. She came to her car and got in, throwing her small handbag onto the seat beside her. Then she backed out and turned around, glancing in the rear-view mirror. The man had put down the mop and bucket and was writing her license number on a slip of cardboard he had ripped from the end of a Brillo box.

Marta drove through the small grove of orange trees, the dust moving through the trees like a pesticide that had been sprayed on the orchard. The man finished writing on his scrap of paper, and then he simply stared, his expression seemingly blank but somehow still conveying a barely concealed fury, as though something that was rightfully his had slipped through his fingers.

She went back through Malibu Canyon, the salty smell of the Pacific fading quickly in the scent of eucalyptus trees. The stands of eucalyptus and the dried grass suggested a savanna. Then she came to the valley, the clutter of it stretching out in one contiguous accumulation of objects which, when seen from a distance, appeared like scraps or some residue left by the action of greed or folly. She told herself everything was fine, that she had been overwrought. That's all there was to it.

The Search
for Romance

THE YOUNG WOMAN came into the *Romance Advertiser* office and stood at the threshold, the door half open. She was twenty-three or -four and had short, bleached hair. The skirt she wore was short and made of leather, or something that looked like leather. She had on a purple blouse and high-heeled shoes and stockings with a seam down the back of thin legs. She was carrying a copy of the *Romance Advertiser*, the pages turned back to the section that described how to place an ad.

Everything about the young woman suggested someone who had come to a critical moment, and that it would be just as possible for her to turn and run as for her to come in and sit down. The office of the *Advertiser* was a little more gritty than she had imagined. There were travel posters on the wall, one showing the dusty, home-like hills of Italy, and another of Greece, with houses as white as blocks of Ivory soap and the sea as blue as a morning glory. There was a rubber plant, too, in the pot of which people had put out their cigarette butts. There were two sofas beyond a courtroomlike divider, behind which Marta sat at her desk. Marta was still thinking about the Pacific and the house in Malibu. Then the young woman sighed, let the door swing shut behind her, and said to Marta, "Hi."

Marta turned toward her and said, "Hi."

"I've come about an ad." The young woman held out the *Advertiser*. It was a small magazine, made of newsprint, and while the cover was printed in three colors, the inside was filled with long lists of advertisements, either twenty-four or fifty words long, in which people described themselves.

The young woman swallowed and licked her lips and ran a hand through her bleached hair. Marta watched as she came through the swinging door of the divider and approached her desk.

"My name's Sissy Blackburn," said the young woman.

"Hi," said Marta. "What do you want the ad to say?"

"I don't know," said Sissy. "I can tell you this. L.A. is a tough place to meet people."

Marta looked at her, thinking it over. Then she said, "I guess that's right. Where are you from?"

"Oregon," said Sissy. "I came down here with my boyfriend. From Coos Bay. You know what he always wanted? He always wanted a dog. A shepherd. So I went out and got him one. Then I had to go up to Oregon for a visit for a couple of weeks. And you know what? While I was gone he spent the time with a girl I had met, kind of a friend of mine. They went to Mexico. While they were gone the dog starved. Made a horrible stink in the apartment. So you know what I did? I went out with my boyfriend's best friend. I gave it to him righteous. Made my boyfriend real mad. Then I thought I'd better start over, so I came in here."

"Are you living in the valley?" asked Marta.

"How'd you know?"

"Just a guess."

Marta rolled a form into the typewriter on her desk, and as she started typing, the sound of the letters striking the roller seemed very loud. She glanced up at Sissy's bleached hair, her blue eyes with mascara around them, her entire presence a mixture of the inflammatory and the desperately innocent. There was something else as she sat there, her skirt above her kneecaps, which were a little white with pressure under the net stockings. Marta had the sensation of somehow being fraudulent, if only because by sitting there she implied she could take care of the problems that walked through the door. She remembered the sirens she had heard at 3 A.M. as she tried to sleep while she lay in the light from the street lamp outside her window. It fell across her in a rectangular sheet, defining the musculature of her underarms when she put her hands behind her head. Sometimes, at this hour, she smoked a cigarette, the plume of smoke moving into the soft glow, the spreading cloud seeming to her to suggest the lonely ease with which the silence of this hour sneaked up on her.

For a while now she had been facing the advertisers, like Sissy Blackburn, with a businesslike approach. This, she supposed, was the best thing, but she wasn't sure it was doing her any good.

She looked up at the wall, where there hung eighty or so small photographs of people who had just gotten married. They looked happy, each couple smiling. Each of the photographs was signed and inscribed to the *Romance Advertiser*. The pictures looked nice, although Marta's boss had got them when the *Los Angeles Herald* had been cleaning out its files, and he and Marta and Elaine, who also worked in the office, had signed them, changing hands and handwriting styles to make them look different.

Sissy Blackburn started talking now, as though words would somehow make everything better. She seemed to hope that if she was intimate enough, why then her reason for being here would be obvious, reduced to a commonplace need which could be filled easily. She worked in a "specialty" mail-order house on Santa Monica, a place that sold envelopes of fake dandruff and cans filled with spring-loaded snakes, devices that were put under a toilet seat and squirted water on the person who sat down. She was looking for another job. She'd applied to a therapist who was going to treat cats and dogs for the trauma of their previous lives, but he was only just beginning. He thought everyone should take a carrot juice and coffee enema.

Her ad ran: "SWF, likes long walks in the country, the beach, vitamins, hard-driving rock-and-roll, good food (if it's instant or quick cooking), going to the malls, interesting clothes. No mouth breathers."

Sissy went out, the sound of her voice as she turned at the door and said, " 'Bye," suggesting that hope and disaster went hand in hand. Marta listened to the diminishing footsteps in the hall, afraid that the only difference between her and the people who came in here was that she was just more careful about the words she used in describing herself.

An office had been built into the corner of the room. The

outside walls were covered with plywood that had a veneer to suggest paneling, and the door had a black sign with white letters that read, "Bobby Salinas." Bobby came out now and stood in the doorway, looking at Marta. Then he said, "Come in here. I want to talk to you."

Marta marked up the ad with copyediting marks and put it in the box for the printers. Then she stood up and went into the office, closing the door.

Bobby Salinas was forty-three years old and had a tattoo around his neck, a line of perforations and, in the middle, the words "Cut Here." He was very tan and had curly hair, and on his bald spot he was using a paste of powdered rhinoceros horns he got from a healer in Santa Monica. He worked out in a gym and was large in the arms, but he had a belly which hung over his ninety-dollar jeans. Recently he had put some money into a marina development down toward Laguna and had lost his shirt. He had a copy of Camus's *The Rebel* on his desk, only a little of which he had read. He assumed the book meant he could do whatever the hell he wanted, in a Frenchified, somewhat aloof kind of way. What he really liked to do was go down to New Port, where he kept his boat. It was what is known as a "cigarette boat," in that it had been used to smuggle cigarettes; it had close to a thousand horsepower and was long and slender. Bobby Salinas liked to get a cooler of beer on board and go back and forth between the mainland and Catalina, throwing a beer can at a whale when he happened to see one breaching from the green Pacific. He had been in primal scream therapy, but after a while he realized he liked the boat better. In the long run, it was probably cheaper, too.

He owned the *Romance Advertiser,* and he also had some other things going. For instance, he had a business that exported secondhand auto parts, which he got from junkyards in southern California. He sent the parts to India by ship and imported cloth and clothes in return. Every now and then he'd make thirty or forty thousand dollars this way, and then he'd look at the Camus. He guessed the French guy was right after all: Do it to them before they do it to you.

"Did you get the box this morning?" he asked Marta.

"No," she said.

She stood in front of him and he looked up at her. He was sitting at his desk with his legs over the corner.

"Did you go to Malibu?" he asked.

"Yes," she said.

"Explain yourself," he said. "If you asked me to go out and get you an ice cream cone, and I came back empty-handed, you'd say, where the fuck is the ice cream? Isn't that right?"

Marta stood straight now, thinking about the flies as they rose in the bedroom of the house in Malibu. She closed her eyes for a moment, and then she looked out the window, through which she saw the hills. She could even see the dome of the observatory, green and reassuring against the hillside.

"I wouldn't ask you to get me an ice cream cone," said Marta.

He stared at her for a while.

"Do you like working here?" he asked.

"It's all right," she said.

"Do you want to go on working here?" He took his feet off the corner of the desk and put them on the floor and then he leaned forward, his expression bland. He was already shaking his head a little, in a gesture she recognized as being an essential part of the man in that, whenever he fired someone, he felt that he had been victimized. He was still pissed off that he had almost lost his driver's license when he had gotten drunk and sideswiped three cars on the Pacific Coast Highway. What the hell were they doing there anyway? For a moment Marta felt herself drift toward a kind of barrier: she imagined it to be like a large piece of transparent plastic, and the sense that she could pass through it, just by telling this man to take his job and shove it, brought with it a mixture of elation and despair in that, even as she was cleaning out her desk, she knew she'd be worried about the rent. Marta just leaned up against it, recognizing the danger in his expression.

"Yes," she said.

"Then tell me what happened down there."

"There was no one around. The place was empty."

She wanted to talk about the atmosphere there, the stains, the buzzing of the flies; she was even willing to try to talk to Bobby Salinas about it. She raised an arm and made a gesture, opening her hand and then letting her wrist go limp. He made the same gesture.

"What's this supposed to mean?"

"Nothing," she said. "I just went down there and no one was around. That's all."

Bobby Salinas sat, staring at her, thinking things over.

"Earl Graves has got a place above Silverlake. Up toward Ferndale. I want you to go up to his house and ask for the box of film. This way it's nice and polite, you understand? I'm not sending a couple of fucking guineas up there who would break his legs for fifty bucks. It's polite. He'll understand that."

Marta looked out the window again. She didn't want to walk out of here with the certainty she'd have to start looking for a job on Monday. The outcast mentality set in so quickly, especially when she was driving around in her car, watching the gas gauge and looking at the newspaper on the seat, open to the classified ads, a number of them circled in bright red ink. She knew she was being asked to do something else here, too, and that she was about to cross another threshold. She was reminded of those times at 3 A.M. when she lay in the light from the street lamp, feeling it almost as an impossibly thin sheet over her skin. Then the sense of isolation left her with an impulse to lash out, and now the impulse of the nights combined with the anger of the moment, the two intermingling perfectly and leaving her saying, louder than she meant to, "All right. I'll get the box."

"Good," said Bobby Salinas. "I knew I could count on you."

He nodded, as though his suspicions had been proved right. He figured she was secretly hot for him.

"Go up there tonight," he said.

"Have you got the address?" she asked.

"You'll have to get it," he said.

"How?"

"You're smart. That's why I hired you. I figured anyone who had gone to Berkeley would be smart enough to do some jobs around here. Say, did you ever read Camus?"

Marta glanced at the book on the corner of the desk.

"No," she said. "I was never interested in stuff like that. I'll get the box."

* * *

Marta went into the outer office and sat down at her desk, rubbing her lips across the back of her wrist as she tried to be clear about what was happening. She imagined that she was caught in a kind of suction, an irresistible current that pulled in a direction she didn't want to go in, and it wasn't driven by her own desires so much as by the thwarting of them, by exasperation. She wasn't sure it was a good idea, but before she thought any more about it, another woman walked in to the *Romance Advertiser.*

* * *

The advertisers finally stopped coming in around four o'clock. Marta got up and went out into the hall, where it was quiet and the air was stale. Then she walked down to a frosted door on which a sign in black letters read, "Pete French, Private Investigations West."

The waiting room behind the door had three chrome and leather chairs, and next to each one there was a stand that held a small metal bowl with a chrome trap door, through which, at the touch of a chrome button, cigarette ends disappeared. There were framed sketches of Sherlock Holmes and a newspaper account of a murder that had been cleverly solved by a detective named Pete French. There were some imitation roses in a vase in the corner. All in all the place suggested the waiting room of a dentist whose white jacket was never quite clean.

French was a tall man, over six four, about fifty years old. His face was angular, although he was a little fleshy, and his profile, with his grayish skin, resembled an axe that has been ill-used. He wore a short-sleeved shirt made of a synthetic material, polyester probably, through which his basketball-player-style undershirt was visible. He wore green pants that were shiny on the seat, and when he went out, he wore a brown and white houndstooth sport jacket. Some years before he had been shot in the stomach, and he didn't have much intestine left. He couldn't eat a large meal, so he constantly chewed beef jerky, and he drank a couple of chocolate milk shakes every day.

Marta listened at the door of his inner office for a moment, and French said, "Come in. I'm not busy."

Marta came in and sat down in the chair for clients.

"Hard night?" asked French.

"Why do you ask?" said Marta.

"You look scared," he said. "Sometimes a bad night leaves people looking that way."

"I'm OK," she said.

French went on looking at her for a while. There was a copy of the *Scandal Sheet* on his desk, which was open to the scandal column.

"How's business?" said Marta.

"Can't complain. Listen. I don't mind when a friend is scared. I mind when she lies about it."

Marta looked back at him. She wanted to say something about Malibu, but the truth of the matter was that all she had was a few details which had been filtered through a bad morning. There didn't seem to be any words to convey the problem, and she didn't want to say anything that could be easily picked apart or dismissed. She glanced up, suspecting that she was only anxious, but she resisted discarding her uneasiness this way, if only because, putting distortions aside, she was certain something was going on. The evidence of it did not exist in just a detail but was made up of an accumulation of small things.

So she waited for a moment, searching for the right words, and as she sat there, she looked at the wall behind French. It was covered with bookshelves made of wood with imitation worm holes in it, and the shelves held law books and others with titles such as *Fingerprinting for the Practical Detective, Disguises and the Assumption of Identity, Starting Over: The Complete Guide to False Identity, Calworth's Standard Directory of U.S. Identity Papers (Including Puerto Rico, Hawaii, and Alaska),* and *Calworth's Standard Desk Reference of U.S. Police Departments.* There were two framed Audubon prints on the wall, one of canvasback ducks, the other of a red-tailed hawk, the eye of which seemed particularly keen and a little vicious.

On the wall to his left there was a sign that read, "No One Ever Raped a .38," and on the other there was a piece of needle-point, the kind that usually says, "Bless This Happy Home," although here the square, neatly stitched letters read, "Expect No Mercy."

"How's the romance business?" he asked.

"OK," she said. "The people come in pretty steady."

"Sure," said French. "Hope springs eternal."

"I guess it does."

He looked out the window. It was a hazy day, the air a gray-yellow color that always reminded Marta of the fur of a coyote. In fact, more and more, the coyotes had been moving into the hills around Hollywood. There were even reports of them getting into garbage cans right in the city, on Santa Monica Boulevard. French looked at the air and at a barometer on the wall: he believed a falling barometer brought about behavior that was difficult, erratic, and sometimes outright criminal. On days when the air pressure was low, he was almost sure that when he got to his office there would be someone sitting in the waiting room who would want him to do something ugly and then would argue with him about his fee.

"Have you noticed any correlation between romance and weather?" he asked.

"I guess more people come in when it's raining," she said.

"You see," he said. "It's all in the barometer."

"I don't know. They always say they stopped in on a rainy day because they could find a place to park."

"The barometer's falling," he said. "Plain as the nose on your face."

She stared at the thing, wondering what kind of weather made people most romantic. She guessed the truth was that people came in in the fall, when it was foggy, and in the spring, when the hills had a short-lived, beguiling green tint.

Then she turned to French and said, "I came to ask you a favor."

"Sure."

"I need the address for a man named Earl Graves. He lives up in Ferndale."

"Naw," said French. "You don't want to go see a guy like that. A nice young woman like you?"

"Bobby wants me to pick something up," said Marta.

French sat there for a while, his eyes a pale, flat gray, about the color of fish scales.

"Quit," said French. "Tell Bobby Salinas to go shit in his hat. Hell, he does it every morning, doesn't he?"

"I don't want to start looking for another job," said Marta. "I just want the address."

"Listen," said French. "You can find another job. You got an education, don't you?"

"I dropped out at Berkeley."

"Then why don't you go back?"

"I wasn't learning much."

He looked at her for a minute with the same flat expression as his eyes moved over her.

"Yeah," he said. "I guess that's right. You going to be in your office for a while?"

She nodded.

"I'll drop down in a little bit," he said.

Then he turned and looked out the window.

"What's there to be afraid of?" she said.

French stared at her again.

"Yeah," he said. "Sure. That's one way of looking at it."

Marta went into the hall. It was empty, and the sheen on the floor and the lingering odor of cigarettes contributed to her sense that when human beings leave a particular place, a reminder of them stays there for a while. The silence of the hall made Marta think of an archaeological ruin which for centuries had existed only in the quietly brooding passage of time.

She took two more ads, and then French came into the office. He was very tall, and his clothes never seemed to fit right. He got a lot of them through a Tall Man's catalogue, which, from time to time, he and Marta would look through together, Marta picking out things which he rejected, usually saying, "I'm not a banker, you know? I want to look like a brush salesman. That's the best thing." As he came through the door, he held out a slip of paper. Then he walked up to her desk and said, "Here."

"Where did you get it?"

"Got the number from directory assistance. Then I called Graves and said I had a check to send him. Telephone company refund. Before he had time to think, he came across with it."

She reached out and took the piece of paper, folding it and putting it in the pocket of her blue jeans, and as she pushed it in, French said, "Come on. You're finished with romance for the day, aren't you?"

The *Romance Advertiser* was in a building on Santa Monica Boulevard. There was a sign in the street that stuck out from the wall so that it could be read from both directions. It was a yellow plastic sign with red plastic letters, the kind usually seen in front of a discount hardware store or an inexpensive Indian restaurant. The *Romance Advertiser* was on the second floor, which was reached by a long stairway with a short landing in the middle.

Sometimes men spent the night downstairs, and they left behind a Sneaky Pete or two and the unmistakable odor of urine. An expatriate Bulgarian, Joe, was the janitor. He had large forearms, and he wore a blue jumpsuit and sandals, and when he smelled the stink in the hall, he usually stood there for a moment, his arms crossed, as though by standing up to the odor he could do something about the men who made it. When Marta came in in the morning and found him with his arms crossed, his nostrils opening and closing as he took breaths, his anger feeding on the odor like a crow on carrion, he would say, "They got in last night. Again. One day I'm going to catch them when they come in here to piss. Let me tell you, they'll wish they hadn't."

"I don't know what things are coming to," said Marta.

"I know," said Joe. He stood with his arms crossed, looking out the window at the cars on Santa Monica. "I know damn good and well what they're coming to."

French and Marta went down the stairs and into the street, Marta wearing a sweater she had brought in that morning. Outside it was beginning to cool off, the hazy yellow afternoon light making an icelike glare on the rails of the track that ran down Santa Monica. Marta turned in to the coffee shop where she usually had a cup of tea while French had a milk shake, but he stopped her and said, "Let's go further up."

"OK," said Marta. "Where?"

"The church," said French. "My mother's sick. She's getting old. I want to pray."

Marta glanced at him.

"Do you?" she said.

"Yeah," he said. "I don't know what else to do."

The church was a large stone building, the blocks of granite looking out of place against the palm trees and telephone wires that ran down this part of Santa Monica. The tracks in the middle of the street were all that was left from the days when there were streetcars in Los Angeles, and there seemed to be something equally forlorn about the tracks and the church. Marta and French climbed the steps and went through the large, arched doorway, French glancing over at her once and saying, "I think you should pray, too. That is, if you're going to see Earl Graves."

Blanche Brooks and the Foggy Bottom

I N T H E C H U R C H Marta thought about her mother. The scent of hymnbooks and Bibles, the odors of polish and dust, the texture of the air, which was so caressing as to suggest silk, all were reminders of Blanche Brooks. Marta clasped her hands together on the back of the pew in front of her and leaned her head against them. Around her there was a devotional serenity, disturbed only by the whisper of French's prayers. The place was as quiet as those churches in which she and her mother had attended the funerals of strangers.

In fact, she might even have come to the funeral of a stranger in this church. Marta looked up and glanced around. She was pretty sure she had been here, especially since she and her mother had gone to almost every church within a thirty-mile radius of Beechwood Canyon, where they had lived.

Blanche would go to the funerals in her costume jewelry and her black dress and her shoes that showed her toes. Marta always wore a dark blue dress and black shoes and stockings. The two of them would come out of their small, imitation Tudor house with the lawn that was mowed once a week by a Chinese gardener, Blanche walking with her shoulders back and her jewelry clinking ominously. She carried herself as though she were an instrument of fate who had come to sit in judgment on the ceremonies for the newly departed.

They would get into Blanche's car, which was parked at the curb in front of the house — a Buick, a red Roadmaster with the chrome exhaust ports in the front fenders. Blanche's costume jewelry jingled as she pulled the door open and said, "In you go, kiddo."

Usually Marta and Blanche would go to a stranger's funeral after Blanche had been waiting around for a boyfriend to call. At a certain point, almost by the quality of the silence in the house, Blanche knew more waiting was a waste of time, and rather than brooding about being dropped by another man, it was better to get out of the house. Then Blanche would look into the obituary pages of the *Los Angeles Times*.

She read the announcements aloud, going from one to another the way a movie fan looks over the entertainment section of the paper. As she went over them, she had a large black grease pencil ready, with which she would circle those announcements that had possibilities. She would do this with a steady, even somewhat cheerful ceremony, as though the deaths she contemplated somehow compensated for her own keen disappointment. Sometimes she would hum, "I wanna be around to pick up the pieces . . ."

She would pick a funeral to go to. Then she would look up at the mantle, on which there was a photograph in a silver frame. The photograph was of her husband, Marta's father, who had gone off to the Korean War and had not come back. He appeared in his dress whites, wearing his cap, his smile dignified and even wise. Marta had never known the man, but she still felt a profound attachment to what she imagined he had been like. At least, she was convinced that her father, as pictured in his dress whites, wouldn't have made a stink in the bathroom like her mother's boyfriends, who sometimes spent the night and then left, giving Blanche a peck on the cheek and an affectionate squeeze at the door. And Marta was convinced, too, that if he hadn't been killed in Korea, she wouldn't be spending mornings, afternoons, and evenings sitting in churches while men, women, and children got ready to bury someone.

The photograph of the man in the dress whites sat on the mantle like an icon, and when things were difficult (if Blanche had an argument with the neighbor, or when there was money trouble, or when the Buick Roadmaster had a flat tire or needed a new fuel or water pump), Marta and Blanche would sit in the living room on the overstuffed green chair and sofa that Blanche had inherited from her mother. And as they sat there, worrying about the Roadmaster's fuel pump, or the results, which they had not yet received, of the medical tests Blanche had from time to time as a matter of tempting or even daring fate to do its worst, they would glance at the picture of the man in the dress whites: his eyes were large and had that peculiar transparent quality which blue eyes have when seen in a black and white photo. His nose was straight, and his jaw and cheeks had been so closely shaved as to give the skin a smoothness that was almost a sheen. His lips were a little thin, but they were set in a restrained expression that suggested not only understanding but a capacity for great passion, too.

The more Marta looked at his face, the more she was convinced of the man's love and concern for her, which, as far as she was concerned, was conveyed by a kind of photographic telepathy. There was something in the man's smile that suggested he knew the difference between things that were dangerous (and should be guarded against) and the phantoms of anxiety.

So after Blanche and Marta looked at the photograph, they would go out to the car. Then they would drive through town, Blanche liking to pick out funerals in different churches, each new building seeming to bring with it not only the spiritual dispatching of the last boyfriend, but the hope that a new man, the right one this time, would finally appear. And, as they drove, Blanche would review the flaws of the man they were saying farewell to, pointing out that "his teeth were too big," or that he "came like a Filipino," or worst of all that he had a "pinched soul." This malady usually revealed itself by the way in which the man spent money on Blanche.

They would park and go in. For years Marta assumed that crying smelled like flowers. Blanche would sit at the back, shoulders square, jewelry making a stern Old Testament jingling, and while she maintained this posture for as long as she could, the eulogy soon touched her, particularly if it was for a decent man who had been a good provider and an affectionate father, and in the general grieving, in the tears of the mourners, Blanche was able to admit how troubled she had been when her last boyfriend had said she was "the hottest thing in town for men over forty," or that he had actually tried to give her money rather than taking her to the Foggy Bottom, a steak house where Blanche liked to go for a "blood rare" steak ("black on the outside and cold in the middle"). Then she would start to cry, muttering in a voice loud enough for the mourners to hear, "That son of a bitch. May he rot in hell."

Whenever one of the mourners gave her an appalled look, Blanche took this as a comment on the ease with which she had gotten herself into another "bad relationship," and she cried all the harder, since being accused on top of her misfortune was a little more than she could take. It added to her resentment of the last boyfriend who had shown his bad manners and lack of taste by discarding Blanche in favor of another woman with a bathroom to stink up and an appetite for the Foggy Bottom's steak.

Outside, Marta would ask, "Do you feel better?"

"Yes, I do," Blanche always said. "Never underestimate the power of a good cry, Marta. Your father used to cry all the time."

"He doesn't look like the kind to cry much."

"Well, he did."

Then they would get into the Roadmaster, neither one saying a word, and when they got home, they usually sat for a moment, both of them looking up at that photograph on the mantle of the man in the dress whites. And after Blanche had satisfied herself, by looking at the picture, that perfection was possible and that she had been cheated out of it, she would take out a copy of the Los Angeles telephone directory, and after she had looked up the name of the man whose funeral they had just attended, she would take a black pen and a metal ruler, both bought especially for this purpose, and draw a straight, sharp line through the entry in the phone book, as though the accounts on another injustice had finally been closed. Then she would look at Marta and say, "Well, at least that's over."

On those occasions when Blanche had been more offended than usual by being dropped (especially when she had "stooped beneath herself" to get involved with the man to begin with), she would begin to consider the people who would come to her own funeral. She went about this not in a dreamy way, but with the practiced authority of an accountant.

She made lists of prospective attendees, writing the names carefully in black ink with the same pen she used to obliterate names in the phone book. Blanche kept the lists on tablets of yellow foolscap. Each year she sent out Christmas cards to the people she thought of as prospective mourners. Then she waited to see whether or not the people she sent them to would send her one in return. She gave them three chances. If she did not receive a response the first year, she put a cross next to the name of the person she had sent a card to, and if she didn't receive a card the second year, she put a check next to the name. And finally, if in the third year she didn't receive a card in which there was glitter spread over glue that said, "Merry Christmas," Blanche put a large X next to the name, knowing as she did so the exact number of names that were left. The operation was carried out with the air of cutting one's losses. She performed this chore under the eyes of the man in the photograph on the mantle.

In fact, though, Blanche knew nothing about the man in the photograph. It had come from a secondhand furniture store on Santa Monica. Blanche had gone there looking for a piece of furniture, an old wardrobe she could use to store Marta's clothes. Marta had been five at the time.

Marta's father had been an engineer for an oil company whom Blanche had met at the Foggy Bottom. His name was John Sanders. He had had a convertible, and they had driven down to the beach. They had gone "tea dancing" together on the strip, and had even watched the grunion run on the beach at night, the silver fish looking like animated moonlight. After Blanche had told Sanders she was pregnant, Sanders had said, "Well, you can do one of two things."

"What are they?" asked Blanche. She rubbed the second finger of her left hand, already imagining the caress of an engagement ring.

"Go to Mexico for an abortion," he said.

"What's the other?" said Blanche. She had stopped rubbing her finger.

"Try to bring it up yourself. But count me out."

They were at the bar of the Foggy Bottom. Each of them had a margarita in a glass that had been dipped in salt. It was a specialty of the house, and Blanche, tasting the salty bitterness of the drink, said, "I'm not going to Mexico. Why don't you go fuck yourself to death the next time you're in the mood."

She reached into her handbag and, pushing her compact and lipstick and a pill case aside and then finally dumping her keys, wallet, address book, and Tampax onto the bar, where they formed a kind of monument to intimacy gone wrong, she reached into the pile and found the ten dollars she kept at the bottom as "mad money" (and which she insisted that Marta carry when she was old enough to go out, the ten dollars pinned to the inside of Marta's coat pocket as a kind of furious memory of Marta's patrimony). Then Blanche slapped the ten dollars down on the bar and scooped her things back into her bag, saying, "Here. That's for my share."

Then she picked up her bag and got off the stool, still tasting the salty bitterness. She stared back at Sanders, wondering what he would do. She looked at the bartender just to make sure there was an audience (or, as she thought at the time, a "witness"), but the bartender looked back at her with a distinct lack of interest, since he had seen just about everything people could do in public and not be arrested and a lot of things for which they probably should have been. Sanders reached out and took the money, saying, "Thanks."

"So, you're going to take it?"

He shrugged. Then he held the bill out.

"Do you want it?"

"Oh, God," said Blanche.

"Look, this is a little messy. But, believe me, a clean break is the best thing," said Sanders.

At the age of five, Marta began to ask detailed questions about her father. Blanche answered without hesitation, her descriptions of the man not really lies so much as carefully incubated hopes and dreams. Blanche and Marta would sit together on the green sofa made of fuzzy material, Marta with her legs sticking straight out since they weren't long enough to reach the floor. Blanche would put her arm around Marta's shoulders and speak in a voice that revealed a mixture of happy memories and a keen, constant regret: these moments were precious to both of them, their voices, the fuzz of the sofa, the quiet house all blending together into a physical sensation of intimacy. Sometimes Marta had a 7-Up, and the tickling of the bubbles in her nose reminded her of the foam of the ocean, where her father had sailed as a navy officer. Blanche couldn't even have said why she had settled on this as part of the identity she had manufactured, but she liked men with blue eyes, and she had recently seen a movie about a naval officer in the Pacific. Blanche even cultivated some nautical expressions, saying, when Marta fell down or hurt herself, "As your father said, 'Don't jib in a strong wind,'" and when Blanche drove the Roadmaster, she would say, "There's a parking spot. On the port side. Behind that station wagon." Or, when she read the paper or watched the news on TV, she said, "What a lot of bilge." She had learned from her uncle years before how to tie a bowline, and she practiced it and then showed Marta how to tie it, too.

Blanche had seen the photograph almost the minute she had walked into the antique store. It was in the silver frame, although the silver was tarnished, and Blanche was already thinking she could polish the thing in no time at all. She liked to polish silver, since the brightness always left a suggestion that things were as they should be. She didn't even think twice, since the man in the photograph did not seem to her a stranger who had nothing to do with her life. She looked at the picture with a sense of recognition: the naval officer's smile, the intelligence in his eyes, the deep angel's kiss in the middle of his lips suggested the very thing she was looking for, which was the image of a man, a kind of Ulysses for whom she could wait forever. The presence of the man was so real she even imagined that through some miracle he might actually walk into her life. Stranger things had happened, although offhand, Blanche couldn't think of one, and when she tried to do so, she was reduced to thinking about flying saucers, which somehow spoiled the effect of looking at the photograph.

The frame was sitting in a collection of dusty photographs, next to some framed ribbons for poultry raising that had been won in the Sandwich, New Hampshire, fair. There was also a trophy, the brass worn away, for a second-place finish in 1936 at a motorcycle race in Michigan. The ribbons and the trophy all seemed to come from a more innocent age, and instead of seeming ridiculous, they added to Blanche's idea that there was a world from which she had somehow been unfairly excluded, but which she still longed for, just as a Russian immigrant, say, at the turn of the century ached for the birches and the wide rivers of home, where the ducks paddled, leaving small, V-shaped wakes just at dusk.

Blanche brought the frame home and cleaned the glass with Windex and used silver polish on the metal, not knowing for whom, exactly, the thing had been bought. All she knew was that when the light came off the polished frame, which was as bright as a newly minted half dollar, she felt an elation that was pierced by an almost pleasurable pang of sadness and by a hope that was unrelenting in the face of her own experience.

She put the frame and the picture on the mantle. Marta came home from school and asked, "Is that Father?"

"Yes," said Blanche. "Yes. That's right."

"Can I take it down? Can I touch it?"

"Of course, sugar. I've just swabbed the frame and got it shipshape."

Marta sat on the sofa, feeling the weight of the frame on her legs. The scent of Windex and polish, the bright metal, the gray color of the man's obviously blue eyes, the neatness of his haircut, the shape of his jaw and chin and the angel's kiss in the middle of his upper lip somehow seemed right, so that Marta apprehended the image of the man with a sense of recognition not so different from what her mother had felt when she walked into the junk store and saw the photo among the ribbons from the Sandwich fair and the tarnished trophy from the motorcycle race.

Blanche didn't think she'd keep the picture on the mantle forever. In fact, she already imagined the day when she would put it on a shelf in the closet or simply drop it into the trash, but after a few months, or even after the first week, she realized it wasn't going to be that simple. Marta and Blanche would sit on that fuzzy sofa regularly, usually on Sunday afternoon, the two of them becoming more intimate after each occasion, Blanche with her arm around her daughter as she told stories about the man in the photograph. She simply made them up as she went along (being careful to remember each new episode). Or she would use details from movies she had seen. But as time went on, she included stories of her own, of men she had met and with whom things had not worked out. But here, as Marta sat next to her in the smallish living room in Beechwood Canyon, a eucalyptus fire burning in the fireplace, sparking from time to time in counterpoint to the lies Blanche told, Blanche's own history took on the order and the appearance of success, the proof of which was the photograph on the mantle. A sailing trip to Catalina, a drive to see the tallest redwood in the world, a beach in Santa Barbara where she had sipped champagne in the moonlight (as silver as the frame on the mantle) had previously been memories which had caused her to flinch with regret at what a fool she had made of herself, but now, through a kind of legerdemain of rearrangement, these things weren't painful anymore, and in fact were pleasurable to recall. With the passage of time and with each new repetition of these stories, both the ones she made up and the ones she included from her own life, they became almost indistinguishable from Blanche's apprehension of fact. So Marta and Blanche sat on that fuzzy green sofa, their intimacy warm and cozy and giving them strength, the fact of which Blanche needed so much as to make her disregard the falseness of the source from which it was drawn.

There were times, though, when Blanche decided enough was enough, that the picture on the mantle was a monument to all her failures, and that the lies she had told, no matter how innocently meant and no matter with what comforting effect on her daughter, were still somehow wrong. Occasionally Blanche thought the problem was in the object itself, and if she could just get rid of the damn thing, why then the lies would somehow vanish with it. Once she even took it out and threw it into the trash while Marta was at school, but even as the frame left her hand, she knew there was no use. Soon, she was digging it out of the coffee grinds and wilted lettuce, wiping it clean, and putting it back on the mantle.

At her worst, Blanche even thought of burning down the house, the flames consuming it and the picture, too, the fire burning in a bright, honest cleansing that would set her free. If nothing else, she'd never have to look at that handsome, understanding, quietly passionate face again.

After a day of wringing her hands and trying to decide what was right and what was wrong, looking at the problem not only from the point of view of practicality (as in how to get out of a serious lie without getting caught) but from the point of view of abstract moral considerations (which, in Blanche's case, was a mixture of astrology, the Girl Scout code, and the last shreds of a gloomy Calvinism which her mother had brought from Providence, Rhode Island, to California). Then, making herself a cup of tea and pouring some bourbon into it, she decided the best thing was to keep her mouth shut.

This appeared to be the best course. Things went along smoothly until, when Marta was sixteen, Blanche received a letter from Marta's real father, John Sanders, saying he was going to be in Los Angeles, and that he'd like to drop by and see Blanche and his daughter, too. He wrote that he had never really forgotten Blanche or the fact that she had had a child, and while it was true he had gotten married himself, he hadn't realized, until he had children of his own, how curious he was or how important it was to him to see the child that he and Blanche had had together. He realized how irregular it all was and how the best thing was probably for him just to drop the entire business, but the truth of the matter was that he had been thinking about it for years, and as time went by, he found himself thinking about it more and more rather than less and less, and since this was the case, he thought he would come by the house the next time he was in Los Angeles. He said he was sorry that he had behaved the way he had; he had been too young, really, to understand. He signed himself "respectfully."

Blanche read the letter as she sat in the living room, almost dizzy by the time she got to "respectfully." But, through the dizziness, she began to think it was right for Marta to be seen by her natural father. This impulse was somehow mixed up with wanting the man to see what he had missed, since, if he had missed a lot, Blanche would be proved, in her peculiar summation of these things, somehow right. Then Blanche got up and went into the kitchen, where she made herself a cup of tea, pouring into it a double slug of bourbon.

It was hard, though, for Blanche to know what to do, since the letter had produced a kind of mental dissonance. Many of the stories she had told Marta were about Blanche and John Sanders, and now, with the letter in hand, these stories came back as they had actually happened, and so they existed in two ways simultaneously, once as her own history and once as the history, which had produced such warmth and intimacy, that Blanche had provided for her daughter.

Marta looked older than sixteen. She had long legs and broad shoulders, their thin bones running straight out from the base of her long neck. Her eyes were a yellowish green and her skin was clear and light and her lips were full.

When Marta came home, Blanche looked at her, thinking that the last thing in the world she wanted to do was to hurt her daughter, and so, for a while, Blanche sat in her chair, drinking the tea and tasting the bourbon and feeling that sure tendril of panic which rose out of her sense of being caught by what had been nothing more than her own broken heart and the best possible intentions toward her daughter. The entire thing gave her a feeling of being in an elevator that dropped away quickly and without warning. She looked at Marta, wanting to speak now, but instead she glanced at the picture on the mantle. Then she said, her voice filled with regret, "I think I'd like to go out."

Marta looked up, and without giving it a second thought, she brought Blanche a copy of the *Los Angeles Times,* neatly folded back to the page where the funerals were listed.

Blanche picked out a funeral in North Hollywood at a Unitarian congregation, which, on general principles, Blanche was opposed to. Mostly Blanche liked Episcopal services, and there were times when, in a deep voice, she would recite passages from the Book of Common Prayer. What she really wanted was to see the funeral of a king, an Anglican ceremony with "all the pomp and whistles, you know, with embroidered robes and the bishops wearing those pointed hats." Now, though, when Blanche mentioned the church, which she usually described as a place where people spoke the same language as a used car salesman, Marta said, "You haven't gotten a disease or something, have you? What's his name, that Frank guy you were seeing for a while. Did he give you something?"

Blanche closed her eyes.

"No," she said. "It's more complicated than something like that."

They drove over to Laurel Canyon, Blanche slowing down at the bottom of it and considering the effect of the climb on the Roadmaster.

"I just don't want to get stuck," said Blanche. "We'd be trapped if the car overheated. I hate being trapped."

At the top of Laurel Canyon the car began to steam. Blanche pulled over and sat, staring at the wisps of white mist that rose from the front of the Buick, the shreds of the vapor undulating in a slow, thin, almost rhythmic movement that had about it a suggestion of just how untrustworthy things can be, lies included. The steam rose, and the car made noises Blanche had never heard before, but as she sat there, glancing at the shreds of white mist and hearing the ominous ticks and groans from the engine, she stumbled on an undeniable fact: she wanted to see Sanders herself, if only to take a quick estimation of just how the years had treated him.

"OK, kiddo. We'll coast down. The Roadmaster will be as cool as a cucumber by the time we get down to Ventura. I'm going to come hard to starboard."

The car gained speed, and as they went, Blanche felt the effect of gravity, which seemed to be drawing her, the car, and Marta down in a familiar, inescapable grip. Blanche rode the brakes, wanting to do something, somehow, about the long, seemingly unstoppable course of events. Marta stared at the purple San Gabriel Mountains on the other side of the valley, the blue line of them looking like bison, all humped up with their heads down. She hoped her mother wasn't lying about the disease. There were antibiotics for gonorrhea. But what about syphilis? Weren't there new drug-resistant strains?

They arrived at the church. Blanche picked some seats at the back, rattling her jewelry from time to time like the first gentle tinkling of doom, if only because now the unavoidable seemed to be hovering not around the expensive casket with silver handles but at the back of the church where Blanche sat. They stood and sang the hymns, Blanche's voice strong and vibrant, bringing to the music a genuine feeling. Then, when she was done and they were sitting down, Blanche said to Marta, just whispering, "Well, you can't take it with you, not even one red cent," as though this was somehow compensation for not having it here, either.

Then they came out into the air, Blanche seeming a little worse for the experience. The Roadmaster had cooled off, and Blanche had been able to find a place to park in the shade so that the seats were cool, although when they started the long climb over Laurel Canyon, Blanche went back to listening to the car and watching for steam.

They parked in front of the house. Blanche stood in front of it, examining it from the point of view of a man coming from Phoenix, say, where Sanders lived. The grass had just been cut, and there was a pattern in it where the lawn mower had gone back and forth. The house had a slate roof and casement windows that were imitation leaded glass. The place always reminded Blanche of her mother, since the house had been bought with money that Blanche had come into when her mother died.

Blanche jerked the door of the house open, almost as though she had been dared to do so, and then she went into the cool living room and sat down. Marta did, too. The fireplace was empty, nothing more than a black brick box filled with ashes and showing at the rear some clean bricks where the eucalyptus coals had burned very hot. Marta wished it was Sunday afternoon and that they were going to spend it as they had when she was younger, Blanche's arm, scented with her Chanel no. 13 powder, tucked around her, the stories of Blanche's courtship as comfortable as a warm bath.

The room was silent. Occasionally a bird walked across the roof, the *tick tick tick* of its scaled feet sounding like a clock that had been running badly for a long time and was finally coming to that inescapable moment when it would stop. Blanche and

Marta turned their eyes to the mantle, as they almost always did when things were difficult and when one or the other of them needed moral guidance. They had sat beneath the picture and sipped champagne when Marta had gotten her period. At the time Blanche had said, "Your father would have been so proud of you."

It was early evening, about the time when Blanche usually turned on the television news to get the "scuttlebutt," but now she sat, contemplating the hardwood floor at her feet, the pieces of wood fitting together neatly, and as she stared at it, she imagined trying to put the pieces of her own life together as neatly as that. She made the effort to do so, but all she felt was the sharp edges of details that clashed against one another.

"You're sure it's not a disease?" asked Marta.

Blanche shook her head. "It's not a disease. I told you."

Marta thought maybe she should go down to the Canton Dragon, the Chinese restaurant on Ivar, and get some food to bring home. She knew from long experience that fried dumplings and shrimp in lobster sauce and some mu shi pork could work almost medicinal wonders when Blanche hadn't got the full therapeutic effect from a funeral.

When Marta seemed upset, Blanche usually said, "Hey, kiddo, you look like you've shifted your ballast," and now, as a way to open the discussion about the Canton Dragon, Marta said, her voice implying all the old intimacy of those Sunday afternoons, "Hey, you look like you've shifted your ballast."

Blanche closed her eyes now.

"Maybe I have," she said. "You've got to believe, though, that I didn't mean any harm."

Marta sat quietly. Blanche started to cry. Marta was reminded of the air raid sirens, which the Civil Defense in Los Angeles used to test on the last Friday of every month and which had left Marta contemplating the panicky disorientation of something new entering her life.

Blanche looked out the window at the Roadmaster, which was parked at the curb in front of the house.

"That goddamned fuel pump in the Buick," she said. "You remember when we got stuck that time at the beach? It must have been a hundred and fifty degrees. You pushed the car and I steered. You remember that?"

"Yes," said Marta.

"Listen," said Blanche. "Things break down. That water pump. Other things."

"What other things?" asked Marta.

"Some of the stories I told you," said Blanche, "aren't true. The ones on Sunday afternoon about me and your father."

Blanche looked at the face on the mantle.

"That's just a picture I bought someplace," she said.

Marta looked at the photograph now, the features seeming a little shocked, as though this information came as a surprise to the man in it, too, and as Marta stared at him, she had the sensation of emotional dissonance, just as Blanche had had when she confronted the two versions of her life.

"If that's not my father, then who is it?" she asked.

"I don't know," said Blanche. "I bought the picture in a junk store. They were selling it for the frame."

Marta looked around the room as though she were trying to put each thing back in the place where it already existed. The bird continued to walk across the roof, its feet still making that same broken-clock sound. Blanche had the sensation of Marta streaming away from her, as if she were flying through space, and Blanche wanted to reach out and take her hand to keep her from the endless long fall. The silence of the room, broken only by the ticking, seemed to Blanche to be like that which surrounds an object, a piece of metal, say, that is thrown off a ship and then sinks to the bottom of the continental shelf.

"Well," said Blanche. "Don't you have something to ask me?"

"Yes," said Marta.

"All right," said Blanche, with the air of taking her medicine. "Go on."

"Are you going to tell me the truth?" asked Marta.

Blanche nodded.

"I wish we could do something about that bird," said Blanche. "Maybe we could put out some d-Con. That'll settle its hash."

"Who was my father?" asked Marta.

"He's a man I met some years ago. When I got pregnant, he wouldn't marry me. Your father — your *real* father — sent me a letter. He wants to visit. And you know something? You know what I really want? I want him to get a look at us that will knock his socks off."

Marta looked up at the photograph.

"He was a handsome man," said Marta.

"Him?" said Blanche. "Oh, I guess so."

She took a Kleenex from the box at the end of the sofa.

"It's just the uniform," said Blanche.

"It was nice on those Sunday afternoons," said Marta, "wasn't it?"

"Yes," said Blanche. "I guess so. But listen. I've thought about it. We could paint the living room and clean the furniture and get some nice flowers."

Marta looked down now.

"Listen," said Blanche. "You remember that dress you wanted at I. Magnin's? Remember? We'll get it."

"That's all right," said Marta.

"What?" said Blanche. "How could anyone not want it? Listen, maybe we could save up and take a trip to Hawaii."

Blanche got up and hummed, "My little grass shack . . ." She swayed a little, her jewelry jingling, the tears still on her face.

"We'll have a wonderful time."

"Sure," said Marta. "I'm going out for a walk."

"You're not upset, are you?" asked Blanche.

"No," said Marta. "I'm going out for a walk."

* * *

It was dusk now, and the sky overhead was a purple blue pierced by stars, and at the horizon in the west the last light of day was the color of a dim white fluorescent tube. The usually warm breeze was cool, as though it was blowing right off the Pacific. Marta went down to Hollywood Boulevard and walked west, coming up to the first brass stars on the sidewalk, going over the names, which she recognized more as part of the sidewalk than as memorials. Up ahead there were the theaters — the Hawaii, the Pantages, the Hollywood — their marquees bright, the names of films displayed in movable red letters.

She went as far as Grauman's Chinese, where she looked at the impressions of hands in concrete, which seemed so much like fossils, the people who made them having a mythic existence, about as real as a fish which, fifty million years before, had been trapped in some newly made sandstone. Marta looked at the sky, now dark blue, and then put her hand into an imprint, Greta Garbo's, seeing that her hand was almost a close match. There was something comforting in this, as though Marta's disorientation from the afternoons of lies had somehow been stopped by putting her hand into the cool concrete.

In the springtime, cement had been poured in the backyard of the house on Beechwood Canyon, and Blanche and Marta had put their hands into it before it had set, although now Marta had a horror of trying to put her hand into the impression she had made, since she seemed so different from the young woman who had kneeled in the bright March sunlight and giggled at the cool ooze between her fingers. At Grauman's Chinese she felt about as real as the ghosts of the actors and actresses who seemed to hover around the impressions in the concrete.

Marta walked away from Grauman's and down Hollywood Boulevard, passing under the marquees, their lights suggesting how things you thought were real and dependable could simply vanish. Under the marquees' light Marta felt as though she was passing through cobwebs, as though her life was nothing more than long, thin strands that simply trailed behind her. Then she walked back up to the house and opened the door.

Blanche was sitting in the same spot, singing, "I wanna be around to pick up the pieces . . ."

"All right," said Marta. "When's he going to arrive?"

"Next Wednesday," said Blanche.

Marta nodded, the slight repeated movement suggesting that something was being confirmed.

"Will you help?" asked Blanche.

"Yes," said Marta. "I'll help you. Maybe I'd like to see him myself."

"Then you're not mad?" asked Blanche.

"I didn't say that," said Marta. "Let's go down to Ivar. We've got to eat something. How about some mu shi pork? Shrimp in lobster sauce? How about that?"

"Why, sure, kiddo," said Blanche. "We've got to keep up our strength. Everything's going to be shipshape. You'll see."

"That's right," said Marta. "We'll see."

* * *

They went to the hardware store and stood among the brushes and hammers, bright new saws and drills, the extension cords and bulbs in small cages, the levels and C-clamps, the plaster of Paris and rat traps. Then Marta and Blanche found the paint section and a large piece of cardboard on which there were small rectangles of color. Blanche was sure she wanted latex, since it was easy to clean up and it dried fast. Speed was everything, Blanche pointed out. "No fuss no muss, right, kiddo?"

"Whatever you say," said Marta.

"That's my girl," said Blanche. "We're the Two Musketeers, right? What colors do you want?"

Marta immediately wanted to say red with black trim, the two suggesting to her the hottest flames imaginable, at the end of which there was smoke, the color of a cloud that rises from a burning tire. She even imagined taking a roller soaked with paint and making the first red slash over the walls. She was about to speak when Blanche said, "Something pretty. Maybe even something a little clublike. You know, Brittishy. How about mist-green walls with white trim?"

"I don't know," said Marta.

They loaded the cans of paint, the plastic drop cloths, the rollers, paint pans, and long sticks that could be screwed into the handle of the rollers into the back seat of the Roadmaster, and then they pulled into traffic, the conglomeration of things in the back seat looking like hope itself.

Marta was comforted when they started working. The paint was a beautiful green, something like that first tint of spring on the otherwise dry hillsides of California, that vernal blush which occurred only after the meager rain of February, and just the sight of it brought something like euphoria. But even so, in the tearing sound of the paint-filled roller going over the walls, she thought, "So, he wants to come here, does he? Is that right?"

The photograph of the man in dress whites was in Blanche's bedroom now, dumped into limbo there, since neither one of them knew quite what to do with it. Sometimes Marta stood in the doorway, her cheeks almost symmetrically marked with paint, like a primitive getting ready for war, and she looked at the photograph with exasperation and a sense of furious betrayal, as if the man in the picture had somehow consciously gone about deceiving her. Then she thought of John Sanders, and as she went about finishing up, she was glad there wasn't a pistol in the house.

They attacked the furniture, too, giving a shampooing to the overstuffed chairs and sofa. Blanche worked on the sofa with a steady, quiet insistence, since it was covered with stains that had come from those occasions when she had entertained one of her boyfriends in the living room. So now, with the shampoo, Blanche felt that, as the spots disappeared, she was not only giving the sofa a good cleaning but was getting rid of the reminders of those occasions that had left her wishing for more than a gasping embrace in the living room and the steak dinner her boyfriends usually bought her.

Blanche went to the drug store and bought cosmetics at an expense that would previously have made her ashamed (particularly when she recalled the size of the check that came, once a month, from the bank that managed her small inheritance). But now, telling herself she would get a job in a restaurant downtown as a hostess or as a typist at a temporary agency, Blanche bought nothing but the best — face creams and mud packs and soap. She lay in the tub for hours, working the knobs for hot and cold water with her toes while she sat with her face in a gray mud pack which made her appear as though she were wearing a new kind of hockey mask.

Sanders had written to say he was going to arrive on Wednesday. That was the next day. The envelope had been postmarked in Los Angeles, and Blanche noticed it had been mailed downtown, which she supposed meant he was staying in one of the older hotels there, places where she and Sanders had gone years before on those bright evenings when the lights themselves, in the hills, along the roads, at the edge of the harbor, had all suggested, for a while anyway, that they were living in a world that was filled with the guarantee of unimaginable success. Blanche looked at the postmark and said, "He's staying downtown."

"Is he still coming?" asked Marta, her eyes steady on her mother's face.

"Oh, yes," said Blanche. "Yes. He's going to go through with it."

*   *   *

By Wednesday afternoon the walls of the living room were only faintly redolent of fresh paint. There were flowers on a table at the end of the room, in front of the window, on either side of which newly washed and starched curtains had been hung. Marta wore a blue dress and low-heeled shoes, her short hair brushed back, her skin glowing in the dim lighting of the room which Blanche favored. In the unfriendly comparison she was going to make between herself and Sanders as far as the effects of time were concerned, she thought such lighting might give her a leg up. They had brought in some tea sandwiches from the delicatessen, and Blanche had a bottle of scotch in the cupboard. They sat opposite each other, glancing from time to time at the blank space on the mantle. The tea sandwiches were in the refrigerator with a sheet of clear wrap over them. The tea service had been polished, and it sat on the kitchen counter. Marta had arranged the tea sandwiches, taking the plastic off, never thinking the order of them was quite right, and as she picked up the diminutive pieces of bread on which there was salmon or thin slices of cucumber, she willed her hands to stop the shaking which reminded her of the flutter of a moth's wings. She knew no one would sell her a pistol, and she realized as she touched the tea sandwiches, which were as delicate as the color of the living room walls, that she had changed her mind. She wished she had a gun.

A car stopped outside.

"Oh, God," said Blanche. "I've gotten old."

There were steps on the flagstone walk that led from the curb up to the house, and as they came, Blanche stood up and put her hands together, turning one way and then another, and then finally going up to the door, where she stood, her hand on it so she could feel the steady, polite, and formal rapping, as though the man on the other side of the door were coming for a blind date he was not entirely keen on. Marta stood up. Blanche opened the door.

"Well," said Blanche as she looked at the man who stood on the step. It was a sunny, hazy California afternoon, a mixture of gray smoke and yellow light that left everything looking as though it was not quite as warm as it should be.

"Hello, Blanche," said Sanders.

"Hello," said Blanche.

"May I come in?"

"Well, sure," said Blanche.

Sanders was of medium height, and his gray hair was thinning and combed straight back over a shiny bald spot. He had a small mustache, a thin one that looked almost like pencil lines drawn on his face. His face was jowly and very tan, too, since he had obviously spent time in the sun in anticipation of coming here. Now, as the two of them stood side by side, Sanders looked at Blanche with the complicated expression of a man who has discovered, only partially to his surprise, that time has treated both himself and an old acquaintance with a kind of democratic ferociousness. He ran his hand over his head, and Blanche straightened her dress a little, each doing so absently, as though adjusting armor.

"You look wonderful," said Sanders.

"Do you think so?" asked Blanche.

"Well, we're all getting older."

"Yes," said Blanche. "I suppose that's right, isn't it?"

"Don't be that way," said Sanders.

"What way?" said Blanche.

"I didn't come here to be unpleasant."

"Well, what did you come here for?"

They stood opposite each other.

"I wanted to see you," he said.

"Well, that's great," said Blanche. She turned to Marta. "You hear that?"

Marta sat in a chair at the end of the sofa, the material of it that same fuzzy cloth with which she had always associated comfort and those stories of Sunday afternoon. She sat with her legs crossed, her hands in her lap. She was wearing the dark blue dress that Blanche had bought at I. Magnin, and the color made her skin seem very white, and her eyes, which were greenish, were now filled with a dark reflection from the blue cloth of the dress. Her lips were a little pursed, as though she had seen something that amazed her. She stood up, facing John Sanders. As she did so, she had the sensation of things not quite fitting, and she was reminded of that moment when her hand had almost, but not quite, fit into the imprint of Greta Garbo's.

Sanders stared at Marta. Her shoulders were square, her feet together, the calves of her legs defined by the shoes she wore. Her lips seemed very full and pink, and there was about her the atmosphere of youth. There was something else about her, too, which Sanders couldn't put his finger on. If anything it was a contradiction, if only because he had never seen anyone who was at once so attractive and so angry.

Marta said, "I'm glad to meet you."

He put out his hand, and she looked at it. Then she put out hers, the tips of her fingers trembling, but even so she took his hand and gave it a sure, firm shake, which seemed to be a reminder of the fact that she was finally facing him after all.

"Well," he said. "It's nice to meet you."

"Is it?" she said.

Sanders turned back to Blanche.

"Is it all right if I sit down?"

"Sure," said Blanche. "Go ahead."

"I just wanted to do this with decorum," said Sanders.

"With what?" said Marta.

Sanders looked back at her and smiled now.

"Look," he said. "I've made mistakes. I'm sorry."

They sat down. Sanders's face was a little saggy, and his coat did not quite cover the belly he carried. Blanche sat up very straight, her costume jewelry jingling a little as at a funeral.

"I need a drink," said Sanders.

Blanche stared at him. He looked directly back, and for a moment it seemed that in the glance there was a struggle over the way each of them perceived the last seventeen years, and there was the illusion, too, as far as Blanche was concerned, that if she stared him down, then a moral victory of sorts would be hers. Finally, though, she got up. She wanted a drink, too.

"Do you still have it over ice?" she asked.

"Yes," he said. "I'm surprised you remember."

"Oh, I remember a lot," said Blanche.

Blanche went into the kitchen, where she took an ice tray out of the freezer and held it under the hot water; the tray made a cracking sound as her fingers became unstuck from the bottom. She put ice into two glasses and poured the whisky over them, hearing the ice snap again. Then she put the bottle, some soda, and an ice bucket on the tray and brought them in.

Marta sat with her hands in her lap, looking Sanders over.

"Well, well," he said to Marta. "I've thought a lot about you. Did you ever think about me?"

"I thought you were dead," said Marta.

She heard the rattle of the ice in Sanders's glass as he lifted it with both hands and took a sip, holding it in his mouth as if he were getting some sense of relief or at least something he could depend on just from the bitter taste of the alcohol.

Sanders turned to Blanche.

"Why did you tell her that?"

"What difference does it make?" said Blanche.

"It was a lie," said Sanders.

Blanche shrugged, as though this was of no consequence. Marta turned her glance from Sanders to Blanche. Then Marta looked up at the mantle, where the photograph usually sat, and as she looked, she imagined her hand going into the cool cement of the imprint at Grauman's Chinese Theatre, but what she remembered was that little bit of difference between the shape of her hand and the imprint of Greta Garbo's, the slight disparity between the two coming to her as a reminder of the difference between what she wanted and what she had. Then she looked back at Sanders. He finished his drink and poured himself another, splashing the liquor over his barely melted ice, and then all three of them sat there while he quietly got drunk. Blanche smiled once, just a little, since it seemed to her that where the effects of time were concerned, at least, she was able to console herself that she hadn't done so badly after all. If nothing else, she was glad he had been paid off with a pot belly and a balding head, but she still felt somehow outraged by the sight of a man whom she had once loved and who was now being slowly if not fiercely diminished.

"Tell me. Why did you leave my mother?" asked Marta with a beguiling, almost innocent frankness.

Sanders looked directly at her, and then, as though trying to form an answer, he looked at the drink between his hands. He stared at the ice cubes. It occurred to him that he had measured out the years of his adult life in melting ice cubes, and as he looked at them he seemed as bewildered by his presence in this room as Blanche was. It was as though the mystery of life coming into the world was so enormous that he still couldn't comprehend it, even after sixteen years of thinking about it. Now, though, his entire expression was frankly truthful, if only because in the disorientation of the afternoon he couldn't tolerate one more lie. He needed something to hang on to, too. He said, "I was scared. I thought I could do better."

"Better," said Marta.

Her face was illuminated by the sun, which was setting beyond the window, its rays making her eyes bright, her skin pale, her lips swollen, raspberry-colored, more pinkish than ever with fury.

"Did you do better?" she asked.

Sanders looked back at her.

"I don't know anymore," he said.

They were only about three feet apart. She wasn't even thinking, really, when she felt her arm rise, seemingly of its own volition. In fact, the sensation was one of buoyancy, of a heliumlike lift, not only in her arm but in the rest of her body, too, as she found herself half standing, moving toward him. It seemed to her that it took a long time and that there was time to think about a lot of things. In particular, she thought of the sound of the rollers as they went back and forth over the wall, making that tearing sound, and as Marta half stood, she finally realized why the sound had affected her: the ripping sound of the paint being applied had about it a suggestion of the violence that had been done to her own ideas about herself, of where she had come from. The sound was like that of a butcher ripping fat away from meat. Sanders looked back at her, uncertain what she was going to do, and, in fact, he had an expression of hope in his eyes, since he had imagined she might be so affected by meeting her father that she'd want to embrace him. He realized, as he watched her, that this was what he had been thinking of during that long drive from Arizona, the feeling of her trembling against him, relieved to meet her father after all.

Marta ran her fingers under the lapel of his jacket. It was a middling expensive coat, a tweed, and she thought about it, running her finger over the texture of the cloth. With that same buoyant quality, and with the sensation that the room was very bright, not to mention filled with the lingering scent of the paint, she took the lapel, holding it now in the center of her fist. She leaned a little closer, their faces almost opposite each other, Sanders's eyes a little bigger now with a mixture of fear and curiosity. She put her lips close to his ear and whispered, her sweet breath warm against his skin, "You were a coward."

"I wouldn't put it that way . . ."

He felt her trembling in the tautness of the cloth she held.

"Well," she said. "You've taught me something."

"What's that?" he asked.

"Never be afraid," she said. "Never."

She let go of his clothes. There were some flowers on the mantle where the picture used to be, and she turned toward them, somehow wishing that the understanding face was still there.

"I can respect that," he said.

He swallowed.

"Please," said Blanche. "Let's calm down."

"Here," said Sanders. "Would you like to see a picture of my family?"

He took his wallet out and removed a photograph of a tired

blonde and two children, both of them younger than Marta. They were standing in a bare yard in front of a dusty looking house. Blanche glanced at it and passed it to Marta, who took a look and passed it back. Sanders put it away, and then they all sat, listening to the long, slow tearing sound of a car that went slowly by in the street.

"I was hoping we could do something," said Sanders.

"Like what?" asked Blanche.

"Maybe we could go to the movies."

"God," said Blanche. "Oh, God."

"What's wrong with that?" he asked. "Maybe Marta wants to go to the movies."

"Without *me*?" said Blanche. She started crying now. Blanche put her drink on the floor and cried with both hands covering her face. Sanders got up and began to approach her, putting out one hand, but then he stopped, his hand still out, just looking at her.

"I'm sorry," he said.

"What are you sorry for?" asked Blanche.

Sanders looked around the room, his expression that of a man who has had an automobile accident and is surveying the damage with an air of mystification.

"Everything. I'm sorry things are confused."

"Listen," said Marta. "You know what I think?"

"No," said Sanders.

"You'd better get out of here," she said. "That's the best thing."

He turned to Blanche. "You want me to go?"

She cried harder now.

"We've gotten old," said Blanche. "What the hell happened?"

"I don't know," said Sanders. "It seemed like we were just having fun and suddenly . . ." He stopped, lifting one hand, as if to gesture toward something he didn't understand.

"You'd better go," said Marta.

"I don't know," said Sanders.

"Don't come here anymore. I'll buy a pistol if you do," said Marta.

"What?" said Sanders.

"You'd better go," said Marta.

Blanche sat with her face in her hands.

"Well," said Sanders, standing up now. "It was nice to see you again."

Blanche didn't look up.

"All right, all right," she said. "My makeup's all streaked. I look like a raccoon."

Sanders nodded. Marta stared at him.

"All right," he said. "All right."

Then he turned and went out the door, pulling it shut behind him with a final, unequivocal thud. Marta stood next to her mother, looking at the door, and then she went to the window, through which she saw the smoky California sunshine. There was something about the banana-colored light that suggested early Technicolor movies in which the landscape always seems a little dusty and pale. Marta watched the man go down the walk, passing the grass that had been mowed into a civilized checkered pattern.

Blanche's glass had a lipsticky imprint of her lips on the rim, and she glanced at it as she swirled around the last of her half-melted ice.

"Tell me," said Marta. "Where is it?"

"In the closet," said Blanche.

Marta went across the room and opened the door, seeing inside the plastic drop cloth, which they had folded up and put away, the paint still wet inside, the pans and rollers and brushes, and above them, on a shelf on which there were hatboxes and an iron that didn't work anymore and some plastic containers in which to keep washed lettuce, the photograph of the man in dress whites, which was now wrapped up in brown paper. Marta reached up and took it down, stripping the paper off and dropping it, and without closing the closet door, the junk inside like the conglomeration of her mother's secrets, Marta went across the room and put the photograph back on the mantle, slamming it down and then propping it up carefully, her outstretched fingers stiff from trembling.

* * *

The next day, and the day after, the sensation of having been intruded upon lingered. Both of them felt it when they had their tea in the morning and when Marta came home in the afternoon and they sat together, neither one of them saying a word. The entire episode had left a sense of isolation. They went to a funeral and sat in the back, but somehow it wasn't the same. They came home early and went to sleep, each facing bed as though it was a lifeboat and the house a sinking ship.

In the morning Marta woke at first light. She sat at the edge of her bed, watching the sunrise and biting her lip at the beauty of the light that came through the window. It entered the room in a direct ray, and it lay in a sheen on her dresses, on the patent leather shoes in the corner, on the bottles which sat on the mirrored surface of her dressing table, on the white curtains and the underthings she had dropped in a pile on the floor before going to bed. Here and there, at the edge of the mirror, over some sugar that had spilled when she had brought up a snack, the light appeared as small filaments, the collection of them suggesting something as ephemeral and delicate as highlights in human hair. The room was warm and golden, and Marta stood up, seeing her shadow as though cut out of black paper in the golden haze on the wall opposite her. Then she turned away and got back into bed, but through her closed eyes she saw a mixture of red and gold, which made the longing to get away seem all the more keen.

*   *   *

In two years Marta went away to school, to Berkeley. She studied biology and English, philosophy and French. She took the mandatory health class and learned to sail, and as she went to her classes, carrying her books, she heard the bells in the Campanile. At the beginning of her second year she rented an apartment by herself on Channing Way. In the evenings, she found herself looking across the bay at the city.

At first she just took the bus across the bridge and wandered around San Francisco, looking into store windows and having a meal by herself, telling herself that the strangeness of it was sufficient and that it satisfied her desire for . . . well, she didn't know what to call it. A special treat. But soon, with a kind of frankness and a refusal to be afraid, she found herself going back, the fear of walking into strange places somehow being perfectly balanced by her refusal to give in to it.

She picked up a man in a bar in the financial district. He had left his car in a parking lot, and they walked out to it, the fog surrounding them with a gray and damp embrace. There were cars parked in the street, and the fog had left them wet, the rivulets running down the windshields and across hoods and trunks, the small streams slick in the light from the restaurants and bars and streetlights.

His car was a station wagon, a four door. In the back there hung some dresses, wrapped in a dry cleaner's plastic, which obviously belonged to his wife. Marta sat against the door, saying nothing, aside from giving a few directions, but the man knew the way to Berkeley anyway. The lights on the Bay Bridge were yellow, and they formed fuzzy globes in the fog. In Berkeley the strings of yellow street lamps along the avenues reminded Marta of jewelry, pearls, for instance, as they ran down to the bay, the lights stopping abruptly at the darkness. They were reflected a little at the edge of the bay, smeared on the wet mud of low tide, but then there was just the black water, which suggested a precipice, a darkness that was infinite.

The man had a kind of sandy, lean respectability, but when he glanced over, half of his face in darkness, half lighted by the yellow lamps of the Bay Bridge, there was something in the dark eye that made her sit straight up in the seat. Marta pointed up ahead, her finger trembling a little, saying, "Turn there. I'll show you where to stop."

They got out of the car, and she walked ahead of him, going around to the front of the building and climbing the steps, aware of his face just behind her as she climbed, and as she stood in front of the door, fumbling for her keys, she wondered just how much of what she was doing was a mistake. Certainly, though, she wasn't going to be afraid.

Inside, she closed the door behind them. There were window shades in the bedroom, and now she let them roll up with a *snap* like elastic against skin. She ran her finger over the semigloss of the windowsill, the slickness of it reminding her of the touch of skin through a run in her stocking. She threw the bed covers on the floor and reached over and let up the shades by the bed, too, so that the light from the city came into the room. She sat down on the white sheets, which glowed now like the moon, and took off her shoes. He helped her with her stockings, which he picked up and held between them, kissing her through the scent of powder and sweat, the fragrance and the texture of the nylons reminding her of her consideration of danger and its attractions. The pale light from the window made her lips look dark, almost black.

He left before eleven, and she lay in bed, aware that he had been an ordinary man who was hurrying home to his wife. She lay back, propped up on two pillows, one leg drawn up, the other straight out before her in that pale light that came in through the window. The room was in whites and blacks, the shadows streaming away from the end of the bureau, the side of the bed, the windowsill in black triangles of precisely the same shape.

Somehow, getting the better of danger and having a thrill from it helped, although, even then, she told herself there was a difference between not being afraid and being plain stupid. This didn't stop her, though, from going back to the city again, although now she was at least smart enough to take the man to a hotel room rather than bringing him to the place where she lived. But through it all, in those moments when she went down strange halls in hotels, some of which weren't the best, there was still some turmoil, some longing, beneath the thrill and the danger. Then she would take the bus back to Berkeley at three or four o'clock in the morning, watching the yellow lights on the Bay Bridge through the mist of fog and trying to read her Kant or Hegel or *The Voyage of the Beagle,* but not having much luck with reading. She told herself she didn't want ever to sit around and wait the way Blanche had. That wasn't for her. But then, when she crossed the bridge at four in the morning, exhausted, her book in her lap, she began to think about the curse of the empty rooms of her apartment. Men her age scared too easily.

She went about her business, waiting in line at the library, going to lectures or the movies, making a few casual friends, taking exams, cooking for herself, but all the while knowing the city was waiting for her.

She didn't tell Blanche about these occasions in the city, although when Marta went to visit, Blanche now looked at her and said, "Well, I'm glad you're getting a chance. That's something I never had." Blanche said this with a new bitterness, one that was even worse than when she crossed off a name from her list of people on whom she could count to attend her funeral, saying, as she did so, "There's another untrustworthy bitch." After crossing the name off the list, Blanche would pick out a funeral as if to console herself for the loss of another attendee, and then Marta would go along, simply putting her head down and trying to think things over. Blanche would watch the proceedings with a critical air, whispering to Marta what she was "going to have," and what she was "not going to have." Readings from the Book of Common Prayer, flowers from Wilson's.

Once, on the way home from a funeral, Blanche spoke about growing up in New England. She remembered visiting her grandfather, who had had a farm, a place with white siding and green shutters and a real slate roof, and in the early springtime, when there was still snow on the ground, Blanche had seen the sugarhouses, the interior of them filled with a white, sweet steam, the moisture of it, the heat, the milky and caressing fog all suggesting to her the hope of romance or love or some sweet, enveloping thing. Marta looked across the seat, listening carefully. Blanche described how the warm, moist, sweet mist had made her skin feel, how it seemed to get under her clothes, how it made her think of . . . oh, she didn't know what.

They pulled up in front of the house, and inside Blanche changed into a housedress, a kind of flowered bathrobe, and then she looked at the phone from time to time, obviously wondering when one of her boyfriends, whom she usually described as "big shots" who were "way up" in some company, would call to take her out for a drink and a piece of steak. But none of them called anymore.

So, in a way, it wasn't even a surprise when in the spring of Marta's third year she received a phone call. It came on a Sunday morning in February, just when it was absolutely certain that all the Christmas cards from the previous year had been accounted for by Blanche and that there was no possibility of one showing up late by accident. Sunday morning had always been a hard time for Blanche, especially if she had spent Saturday night alone, and the quiet, restive gloom of the morning not only seemed to be a shadow of the previous night but held the certainty that there wouldn't even be a good funeral until afternoon. Marta answered the phone. An official voice, one that would say "vehicle" for car or "precipitation" for rain, told Marta that Blanche had taken "an apparent overdose of sedatives."

*   *   *

Marta got on the plane and took a taxi from the airport, and when she came into the hospital room where Blanche was lying, she stood there, looking at her mother, who said, "Oh, you shouldn't have come." For a moment Marta wondered whether or not her name had ever been on the list of mourners and whether it had been crossed off.

"Don't be angry," said Blanche.

"Don't be angry," said Marta.

"All you do is repeat what I say," said Blanche. "Oh, honey, don't be that way."

Blanche put a hand to her bleached hair. She blinked and looked around the room, at the white nylon curtain hanging from a runner on the ceiling, drawn back to expose some electronic monitors, at the stainless steel stand from which there was suspended a plastic bag of clear glucose, the conglomeration of the eerie machinery of medicine making Blanche feel a little disoriented, as though here, in the clutter of stainless steel and the scent of disinfectant (something like the eucalyptus logs that she had burned in her fireplace), Blanche needed to drop all illusions, if only to have something definite to hang on to. So, she looked back at Marta and said, "I was afraid."

"Afraid," said Marta.

"Yes," said Blanche. "Of being alone. Of getting old . . ."

Marta stood there, feeling her fingers tremble against the cool rail of the bed. In other parts of the room there were people behind curtains, and from time to time a small, piercing buzzer went off, and then a nurse came in, not hurried, not running, just businesslike and quick. There was the quick *screech* of the curtain hooks scraping against the overhead rail, and then there were whispered sibilants or groans.

"Don't you love me?" asked Blanche.

"We're not talking about love," said Marta. "We're talking about being a damn fool. This is stupid."

"Please, honey," said Blanche. "Don't be so mad at me."

Marta listened to the sounds from behind the curtains, the quiet steps and a voice, insistent now, quiet, its sibilance like the evidence of a secret. In the moment, in the stainless steel clutter, the buzzers, the red lights on instrument panels, the screens on which heartbeats rose and fell like a series of infinitely repeated mountain peaks, all of the bright, hard medical equipment seemed to be an expression of the disorder which had been part and parcel of Blanche's life, right down to Marta's conception. And now, as Marta stood there, the disorder and isolation from which she thought she had been so safe seemed a little more inescapable, if only because of the passage of time and the complicated gifts that are handed down from mother to daughter.

She went back to Berkeley and finished her exams and then withdrew from school. She moved back to L.A. so she could keep an eye on her mother, but she wasn't going to live with her. Marta packed her things and rented a car and drove home, leaving her books and clothes in Blanche's house. The house made Marta more exasperated than ever, if only because it seemed to be evidence of all the things she wanted to avoid, but which still had a claim on her.

On the morning of her first day in Los Angeles, Marta bought a secondhand car. Then she rented an apartment on a side street off Western Avenue, south of Santa Monica, a one-bedroom place at the back of a house that had been divided into apartments. There was a back porch, and she could use the garden, too. She stood in the yard, in the weeds in the garden, already thinking, with a kind of desperation, that she might be able to grow something there. Then she started looking for a job.

By the second day she found herself driving from interview to interview, making telephone calls (trying by an almost devotional display of intelligence and cheerfulness to get hired), and reading the want ads with an unshakable notion of being an outcast, of being someone who was just barely treading water and for whom, in time, there would be nothing but the prospect of sinking without leaving a trace. The best part of the day was in the morning, when she had appointments, when she got into the car, the scent of her shower still on her, and before the smog had gotten bad. By afternoon, though, the smoky heat had come, and she drove with the want ads on the seat next to her, crumpled up and circled here and there with a ballpoint pen. The mornings weren't so hopeful anymore. The ads in the paper became repetitive, useless. Then she found herself standing on Santa Monica Boulevard, looking up at the sign that said, "Romance Advertiser."

*　　*　　*

So now, in the church next to French, she put her head down, thinking of the funerals she had gone to with Blanche, of the cool, flower-scented churches, of the sheen on the polished seats, of the reassuring weight of the hymnbooks, and the scent of the leather that covered the drop-down stool to kneel on when she prayed. French looked up and swallowed. Then he said, "Are you done?"

"Yes," said Marta.

They both stood, French getting up on one knee and then another, turning and walking with a slight limp as he went out into the yellow California light of afternoon. It was like walking into a splash of gasoline.

"Did you pray?" asked French.

"Yes," said Marta.

"Is that why you're crying?"

"I guess so," said Marta. "I don't know."

"Well," said French, looking over at her. "It's a good thing you prayed if you're going to see Earl Graves."

Marta looked at the rails of the trolley track in the street, the long, straight edges of them disappearing together in one bright spot in the distance.

"I'm just going to pick up the film he was supposed to give me in Malibu," said Marta. "I'm not going to have anything to do with him."

"Uh-huh," said French. He nodded. "Uh-huh."

Then he walked down the steps of the church.

"Well, it's a good thing you prayed," he said.

The Scandal Sheet

CLASSIFIEDS

ZIMBA, Asian Elephant, can put a little pizzazz into your parties, promotions, and what have you. Call Raj, anytime, 398-1289, Encino.

VITAMIN PURVEYOR TO THE STARS, supplements, trace elements. Improve memory (special mixture for actors learning lines), hair sheen, skin tone, love life. 90-day special program. 398-2369, days, Venice.

IS PLASTIC SURGERY RIGHT FOR YOU? Just missing that big part? Profile not quite right? Bustline not perky enough? The pros use all the tricks. Tucks, chins, noses, lifts, Dr. Sam Franks, 323-0914, by appointment only, Canoga.

MAN WITH HORSE, PALOMINO, can add, subtract, take hats from head, the works. Also, two bulldogs, cute as a button. Macaw, green and blue, can sing "Somewhere Over the Rainbow," 987-6789, West L.A., mornings.

EDITOR, needs work, desperate, will travel. Have big-budget porn credits. Smiley, 890-6791, Silverlake, anytime.

ACTING LESSONS, "Only the Strong Survive," Hutch Mc-Ewane, "The Steps to Dedication," film and TV credits, Royal Shakespeare Company, Visa and Master Charge accepted, 890-6817, West Hollywood. After noon.

FOOLPROOF GAGS. Knew Marx Bros., "What's the difference between a broom and a horse . . . ?" Get the answer when you call. The Humor Doctor. Sunny Acres Retirement, Santa Monica. Early riser. 780-4681.

DISC JOCKEY, good voice, waiting for chance, no objections right-wing station. Will send tape. References from AA. Burbank, 367-9012, anytime.

ANIMAL TRAINER, with python (name of Pete), available all acts. Valley, 396-4124.

JACK HAWK'S AROUND TOWN, *Scandal a la Mode*

First, the Police Blotter. **Will MacKechnie** of TV's *Lonesome Rider* was arrested for shooting a deer in his backyard on Mulholland Drive (police were called when neighbors reported Will finishing the deer off with a tire iron). **Dorothy Calsum,** out of work since *On the Sunny Side,* arrested for making harassing and threatening phone calls to her ex-agent, Hollywood Heavy **Sharon Macmahon. Dorothy Twilly,** of TV's *Family Ways,* for disorderly conduct at Warriors, lesbian leather bar, arresting officer using Mace.

OBITUARIES

Mike Nelson, cowboy singer best known for role of chuckwagon cook in *Montana Fear,* of cirrhosis of the liver, in Glendale.

Gloria Beaveridge, columnist for *Insider's Hollywood,* in an automobile accident after a drinking spree in Rosarito Beach, Baja California.

Hep Keller, stuntman, on location.

The Heart
of the Matter

MARTA'S APARTMENT was filled with the day's dry heat. From the window she could see the Griffith Observatory, its green dome cool and aloof against the darkening hillside. Marta stared at it, the sight bringing her a momentary sense of ease, if only because it made her think of men who spent their lives looking into the depths of space, into the glittery sheen of the stars and the dust of the universe. She imagined the sidereal lights, on the clearest of evenings, as being like pieces of a broken headlamp sprayed over black asphalt. And, as she looked at the cool copper roof of the building in the distance, she wondered if she should take a knife when she went to Earl Graves's house.

She had a knife that a friend had given her at Berkeley, and now she opened the drawer of the plain, unpainted desk and looked at it lying in the hot shadows, the handle black with a gleam to it. It had a button that made the blade flick open. She closed the drawer, leaving the thing there, not wanting to give in to the desire to take it, which she recognized as the first impulse of panic.

She went out to her pale two-door Dodge, the color of it like the sky on a day when the sun just won't come out. The previous owner had lived near the beach, and there were streaks of rust, as if from the scuppers of a ship, around the bumper and the locks of the doors and on the trunk. As it sat at the curb, it looked like an idea that hadn't quite gotten a fair hearing and was somehow slowly falling into disrepute. Marta got into the car, putting on the seat next to her the slip of paper with Earl Graves's address on it. She bent forward, leaning her head against her hands, which rested on the wheel. In the silence of the car, in the heat of the late afternoon, she was surprised by the loudness and the suggestiveness of the throbbing of her heart, which she felt in her head, at the temples and in the back, too.

She had a pretty good idea where Sherwood Terrace was. Up toward Ferndale. As she drove out Franklin, she thought the best thing would be to keep everything low-key with Earl. No talk about Malibu. The thing was to walk in, just as though they had always planned to meet in his house, and ask for the film. Keep it simple. No trouble. Nothing personal.

It was almost evening and the red glow of the signals on Franklin seemed raw. Marta glanced at the color, trying as a distraction to decide what it reminded her of. After a while, she guessed it was the way the sun looked when it set through the smoke of a bad brushfire. Then she thought about the Pacific as seen from Malibu, the shimmer of it in the sunlight, the light in the chop like curls of silver. Well, she would try to do her best. She'd been pretty good so far in not opening too many wrong doors. Even in the depths, in her own personal shadows where it was hard to see clearly, she would do her best.

The house was set back from the road, a small place, really, a story and a half, covered with graying shingles and surrounded by elms at the front and eucalyptus trees at the back. There was a hedge along the sidewalk, about six feet high, although it hadn't been trimmed for a while. On the lawn, just a little of which could be seen as Marta drove by, there were two white chairs and a white wooden glider, all sitting in grass that needed to be mowed. She got a glimpse of the house, two windows in front with a door between them, a black one with a brass knocker. There were flowers growing in the beds by the door, pansies it looked like, or maybe morning glories, the petals collapsed now, shriveled up in the blue glow of twilight. The yard, the house, the door, the lawn furniture all went by in a blur, but as Marta parked the car, something about the yard and house lingered, and as she considered it, she wondered whether or not malignity existed almost as a variety of gas, and if it might make the siding of a house gray, operating as a kind of weathering. Maybe it could be seen in the gloom of the yard, in the peeling paint of lawn furniture, or even in the wilted shapes of flowers by the door. Then Marta shook her head, thinking, Keep it simple. Nothing personal. No recriminations.

Even now, she knew she could simply start the engine of the car and turn around. In the morning she'd tell Bobby Salinas she wasn't sure she wanted to work there anymore. Put the ball in his court. Let him see if he had the stuff to fire her. But then, she wasn't even certain if this was a matter between her and the man she worked for. In fact, for a second, she thought that her refusal to be scared off would make her free: it was a way of looking into the face of everything that appalled.

There was a light on in the house — not in the living room, which was obviously near the front door, but further back in the house, perhaps from the kitchen. Marta went in through the hedge and passed the lawn furniture, on which, for a moment, she had an overwhelming impulse to sit. Instead, she went up to the door, the surface of which was newly painted a glossy black, like an oil slick. She picked up the brass knocker and banged twice, feeling the sound roll into the shadows of the house, the clack of metal on metal seeming to have about it the *boom* of someone hitting an empty oil drum.

No one responded. She faced the door, having the sensation that she was being watched. There were only the darkened windows at either side of the door, and when she saw a slight movement just out of the corner of her eye, it was with a maddening imprecision, just a black flick with the cadence of a bat's wing, or maybe the panel of a silk bathrobe being closed and tied with a silk sash.

She looked over her shoulder at the lawn furniture. It had a blue-white tint from the last of twilight. Next to it the concrete walk cut through the grass. The hedge, in the failing light, looked like a black, impenetrable wall. Marta shook her head and swallowed and, after thinking, Keep it frank . . . Just business . . . Dull and ordinary, she reached out and used the knocker again, surprising herself by how hard she brought the piece of metal down.

A light went on behind the door.

"What do you want?"

Graves's voice was precisely as she had expected, not arrogant exactly, a little deep, absolutely sure of itself, or at least reflecting the fact that Graves wanted to make sure of what was on the other side of the door before he opened it.

"I came about the film," said Marta.

"Is anyone with you?" asked Earl Graves. "Are you alone?"

She tried to be equivocal when she spoke, but it was useless. Anyone could tell she was telling the truth when she said, "Yes."

Graves opened the door and said, "Come in."

He stood on the step above her, lighted by a fixture on the ceiling of the hall and by the yellow glow from the back of the house. When he turned to the side to glance into the yard, Marta looked at the features of his face, the nose that was a little flattened, the rough skin, the full brows, the thin lips set in an expression of thinking things over.

"I'll wait out here," she said. "I just want the film."

He turned away from the door and walked into the hall, where she could see the undulant movement of the shiny robe around his legs. He walked with a quick gait, the padding of his feet in his slippers having a quality which, after a half second's reflection, Marta recognized as somehow domestic. Then he stopped and said, "Come in."

Marta waited, feeling the warmth of the light on her face. The darkness of the yard had crept up on her, and now, as she waited, she could feel the presence of it behind her. She heard the padding of his feet, and his voice, too, which at least seemed neutral. She stepped into the hall.

"Close the door," he said.

She moved over and gave the door a shove with her shoulder. It seemed to take an eternity until it hit the frame with a subdued slam.

"You never can tell who's going to show up at the door," he said. "People trying to sell you something. Fuller Brush is around all the time. And then some people who want to tell you about God. You want to know what I think about God?"

"I just want the film," she said.

"Come in here," he said.

There was a doorway to his left, beyond which there was a

kind of library, the shelves of it filled with books and magazines. There was a desk with a dim green light. The desk was heavy and of good quality and behind it there was a modern chair. The room had the air of a place where decisions are made.

"Sit down," he said.

"Listen," she said. "I just came for the film. That's all."

"I understand," he said.

"Then pass it over," she said.

He sat down and looked directly at her.

"Were you in Malibu this morning?" he asked.

"Yes," she said.

"You went into the house?"

"Yes," she said. "Just in the doorway."

"That's all?"

"I just pushed the door open and saw there was no one there. Then I closed it and went home."

"It's a mistake to lie to me," he said.

"What's there to be devious about?" asked Marta.

She sat down. The room was completely silent, not a rustle of paper or the indication of movement of any kind. From the kitchen came the sound of water dripping into the sink, the *pink pink pink* insistent and irritating, too, since, as she sat there, she had the impulse to get up and turn the faucet off, hard, if only to make the sound go away. She wondered why it cut into her so much, and then it occurred to her that it was the unavoidable sequence, the steady ticking, that made her think of how she had got up this morning, lying there in the warm room with the sun in strips over her hips and back, of getting up and getting dressed, of taking one action and then another, all of which seemed random but which she now knew had led, like links in a chain, from the moment she had opened her eyes to the moment where she sat listening to that steady drip.

She sat back in the chair and crossed her legs and tried to appear bored. But, as she looked around, she was reminded of something. Knitting her brows for a second as she concentrated, it took a moment, but it came to her: the buzzing of those green flies in that room in Malibu. She couldn't even say what it was that made the connection, maybe nothing more than the scars on the face of the man who sat on the other side of the desk.

"The only thing that's going to make me angry is a lie."

"All right," she said. "I understand."

"Good," he said. "What did you see when you went into the house?"

"Nothing," she said.

"Oh?" he asked.

She nodded. "That's right." Marta swallowed, thinking of the heat in the room, the flies that rose in a blue-green shimmer. She remembered having been told once, when she was a child, that she shouldn't be frightened around a dog because the dog could always tell. Marta looked at Earl Graves, not wanting to move her eyes away.

"I didn't stay long," she said.

"What rooms did you go into?"

"The living room."

"Just the living room?"

She nodded.

"I thought we weren't going to tell any lies," said Graves.

"All right," she said. "I guess I went down the hall. Why don't you let me have what I came for?"

"Down the hall?"

"Yes."

"And you went into the bedroom?" he said. "And you saw a stain on the wall. Isn't that right?"

"There were flies in the room," she said.

"You should have stayed out of there."

"I left after that," said Marta.

"And now you want to leave here?"

"Yes."

Graves shook his head and then rubbed his chin and a cheek with one hand.

"Let's look at it clearly," he said.

"I don't need to do that."

"Be nice," he said. "Listen. Say I hired someone to make some movies for me. Your boss pays me and I promise to deliver, but

I don't actually make the movies myself. I hire a kind of pro. Out-of-work cameraman. Maybe I've been working with him for years. We make good money together. I think I can trust him. We even go out together. We go up to Vegas."

"I understand," she said. "You were friends."

"I won't go that far," said Graves.

"So why can't I just have the film and then I'll go," she said. "No big deal."

"Sure," he said. "But let's go through the whole business, all right? Then maybe you'll see my point."

"Well, I don't know," she said. "I've got to get going."

"Uh-huh," he said. "Let's just say I trusted him. Up to a point. And one day I do a little checking and find that he is copying the movies he makes for me."

Graves looked into the shadows of the room, his expression showing he had confronted something with an almost mathematical certainty once he had done a little checking on the man with whom he was doing business. If anything, he looked relieved, in the same way anyone does when his theoretical considerations have been proved right after all.

"So," he said. "What do you think the guy is doing with the copies?"

"Listen," said Marta. "I've really got things to do this evening. I'm late already. I just want the film. There's no big deal about anything."

He nodded, looking at her, raising a brow now, the atmosphere in the room changing from that around a man who has just been proved right to one of malevolent scrutiny.

"I asked you a question," he said.

"What is this?" she said, "a guessing game?"

He went on staring at her.

"All right," she said. "He was selling them to someone else, right?"

Graves made his hand into the shape of a pistol, three fingers tucked back, one pointing at her, the thumb held up like the hammer. He aimed at her and fired.

"Right-o," he said. "What should I do about that?"

"I don't know. That's not my problem."

"It's hard to say," he said.

The water went on dripping, and Marta swallowed. She hadn't smoked a cigarette for a while, but she now had the desire for one. She thought of picking up the dry, light, small round tube of paper, so neatly filled with tobacco, of striking the match, of the tug of her lips against it, all of it coming as a small relief in the face of the atmosphere in the room. She concentrated, trying to understand exactly what the essence of the room was. The books on the wall, the contact sheets of black and white photographs on the man's desk, the figures in them barely discernible, men and women it seemed, all combined in such a way, along with the presence of the man opposite Marta to suggest a world she had always known existed but from which, starting with her earliest years in California, she had just been pretending she was somehow immune. Even the air seemed a little different, a little heavier, as though this new world required a lot more effort than the one in which she usually lived.

"Look," she said "I'm not going to say anything. I mean about the bedroom in Malibu."

"I know," he said.

She turned her head toward the kitchen, where there was that steady *pinking* sound.

"Can I turn that dripping off?" she asked.

"Sure," he said. "Go on. Maybe you want something to drink?"

She stood up now, feeling the weight of the atmosphere in the room. The room was lighted only by a small lamp on Earl Graves's desk, and the shadows had a brown-gray staleness; she realized this was the thing that distinguished the dread she felt, that very staleness, like the smell of an old sock. She started walking toward the kitchen, going through the door, glad to come into the light. She heard his steps behind her, coming out of the library, his careful padding suggesting precision, like that of a man walking on a high wire.

The kitchen was large, with a double stainless steel sink, some shelves and cupboards, a stove, a refrigerator, some pots and pans hanging from hooks, a calendar on which there was a picture of a dog, a poodle of some kind with a ribbon tied in a bow on top of its head, and in the corner there was a breakfast nook, which had been painted yellow. There was something antiquated about the room, a kind of old-fashioned domesticity in which a young wife would wear an apron and serve large breakfasts.

Earl Graves came into the room and said, "You saw something in the room in Malibu. It wasn't just the stain, was it?"

The dripping went on as she turned to look at him, that *pink pink pink* louder than before. She turned her back on Earl, a cool sparkling sensation coming over her skin as she did so. She took the large faucet handle and turned it hard. The dripping stopped. Marta glanced around and, oddly enough, everything seemed a little brighter than before: the curved chrome handles on the cabinet, the pans with the copper bottoms hanging from stainless steel hooks, the faucet itself. Out the window she saw the city, the lines of the avenues stretching away in long golden chains between which there was an erratic glitter of lights, just little pricks of it, like the individual points in the sheen on the side of an eel. Marta concentrated on the lights, thinking, Just business. Nothing personal.

"I've got to go," she said. "Where is the film?"

"You didn't answer," he said.

"You're not giving me the film," she said. "That makes us even."

"Don't be smart," he said. "Don't you see? I'm trying to get your attention. I'm trying to tell you something."

"What is it?"

"Don't lie. I've got to make decisions," he said.

She had the desire to reach around and turn the faucet handle a little so that it would start dripping, and then she was alarmed by trying to find comfort in something as mundane and ridiculous as that. She tried to take some solace in refusing to give in to anything chaotic, like panic.

"What do you think I should have done about the guy who was making copies?" he asked.

"I don't think much about it at all," she said. "I'm just running an errand. Nothing more. Nothing less. None of this is any skin off my nose."

He sucked his cheek. "I want you to understand my perspective. I got all kinds of problems in my business. One of them is credibility. It's something you just got to have, right?"

"I wouldn't know."

"Come on. You're smart," he said. "You know what? Bobby Salinas brags on how he's got a kid from Berkeley working in the *Romance Advertiser*. He says it gives the place tone."

"He doesn't pay much for it," she said.

"Would you like something to drink? Maybe that would help you calm down. Maybe tea. Or a shot of something strong."

"Look," she said. "All right. The atmosphere in the room was bad. But so what?"

"Yes," he said. "Let's talk about atmosphere. It's a strange thing, isn't it? Something happens and . . . well, maybe there's a smell, or a little dirt, or just something that's not quite right and you can tell, can't you? So, you're pretty sure someone . . . had some trouble there, aren't you?"

She stood with her back to the sink. He was opposite her, standing in the entrance to the room. Behind him there was a door that went outside, into the back yard. In the silence of the house, in the gaze of Earl Graves's eyes, in the almost unbearable beauty of the city (if only because it was so far from this room), she heard herself say, with something like defiance, "Yes."

Earl Graves took a little gasp of air. Then he shrugged and said, "How would you like to make some money?"

"I'd like to leave," she said.

"Let's talk about making some money," he said.

"I've got nothing against money. But if I'm not getting the film, I'm going to go."

She didn't move. Something about the posture of each of them in the kitchen seemed to suggest they were at a juncture, some boundary, and that if Marta didn't want to cross over, she should be absolutely still. Her concentration was like that of a sprinter in the blocks, waiting for the sound of the starting gun.

"What I'm really doing is trying to find a way to trust you. You want that, don't you?"

"I don't know," she said. "Sure, I guess so."

"You've got a special kind of good looks," he said, "a kind of sultry . . . cleanliness."

"I'm flattered."

"Are you?" he said. "That's what I mean. I'll bet you can still blush, too. Isn't that right?"

She blushed, the color coming into her cheeks with the tint of rouge.

"Yeah," he said. "That's the quality I'm interested in. Now on film, that will be dynamite."

"I'm going to go now," she said.

"Wait. We're talking business now. Don't you understand? You got a problem here. I got a problem. So, what we've got to do is to find some common ground. We do that and everything's fine." He smiled. "I'll pay you good money, too. You like money, don't you? We can work this out. I don't want to get rough or anything. Come on, be sweet."

As Marta stood in the kitchen, the depths of a kind of horror seemed to fall away before her. She couldn't tell whether she was really in danger, if the man opposite her was really concerned about what she had seen, about that room in which the green flies buzzed, or whether he was just using the possibility of her fear to get control of her. Perhaps nothing had gone wrong in the bedroom in Malibu. It was entirely possible that in the making of a pornographic movie someone had been cut . . . maybe someone had fallen over a camera case and broken a nose and had leaned against the wall. It was possible everyone was high and sloppy. Just as it was possible that her fear, which might be based on nothing more than an illusion, was something Graves was preying on. The possibility left her sifting through what she knew, trying to decide, or at least to come to some estimation of how things really were.

She turned and looked out the window, seeing the lights, the cool yellow pattern, like a grid. She tried to keep in mind that each light was evidence of a human being going about some ordinary task.

Then she glanced back at the kitchen counter, past the old-fashioned toaster, the juicer, a line of canisters which must have held tea, coffee, flour, sugar, the very names coming to her mind as an indication of just how far away she was from anything like domesticity, but then she went on looking down the counter, seeing a bread board, a wooden one with raised script that read, "Our Daily Bread," and a bread knife, and next to it there was a rack, a wooden one out of which stuck a number of knives, all of them with black handles, which, for some reason, made Marta think momentarily of the color of an umbrella. Then she turned back to Earl and said, "I came here to do business."

"We're doing it," he said.

"No we're not," she said.

"I'm making you an offer. I'm giving you a chance. Be sweet, now. Everything will be all right. You'll be doing yourself a favor. We'll make some movies. I'll get it set up. Good money. I'll bet you could use some. What kind of car are you driving?"

"A Dodge."

"How many miles on it?" he said.

"Ninety, ninety-five thousand."

"I bet it burns oil," he said.

"A quart every thousand miles."

"Yeah, that's the way I figured it. Let me get a look at you."

He unbuttoned the top of her blouse. She felt only the dry, fumbling pressure as he undid one button and then another, and even as she felt this, she hesitated, having the peculiar sensation that she wasn't really in the kitchen or that this was not quite happening: it was as though she existed in that long, falling moment in which she was not fully asleep, not dreaming, and yet not fully awake. She heard him whisper to her, explaining how things were, that he wanted a sign from her, some reassurance, something definite . . . a kind of bond. That was the critical thing. They had to understand each other. She wasn't going to leave until that was clear. She had put him in this position, and, of course, she could get them both out of it. It was her decision to make.

He undid a second button and a third, exposing her skin. She didn't really remember reaching around to the wooden knife rack. There was a movement and some noise. Had he shouted at her, had he told her he was used to things like that knife? Hadn't she heard the story about how, when he was young, he had used safety pins to put himself back together after he was cut across the stomach? He had boiled the safety pins and then used them. Hadn't she heard that? It seemed, for a moment, that they stood directly opposite each other, the two of them not yelling, not raising their voices, almost whispering, hissing at each other. Even now, she thought, Just business. Just ordinary. Nothing personal. The air was cool on her skin where her blouse was open. He said, "You should be a lot more frightened than you are, you know that?"

She had waited a moment, during which she had the sensation of almost handling the words, touching them with her palm and fingers, as though they were marbles she held in her hand. She had looked at him and said, "I'm not afraid at all."

What he said was lost in the pressure that seemed to grow in the room. Marta couldn't remember the words exactly, but his voice was frank: nothing overtly threatening, just a flat, matter-of-fact tone. And, as they stood in the kitchen, before they actually began to struggle, it seemed to her that the lights grew dim, becoming piss-colored.

He said something like, "Oh? You're not afraid?"

Later, the kitchen looked as though there had been some trouble in it. In particular, she remembered seeing the spilled canisters of flour and sugar, the white powder spread across the Formica-covered counter, the flour rising into the air like smoke from a fire, the sugar sparkling like stars on a clear night in September. In the crash of breaking glass, which sounded so much like a domestic argument that had gotten out of hand, she even thought of the observatory, of those men who spent their lives staring into the sky, where the stars appeared like bits of shattered glass.

There had been ice in an ice bucket, and somehow that had been knocked over, the slippery, half-melted cubes sliding across the counter and falling, dozens of them, hitting the floor and shooting into raylike patterns in front of the cheerful yellow nook.

Perhaps the ice on the floor had been part of the problem. He had walked through it in his slippers with leather soles. He had been coming toward her, putting his feet into the confusion of ice. He had lunged toward her, his legs going out behind him, making him appear like a man who was flying, like a skydiver, if one could be imagined in a blue silk bathrobe, the panels opening, the sash streaming away from him. He had fallen against her. She remembered the hard, sweaty shock of him.

Now, she sat on the floor, against the door, her head in her hands, hearing a steady, repeated drip, which at first she thought was from the sink and which she almost got up to turn off, but then remembered she had already done that. There was water on the floor from the melted ice, and mixed with it there was a pinkish, roselike hue. In the melted water roseate threads moved with a serpentine motion in the moisture, responding, as they turned one way and then another, to something in the water, or perhaps to an almost unnoticeable welt in the floor. She stared at the melted ice as the long pinkish threads worked through it. One of her wrists felt strange. After a while, after she had closed her eyes and concentrated, it came to her: it felt like a wrist burn a playmate had given her when she had been eight years old. Had Earl had time to grab her wrist?

She wanted to be certain about what had happened. Earl had come toward her. She had been standing in front of the breakfast table, and he had slipped on the ice. He had fallen into her, and when she had tried to step aside, she hadn't been able to get the knife away, too. There was something about how the man had fallen, his weight bumping her and trapping her hand against the table, that had seemed to be part of the claustrophobic atmosphere of the house. As nearly as she could remember, she had barely had a grip on the knife as Earl's weight had slid over it.

She buttoned her blouse, still sitting against the wall, and looked at the disorder of the kitchen. Even now she had to be precise, since she didn't want to have any doubts about anything, and she sat there, puzzling over the suddenness of the event. As she tried to make sense of it, she came up against a palpable novelty, or at least something that she had never dreamed possible, and this was a sense of isolation so large as to be . . . well, she thought again of the observatory. Sidereal. That was the word she was looking for. There was a gurgling sound from the breakfast nook, just like the noise someone's stomach makes when he is hungry. There was another sound, too, a more flatulent sound. The dead man was still making noises.

She stood up now. Her neck felt hot where her collar had been jerked. Her blouse was wrinkled, but that was all, and in an instinctive gesture, trying to straighten herself up, if only so she could think more clearly, she unzipped her blue jeans and tucked the blouse in, zipping them up and buttoning them again.

Marta didn't know what scared her the most, that she was in this room or that some basic component of her personality, maybe nothing more than an idea of herself, was slowly threatening to abandon her, leaving her frightened and a stranger to herself. Then she swallowed and looked around.

The thought of having the police in front of the house, with the red, white, and blue lights flashing on top of the police car, left her looking for a way out, a back door. The ice was quickly turning into water. Would they believe there had been ice on the floor? By the time they got here it would be water. Even thinking about trying to explain brought on that real, new fear: how could she tell them she hadn't meant to do it when she wasn't even sure herself how much had been accidental?

She stood in the kitchen, concentrating, looking out the window at the lights of the city, the accumulation of them bright and having a mysterious quality, as though just by the enormous number of people the place was somehow overpowering, grand and having an almost otherworldly scale.

Her hands were open now and she looked at them, surprised to find they weren't stained and that there wasn't anything on her clothes, either. It occurred to her that she had never been fingerprinted. Then she tried to remember, too, what she had touched. Earl had opened the door. There had been only the knife. And the faucet. She took a paper towel from the roll above the sink and wiped the faucet, and then she stood in front of Earl, who lay on the seat in the breakfast nook. After she was finished, she put the paper towel in the garbage disposal and turned on the switch and the water with another towel, which she used to turn them off, too, and then dropped it in the waste-basket. As she did this, a man came into the room.

"Hi," he said. "My name's Victor Shaw. I saw the whole thing. I think we'd better get out of here. Right now."

BOOK
2

The Scandal Sheet

CLASSIFIEDS

ZIMBA SPECIAL! Emergency Medical expenses require immediate attention. Two Weeks Only! Zimba at three-quarters price. Pick your occasions. Now is the time to have the jungle come to you. Call Raj, anytime, 398-1289, Encino.

WRANGLER, can handle horses, snakes, baboons, chimps, and dogs. Can sing. Reseda, evenings, 367-8761.

ACTRESS, has it all, what can you do with it? Serious offers only. Santa Monica, mornings, leave message with female voice only, 987-2146.

ACCORDION ARTIST, good for atmosphere, authentic German, Eastern European. Dependable. Played with Harmonicats. Redondo. After six, 897-2387.

STUNTMAN, no stunt too crazy. Long falls a specialty. Can make automobiles talk turkey. West L.A., leave message with service. Price-per-stunt basis, 652-9871.

The St. James Infirmary

THE MOMENT Victor Shaw had reached down and opened the wooden cabinet in the psychiatrist's office and found the tape recorder, he had known what it was for. The psychiatrist, whose name was August St. James, used it to record the things his patients said, and as Victor looked at it, he knew he was facing an opportunity. The machine sat on the shelf, right in front of his nose, so obvious Victor began to sweat. His face was warm as he started considering possibilities so large and so various as to represent a kind of disorder, although from Victor's point of view, disorderly or not, infinitely various or not, mysterious as to practical implications, these possibilities still had a whiff of something that connected them all. It took a while for Victor to realize what it was, but after a few minutes he recognized the sure, definite tug of the mercenary.

Victor Shaw had just gotten out of Soledad and had moved to Los Angeles to start over. He was twenty-seven years old, was tall, and had auburn hair and blue eyes. His appearance suggested an all-American boy, as though he had grown up on a farm, or better a ranch in Montana. He arrived in Los Angeles by bus, getting off at the Hollywood station with his one leather suitcase, which was held together with two pieces of clothesline he had bought at an overpriced hardware store near the bus station in San Luis Obispo.

Shaw had a friend in Los Angeles, a man he had known in Soledad and with whom Shaw wasn't supposed to have anything to do. As a condition of his parole, he was supposed to avoid "convicted felons and other associates of a criminal bent." His friend's name was Nicky White. Nicky had curly hair and was tall and dark, and there was about him an unmistakable charisma, although this was something Nicky had put a considerable amount of work into. He had grown up in Los Angeles, and he knew a fair number of people in the movie business, directors and actors and screenwriters, most of whom liked to invite Nicky to a party if only because of his shock value. Once, when Nicky was asked by a studio executive, who was wearing three thousand dollars' worth of casual clothes, what Nicky did, Nicky said, "I steal cars. What about you?"

The studio executive had said, "I make pictures."

"Yeah?" said Nicky, "Is that right? I understand. You steal money from film budgets, right? Listen, maybe I can interest you in a Mercedes 320 SL. Low mileage. I mean, we're talking in the low five figures. Full documentation."

Nicky lived in an apartment building on Highland. It was two stories tall, built around a swimming pool and a couple of palm trees. There were gold specks in the stucco of it, and at night two lights, a red and a green one, shone on the front of the building to make them glitter. Nicky said it gave the place "a little touch of Vegas, without all the sleaze."

Victor Shaw walked the distance from the Hollywood bus station to Highland north of Hollywood Boulevard, carrying his bag, which kept knocking against his leg. He went right by the liquor stores and the movie theaters on Hollywood Boulevard, although he glanced at the front of Grauman's Chinese. When Nicky answered the knock on his door, he found Shaw standing there, sweating, still carrying the suitcase. Nicky said, "Well, well. It's the mathematician. Well, well. Does the LAPD know you're here?"

"No," said Victor.

He put his bag down and stood in the fragrance of the chlorine from the pool, and even though he had walked from the bus station in the shadowless heat of an early June day, he tried to maintain his sense of being cleansed somehow, in the way a recruit feels changed, maybe even for the better, by having gotten through boot camp.

"I just want a job and a little peace and quiet," said Shaw.

"Sure, sure," said Nicky. "I'll give you a hand. No recidivism here, buffo. If we don't hang together, what happens to us? Sure, I get you. Hats off."

"My past is behind me," said Victor.

"Well," said Nicky. "I wouldn't go that far. I can give you a hand. I know a guy who can help you."

Nicky said it would take a couple of days to get things set up. You can't move mountains overnight, right? Maybe Nicky could find Victor a warehouse job, maybe driving a forklift. How did that sound? Victor said he thought that would be pretty good.

"Good?" said Nicky. "It's gonna be great."

Victor got a copy of the L.A. *Times* and started looking for an apartment, and after he had seen three or four that were almost identical, right down to a peculiar odor like dirty laundry, he rented a place on a street just off of Western. Then he dropped by to see Nicky.

"It's all set," said Nicky.

"That's good," said Victor.

"Well, it's a start," said Nicky. "At least I can say that."

"What's wrong with a warehouse job?" said Victor. "I thought you said you knew a guy who could get me a job in a warehouse."

"It's not a warehouse," said Nicky. "I got to tell you that."

The Southwest Maintenance Corporation was in Watts. Victor had to take two transfers and wait at the bus stop on a gray, misty California day, the air not getting ready to rain so much as just becoming dirty. He stood absolutely still at the bus stop, looking into the distance, his figure suggesting a mixture of patience and barely subdued defiance. He wore new blue jeans and a secondhand shirt, the sizing from the blue jeans that were worn right off the shelf having about it a particular odor which Shaw supposed was the miasma of fate just waking up to new possibilities. While he waited for the bus, he added this to the things he'd have to endure: being in L.A. without a damn car.

So he stood there just as if he were in the food line at Soledad, waiting for a gray metal tray, but now he went over the things he had learned while waiting to get out: Keep your mouth shut.

Don't let anybody know what you're thinking. Find the right opportunity. Make sure it's the right one. Then take the chance. The word "chance" reminded Victor of those summer nights at Soledad when everyone was smoking cigarettes in the dark: that was the worst part, feeling that darkness.

Southwest Maintenance was in a one-story building surrounded by a cyclone fence which was topped by rolls of razor wire, the blades of which flashed like new steak knives.

"You're the only white boy we got working here," said the manager.

"Is that right?" said Shaw.

"You haven't got an attitude, do you?" said the manager.

"No," said Shaw.

There was a calendar on the wall, the days carefully X'd out, and against the wall there were bundles of brown paper hand towels that went into dispensers in public bathrooms. There were three other men in the room, all wearing green work clothes, and they glanced in Shaw's direction but not at him, their eyes simply not acknowledging him, the glance not hostile but, more than that, simply consigning him to oblivion. He stood still, patiently staring at absolutely nothing at all.

The manager gave Shaw a mop and a galvanized bucket with a built-in mop squeezer, set on small black casters.

"You can take that out to the van," said the manager. He held out the bucket. "You got it?"

"Yes."

"You sure?"

"I said I got it."

"OK," said the manager. "I'll take you up there to Beverly Hills and break you in."

At night, Victor Shaw cleaned the building in which August St. James had his office. It was on North Rodeo Drive in Beverly Hills, and St. James's practice was made up of people who were in the movie business or who just had money. There were eight offices in the building, but the one Victor liked the most was St. James's. He gave it a good going over the first night, hoping he might find something interesting, a pad he could use to write himself a prescription or two, say; but then he thought it might be better just to do his job. So he didn't find the tape recorder the first night. It took about a week, and when he had opened the cabinet, as a matter of idle curiosity, he had found the tape recorder and had stood there, back from the cabinet, just looking at it.

The cabinet stood next to the couch in St. James's inner office. The couch was a chaise, covered with black leather, not Naugahyde, and the frame was mahogany, the leather held against it by a long line of brass brads. The thing had feet like a lion's. There was a chair at the head of it, also covered in black leather, but it had a curved, laminated back. Victor had only seen such a chair in advertisements for liquor in the magazines in Soledad that printed photographs of nude women. Usually the pages were stuck together.

The tape recorder had a stainless steel surface and a lot of dials and gauges and knobs. Above it, on a shelf, were rows of cassettes, each one with a little sticker on the case. Each sticker had a number written on it. A wire ran from the tape recorder to the chair where St. James sat while he listened to his patients. Beneath the carpet, where the wire ended, there was a little switch like the kind old houses used to have on the floor at the head of the table so that someone could summon help from the kitchen.

Victor sat down in St. James's chair and thought about the little stickers on the cassettes. What good were the tapes going to do him if he didn't know who was on them? Victor suspected that good fortune was trying to come his way, but somehow red tape, or some invisible hindrance, was making it difficult. Then Victor thought about a man he had known at Soledad. The guy's name was Jerry or Berry, had warts all over his hands and talked about flying saucers all the time. He told Victor he could recognize the brands of flying saucers, just as Victor could tell by looking at a car whether it was a Dodge, a Ford, or a Mercedes. The flying saucers had names like *Zobe* or Z-42. Just a cheap second-story man. But he told Victor that educated people like to hide things under horizontal surfaces. Like an accountant will think taping something to the underside of a toilet-tank cover is a great idea.

Victor got up and went into St. James's private bathroom, but it had a flushometer. Then he went back and stood in the office with the couch in it. Well, at least there wasn't a lot of stuff to clutter up the place. Victor started looking on the underneath of the inside of the cabinet, although he didn't find anything. But, on the underside of the one drawer of the modern desk there was a kind of leather pouch with a little cover and a snap, and inside there was a small loose-leaf binder, a black one with a flexible cover. Victor opened it up and found a list of names that went with the codes on the cassettes.

The writing in the notebook and on the cassettes was in clear, black letters that reminded Shaw of the script librarians used to put numbers and letters on the back of a book. He went down the list of names again, recognizing those of directors, actors, people he knew from the gossip columns, a congressman, a senator. He went along until his finger stopped at the name of Beverly Mason.

Beverly Mason was an actress. Shaw had even seen a couple of her movies, although it had been a few years since she had made a new one. Nicky would know about her. Mason was one of those slender blond women who look a little like Lauren Hutton, only more sultry. She had a little something wrong with her eyes, like Lauren Hutton. Maybe she looked more like Cybill Shepherd. Anyway, Shaw knew she had gotten into trouble. Everyone tried to hush it up, but it had been bad. Beverly Mason had had a bad night — even by Hollywood standards. And just think of those nights, thought Shaw, just think of them. Those hours spent in beach houses or in the hills or canyons with the white powder everywhere and a body on the floor. Fortunes hung in the balance, or by the most delicate thread. There was Charley MacKlay, for instance, and his swimming pool (the girls underage at best), or Matinee Cantwell and her tricks, or Fatty Arbuckle in a hotel room in San Francisco. Shaw knew all these nights had a definite atmosphere, like a half-remembered scent, something like romance hovering around the bits and pieces that are left, the broken glass, the mess . . . Yeah, Beverly Mason had had a bad night. She was sultry. Shaw remembered that. She had a way of sitting down or walking or just looking across a table . . . Well, maybe there wasn't any need to mention her to Nicky.

Shaw put the notebook away and decided he'd better think the whole thing through, so he went out to the waiting room. It had off-white walls. There were paintings hung on them, oils in a style that was an imitation of Monet done by an ex-patient of St. James's who had been arrested for molesting a teenage girl in Venice Beach. St. James had got the paintings for nothing when he had posted the patient's bail.

The waiting room had two sofas arranged at right angles so that if two people were in the waiting room at the same time, they wouldn't have to face each other. The sofas were off-white, too, with a comfortable nap, and in the corner a rubber plant stood in a ceramic bucket. There were some *New Yorker* magazines on the table, arranged one on top of another, like cards in a game of solitaire. As Shaw looked around, he wondered what St. James and his women patients did on the couch in that private room . . . Yeah, well, maybe some of that was on the tapes. He thought this over, too, as an additional possibility.

He sat down on one of the sofas and opened one of the *New Yorkers*, and as he did so, he admitted to himself that he was coming up to a threshold. Again. He took his lunch, a sandwich and a Twinkie, out of the pocket of his jacket, the two objects like the remains of a life that had had, at one time, real possibilities. Shaw considered the man who ate such a lunch, and he didn't like what he thought about him. He guessed it was the effect of the office that made him pensive about how he had come to this particular place at this particular time. The office felt so safe, it even smelled like the paper that money is printed on. And as Shaw resisted the comforting atmosphere, so conducive to rumination, he went through the list of things he had learned at Soledad almost as articles of faith: Keep your mouth shut. Don't let anybody know what you're thinking. Find the right opportunity. He sat back on the sofa and closed his eyes. Yeah, that sure felt nice, didn't it? Jesus, the people who came here didn't have the first idea about trouble. Not real trouble.

* * *

Victor Shaw had had a gift for mathematics. From an early age — ten, eleven — he had always been good with numbers. Sometimes he went to the supermarket in Los Angeles, where he had grown up, with his mother, who was a cocktail waitress at Diamond Jack's on Hollywood Boulevard. His mother put things in the cart without keeping track, and then sometimes when they got to the checkout counter she didn't have enough cash. Then she would turn to Victor and say, "Vic, honey, can you run this peanut butter and this steak back? We don't want them anyway, do we?" It didn't take long for Victor to start keeping track of what his mother bought, asking beforehand how much was "in the bank." This way they sorted out what they could afford before they got to the cash register. His mother had always bought him Twinkies, though, going without cigarettes sometimes. It had been a secret between them. When they were running out of money, Victor kept his head down, mumbling about how much money was left "in the bank," his uncertainty about whether or not his mother loved him coming right down to that moment when she put back a package of cigarettes rather than making Victor take the Twinkies back to the Hostess rack. It was the best memory he had.

There were others that weren't so good. He'd done plenty to get into Soledad. In fact, they hadn't even caught him for most of it. Well, he'd tried one thing and another. One thing and another.

Shaw knew that soon he would get up and go into the room with the leather chaise and listen to the first tape. He thought, at least he should eat his lunch first since it might be a long night. He ate slowly, taking small bites, chewing. He remembered Soledad and those dark, hot nights of July and August and September. Then he cleaned up his lunch, crumpling plastic wrap and the brown paper bag, the crunching of it making him stop: it seemed loud and sudden. Gradually, as Victor spent his nights alone, he was getting jumpy about sounds. He couldn't say exactly when it happened, since it was a process as slow as a bucket filling up with water one drop at a time, but still, it was there. Certain sounds were getting to him, the sucking roar of a vacuum cleaner, his mop hissing across a floor, the crunch of ice breaking out of an ice tray at five o'clock in the morning when he got home and made himself a drink. Then he would sit in his kitchen in a small apartment in a converted house off Western Avenue. The kitchen had one table and one chair. There were other sounds, too, he would flinch at: the barely audible hiss as he opened a can of peas, which seemed to be just a quieter version of the hiss of a hamburger frying in his cast iron pan. Sometimes there was the digging, scratching sound of rats working in the walls.

Usually, Shaw took the bus home from work. There was one that went down Sunset that he could catch at 4:30 A.M., the bus coming out of the west with the sky purple behind it, the city seeming deserted at this hour, not just empty but as though no one was ever coming back. Shaw once sat behind the bus driver, and when he said, "Looks like it's going to be a beautiful day," the driver said nothing, didn't seem to react at all, aside from pointing at the sign above the windshield, which read, "Do *not* converse with the vehicle operator."

Victor's apartment had a folding table, a chair, a bed, and a sofa from the Goodwill store. The sofa had some stains on it which he tried not to notice. He moved his chair back and forth between the kitchen and the living room, depending on where it was needed. Next to the sofa was a wooden packing crate on which there was a handbill, an advertisement for the Big Brothers. It showed a picture of a kid with freckles who was about twelve years old. Next to him there was a shape the size of an adult, and around it were little lines like the ones that have "cut here" printed next to them. The caption read, "Put yourself here. Be a Big Brother." Sometimes Shaw thought he would go down to the Big Brothers office and maybe have the courage to go in this time. He figured he'd be able to tell kids a few things, like about losing your head over a stupid idea or about getting yourself sent to a place like Soledad. He might tell them what it was like living with nothing but noises, as he did now, while looking for the right chance.

Shaw went into the inner office and turned the machine on, the two rows of lights on it, one green, one red, beginning to flash in a steady, mildly impatient cadence. The thing that surprised him, after he started listening, was how quickly he became attached to the patients. He got to know them just by the sound of their voices, thinking, "Oh, yeah, him, drinking too much and doing something funny at the stock exchange . . . Jesus, hope he didn't have another argument with his wife . . ." Or, "She's the one who banged her boyfriend's best friend . . ." And he found, too, that if they did something stupid he was disappointed, and he was pleased, in a way he didn't really understand, if one of them cut down on tranquillizers, got some exercise, or broke off a destructive affair. Sometimes, after listening, he said, "Way to go, Jack. You don't need that Valium." Or, "That's hanging tough, Barbara. Don't let him pull the wool over your eyes."

He waited for a couple of nights before listening to the tapes of Beverly Mason, if only because he wanted to make sure he understood what was going on. Everybody had a special language — cops, engineers, doctors, even patients. There were words the patients used for things they didn't like to talk about, and they used phrases like, "You know, the thing I did that time," or "before it happened," or "after it happened." Now, though, he put the first of Beverly's tapes into the machine. There were two good speakers, and they made the voices seem a little louder than when the patients were actually in the room.

There was a leathery squeak as Beverly Mason sat on the chaise. It was slow and languid, as though she had sat at the side of the couch for a moment, uncertain as to whether or not she was going to continue, and then, with a quick impulse, swung her legs up, as though she had decided to go through with it after all. She breathed steadily, slowly. She didn't say anything for a while. Shaw imagined her large, bee-stung lips, slightly chapped maybe, just touching as she waited. Then St. James said, his voice impeccably neutral, "You can begin."

She shifted her weight again. Shaw leaned a little closer. Her voice had a whispery, throaty quality, which seemed natural for a confession. She said, "You remember that old Mae West line about how when I'm good I'm good but when I'm bad I'm better?"

"Yes," said St. James.

"I always laughed about that," said Beverly. There was silence. "Or at least I used to. Well, there's something I'd better talk to you about."

The details left Shaw opening his eyes a little wider, although some of them left him puzzled, especially some French words that were used to describe what she did in bed. He knew he'd have to get a French dictionary to figure out just what the hell she was really doing. Her voice filled the room with a sultry quality which left him trembling if only because, after listening to her, he realized how paltry his own experience had been. He put this paltriness in the same category as being in L.A. without a car.

He thought he and Beverly were a lot alike. After all, they both had gotten some crazy ideas and had acted on them, and they both had gotten into trouble. Beverly had been in a house where someone had gotten killed. She hadn't been charged, but still, there was something about the entire business that had made her less desirable as an actress. She had made a B movie. After that, she got even fewer calls than before, which is to say, no one called her at all. How could she take control of things again, the way she had before the trouble? Beverly could remember the freshness at the beginning when people were so taken with her. There wasn't any other feeling like it.

It took about a week of listening to Beverly's tapes before she said the thing that Shaw was looking for. He had cleaned up and had sat down, eating just a sandwich (having given up the Twinkie to save money for a car, because he knew, no matter what he was going to do, he had to have a car). He put a new tape in and turned the machine on, hearing the hum in the speakers. Then there was the leathery squeak as she sat down, her voice coming into the room with a disorienting rush that took him half a minute just to get used to.

She stretched out on the chaise. Then she said, "It's hot. Do you mind if I take off my skirt? I've got a pair of pantyhose on."

"I can turn up the air conditioner," said St. James.

"That will take too long," said Beverly. "I'm asking you a direct question? Will it bother you?"

St. James waited for a moment. "No. Make yourself comfortable."

There was the sound of a short zipper being run down and then a rustle and a squeak as Beverly stood up. Shaw guessed she was folding the skirt. There wasn't a chair to put it on, and he looked around the office, wondering where Beverly had put it. Maybe on the shelf or just at the end of the chaise. He imagined her standing in black stockings and high-heeled shoes, bending over, the nylons with a little sheen along her calves and thighs. The chaise squeaked again, and she said, "God, it's hot, isn't it?"

"It's warm," said St. James.

"What really scares the shit out of you?" said Beverly.

St. James didn't say anything, and there was only the sound of Beverly's breathing. This was the way he dealt with questions he thought were too theoretical. He simply waited. Shaw wondered what was going through his mind. He said, "Continue."

Beverly sighed. She sighed again. The sofa squeaked. She began to talk in the flat monotone of confession. She said she had grown up in Antelope Valley, which was a hundred miles or so north of Los Angeles. Her parents had been caretakers of a hunt club and ranch there. Men from the city had put up some money and bought the place so they could shoot pheasant there and hunt deer. There was a farmhouse in which Beverly had grown up. Her father had been a failed farmer, and her mother had gone to beauty school. Beverly had stood and watched when she was thirteen, fourteen, and fifteen years old as those cars came up from the city and the men got out and took their dogs and went after pheasants, the *bang bang bang* marking Saturday mornings in the fall. Or later, there were the deer hunters who came, and they brought their bucks in and hung them in the tree in front of Beverly's house, the animals swinging back and forth in the wind, the chest of each one propped open with a stick where the lungs and heart had been removed, the dark eyes moving in and out of the shadows.

The summers were different, though. Then the hillsides turned brown, and when Beverly walked through the tawny grass, she saw the silver lines, like needles, on the stalks where the July and August sun was reflected. There were eucalyptus trees on the place, and she remembered the scent of them, like Mustarole. When she was sixteen, she had a boyfriend. In the summer they took walks along a creek bottom that was a half mile or so from the house and barn. In July the water was low, and the stream ran between rocks and sandbars that were like small beaches. It was so long ago she could hardly remember the romance of it. Or the innocence. The two of them sat with their feet in the water, which in the noon sunlight of July had the color of silver. Beverly had wanted to be an astronomer, and at night the two of them would come to the stream. In a still pool the stars appeared as a handful of silver flakes, as though pieces of foil had been dropped into the water. Beverly had tried to pick out the constellations in the stream, but everything had been backwards.

One day they sat by the stream. In the distance, through the glare of the creek bed, they saw the barn, its roof dark with old shingles, the planks of the front wall having a reddish cast, as at sunset, from the red paint that had been weathered away even before Beverly and her parents had moved here.

They stood and started walking toward the barn. The heat seemed to exist as a kind of essence, hot, searing on the skin, and both of them wanted to breathe more deeply, as if there weren't enough air. The sky was almost a purple-blue, like morning glories. The road from the creek was dusty in the ruts, and it felt like warm talcum powder on their feet. Occasionally a breeze made Beverly's skirt billow.

The barn had a triangular shadow in front of it, and when they came into the shade their eyes were filled with minute sparkles disappearing like bubbles at the surface of champagne. Beverly opened the door and said, "Let's go up to the loft." She had blushed; she still remembered the heat of it and the sudden tearing of her eyes.

She spread her white skirt and blouse on the hay, putting her white cotton briefs down alongside his shirt and pants to make a place where the hay wouldn't scratch. The sun came in through the open loft door, the yellow light angled down in a rectangle. She stood in it, feeling it on her skin, looking out at the creek bed where there was that silvery ribbon of water, the heat of the sunlight like a broad, flat pressure, like leaning up against a warm sliding glass door. His skin was as smooth as the powder-like dust that had been in the road.

The moment was an antidote to the confinement of being the caretaker's daughter. As Beverly felt the heat and the sweaty slickness of her skin, she remembered those times when her father had bowed and scraped to the members of the hunt club. They had ordered her father to bring them drinks, and Beverly had hated the confinement of standing there while her father trotted off to get them. She would have done anything to break the expression of smug anticipation on the face of the men who had watched him trot off through the late afternoon shadows. In the heat of the barn she had even said, "Anything."

The dust from the hay floated out of the shadows and emerged into the light, where it was suddenly illuminated, golden, as it hung in the air and then simply vanished, winking out as the bits turned back into shade. Beverly watched them at the border between the shade of the barn and the light from the loft door, and it seemed to her, in the moment, that she existed in a pleasant thrill of points, indistinguishable from the flecks that emerged in the sunlight, one and then another, the accumulation of them small, delicate, constant, making for a tingle or a chill. There were flecks in the boy's eyes, golden bits in his otherwise gray irises, and it seemed for a brief moment that the mite-filled air, the scent of the dried hay and the heated wood of the barn, the beating wings of pigeons as they landed on the roof, the slickness of her boyfriend's skin and her own all blended into one moment in which she was unable to speak. She started to cry.

"What's wrong, what's wrong? Oh, please. Did I hurt you?" the boy said.

She moved her head from side to side, shaking it, trying to let him know that it wasn't that there was something wrong so much as that she couldn't speak, that she was at a loss. They lay in the rustling hay, feeling the slow, constant dust of the place as it settled on their skin, making them feel not dirty but just a little gritty. They fell asleep in the heat. The breeze blew across them, warm as the breath of a cow. Outside the grass rustled, the dry hush mixing with the occasional flapping of the pigeons' wings and the buzz of the wasps that made their nest under the eaves.

Beverly woke to the slam of the door downstairs. Then she

stood, sick with sleep, and looked below. The loft was made of planks, and between them there sifted those bits into the darkness below, although now the bits that glowed in the afternoon sunlight weren't so beautiful or reassuring.

The hunt club bought hay for the horses they used in the fall to hunt deer, and the hay was delivered by a man who now stood on the hard-packed floor below the loft. He was a preacher in a local sect, and he wore a pair of black pants and a white shirt and a black jacket, too, not new but clean. His hands were large and the fingers were square, obviously calloused, and having the texture, if you touched one, of an unmilled pine board. He was about sixty years old, had gray hair, and wore large boots the color of iron, tied up with black laces. The light came through the cracks in the barn, making a pattern of strips, and they lay at a slanting angle across the man's face, chest, and arms. His eyes were a flat lizard green, and as he looked up, one of them was filled with a point of sunlight as though the man were having a vision of the divine.

He had a can of snuff in one hand and held a pinch of it in the other, his mouth open, hesitating, showing his stumps of black teeth as he stared at her.

"You know your Bible?" said the man.

Beverly shook her head. For a moment she had the impulse to put an arm across her breasts, or to put a hand between her legs, but she stood there, resisting it, somehow knowing that by refusing to be humiliated she hadn't lost everything. Her figure appeared in a dark outline in that aureate light, the air around her more filled with bright motes than before since she had stirred the dust up by walking across the loft. His eyes went slowly over the white skin which showed the shape of her bathing suit, moved up to her broad shoulders, and finally rested on her eyes.

So he waited, realizing this was a kind of challenge, or at least a refusal to give in to his own furious glance and the gloom he seemed to carry with him, as if when he walked into a room he was able, through a kind of dark suction, to remove the light. He went carefully over her again, lingering on the bits of hay in her hair, in the slight dusting of her sweating skin. He raised a hand to strike or at least to make a curse, a quick drawing of his fingers one way and then the other, as though he were personally responsible for bringing damnation to this moment. He looked her in the eyes and put back his head and began to laugh, the sound harsh, repeated, and then, keeping his eyes on her, he said, "Oh, I see you all right. I can look right down into your heart. I can see every corner. Do you think I can't?"

Then he turned on his heel and walked outside, where he stood in the sunlight, looking at the house where Beverly and her parents stayed. The barn door was open, and as the man walked toward the house, the door swung in the breeze, its rusty hinges making a long, slow creak.

Beverly got dressed, keeping an eye on that heavy-booted, black-coated figure who made his way through the dust.

Her father came to the door, instinctively keeping the screen door between him and what was approaching. Beverly started walking to the ladder at the edge of the loft, already hurrying, not knowing what she would say but somehow wanting to find a way to be able to stand up to the hay man who now walked across the yard in a cloud of his own gloom, giving the barn one furious glance over his shoulder.

"Well, hell. Wouldn't you know it?" Beverly's boyfriend said as he went down the ladder and out the back door of the barn, simply disappearing into the shimmering light. Beverly went out the front door, hearing the hinges creak like the sound of some insect.

She walked with her head up, feeling the sunlight. Her father still had the screen door between him and the man in the black coat. Her father was a thin man with a small wisp of hair, almost like a forelock, that hung over his forehead. He had gray-blue eyes and a gray complexion, an unhealthy cast to his skin that had come slowly as he had lost his own place, his skin seeming to turn a little grayer with each new note he had signed at the bank and with each new plan (soybeans, barley, feed corn) that had come to almost but not quite enough. But even during the worst times he had always picked up Beverly, when she was young, and said, "You're my girl. My girl." And when they had finally lost the piece of land down the road, which they all tried to avoid passing, Beverly's father had taken her out to the ice cream store in town and let her order anything she wanted, and then, when she had finished he had looked out the window, not crying exactly but just letting the tears run down his face for a moment.

So now Beverly approached, seeing that her father had stepped out from behind the door. She couldn't hear what it was that the man in the black coat said, but she saw her father slam the door behind himself and come out into the yard. There, under the apple trees, where the leaves dappled the dust like the shade from a moth-eaten umbrella, the two men seemed about to collide. The hay man stood above Beverly's father, his voice loud now, the words "Jezebel," and "Gomorrah," floating on the air of the dusty orchard around the house, and as the man spoke and pointed, as if from a pulpit, Beverly's father stepped up, short, thin, one hand lifted, as though with his diminutive, raised fist he was striking out for every slight, every failure, every insult he had quietly endured. The hay man knocked him down. Beverly's father got up again. The hay man was waiting for him. Beverly ran now, coming out into the meager shade. Her father sat in the dust, his eyes having a gray, tired defiance, behind which there was shame.

He bled from the nose and mouth, and Beverly turned toward the hay man, screaming now, telling him to get the hell away. She knelt next to her father, holding his head, his nose and mouth dripping onto her white skirt like red paint dripping onto a white cloth. Then the hay man said, "Get your feed someplace else."

He turned and walked away, his figure retreating, diminishing, finally being absorbed into the glare off the windshield of his truck, as though he had disappeared into the center of the sun. There was the sound of the engine of his truck, a loud popping, and after he backed up and turned around, he left a trail of dust, the truck turning onto the paved road and finally disappearing into the quicksilver shimmer of heat.

Beverly's father sat in the dust, his forearms on his knees, saying, "Bev, oh, Bev, I'm sorry. Look at your skirt. Oh, Bev."

"It doesn't matter," she said.

"Is that right?" he said. "We saved up to order it from the catalogue. Don't you remember?"

"Don't worry about it," she said.

"I don't know. I think I want to be alone for a little."

"I'll stay with you," she said.

"No," he said. "I want to be alone."

Beverly sat in the dappled light of the trees, hearing the wind that came up and the slam of the door as her father went into the house. Then there was the sound of her father opening the ice box and the sad, lonely tinkle of ice cubes being dropped into a glass and the slight *pop* (like the one he used to make by putting a finger inside his cheek) of the cork being drawn from a bourbon bottle. She looked down at the blood on her skirt, and went inside and put meat tenderizer on it, hoping this would get the stain out. Then she put cold water on it in the upstairs bathroom and scrubbed the cloth, rubbing it between her knuckles.

"But don't you see?" said Beverly to St. James. "That's the man I'm afraid of. The hay man. When I think of someone like that, a redneck preacher, a creature of the anonymous parts of the world, existing at the edge of strips and shopping malls . . . that's the one I'm afraid of. Just thinking about him makes me feel like when I was washing my father's blood out of my skirt. Do you understand? I see him in my dreams, coming to get me. I'm afraid of him coming to get me."

"Get?" said St. James.

"Yes," she said. "It's worse than hurt. It's like something from a dream, a terror without a name."

There was silence in the office for a minute, and then a squeak as she squirmed.

"But that's a little vague," said St. James. "Tell me about the 'getting.' What are you afraid of?"

"Do I have to?" asked Beverly.

"It's your decision," said St. James.

There was another squeak, like a saddle, as Beverly moved, squirming now, turning one way and then another.

"I don't like this couch," she said. "I can never get comfortable here."

"You don't have to tell me," said St. James. "It's all right."

"No," she said. "No. It's not all right. No."

St. James waited now. Victor imagined the office as quiet as it was at night, although even in the recording there was something in the air. He strained, trying to decide what it was. Like on an airplane that's falling a thousand feet.

"First, I'm afraid he would catch me," said Beverly. "He'd have me alone someplace. Maybe in an isolated house. Maybe in my own house when my husband was gone for a week. We'd be alone. He'd take me into the bedroom. He might have a knife. Probably a hunting knife with a bone handle, one with a sharp, polished blade. He'd have tattoos probably, and he'd have pocked skin, and he'd be balding, and he'd look as though he had a kind of genius for the wrong thing. He'd probably stink. He'd have a six-pack of beer with him. He'd probably have some rope. He'd tell me how bad I was as he began. He'd know everything I've ever done, and he'd start . . . making me do things, always having another idea for me."

She moved again, making that squeak.

"Continue," said St. James.

"But that's not the horror. That's just the beginning," said Beverly.

"What's the horror?" asked St. James.

"That I'd help him. That somehow, in a way I couldn't control, I'd want him to continue, that the part of me that delights in things going wrong would blend with him, and that with each step down, as things got scarier, I'd want that much more to continue. So there we'd be, the two of us, hating each other, embraced, going on until I was glad, insisting that he kill me. That's the horror. That's the real horror. That I'd become part of him. That I'd be lost . . . Really lost. It's like I can smell it on his breath, cigarettes and beer and something he'd eaten, something he'd devoured . . . The entire idea affects me like a gas, one that's leaking out of the ground and making me sick. I can't stop it."

It was quiet for a while, and then St. James said, "All right. Until Thursday, then."

* * *

Victor went to see Nicky on Sunday evening, one of his two nights off. The front of the apartment house was lit up with the green and red lights, and the palm trees by the pool were covered with the aquamarine shimmer from the slowly lapping water after the evening swim of an airline stewardess who was one of Nicky's neighbors. Shaw walked around the pool, smelling the chlorine and seeing the slowly drying footprints of the woman, who had gone back to her aparment. Then he knocked on the door, and in the hollow sound he knew that if he talked to Nicky about what he was thinking, he wouldn't do it. If he talked about it, that would mean it wasn't really very strong. So coming here was a way of figuring things out.

"Hey, it's Einstein," said Nicky. He was wearing a pair of gold pants and a see-through black net T-shirt. "Or is it Niels Bohr? Who was the better scientist?"

"Listen," said Shaw. "I got to talk to you."

"Sure, sure," said Nicky. "Come in. Just got back from Santa Anita. I hit a quinella you wouldn't believe. There was this horse in the first race called Rainbow Bob. Now, the charts say —"

"Are you alone?" asked Shaw. He stepped inside.

"Yeah," said Nicky.

Shaw closed the door.

"You want something to drink?" said Nicky.

"No," said Shaw.

Nicky had a tank in which he kept some tropical fish, big blue ones with black stripes and pointed tails and whiskers around their snouts, and they floated back and forth in the water which was colored by the blue wall behind it. Shaw stared at the fish and then looked at Nicky.

"You don't look so good," said Nicky. "You know, I think you aren't getting out enough. How would you like to come to a real Hollywood party? Get with a better class of people."

Shaw looked at the fish and thought about this for a moment. From what he had heard on the tapes, he wasn't so sure Hollywood people were that different from a lot of guys he had known at Soledad, especially considering what went on during the hot nights in July and August. Nicky put a little fish food into the tank, which spread out on the surface, and then the blue fish slowly rose toward it, infinitely languid as they took one flake and then another out of the film on the water.

"You know," said Shaw, "I'm always looking for a possibility."

"Who isn't?" said Nicky. "Like the quinella today . . ." But he stopped, his eyes resting on Shaw's face. "Like what kind of possibility?"

Victor shrugged.

"Hey," said Nicky. "How about some pineapple juice? You aren't getting any vitamin C. I can see it in your face."

"OK," said Shaw. "A little pineapple juice."

"I get it down at the farmers' market. Costs like three dollars a quart."

Nicky went to the refrigerator in the kitchenette and poured the thick, syrupy juice into an ugly glass and brought it back.

"Here," he said. "I can see you aren't taking care of yourself. You aren't eating right, are you?"

"I'm saving up to buy a car," said Shaw.

"Well, take a supplement then," said Nicky. "You can get them at the rack at Hughes. Drink up."

Shaw drank the juice, surprised at the freshness of it. It had been a long time since he had had anything that wasn't out of a can. He wanted to be able to afford some fresh food every now and then rather than eating like someone who was living after they dropped the H-bomb. The fish drifted back and forth, as slowly as a cloud.

"Pretty good, huh?" said Nicky.

"You can feel the health in it," said Shaw.

"Sure," said Nicky. "What kind of possibility were you talking about?"

Shaw stared at the fish.

"You got to be careful about what you do," said Nicky.

"You're telling me?" said Shaw.

"Well, yeah," said Nicky. "Sometimes you don't really know what you've got. Like, you remember Sammy and Blind Frank at Soledad?"

"Not really," said Shaw.

"Sure you do. Blind Frank was a fat guy from Frisco. Could see just a little. Shadows and bright light. Sammy was his pal. Once they took a funny-looking suitcase out of a van in Frisco. The suitcase was aluminum and Sammy said it must have cost a thousand dollars. It had one of those symbols on it for radiation. Like you see in bomb shelters. You know, it's got three prongs."

"Uh-huh," said Shaw. He was still thinking about the taste of the juice.

"They got the suitcase open and there was this big thing inside, a kind of machine with flashing lights. Like a big tape recorder or something."

"Yeah?" said Shaw.

"There was a row of red lights and they were all flashing on and off, on and off. Then the thing began to make a steady beeping. Blind Frank thought it was some kind of warning. Sammy thought the thing was an H-bomb and he was convinced they could get something for it. Find a terrorist, right? They'd pay plenty." Nicky started to laugh. "The thing starts beeping louder and the lights flash a little more. And finally they ditch it in an alley and start running, thinking it was about to explode. They figured they'd read about it in the papers. Don't you remember those two guys who were always saying they stole an atomic bomb?"

"No," said Shaw.

"Well, the thing they had was probably some kind of medical appliance or something. But if they had had a bomb, Jesus, could they have made out."

"People don't leave bombs around in San Francisco," said Shaw.

"I don't know," said Nicky. "Guys have picked up some pretty weird things boosting vans and trucks. I knew a guy who stole a cooler and when he got home he found a kidney. The ice was melting and he couldn't do much with it."

"Uh-huh," said Shaw.

"Well, what have you got going?" asked Nicky.

"Nothing, really," said Shaw. "I was thinking about starting a juice cart, you know. I'd wheel it up and down Hollywood Boulevard and sell orange, papaya, cranberry to the gawkers out there."

"You got two problems," said Nicky. "One is spoilage. The other is license. I don't think you can cut the license with a felony rap."

"Yeah," said Shaw. "I guess that's right."

"That's all that's on your mind?"

Shaw nodded. They both sat and watched the fish. Some green plants rose in strands from the sand in the bottom of the tank, and there was a bubbler, too, the silver balls it made rising steadily to the surface. Nicky looked at Shaw and then back at the fish.

"You're not getting out enough," said Nicky. "I'll let you know about this party. You won't believe some of these Hollywood types. They'll think you're the real thing."

"Will they?"

"Sure." said Nicky. "I'll call you. You'll have a good time. Trust me."

Shaw got up and went to the door.

"Well, OK," he said. "I guess that settles it."

"There's no money in retail anyway," said Nicky.

Shaw opened the door. "Thanks."

"Sure," said Nicky. "And do yourself a favor. Take a supplement, will you?"

A Day at the Zoo

VICTOR KNEW precisely what Beverly was afraid of. At Soledad he had watched a man put a homemade tattoo on his fingers, doing one letter for each year he'd been locked up, starting with an *H* on the little finger of his right hand, and then progressing, each year adding one more letter, an *O*, on the second finger the second year and then an *R* on the middle finger of the right hand the third year, continuing until there were only three letters more to go when Victor arrived at Soledad. The man was short and thin, with brushlike gray hair and green eyes. He had not only the expression of a rat but the angry insistence of one, a singleness of purpose that made men just leave him alone since everyone knew that if you started a fight with him, it wasn't going to be a one-time occurrence so much as the beginning of a long-term struggle that would leave one of the two people involved dead. He was a hard, taciturn man who had come from Oklahoma or Alabama and who was doing time for murder, a man who got up in the morning and ate his oatmeal and stale toast with a slow, constant devouring, as though it wasn't food he was taking in, but the time he still had to serve, which he was making disappear by a steady, unstoppable chewing. The man didn't smile or joke, looked neither to the right nor the left when he came into a room; he went about his days with a furious, efficient resolve, as if getting into this place was only a temporary stop on the way to some other place. He read the Bible, going through the Book of Job, laughing from time to time with a steady "heh heh heh," the sound itself making everyone's skin crawl.

So no one even bothered to ask what the next letter was going to be, although by the seventh year it was pretty clear and almost certain by the eighth, the entire inscription done in blue-green ink and a pin to break the skin. When Shaw was released, it was the tattoo he found himself thinking about. He went into the reception hall of the prison and then out the door, catching the bus to King City, the moaning of the engine somehow all mixed up with the sight of those eight fingers and two thumbs that read, when they were all lined up, "Horror Show."

Shaw thought about this a lot now, especially as he considered what action he should take. He began to feel close to the man with the tattoo, and he didn't like it. He wanted to be smart rather than crazy, and the thought of impersonating Beverly's worst fear left him ashamed. He sat in his living room and looked at the advertisement for the Big Brothers and tried to imagine himself in the space with the perforated lines and the caption "Imagine yourself here." Well, it sure beat sitting around the apartment. Maybe he could do a little good. The apartment had gotten quiet during the days when he had sat there, thinking things over. He wasn't sure of anything, really, but somehow Victor thought he might not be so quick to make a mistake if he started spending a little time with a kid.

Victor went through the list of the patients St. James had taped, dismissing those who, by their criminal records and their compulsions, would have been even less acceptable to the Big Brothers than Shaw. He ran his finger over the neatly lettered names, remembering their voices and flinching at the prospect of some of them even being around a child unescorted. Finally, he came to the name of one who seemed, more than anything else, to be a monument to dullness. The man was a banker who spent every spare minute washing his hands. His name was Harold Carroway. There wasn't anything else wrong with Carroway: sex once a week on Saturday morning with his wife before they did the grocery shopping together, one drink on Saturday evening, measured with a shot glass, a mild crush on a young woman in the bank. He voted Republican with an unquestioning regularity that reminded Shaw of Carroway's Saturday mornings with his wife. Shaw himself was a Democrat, or had been until he got sent up. Well, there was nothing in the guy's record that would keep him from doing some volunteer work. Victor copied down Carroway's social security number. He put "Carroway" on his mailbox above "Shaw." Then he went down to the office of the Big Brothers.

The office was in an art deco building. It was concrete, and across the top on the front it had a pattern of triangles that looked like the skin of the Jolly Green Giant. In the waiting room there were some flowers in a vase on a bookcase, a couple of sofas, and in front of them a table with some magazines on it, *Ranger Rick* mixed in with *Better Homes and Gardens*. There was a woman at a desk, too.

She was in her early forties, had straight brown hair worn with a part in the middle. There was something a little bookish about her which was enhanced by the half-glasses she wore in the middle of her nose. She looked at Shaw, her expression something like that of a woman who can't tell whether the person approaching her front door is selling vacuum cleaners or about to tell her about Jesus.

"Good morning," the woman said. "Did you want to see about being a volunteer?"

Shaw looked around. There were pictures of kids on the wall. He cleared his throat.

"Yes," he said. "That's right. I have a little time on my hands."

She took out an application form and passed it over. He filled it out, taking a pen from his pocket with something like a flourish. She noticed he had his own pen. He was sure of it. Well, that was something he could probably teach the kids: make sure you always have your own pen. Don't ask for one. He used the name and social security number of the banker who was a patient of St. James.

Shaw passed the form back.

"Is it warming up outside?" she asked.

"A little."

"People in the East say we don't have real seasons here," said the woman.

"Oh," said Shaw, "we have real summers in California."

"Where are you from?"

"Up north."

"Where?"

"Near Soledad," he said.

"Gets hot up there, does it?"

"You bet," said Shaw. "Sometimes you can cook a pork chop on the blacktop."

"Really?" The woman looked at him for a moment. "Of course, we'll need a personal reference. A letter."

"A friend of mine's a doctor," said Shaw. "A psychiatrist. Would that be all right? Should it be on his stationery?"

"That would be fine," said the woman.

Then Shaw went out and bought a car. He walked down to Santa Monica and then went east, passing the motels, chain restaurants, the cheap coffee shops and stores, plumbing supplies and magic and hobby shops mixed together in such a way as to make no sense at all. He stopped at a used car lot, a place decorated with small plastic triangular flags flapping in the breeze, and beneath them cars were lined up with prices written in white letters on the windshield. There was a little office, a kind of house not too much bigger than a booth. Under the flapping of the flags (in the sound of which Shaw searched for an omen), he paid cash for a ten-year-old Ford station wagon with stuffing coming out of the seats and three bald tires. Shaw planned on going to Pep Boys for some seat covers, terry cloth ones, and would hope for the best about the tires. The way he saw it, a kid who went to Griffith Park on the bus wasn't going to think much of the man who took him there. The Ford overheated a little on the way home, but Shaw stopped and put some STP stop leak in the radiator, and that seemed to help a little.

When the letter from the Big Brothers arrived, setting up his first appointment, Shaw was thinking about Beverly Mason. It was as though her willingness to talk about her fears had been a catalyst for him, and there were things that had begun to stir in his own carefully sealed-up depths. He could feel them squirm, like eels in a bag. Maybe if he could just spend a little time with a kid, just talking things over, maybe taking a ride out to the zoo, why then he might be able to form a decent, straightforward attachment that would help with his own temptations. The kid would be a lifeline. That was the word Shaw used when he thought about it.

*   *   *

The boy lived between Sunset and Santa Monica on one of those short streets filled with what Easterners called "bungalows." These are one-story California houses with a pitched roof and a large, covered porch. Each had a front yard between the sidewalk and the house, usually about twenty-five feet wide and fifteen feet deep. Some of the houses were on a little rise above the street, on a shoulder that had been made with a bulldozer. The house that Victor was looking for was one of those that sat above the street. The lawn was brown, and there were some white flowers in a bed by the house, although it was possible they were plastic. Victor stared at them, looking closely, trying to see if they moved in the stale air of a California afternoon so he could tell if they were real or not. He guessed they were pretty good phony ones.

Victor had gone to Penny's and bought a new pair of pants and a new shirt. The pants were a light synthetic cloth that looked a little like wool and which in the store had seemed to him to be the kind of thing a fashionable man might wear while he sat in a library reading or something, but now that he had them on, he didn't think they were quite right. His blue shirt was OK, although it was a short-sleeved one made of Dacron. He had seen some all-cotton shirts, but he didn't think he could afford them. He hadn't had the money to take the shirt to the laundry, and it smelled of sizing. Victor was ashamed of its newness. It seemed like it was giving him away somehow, that he had had to go out and buy a shirt. He looked down at the pants and thought he shouldn't have bought them, either. God, he looked like a guy who sold vacuum cleaners door to door or something. What would a kid think of that?

So, now he sat in his car looking at the flowers, thinking they were imitation, and as he waited, he looked at the seat covers he had bought at Pep Boys and hoped the car would make it to the zoo and back.

Shaw had seven dollars. He thought they'd each have a hot dog, a bag of peanuts, and a Coke. The hot dogs couldn't be more than a buck and a half. Fifty cents for a drink. Fifty cents for a bag of peanuts. Maybe a buck to get into the zoo. He could do it on the seven. He also had some change in his pocket, about a buck twenty or so.

He got out of the car. The air was a reddish gray with a little yellow mixed in, too, the combination suggesting to Victor a yellow cat with dirty fur. It was hot, too, and the air smelled of distant burning tires. There had been a fire in the canyons, and bits of ash, small, pure white specks, swung back and forth as they drifted to the ground, the side-to-side motion suggesting the precarious existence of unfounded hope.

Victor closed the door of the station wagon and looked across the top of it. The roof was sun-bleached, and the green paint seemed dry and washed out. He had almost gotten a $68.99 paint job at Earl Scheib's, but he had decided against it, since the cars that had one of these jobs looked too much like you'd done it yourself in your back yard with a can of spray paint.

He walked up the three steps in the small hill above the sidewalk, absently running one hand through his hair. Victor had looked in the mirror that morning and had noticed he was turning a little gray around the ears, even though he wasn't over twenty-eight. A glider sat on the porch. There was a screen door, and as Victor approached it, a woman opened the inner door. They stood with the screen between them for a moment, each of them looking the other over.

The woman was about thirty-eight. She had teased, bleached hair, and she had on a short skirt and fishnet stockings, the kind of thing a waitress might wear. She smiled and said, "Come in. You must be from B. B."

"B. B.?"

"Big Brothers and Sisters," she said. "Frank's been waiting all morning. My name is Maggie Teele."

Shaw said his name was Carroway.

"Nice to meet you," she said. "I knew a Carroway once. Over in Pasadena."

"Well, there's a lot of them around."

"Of course there are," she said. "This one sold insurance."

"Some of them are in banking."

"Well, sure. Insurance. Banking. It's all the same." She smiled. "I've got to go to work. You can just drop Frank off here if I'm not back yet."

Frank came into the room. He was fourteen, tall for his age, and he had red hair and freckles and was wearing a pair of black jeans and a black T-shirt. His hair was short, and he had blue eyes, and he came into the room with the slow, careful movements of an animal that isn't sure whether it is really cornered. Victor put out his hand. Frank said hello and let Victor stand there with his hand out. Shaw waited a moment before he put his hand down. OK. That's the way it's going to be. He looked Frank right in the eyes, giving the kid a glance he had learned at Soledad, although he wasn't sure the kid was smart enough to know what it meant.

"Oh, you two will get along fine," said Maggie. "I can see that."

The boy sat down, staring at Shaw as though daring him to do something.

"Frank?" said Maggie.

"What?"

"Try to make an effort to get along, will you?"

Frank shrugged.

"Well," she said, turning away from the two of them. "I've got to get to work."

She went out the door, letting the screen slam. At the sidewalk she stopped and looked back at the house, biting her lips, her figure isolated against the pastel sun-blasted paint of the cars on the other side of the street. Then she sighed and started walking. Victor and Frank heard the tapping of her high-heeled shoes as it slowly diminished into the distance. Well, Shaw knew how to deal with punks like this. He'd seen plenty. You had to find a moment in which everything is made perfectly clear. He thought about the expression on the face of a young man who had been in Soledad, a kid with a chip on his shoulder who looked like a girl. Shaw hadn't touched the kid himself, but he had waited, knowing what was going to happen, feeling that slow, steady windup almost as if it was a cool breeze. Even now, when he thought back on it, he couldn't stand the memory of the kid's crying in the dark, a kind of steady, repeated whimper which seemed so appallingly ineffectual in the face of the world having changed forever. Well, Victor guessed Frank needed to learn some manners. Victor just stood there, looking at a spot just over Frank's head, remembering that sound in the dark. Anyone else in his right mind would have taken a look at Shaw's face and thought twice about being a smart-ass.

Shaw sighed and shook his head. He didn't want to get tough right off the bat, although he sure didn't like that business with the handshake. Well, all right. Try and make a good first impression . . . there was something to it. He figured he'd give the kid three chances.

"Where are we going?" said Frank.

"I was thinking about the zoo," said Shaw.

"The *zoo*," said Frank.

"Yeah. Griffith Park. What's wrong with the zoo?"

Frank shrugged. "OK," he said. "It's OK if you like animals. I can take them or leave them."

They went out to the porch, into the musty shade, the screen door slamming shut behind them. There was a finality about the *bang*, the suggestion of an impenetrable barrier. Then Shaw went into the sunshine and out to the curb, the tinkling of the keys in his hand seeming bell-like and too loud.

"Is this your car?" asked Frank.

"Yeah," said Shaw. He opened the door and got in. "Don't you like it?"

Frank shrugged.

"Let me tell you something," said Shaw. "It beats taking the bus."

Frank looked across the seat with an expression of disgust. Shaw realized he shouldn't even have mentioned the bus. He put the key into the ignition and turned it, hearing the engine grind. It went on grinding for a while and Victor pumped the gas, feeling the sweat beginning to form on his forehead.

"These seat covers came from Pep Boys, didn't they?" said Frank.

"Yeah," said Shaw. He gave the engine a rest. "Yeah, I think they look real nice."

This morning he had been looking at the car with something like admiration, or even self-congratulation. These old Fords really were something, a little boxy but dependable. The terry cloth seat covers went real nice with the imitation wood on the dashboard. It wasn't such a bad deal after all. He'd moved up a notch. It had taken effort. Now, though, Shaw wasn't so sure about the entire business. He looked across the seat and tried to decide whether Frank had used up his first chance. The accounting of them reassured Victor that he was in control after all. He wanted to be fair, though, so now he said in a flat, steady voice, as if he were asking the time, "I'm going to tell you once. I think you'd better mind your manners."

Frank looked over with a pained and mystified expression. "What do you mean?"

"You know what I mean," said Victor. "Like the business with the handshake. Someone puts out his hand, you shake it."

"Oh," said Frank. "Gee. I'm sorry. I didn't mean anything."

"Keep it up," said Victor.

Frank smiled a little, just a smirk that flitted across his lips. Yeah. OK. That's the first chance. Shaw figured that showing the kid what was what in the real world might not be an unpleasant task after all. Then he swallowed and made a long, careful attempt to get a grip on himself. He didn't count to ten, but he imagined a marble at the top of some stairs, a blue one, that rolled off the first step and then slowly rolled off the next step, the *kunk* of it on the carpet as regular as the ticking of a clock. All right. OK. Maybe they could work it out after all.

The engine started. They both sat and listened to it. There was a knocking, a steady, repeated banging. Could be a rod, thought Shaw. The kid had his hand on the cloth of the seat covers, but then he lifted it and put it in his lap. "You got a cigarette?" he asked.

"Sure," said Victor. He held out a package of cigarettes in a box. "You know you shouldn't smoke."

"Then how come you're giving me one?"

Shaw pulled the cigarettes back a little, thinking it over. Shit.

They were right back at it, involved in some kind of skirmish. The kid was just itching for it, just spoiling for it. Well, he'd come to the right place. Shaw squeezed the steering wheel and sighed again. Easy, easy. Take it easy. He gave the kid a long look and then held out the cigarettes again, saying, "Take a cigarette and don't be such a hard-ass."

Frank looked across the seat. Shaw could see the kid was trying to make up his mind. He could go on being difficult and refuse the cigarette, or they could make a kind of deal. The kid would take the cigarette and smoke it and keep his mouth shut. Shaw held the package of cigarettes open. Recently he had been trying to smoke a little less, since cigarettes had gone up a lot and because he had been saving up for the car. Frank took a cigarette with a nonchalance that seemed to imply there hadn't been any awareness of an agreement, although he wasn't too convincing. Shaw could see he'd have to take another whack at getting things clear between them, at least as far as the cigarettes were concerned. But he was in better shape than he had been in before. So, with a slight glow of victory, he put his finger over the lighter on the dashboard, playing with fire here, since he knew the thing didn't work. But he was feeling like a gambler who was on a run of good luck.

"Light?" he asked.

"Naw, I got a match," said Frank.

"Superman, huh?" said Shaw, feeling a little extra boost for having gotten away with the lighter.

Frank looked across the seat, drawing on his cigarette and then letting it dangle from his lips, squinting through the smoke, just staring at him. Then he said, "Sure. I guess that's right."

Well, all right. It was a stupid joke, but even so, Shaw still felt he was ahead on points. He thought maybe he could afford to be generous with Frank, too, about those last two chances. It's amazing how much better a joke made him feel. Then he looked down at the temperature gauge and saw that it was going up. The sound in the engine was a little louder, as though a bushing was wearing someplace. Shaw lighted a cigarette too, taking a book of matches from his pocket. They drove silently for a while,

going out through the Cahuenga Pass, the Hollywood Bowl sliding by on the left. The kid opened the wind wing of the car and
with a kind of practiced gesture flicked his ashes out the window.
So far so good.

They came to the top of a hill where there was a bridge made
of poured concrete. It seemed to be in the same style of architecture as the post office in Hollywood. Art deco. Shaw pronounced
it "dee-co."

"You ever seen *Invasion of the Body Snatchers?*" asked Shaw.
"The original with Kevin McCarthy?"

"No," said Frank.

"It's pretty good. The last scene was shot right here. Right
over there." He pointed toward the side road where the last scene
of the movie had been shot.

Frank looked across the seat.

"What do you do for a living?" he asked.

"What's that got to do with anything?" said Shaw.

"I asked you a question."

"I work at night," said Shaw.

"I didn't ask when," said Frank.

There seemed to be a little steam coming from the car, although it could have been Shaw's imagination. For a moment he
thought what it would be like standing by the car at the side of
the road with the hood open. He wondered if he could get the
kid home in a taxi with the eight dollars and twenty cents. He
had a watch, and maybe what he could do was give the watch to
the cab driver, too, although he wouldn't want to do that in
front of Frank.

"What's the matter?" asked Frank.

"Nothing," said Victor.

"Well?" asked Frank. "What do you do?"

Shaw glanced at his new pants. Goddamn it. They looked like
shit. He should have bought some khakis, maybe a madras shirt.
Except they didn't sell madras anymore.

"I'm an inventor," said Shaw. "You ever see that thing they
advertise on late night TV? A sponge with a magnet so you can
wash the outside of windows? That's mine. Some other stuff. A

water filter. You wouldn't believe what kind of stuff there is in the L.A. water."

"Then how come you're driving this car?"

"I like it," said Victor. He glanced at the temperature gauge. The thing was definitely going up. "I get some of my best ideas in this car. Sometimes I drive out to the zoo and *presto*, there it is. A new salami slicer."

"What do you mean, a new salami slicer?" said Frank.

"You know, you go into a delicatessen. You want a half a pound of roast beef." Victor thought how long it had been since he had had a piece of roast beef. "You got to wait while they walk back and forth between the scale and the slicer. The trick is, you put the scale and the slicer together. Saves a lot of time."

Frank looked at Shaw and then flicked his cigarette out the window.

"We've got a problem with fires in southern California," said Victor.

"I think you're lying about being an inventor," said Frank.

"Think what you want," said Victor. Was that two chances? Was it? Gauge definitely getting hotter, but soon they'd have a downhill. That STP, what a bunch of junk.

"You know," said Frank. "This Big Brother thing was my mother's idea. She's always talking about a 'role model.' You know what that is? A new design for toilet paper."

"What about your father?" said Victor.

"What about him?"

The gauge had leveled off. Maybe there was something to that STP. Lot of guys swore by it. A hot dog couldn't be more than a buck and a half. Tops. Everything would be OK if the kid would shut up and start acting like he was grateful. Did he have any idea the chance Victor was taking?

"What does he think about the Big Brother business?" said Shaw.

"Not much."

"Did you ask him?" said Shaw. "You know, it's important to keep lines of communication open."

Oh, no. Not that. Oh, Jesus, not actually fucking saying that. He'd get on to music as soon as he could. Shaw was trying to think of some young rock musicians, but they all had funny names. Didn't make any sense. Not like the Rolling Stones. Or Jerry Lee Lewis. Or Otis Redding. Nobody could match Otis, especially "I've got dreams to remember . . ." Then, almost like an eruption, the sound of that kid at Soledad crying in the dark came back, and Shaw looked over at Frank, angry at him for being so stupid and so vulnerable at the same time. Well, he better shape up if he knows what's good for him.

"He didn't say anything," said Frank.

"Does he live with your mother?"

"No."

They came to the bottom of the hill and turned onto Barham Boulevard. There was an old place on the corner, a run-down mansion that hadn't been lived in for years. Everything about the place suggested the effects of time working in concert with the unexpected to produce disaster. Shaw turned uphill now and gave the engine a little gas.

"Where does your father live?" he asked.

"Up north."

"I been up that way. What's he do?"

If they could make it to the top of Barham there was nothing to it, since it was just one long downhill to Forest Lawn Drive. They'd take the drive to Griffith Park.

"Can I have another cigarette?" said Frank.

"Something told me you were going to ask that."

"Well?"

"You first," said Shaw. "I asked you what your father did."

It was a hazy day, and the sunshine fell in a way that made for pale shadows, as though everything had a stain around it. From the top of the hill they saw the San Gabriel Mountains in the distance. The valley had a glitter to it, and as Shaw looked at it, the endless bits, the dappled silver, seemed to suggest a constant separation, as though the bright clutter expressed a kind of isolation among the people who lived there, and the conglomeration of an infinite number of barriers gave Shaw a moment's pause. He looked back at the heat gauge. Still hot.

The clutter of the valley reminded him of something else, too: the endless ways in which he had thought about his own life, or the things that had brought him to this particular moment, and as he looked at Frank, he thought the kid was similar to the way he had been, and the recognition made Victor angry, as though the young man sitting next to him were just waiting to do the same stupid things he had. The prospect of each new mistake suggested endless links, all of them forming a chain that bound people to the central, unyielding part of who and what they were. Shaw didn't know what pissed him off more, that the kid was going to do something stupid or that he himself already had.

"Well?" said Shaw. "What does your father do?"

Frank turned his head toward Victor and said, "He's an inventor."

That's two. Definitely two.

But there was something in the kid's voice that was familiar. Shaw went on concentrating, trying to think what it was, and when he looked at the glitter of the valley, it came to him: the quiet, subdued voices of kids who came up to Soledad on visiting days.

"Where up north did you say he was?" said Shaw.

"I didn't say."

"Well, I'm asking you."

"Hey, what is this?" said Frank. "Twenty questions?"

"What kind of answer is that?" said Victor.

He took out the box of cigarettes, flipped open the lid, and put it on the seat between them, although it was close enough to Shaw's side of the car still to be clearly in his domain. If the kid wanted one he would have to reach over, obtaining it as a boon. Frank glanced at it, obviously thinking it would be easier just to give some information and have the cigarette as an object he was entitled to. Shaw drove with one hand, saying nothing.

"Near San Francisco," said Frank.

Well, that was something. Not much though. Victor shoved the cigarettes over a little and Frank took one.

"Does the lighter work?" asked Frank.

"Sure," said Victor.

He pushed it in, feeling, in the tip of his finger, a kind of weight, as though for one minute everything had come down to the pressure of that flat knob against the end of his index finger.

"What has he invented?" asked Victor.

Even as he spoke, he knew he should leave it alone, but somehow, going along Forest Lawn Drive and the Los Angeles River, he couldn't help himself.

"A lot of stuff," said Frank.

"Like what?"

"A kind of surgical table. It has a device on it that holds patients for chest surgery. You can hold them any way you want," said Frank.

Shaw had never thought about the problems of a surgeon before. Maybe it was hard to get the body to stay in exactly the right pose, especially if you wanted to make a cut in the side. He remembered an inmate at Soledad who had killed a man and who told Shaw how hard it was to get the damn body into the trunk of a car. Just like a bag of water. You prop the thing up and look away, and bang, the goddamn thing is on the ground again.

"The lighter's taking a long time," said Frank.

Shaw pushed it in again. The knob was cold and there was no odor of heating metal. So there it was again, things getting out of control. Goddamn lighters. They never make one that lasts.

"Where near San Francisco?" asked Victor.

"What's the big deal?" said Frank.

"I'm asking you a question," said Victor.

Jesus, if the kid doesn't want to talk about it, let him alone. Any fool could see this was a mistake. There was a slight odor of the engine overheating, and Shaw hoped the kid would think it was the lighter warming up. They sat there, both glancing out the window at the distant purple mountains. The hills seemed very dark, as if they were covered with a black-purple fleece. After a while Victor realized the kid was looking at the lighter, waiting; he wasn't going to use a match.

On the left was the Los Angeles River, which was really a concrete-lined trench, at the bottom of which was a smaller concrete trench, now filled with muddy water. The hillside to the right was dry grass and eucalyptus, the kind of thing you saw in Westerns. Forest Lawn was just up the road.

Well, it was time to face up to it. Victor pulled the lighter out, looked at it, and then put it back.

"I guess it doesn't work," he said. "Wonder what's gotten into the damn thing."

Frank looked out the window.

"It's San Quentin," said Frank. "That's where my father is."

Victor drove straight along now, watching the gauge. And that damn cemetery was coming up, too. He should have thought of some other place. Like Disneyland or Pacific Ocean Park. But crowds had always made Victor uncomfortable; just the sheer number of people made him feel a little disoriented and somehow at their mercy.

"How long is he going to be there?" said Victor.

"Fifteen to life."

For a while Shaw looked down at the L.A. River, the amount of concrete there, the mass of it, somehow contributing to his sense of the heaviness of the air in the car.

"My mother and I went to see him," said Frank. "We took the bus. Greyhound. We went straight up the valley. My mother made some sandwiches so we didn't have to spend any money at the bus stops. They charged, like, two dollars and a half for a cheese sandwich."

"You go at night?" asked Shaw. "The night is always the best time to take a bus."

"Well," said Frank. "I don't know. There was a funny guy in the back by the bathroom. You know, he'd say things when the men went back there."

"Well, it's a long trip from L.A. to Frisco," said Shaw.

"Yeah," said Frank.

He flicked the ashes out the wind wing again. Here the road was close to grass and brush, but Shaw didn't say anything about it.

"When we got in to see my father, he was behind a piece of glass," said Frank. "He started crying."

"He missed you," said Shaw.

"He was probably just embarrassed," said Frank.

"No," said Shaw. "He missed you."

Frank shrugged. "I don't know."

"I'm telling you something. He *missed* you. That's a goddamned fact. You hear me?"

"I don't know," said Frank.

"Don't get smart with me," said Shaw. "I'm warning you."

Even Shaw was surprised by this: he hadn't meant for it to come out that way, and so he went on driving, gripping the wheel, reaching down and giving the cigarette lighter a shove in, even though it wouldn't work. Then he jerked it out again. The gates of Forest Lawn appeared.

"You're on thin ice," he said. It was amazing to Shaw that the kid couldn't see what was in front of his nose. Frank's father had probably thought about making a rope and hanging himself. That's what you feel like when your kid sees you locked up. Then Shaw swallowed and squeezed the wheel, thinking, Let's just get to the zoo. We'll just get there and start fresh. Maybe I won't have to park the car and take the kid into the bushes to show him which end is up.

"I told my mother someone was going to give me a lecture," said Frank.

"You'll understand when you're older," said Victor.

Shit. He'd said it. He started shaking his head, his expectations for a pleasant afternoon, even his desperation for such an afternoon, turning into shame at being inept. He put the cigarettes on the seat, the gesture meant to get things back on track.

"Take 'em when you want 'em," said Victor. "I won't say anything."

They went on, toward Griffith Park. On the other side of the wash they saw the Disney Studios, the sound stages painted two-tone, brown and dark brown, like the wall of a hospital. Even though he knew what the answer was going to be, Shaw couldn't stop asking the question, since the answer made him feel a little closer to the kid and helped him keep his temper a while longer. Victor said, "What was it like, taking the bus back to L.A.?"

"My mother cried to beat the band," said Frank.

Shaw went on driving, saying nothing for a while, feeling the car move through the yellow-gray air of a summer afternoon, the stuff itself seeming like an expression of the things that just surround you and require an action you can't be precise about. The car was getting hotter again.

"What's the smell?" said Frank. "Like something burning."

The car was making a low moan, too, in addition to the smell. Shaw thought that maybe the radiator was dry and the engine was getting so hot the rotor was melting. He squeezed the wheel and saw that the needle in the gauge was even higher than before, not in that little orange strip at the top yet, but getting there. Then, through a stand of eucalyptus, the bark the color of a fawn, he saw the parking lot for the zoo. Victor turned into it and stopped in a row where there were no other cars. The Ford sat in the middle of hundreds of parallel white lines. Well, all right. The kid's got one chance left. He mumbled to himself as he took the keys from the ignition. "All right. One more."

"What?" said Frank.

"Nothing," said Shaw. "Let's go up to the zoo."

* * *

Even from a distance Shaw could feel the presence of the animals: it was with turmoil perfectly mixed with an attempt to keep everything normal that Victor heard an elephant trumpet. He couldn't remember if they had any crocodiles here, but he hoped they did, especially if they had those birds, too, that get into a crocodile's mouth to clean their teeth. Victor wanted to watch the bird in the monster's mouth, pecking around those spiked teeth. After a moment's thought he realized why he wanted to see those birds: it gave him a feeling of empathy.

Frank was silent as they walked up to the entrance. Shaw realized, with a kind of disappointment, that Frank was too old to be taken by the hand. He admitted to himself that he had imagined leading a kid by the hand up to the entrance of the zoo. The sun was out, and he felt the caress of muted heat, and as he walked along among the other people on the walk, he heard the elephant trumpet again. Shaw smiled, although, for some reason, his eyes began to fill with tears. He swallowed and opened them wide, thinking, yeah, that's the way you deal with that. Just keep blinking. The elephant trumpeted again.

It was a buck seventy-five to get in. Shaw was glad about being able to work with numbers: he had had eight dollars and twenty cents, including the change in his pockets, and now he had four seventy. As he listened to the elephant, he thought of those times in the supermarket when he and his mother had gone shopping and she hadn't had enough money. Well, at least he understood now why she always got so irritated at him. He looked at Frank. Yeah, the kid is down to his last chance. Definitely.

"Here," said Shaw. "Here's your ticket."

They went through the turnstile, the three stainless steel prongs of it cranking over.

"Well, it's a little hazy today, isn't it?" said Shaw.

"Smoggy," said Frank. "You can feel it when you take a real deep breath, you know?"

"Yeah," said Shaw.

"That's something your generation has got to take the rap for," said Frank.

"What?" said Victor.

"The smog."

"You think I made the smog?" said Victor.

"Your generation," said Frank.

"Wait a minute. I didn't make the smog. Who do you think I am, chairman of General Motors?"

Frank shrugged, as though this was a matter of splitting hairs. "Just look at it," he said.

In the distance, between the zoo and the purplish mountains on the other side of the valley, a layer of reddish-brown smoke hung in the air. It resembled an enormous foxtail. Well, thought Shaw, he's getting close. That's almost three. Shaw figured that he was getting tired of being accused for things like the smog. He'd gone hungry to buy the damn car. He stared at the smog and blinked. He tried to think of that marble slowly rolling off the first step. When he could trust his voice, he said, "If I could stop the smog, I would. Come on. What do you want to see first? The seals? Or a camel?"

Frank wrinkled his nose. "Camels stink. Rhinos stink, too, like some kind of fish."

"What about a penguin?"

"They seem kind of dumb."

The hot dog stand had a red-and-white-striped awning, and

the entire thing was on wheels so it could be moved around. A hot dog cooker sat on the counter. It was an aluminum box with glass windows, and inside the hot dogs slowly turned on stainless steel tubes. The frankfurters were brown and glistening.

"Two hot dogs," said Shaw. He turned to Frank. "You want mustard?"

"Yeah," said Frank. He looked at the browning hot dogs and swallowed.

"Two with mustard," said Shaw.

The man behind the counter flipped open a steamer and forked out a bun and put a hot dog in it. The elephant trumpeted, and Shaw starting blinking again, the shriek seeming to flow through the years just as if it had been one of the sounds of Shaw's own youth, although, when he thought about it, he couldn't remember ever having been in a zoo or anyplace where he could have heard an elephant. Maybe it had been a movie. Sure, that was it. Shaw and his mother used to go to the movies on her days off. She had always liked jungle movies. Sometimes she'd buy Victor a Twinkie, and he'd eat it in the darkness of the theater, tasting the creamy sweetness while watching the African landscape. There had even been a commercial on TV with an elephant in it, a big gray thing with ears the size of flags and legs as big around as trash cans. In the advertisement the elephant stood in front of a supermarket and held a sign that read, "We never forget the shopper." Victor's mother used to wait for the advertisement, and then she sat in front of the TV, watching the elephant and making kissing noises at it, saying, "Oh, honey bear, oh, puss-puss, aren't you going to blow your top? You don't have to be pushed around. No you don't. Not a big thing like you. They think they got you, but maybe they're wrong." What was the dumb thing's name? Zimba. Yeah. That was it. Victor's mother used to say, "That elephant is going to blow his top one day, and then, look out!" but Victor didn't think there was much chance of it. The elephant was broken. Zimba. Probably a phony name, too.

"That'll be five bucks," said the hot dog man.

"What do you mean?" said Shaw.

There were two hot dogs on the counter, each on a piece of waxed paper.

"They're two fifty apiece," said the hot dog man. "Extra long ones. All beef. Extra long roll."

Shaw stared at them, knowing that he was thirty cents short.

"We'll only have one," he said.

"They've already got mustard on them," said the man.

"We'll have only one," said Shaw.

"There's already mustard on them," the man said.

"You know what you do about that?" said Shaw.

"What?" said the man.

"You take a napkin and you wipe it off."

"I already put it on," said the man.

"I just told you how to take it off." Shaw stepped a little closer to the counter.

"Careful what you say to me," said the man. "I got a little button I push right here. It calls a guard."

Shaw swallowed and wiped the sweat off his upper lip as he wondered what would happen if he had to show a guard some identification. What if Frank noticed that the name he was using wasn't the same as the one on his ID? Shaw looked at the man behind the counter with the expression he had learned at Soledad.

"You want me to call a guard?" said the man.

"For two cents . . ." said Victor.

The man reached for the button.

"Calm down," said Victor.

"There's already mustard on the hot dog," said the man.

"I told you what to do about it," said Shaw.

He picked up a hot dog and gave it to Frank. Then he turned around and gave the hot dog man two dollars and fifty cents.

They walked along for a while. Frank wasn't eating the hot dog.

"What's the matter?" said Shaw. "Is there something wrong with it? If there is I'll take it back and shove it right up . . ."

"No," said Frank. "There's nothing wrong with it. I'm just not so hungry now."

"Eat it," said Shaw.

Frank took a bite.

"The monkeys are right up here," said Shaw. "You hear that elephant?"

Frank took another bite, chewing slowly.

"You want a drink?" said Shaw.

"It's OK," said Frank. "I don't need one."

"You got to have a Coke. I just didn't feel like eating anything. I had a big breakfast."

"Listen," said Frank. "It's OK about the Coke."

"There's a place right there," said Shaw. He went up to the counter and got a large Coke, which was served in a red paper cup. "Here."

He held it out.

There was a park bench in the shade, and they both sat down on it. The bench was one of those old-style ones with slats for the seat and the back, too, kind of like the benches Shaw had always imagined there were in parks in Paris. He leaned forward, putting his elbows on his knees, his head in his hands, thinking. Up ahead, at the center of the plaza next to the pool for the seals, three young men were sitting, their hair cut into irregular patterns. They wore black clothes with holes in them. The holes had obviously been cut into the new-looking jeans. Shaw wondered why they were letting kids who were selling drugs into the damn zoo. He wondered, too, what they were selling. Victor hadn't been sleeping so well recently, and a Quaalude or a barbiturate would have helped.

"Look at those kids," said Victor. He shook his head.

"What's wrong with them?" said Frank.

"They look stupid with those haircuts."

"You wouldn't understand."

"Well, all right," said Victor. "So what? Each to his own, OK?"

Frank shook his head.

"They're members of my generation," he said.

"Oh, shit," said Shaw.

"You're too much like my father," said Frank. "You know that? I hate this."

"Listen," said Shaw. "You got to remember. Your father and I are two different people."

"Yeah," said Frank. "Members of the same generation, though."

"No," said Shaw. "Your father's got to be older than me. I'm not even thirty."

Frank shrugged. "When I look at you," he said, "what I see is smog. You're a smog man."

"Yeah?" said Shaw. That's three. Definitely three. "Well, I'll tell you what. On the way home we'll take a little walk, you know? Maybe up above the bridle path."

He stared at Frank for a moment.

"I don't like to hike much," said Frank.

"Sure you do," said Victor. "I'll show you a nice place."

Victor put his head in his hands again and listened to the sound of the elephants. Their cage was just beyond the seals, and their scream had a beckoning quality, as if they were calling for help. Then he got up and walked toward them, up to the heavy wire where the elephants rested their trunks, the ends pink and wet. He guessed Frank was still sitting on the bench, and while the trunks made that asthmatic, wet, and faintly desperate noise, Victor tried to decide what he'd do to Frank on the way home. The kid was just begging for it. He wanted to say, Reality is right here, bub. It's name is Victor Shaw.

There were three elephants altogether, two older ones and a smaller one. There was a pool for them, too, which was filled with greenish water. The elephants put their trunks up to the wire to get a peanut, which they took with an echoey sound, as in a vacuum cleaner hose.

Victor thought about his mother using a vacuum cleaner: she had one that didn't work very well, and she used to get angry at it, beating the tube against a wall, saying, "This is American workmanship? Don't make me laugh."

Shaw turned around and looked at the center of the plaza. The young men with the funny hair were gone, and so was Frank. Victor guessed Frank had just walked over and started talking to them. It didn't seem as though much time had gone by, but then maybe Victor had mooned off a little, standing there in front of the elephants. Well, wasn't that just perfect. Yeah. That was three all right.

In the plaza in front of the elephant cages there were only the seals sitting on their cement platforms, looking down into the irregular concave chop of the water, like the surface of a swimming pool which is slowly calming down. The plaza was at the center of the zoo, and there were paths radiating out from it. One went to the aviary, another to a dry hillside where deer and antelope and llamas lay in the shade of eucalyptus trees. Another path led to the cat house. So there it was: it was impossible to tell which way Frank had gone. Why couldn't the kid understand what he was playing with? Well, all right. He wants a lesson, he's going to get one. In spades.

Victor sat down to wait. The long shadows of afternoon began their slow, unstoppable slide across the plaza, the dark blue lines creeping over the water of the seals' pool, and the seals sat and watched it come with a kind of doglike fatalism. Shaw sat, too, and quietly cursed that damn hot dog. That was what had been the trouble. That two dollar and fifty cent hot dog.

He tried to think, but he kept remembering the asthmatic, sucking noise of the elephants, as if it were the sound of being pulled down into someplace he didn't want to be. Shaw looked up. People were coming into the plaza and leaving it: a young man and a woman, both in blue jeans, holding hands; a guard or zookeeper in a brown uniform carrying a baby kangaroo that had somehow gotten out of its cage. Opposite Victor there was a line of cages for large cats, and they paced back and forth. He couldn't stand to look at the cats going back and forth, so he crossed to the other side of the plaza and sat down again, still trying to decide what to do. What if Frank didn't come back at all?

Shaw looked around at the few people in the plaza, examining their faces, looking for signs, for details that would let him know what he was up against. Then he decided the best thing would be to get up and start looking. He walked along the macadam paths, passing the animals, through the odor of manure and the clouds of dust, the dampness of cages that had just been hosed down. There was a cart filled with meat. He passed coyotes and hyenas, their eyes following him as though they were made more alert by his desperation.

He came to a bench beyond the coyotes and sat down again. What had he wanted to spend time with a kid for anyway? The whole idea had been stupid. Then he thought of the silence of his apartment as it was infused with the memory of Beverly Mason's voice, the breathy words describing her deepest, most secret terrors. Well, he was going to catch that kid and let him understand it was time to stop playing around with Victor Shaw. Definitely time to stop. Definitely. Then he felt the presence once again of the animals in their cages, all of them restless or simply fatigued by being confined. They seemed to be an expression of all his own stymied impulses. The thought left him trembling, sitting on the bench as though leaning over the abyss of his own fury. The way Shaw saw it, someone was going to pay for this. The fact of Frank's disappearance seemed to have its own unavoidable weight, like something he just couldn't shake.

He got up and started walking again. It wasn't dark yet, but the afternoon was advancing. The California days in summer ended with a smoky, gray-blue haze in the distance, the same color as the advancing shadows. Shaw came back to the plaza and sat down. The wet seals in the shadows were as sleek as patent leather. He wondered idly what it would be like to eat a seal. Couldn't be much worse than the stew in the cans he had his meals from.

That goddamned hot dog. Then he began to think it wasn't that: he hadn't been able to reach out to the kid. That was the real problem. He just hadn't been able to do it. As he sat there in the shadows, everything around him seemed imbued with this unmistakable fact; the macadam, the water in the seals' pool, the wire and bars, the locks and metal hinges all seemed a monument to the gulf between Shaw and someone else. He was tired of it. He'd been abandoned again. He counted his money, even though he already knew he had two dollars and twenty cents. Even if he had been able to get something off those kids, like a Quaalude, he wouldn't have had enough money. Maybe he could just take it from them. If he could find them.

It was closing time. Victor went through the turnstiles, which cranked over with a sound like mechanized doom, and then he walked across the parking lot, the gray surface still warm with the heat of the sun. He walked up to the car, thinking, That damn radiator. He went around to the door, opened it with a jerk, and got in. He looked at his hands as he tried to put the key in the ignition: they were shaking so much he stopped and just sat, looking into the shadows of the eucalyptus groves and seeing, as an eerie white in the last of the afternoon, the rails of a bridle path curving into infinity.

Shaw started the engine and pulled out of the parking lot. At least the needle was way down near the C. On Forest Lawn Drive, on the right near the studio, some flats to hold water had been built, and some birds sat around them. The flats took on the pink sheen of sunset. It was beautiful.

Some of the cars coming the other way had their headlights on, their random appearance suggesting to Shaw a kind of disorder: Why should one car have its lights on and another not? Why wasn't there one moment when everyone knew it was time to turn on the fucking lights?

He went down Barham, coasting now with the needle all the way into the red. The deserted mansion was at the bottom of the hill, the back of it visible from this angle, where the shreds of a net across the tennis court hung like something left by a fisherman who had given up the sea and was letting his boat, his oars, his equipment simply rot.

He pulled up in front of Frank's house, the bungalow sitting behind its dark lawn, like the others, the dim light in the living room seeming neither domestic nor cheerful but just weak. The porch was one large shadow, pierced by a little bit of light from the house. Victor got out of the car and went into the shadows and up to the door.

*   *   *

Through the glass of the door Victor saw Maggie. She was sitting on the greenish sofa, her legs up on the coffee table. She was still wearing the short skirt and the fishnet stockings, although she had her shoes off. She was reading a newspaper, a gossip sheet, and she had one hand in her teased hair. She uncrossed her legs, putting the bottom one on top, her face sharp, keenly interested in the gossip column, one hand idly tracing the shape of her kneecap through the fishnet stockings. Victor thought she must be pretty lonely with her husband away. She wasn't so bad-looking, not really. Then he knocked on the door, feeling his palms sweat.

She came to the door in her stocking feet, smiling now. With the door open, it seemed to Shaw that the darkness from the porch behind him had poured into the room. He wiped his hands on his pants.

"Frank ran off," he said.

"Oh, God," said Maggie.

"I don't know what got into him," said Victor. "I wasn't rough or anything."

Even now, though, he still wished he'd had the chance.

Maggie sat down on the sofa and leaned forward, her elbows on her knees in those fishnet stockings.

"What do you think we should do?" said Victor.

Maggie kept her head down, her hands, with her long fingers, pushed into her hair. The moment seemed somehow domestic, difficult but intimate, as though Frank was their kid. Victor thought of taking Maggie by the hand. They could go into the bedroom, where, in the dim light, she'd lift her skirt, exposing the white skin at the top of the stockings as she undid the garters and rolled them off. It had been a long time.

"Should we call the police?" he said.

She looked up at him. He thought of her lips against his ear, the shape of her tongue. Then he tried to think about the police, having them ask him questions.

"I don't know," said Maggie. "I just don't know."

"Frank just seemed to have a chip on his shoulder," said Shaw. "I thought I could do him some good."

"Well," said Maggie, "he's had some trouble with the police."

"Then maybe it isn't a good idea to call them," said Shaw.

She glanced up now and looked him right in the eyes.

"If you could see your way to do that, I'd appreciate it," she said.

"Well," he said. "There are rules about this kind of stuff . . ."

"Please," she said. "Frank's already had some trouble."

"OK," said Shaw. "We'll keep it quiet for a while."

"Thank you," said Maggie. "He came back the last time he ran off."

"Did he?"

"It took a couple of days. Drove me crazy, you know?"

"Uh-huh," said Victor.

He stood there, listening to the sounds of the house, the distant throb from the kitchen, a radio playing next door, a car going by on the street, a voice down the block saying, "Well, it serves you right, doesn't it?" On the table Maggie had laid out her tips, the dollar bills and a few tens and twenties looking orderly. She stood up, and he could smell her perfume mixed with sweat.

"What if he doesn't come back?" said Shaw. "How long should we wait?"

"Oh, God," said Maggie. "Oh, God. Don't say that. Just don't say it."

Shaw nodded. "OK," he said. He picked up a pencil and wrote his telephone number on the edge of the gossip paper she had been reading.

"Call me before you do anything," he said. "OK?"

"Sure," she said.

"Good night," said Shaw.

She nodded and sat down again, and as Shaw went through the front porch, he looked back to the window, seeing her sitting down again, elbows on knees, her head in her hands. Probably was a nice white stripe. Just above the stockings.

Then he walked out to the car and got into it and glanced down at the temperature gauge. Solidly in the red. Had to get some more STP. Some guys swore by it. Yeah, and there was something else he'd have to do, too. Get some money and get the hell out of here. There wasn't much time, either.

Full Documentation

V ICTOR SHAW DROVE up Highland and found a parking spot on the street in front of Nicky White's apartment house. The Hollywood Bowl was up the way, the fountains in front of it on Highland having that same art deco quality as a lot of other buildings in town, all hard slabs and curves that looked like a refrigerator built in 1935. It was just dusk, and the lights on the avenue glowed like coals through the early evening smog. Victor wanted to get inside, off of the street, and he was thinking, too, that he might miss Nicky, who usually started his rounds at about this hour, moving from bar to bar, from place to place, taking bets, doing business, maybe selling a pistol, helping with some paperwork, taking care of stolen credit cards, just doing, as Nicky liked to say, "what came naturally." But even so Victor lingered, standing in the street with the cars going by, the red taillights describing a path that led to the entrance to the freeway.

He turned into Nicky's apartment building. By the pool was a woman who wore a small bathing suit and whose wet hair dripped water down her back. Her tanned skin was beaded with moisture and it had the odor of chlorine. There was something about the woman as she stood alone in the warm air, a quality of delicate anticipation, as though in the face of the city's harshness she was suspended over possibilities, like those of hope, that were at once vast and fragile. She turned and looked at Shaw, holding the towel to her breasts, a sudden chill showing its passage over her skin in a slow, languid wave of goose bumps. Then she tried to smile and Shaw tried to smile back, but neither one of them was quite up to it. He looked away, and the woman went back to toweling herself.

Nicky was wearing a blue shirt, the first three buttons undone, and he had on a pair of leather pants which squeaked. He was wearing a gold chain. Shaw looked at the chain and shook his head, thinking, Jesus, he's still doing that. Shaw went in and sat down and stared at the fish in the tank.

"Hey, Einstein," said Nicky. "Long time no see. What's cooking?"

Victor shrugged. "I don't know."

"You don't look so good. Didn't I tell you about taking a supplement?"

"Yeah. I got some."

"Well, that's something," said Nicky. "Are you taking them?"

"No," said Shaw.

"They aren't going to do you any good in the bottle," said Nicky.

The tropical fish moved with an easy, fluid movement, almost as if the tank were filled not with water but with baby oil.

"I haven't got a whole lot of time," said Nicky. "I'm just getting ready to go out . . . I got people waiting here and there, you know?"

"Uh-huh," said Shaw. "I just wanted to talk something over."

"Sure. How about a drink? You ever tasted Linkwood single malt? I get it right off the boat. Guy in San Pedro always boosts me a couple of bottles. Those goddamned containers, though, they're making pilferage an art."

Nicky poured some Linkwood into a glass and held it out. "OK," he said. "Maybe I can help out. You got something good?"

The Linkwood was so smooth it was like running your tongue over a piece of brown silk. Shaw had never tasted anything like it, and the warmth went right down into that dark sensation of dread. He just sat there, concentrating on the warmth and feeling it in what he now realized was the physical locus of fear. The fear was what he wanted to consider, as though talking it over would help sever the connection between himself and that dark turmoil. He just didn't want to go back to Soledad. Not ever. And yet, aside from taking a chance, there didn't seem any other way to break out of that room he lived in, with the furniture from the Salvation Army and that sofa with the stains on it. He wasn't even getting close to a woman. Women wanted money, and they didn't like somebody who sat in a bar nursing a beer for five hours just to watch the damn TV and hear some voices. He'd picked up a forty-five-year-old woman one night, and afterwards she'd started hitting him and screaming loud enough to wake up the entire building. You could see that gave her a real feeling of the dramatic. Shaw had another sip of the Linkwood, taking a small one to make it last.

"What is it?" asked Nicky. "I can tell you're working on something. Maybe it's too big for just one guy, you know?"

Shaw held the glass in both hands and squeezed.

"Hey, buffo, it's no skin off my nose," said Nicky. "It just feels like you got in pretty far or something. Jesus, don't I know what that's like? Sometimes the world looks like a piece of glass that's getting ready to crack."

"Uh-huh," said Shaw. "This stuff is good." He swirled the liquor around in the glass.

"Sure, sure," said Nicky. "You want some more?"

Shaw nodded, keeping his head down.

"You remember Captain Hook at Soledad?" asked Shaw.

"You mean the guy who ran the dining hall? Only had one hand? Sure. What an asshole. Always putting that hook in the Jell-O. You get your Jello-O and it's all ripped up."

Shaw nodded. "Were you there when we were all eating that meat and we couldn't figure out what it was? It was cooked gray and it wasn't beef?"

"Sure," said Nicky. "It was buffalo. The army thinned out the buffalo herd in Wyoming or someplace and Captain Hook got a deal on it. What about it?"

"That's when I felt being locked up the most," said Shaw. "Eating the buffalo. I liked to think of them running around, you know, out there on the grasslands. Not being eaten in a goddamned prison."

"I never thought much that way," said Nicky. "I was always trying to figure a way to get out. Some smart lawyer move. Or I'd think about the track."

"You ever eat horse?" asked Shaw.

"God, no," said Nicky. "Why would I want to do that?"

"I was just trying to explain about the buffalo, that's all."

"I don't get you," said Nicky. "Horses are horses and buffaloes are buffaloes."

Shaw had another sip of that pale, smoky liquor.

"Look," said Nicky. "You remember that party I was telling you about? Big deal Hollywood guy is going to have a party. They want to have a little color I guess, you know? I want you to come. OK?"

"Sure," said Shaw. "Thanks."

"Well?" said Nicky. "What have you got?"

Shaw shook his head. "I don't know." He shrugged. "I haven't got much time. I tried to do a little good and I don't think it's working out too well."

"Jesus," said Nicky. "Doing good isn't for people like us."

"Are you sure?" said Shaw. "I was kind of hoping . . ."

"Hoping what?"

"That I wasn't completely cut off from ordinary things. Like going to the zoo with a kid. Or something."

"Listen," said Nicky. "What you need is a good party. You might even get laid. You got the willies, that's all. You been spending too much time alone. The party will fix you up."

"I haven't got much time," said Shaw.

"Who the hell does?" said Nicky. "Now get out of here. I got my rounds. I got a guy who's lifted a stamp collection, can you believe it? How am I going to move the damn stamps?"

"I don't know," said Shaw. He finished the drink and stood up.

"Take things easy. One day at a time. When you want to tell me what you got, I'll be right here," said Nicky.

"I haven't got much time," said Shaw.

"Uh-huh," said Nicky. "Fine. If that's what you want to say. Fine. Now get out of here."

*   *   *

Victor went to a stationery store and bought a tablet of paper with light blue lines on it, as anonymous as a bus ticket. A plastic ruler. A dozen pens, Bics, in a plastic sack. He went to a drug store, too, and bought a pair of rubber gloves, doing this in Hollywood, where, God knows, a lot of people had some pretty kinky uses for rubber gloves. The pharmacist didn't even look at him. Shaw also bought some freezer paper, big white sheets of it, which he now spread over his folding table. He knew that he couldn't even lick the stamp, since some guy at Soledad had told him that these days you can be identified by just the residue of the saliva that is left on the stamp. DNA. The stuff was everywhere. Well, he'd tape the letter shut and tape the stamp on it, too.

He wrote a letter, wearing the rubber gloves and making the letters with the pen and ruler, and as he worked he thought of the way that man with "Horror Show" on his fingers ate his breakfast. The letter spoke of Beverly's betrayals, hinted at her most intimate acts. What travesties hadn't she indulged in? Was there any unnatural act she was not capable of? The writer of the letter said his name was St. Elijah. He was coming to get her. The time of whoredom was over. St. Elijah knew what was in her heart, how excited she was, what it was she really wanted. He would give it to her. He had an entire list of things they would do together. The end was going to be the best, and she knew that, didn't she? What would happen at the end? St. Elijah was watching her. Hadn't Beverly read of bodies that had been found on an isolated beach, up toward Ventura? And what about the one up in the canyon, off Mulholland? They were his work. He had left his signs. St. Elijah would know if she contacted the police, or if she spoke to anyone. If she did, he would remind her that God was an angry God, and that St. Elijah was his messenger. St. Elijah had been waiting for a long time. How much the FBI would like to put him in a cage . . . Did she know what the inside of a coffin smelled like? St. Elijah did.

St. Elijah told her, though, there was a chance for mercy. If she wanted mercy, she should take out an ad in the *Los Angeles Herald,* and it should read, "Dear Elijah. You have my love. Contact me about how to proceed."

The letter lay on the table in front of Victor. The odd script, the half-assed neatness of it, all suggested insane retribution itself. He added some symbols, curlicues and crosses the Bible reader from Soledad with "Horror Show" tattooed on his fingers had scratched on the wall of his cell and written inside the girlie magazines. Shaw didn't like adding them, though, since they gave him the impression that the man with the tattoo had clung to him somehow and that his influence, while small now, could easily begin to grow.

He put down the pen and the ruler, and stood up and looked out the window: he could just see Western Avenue, a few cars going by with their lights still on, and in the distance, in the east, there was that semicircular burst of gold. The letter seemed to come from the shadows of ordinary, anonymous life.

At night, in St. James's office, Shaw opened the cabinet that held the tape recorder and turned it on, the lights on the console flashing, and suggesting, in their cold objectivity, both a warning and the thrill of possibility. Beverly came in, walking directly to the couch, and when she sat down there was a continued, jumpy squeaking. She couldn't sit still. Shaw listened to that and her breathing, her sighs, and the long pauses between sentences that were begun and then trailed away. Then there was a keen silence, one that made him reach out toward the machine, as if to comfort her. He sat there, hand out, listening to the silence. There was a scale to it, which suggested that moment when you wake in the middle of the night and cannot abide the darkness of the room one instant more, if only because it is filled with the phantoms of things you have been trying to deny. And when you turn on the lights, they don't disappear so much as just retreat into the shadows, where they wait. Yeah, she'd gotten the letter all right.

St. James prescribed a tranquillizer. Beverly took the slip.

Victor bought a copy of the *Los Angeles Herald* and turned to the personal ads. There it was: "Dear Elijah . . ." He stood there, holding the paper, like an actor looking for his name in a review.

Shaw wrote again, telling Beverly she should get twenty-five thousand dollars, in tens and twenties and fifties. Make a package. Be ready for instructions. If she wanted to go on living, if she didn't want Elijah's touch or his signs left on her, she should put another ad in the newspaper.

He had discovered an abandoned mailbox on Laurel Canyon. He was going to have her put the money in it in the morning and leave it there during the day. He was also going to tell her to come back in the evening. If the money was still in the mailbox, she was to take it home and try again the next morning. This way Shaw figured he could do one of two things. Get it at the mailbox. Or he could be waiting at her house when she came home. He could just step out of the darkness and ask for it. He didn't like that part so much. Anyway, it gave him some flexibility, since she'd probably go back and forth for at least two days.

Beverly put another ad in the paper. She was ready with the money.

At night he listened to her voice. He felt the cool, almost acrid scent of terror, something he imagined as an odor like the smell that came off of dry ice. There was a record store on Sunset Boulevard where you could sit in a booth and listen to records, and Shaw stopped by and listened to Schubert while he sat in the booth and watched the cars outside, the music and his sense of tragedy combining with a kind of beautiful thrill.

He bought some dark clothes. The morning he brought them home and tried them on, the telephone rang. He picked it up and said, "Hello."

"Hello? This is Maggie. Frank's mother."

"Oh, sure," said Victor. "Hiya. Frank turned up yet?"

"No," said Maggie.

"Oh," said Victor.

That goddamned kid. Maybe it would have been a good thing to take him up in the bushes right off the bat.

"I'm worried," said Maggie.

"Sure," said Victor. "I can understand that. What are you going to do?"

"I don't know," said Maggie.

"I think we just got to wait," said Victor.

"I don't know," said Maggie.

"Well, I don't know, either," said Victor.

"He's never been gone so long."

"Well, let's wait a little more. Maybe that's best."

"Maybe. I got to think about it. Maybe you could come by sometime and we could talk it over."

"OK," said Victor. "Sure. I'm a little busy right now."

"I'm worried," she said.

"Me too. Let's give it another week. We don't want to cause trouble, do we?"

"No," said Maggie. "I guess not. I got to think about what's best, though."

She waited for a moment. "Someone's been calling here and then hanging up," she said. "I'm sure it's Frank. If it wasn't for that, I'd go to the police right now."

Then she said good-bye. Victor put the phone down, thinking about time. Whenever you had it, you wanted to kill it, and when you needed it, you couldn't buy it for anything. Sometimes he could feel it move, especially when there was a lot of it; then, when he was alone, it was as if time would hardly budge, like that stuff insects were caught in, and other times it went like something that spilled on the floor, hot oil, say, that would burn you if you touched it. Then he looked in the mirror and saw himself in his dark clothes. Well, it would be hard to see him in the dark.

Victor mailed the letter telling Beverly to take the money to the abandoned box in Laurel Canyon.

*   *   *

He knew right off that he wasn't going to go up there and put his hand into the mailbox to get the money himself. What if Beverly had gone to the police and they were there waiting for him? Victor thought about the possibility of the police waiting for him and the moment, too, when they would put handcuffs on him. Victor knew this was the beginning of a kind of enlightenment about something so powerful and so deep it gave him a chill just considering it. So, if someone was going to reach into that mailbox, it wasn't going to be him.

Victor sat by the window of his apartment and looked across the street. A young woman came out of an apartment building and got into her car. Victor had seen her a lot of mornings at about this time. She was usually dressed for work, her short, golden hair having the sheen of the early California light, her eyes green as the Pacific. And as he watched her, opening his venetian blinds with two fingers to do so, he could almost smell the fresh odor that trailed behind her in the morning, soap and powder and something moist on her skin. She got into her car and drove off.

Victor spent the day thinking about wisdom. Let's face it: there's no substitute for it. The way Victor saw it, wisdom was applied cunning. So, he picked a name out of the telephone book at random and called the number, and when a woman answered, Victor told her that she had won a prize and that it was waiting for her, right up in Laurel Canyon. All she had to do was go pick it up. Then he hung up, leaving the woman saying, "Prize? I've won a prize?"

Around noon he followed a man, a neighbor, who went up to the store on the corner. The man bought a pornographic magazine, folded it, and put it under his arm, walking along with the air of someone who has just bought a copy of the *Wall Street Journal,* but Victor knew better. He had bought the same magazine, one that always seemed to promise some progression, some advancement beyond its pages, but this always turned out to be an illusion.

There had been some fog in the morning, but it had burned off, leaving a kind of salty, oily residue in the air. As Victor followed the man with the magazine, he could barely see his own shadow, and it gave him the uncanny sensation that he was about to disappear. Then Victor went back into his apartment, dismissing the man with the magazine as no longer being a good possibility. Who wants to have anything to do with a jerk-off artist anyway? Victor had seen enough of them in Soledad. Then Victor made himself some beef stew out of a can and poured it into his bowl, which until this moment he hadn't given a second thought to, but which now, with the thin wisps of steam rising from it, reminded him of the kind of dish a dog would eat from. He sat there, letting the stew get cold.

In the evening he looked out the window and saw the young

woman who lived across the street. She was wearing a pair of jeans and a blue shirt, and she carried a white slip of paper in her hand, walking through the last light of the day in a golden nimbus. As Victor looked at her, his fingers holding the venetian blinds open while he smelled the dust on them, he thought, Wonder where she's going?

He was good at following her. Shaw liked to tell himself that he was disappearing into the landscape of southern California, emerging from it only when he had a reason to. Her small Dodge had sun-blasted paint which looked like the sky when the fog was just lifting, and there was a moment, in the blue shadows of evening, when the car almost seemed to disappear into them. She went up to Franklin and turned right, going out toward Ferndale. She drove at the speed limit, and there was something in the way she handled the car which suggested she was trying to keep things from getting out of hand. Well, all right, she was scared, but who wasn't?

The stoplights on Franklin were set to move the traffic along at thirty-five miles an hour, and up ahead Shaw saw five or six lights turn green together: it was a wave phenomenon, the lights coming on and off in a pattern described by a sine curve. Shaw liked to see it, if only because he began to feel that even though the pressure was right up there, everything had begun to flow.

There are a lot of small, curving streets in Ferndale, and it was obvious she wasn't familiar with the place she was going to. She stopped and looked at the addresses, which were painted on the curb, and then picked up the white slip of paper she had put on the seat.

So it was just dusk when she drove slowly by a house with a hedge. Shaw had been confident she was almost where she wanted to go, and he had been taking chances, getting a little too close. She slowed down and turned to look at the dark opening in the hedge and the house beyond. Yeah. That's it all right.

Shaw went up the street and parked, watching in the rearview mirror. The young woman pulled over, too, and turned off the engine. Then she sat in the car, obviously thinking things over. The sky was just a pale blue in the west, but the entire hemisphere of the sky still gave off some light. He glanced at his watch.

The young woman got out of her car. She closed the door with a shove, not hard so much as definite, but then she waited, putting a hand to her hair, seeming to take a small, delicious pleasure in hesitating. Victor got out of his car, too, and, dressed in his black jeans and dark blue shirt and black sneakers, he stood in the shadows, his face marked only by the two spoon-shaped whites of his eyes. He moved from one shadow to another, through the dark blue shade beneath the elms on the street. The young woman went through the hedge.

She entered the house. It was a small, even cozy-looking place, what Shaw imagined as a "Cape Cod cottage." It was sided with graying shingles, and it had a pitched roof, which was covered with shingles, too. There were two windows in front, with a door in between. A dim light was all that could be seen through one of the front windows, and the pale yellow color, as from a low-wattage bulb, lay on the glass like a film. Shaw hesitated, feeling the keenness of the shadows. He wished he could disappear into them so as to be nothing more than an invisible presence, and as he moved along the side of the house, stopping from time to time to listen to the murmur from inside, he put out his hand into the still, cooling air as if it were possible to touch the palpable atmosphere, like an eddy of something that was getting ready to happen. Shaw had the momentary uneasiness of wading into darkened water at night: it left him with a nagging, constant necessity for a kind of faith.

He heard a bang and a rattle. Then there was another sound, too, an exclamation and a tinny crash, and when Shaw moved around to the kitchen, he saw a cloud of smoke, or dust, rising from a flour canister that had been knocked over, the billows making him think of a genie that had finally been let out of the bottle. The young woman's blouse was open. Her lips seemed a little blue, as if she were cold, and she held a kitchen knife in her hand. There were some ice cubes which had tumbled out of a bar bucket onto the floor, the cubes silver and white or clear, all spread out in a pattern like that of a shattered glass. There was a man opposite the young woman, his features set in an expression of disbelief, as if those things he was certain of were being tested. The knife didn't have so much to do with the moment, or so the man seemed to think, as with the fact that things weren't going the way he wanted. The man in the kitchen lunged forward, onto the ice cubes on the floor. Shaw had been stepping up close to the window, but now he stopped at the sight of the man actually flying through the air, arms out, legs up behind him, his entire aspect one of sudden levitation. And when the young woman stepped back, she seemed as confined as though someone had dropped a net around her. She was trapped by the breakfast nook as the man fell against her. The blade of the knife caught the light in the room, the flash of it swinging through the darkness of the yard.

The young woman stepped back from the man, who lay on the seat of the nook. Then she sat on the floor, against the wall, her head in her hands, not moving until she snapped her head up, obviously listening to the steady *pip pip pip* that came from the floor beneath the table.

Shaw waited in the yard, appalled that things had gotten so far out of hand. On the ground around him there were the shadows of the window sashes, which formed separate, elongated boxes, each spreading further out until they reached the shadows of the yard. More than anything else, he wanted to turn and walk away, but he found himself going into the kitchen, if only because, in the face of the unexpected, he was left only with his plan, and on the basis of that he went in, thinking, Well, at least I know how I'm going to get that goddamned money.

*   *   *

Marta walked out the door with him, and they got into his station wagon. Shaw sat behind the wheel. It was completely dark, and the street lamps were on, the purplish light coming through the windshield. Marta was quiet, just sitting there, her short hair dark in the half light and falling over one side of her face.

"I think we should get out of here," he said.

"I don't know," she said.

"Sure," he said. "What else are you going to do?"

"Call the police. Tell them what happened. I didn't mean anything. It just got out of hand."

"Listen," said Shaw. "I've been in a place where there were a lot of guys doing time because things got out of hand. And, anyway, there's a witness. I guess it depends on how he tells it, don't you think?"

She turned her head now and looked at him. She had small dots of light in her eyes from the street, and when she blinked, the movement of her lids made the dots vanish. After a while she put her fingers to the buttons on her blouse, still thinking things over, the tips of her fingers going around the milky whitish buttons.

"What do you want?" she asked.

"Just a little favor. That's all."

"What's that?"

"We'll take a little drive up to Laurel Canyon," he said. "There's something I got to do."

They went down to Franklin and started driving west. At Gower they dropped down to Sunset. Shaw drove at the speed limit, not wanting to get stopped, not now, especially with the California Highway Patrol working this stretch. They made the LAPD look like Girl Scouts. The lights on both sides of the street slipped by, the neon, the reds, yellows, and blues, the pink of a dry cleaner's ("24 hour service. Guaranteed"), the purplish glow of the street lamps, all had about them a random, indistinct quality that seemed just barely to conceal a gussied-up tawdriness. Up ahead, women in blond wigs and short skirts beckoned to men in cars.

"This won't take but a minute," he said.

"Can I go after we do it?" she asked.

"What?"

"Can I go home?"

"Oh," said Shaw. "That. Sure. Sure. No problem."

"You didn't say I could go," said Marta.

"Don't talk so much," said Shaw.

He turned up Laurel Canyon. Even from the bottom he could smell the eucalyptus, the medicinal odor giving him something familiar to concentrate on. Marta looked out the windshield at the cars coming from the valley, their headlights bright and yellow. Then she swallowed and said, "I didn't mean any harm."

"Uh-huh," said Shaw.

The row of mailboxes was in the middle of the canyon, on the Hollywood side, halfway between the top and Sunset. There was a restaurant there which at one time had been a store. A couple of streets came together here, making for a kind of center. The mailboxes sat on a long plank, twenty or so altogether, each one from a different era or of a different make, some having flowers and animals painted on them, others large and functional, a few old and rusted. Shaw guessed it was probably the salt air that had rusted the ones at the end. The dead one was fourth from the end. "The fourth one," he said. "Get out and pick up the package that's in it."

The smell of eucalyptus was very strong, although it was mixed with the odor of exhaust from the cars on Laurel Canyon. Marta got out and started walking, her figure slender, tall, her hair bright in the street lamps.

It was one of those warm California evenings when the temperature has an almost intimate quality. The cars kept coming from the top of the canyon, a few of them sports cars, usually driven by kids or middle-aged men, going fast. When they came down to the corner where the mailboxes were, they were still going fast, appearing as nothing more than metallic and chrome streaks around which there was a high, tearing sound of the tires barely holding on to the concrete.

If the cops are going to grab her, it'll be now.

There were shadows of saw-toothed leaves on the pavement, and Marta went through them, her blouse winking out in the shadows and then brightening up again when she came into the direct rays of the streetlights. She stood in front of the fourth mailbox and opened it up. Then she put her hand inside and brought out the package, which was a can wrapped up with white tape. For a moment she just stood there, under the street lamp, her shadow at her feet like a black slip she had just dropped. Then she straightened up and started walking back to the car.

Shaw started the engine. Halfway down the hill he told Marta to open the can and show him what was inside, and then she sat there with the bills lying across her hand.

"Throw the can out the window," he said.

She threw it out, and as the can hit the ground, tumbling end over end, the sound of it reminded him of something. He swallowed, holding the wheel. A beer can. That was what it was like, a beer can being thrown out of a car. Shaw wasn't sure exactly why, but people didn't seem to do that so much anymore. All this talk about the environment. What everyone needed was a good war to make them shut up. Then he turned and looked at Marta.

He hadn't planned on this part, the two of them being together after having actually got the money. He realized now that, through a fatalism he had never even admitted to himself, he had always supposed that the police were going to be waiting, and that instead of being in this car with a young woman and some money, he'd be driving fast, trying to get away and reckoning just how far he was from the Mexican border. Well, how was he going to get rid of her? She'd seen him and his car.

She glanced over at him.

"I hadn't figured on this," he said.

"Figured on what?"

"Nothing," he said. "Nothing."

"Listen," she said. "Just drive me back to my car, will you?"

"No," he said. He looked at her. Goddamn it. Everything always has something in it that's just got to go wrong. Maybe he could make her take half the money; that way they'd be partners, wouldn't they? Maybe half was too much, maybe a fifth. That was more like it. But he didn't want to do that. Anyway, he had enough on her, didn't he? But what if she got to thinking some honesty is the best policy stuff; what if she just went to the police about what had happened in that house in Ferndale? What then? There was a word he was looking for . . . options. Yeah, what were his options? He didn't want her around, but he didn't want to lose sight of her, either.

"I didn't figure on this, you know," he said.

"I just want to get back to my car."

He nodded, thinking, Yeah. Got to do something.

"You can't go home just yet," he said.

"Why not?"

"There's a party," said Shaw.

"Oh, God," she said.

"You've got to come. That's all there is to it."

She glanced over at him.

"Don't start crying," he said.

She swallowed and then put her head in her hands.

"I've got to think," she said. "I just need to think."

"Sure," said Shaw. He looked over at her. "I'm thinking, too."

"What are you thinking about?"

"One thing and another," he said. "One thing and another."

He went on driving, going down Hollywood Boulevard and up to Highland. There he stopped in front of Nicky White's apartment house, the aquamarine glow of the swimming pool lighting the building as though by foxfire. Nicky was waiting out front, and he came over to the car.

"Who's that?" asked Nicky.

"This is my friend Marta," said Victor. "We've been friends for a while."

"No kidding," said Nicky.

"Yeah. Marta, this is Nicky," said Victor.

"Nice to meet you," said Nicky.

Marta looked out into the street. Then she turned to Victor and said, "All right. I'll go to the party. But that's it."

"Sure, sure," said Victor. "That's the deal."

"Not too friendly, is she?" said Nicky.

"She's a little tired," said Shaw.

"Well, this party will fix her up," said Nicky. "We'll go out the canyon to Malibu. Let's take my car. Yours doesn't look like much, does it?"

"I'm getting a new one," said Shaw.

"Yeah?" said Nicky. "Maybe I can help you out. I can get you something with low mileage. Full documentation."

The Scandal Sheet

CLASSIFIEDS

ZIMBA. Sale! Zimba at half price. Bring the jungle home. Call Raj, anytime, 398-1289, Encino.

OPTED FOR CREMATION? Ashes spread over the Pacific from airplane. Reliable. No mixed flights. Call the Baron at Last Flight Flying, 679-3843, San Pedro.

METAL DETECTORS. Pay for your vacation at the beach by finding objects lost in sand: rings, watches, money! Credit plans available. Also, super ribbed condoms, buy by the case and save big bucks. Plain wrappers to assure your privacy. Novelties. Box 6892, Santa Monica.

ACTRESS, desperate. Late thirties. Can sing. Leave message at Universal Answering for Chantilly. 768-9018, Reseda.

SWEAT EQUITY FILM. Everybody shares in profits. Technical people needed most. Call Dan, evenings, 760-1245, West L.A.

NEED RESPECTABLE MOTHER OR FATHER TO STAND UP FOR YOU AT YOUR WEDDING? Many people are out of touch with their families, but why let that spoil a traditional wedding? Call The Family Shop for mother, father, brothers, sisters. Packages available. 237-9071, anytime.

ACTORS. ACTRESSES. Need a quick jowl lift for a tryout? Don't let age cheat you out of a part! Tape and tie. Lasts days. Call Valley Cosmetology, 590-2356, Van Nuys.

SCANDAL SHEET SPECIAL!
Interview with the Advertiser.
ZIMBA!

There's a lot you didn't know about elephants. Zimba, advertised here for parties and commercial appearances, including films, eats over five hundred pounds of food a day. Zimba is an Asian elephant (*Elephas maximus*), born in the wild and captured at the age of eight. Elephants do not breed well in captivity and usually they are caught in the wild and then trained by other domesticated elephants. Of all the animals in the circus, the elephant is the most dangerous. Mostly, in Asia, they are used as draft animals, but they have been used in war, too, particularly by the Carthaginians when they invaded Rome in the Second Century B.C. It was the Indians who first used these animals for war, but elephants were also used in Persia by the Fourth Century A.D. Elephants are valuable from a military point of view because of their willingness to charge both men and horses. They were even used in the Second World War in Asia!

Elephants have been exterminated by man from Iran, Iraq, Afghanistan, northwestern India, much of the Malay Peninsula, greater Borneo, Sri Lanka, and much of Africa, where poachers kill them for their ivory. Hairs from the elephant's tail bring good luck. Poachers have been known to chase elephants with a jeep and a machine gun.

The animals live about seventy years, and are only really dangerous during their *must*.

Zimba's owner, Raj, says, "We've made a good thing out of the elephant. Zimba has appeared in films, advertisements, openings for shopping centers, and in corporate promotions. Elephants are patient and dependable. And, there aren't many left in the world."

A Trip to the Airport

MARIO DESANTIS thought about the day he had married Beverly Mason: the ceremony had taken place in a chapel on the coast, in Ventura, a place with glass walls so you could see the Pacific when you turned away from the altar. The chapel had even been used as a location for a movie, and somehow this was reassuring to DeSantis. *All the Way to Heaven* with Geordie Michaelson and some young actress had been shot there. What was her name? Anyway, Beverly had worn a white dress and a veil. Her hands had been cold and they shook. Around her, in her hair, on her skin, there had been the sweet, fragile scent of orchids. A limousine had driven them away from the church, and in the back seat Beverly had hiked up her skirt and had scratched her thigh, the white bridal underthings exposed for a moment in a cloud of chiffon. Then she had said, "A lot of people came. Couple of agents. Jimmy McGalley. Byron Arlington. Schwarzkopf. And what's his name from International."

DeSantis was sitting on the terrace of his house, looking out at the city. He wore a pair of white flannel pants, a work shirt he had paid a hundred and fifty dollars for, and some carefully polished brown shoes. There was a chaise longue next to him, but when he was thinking, he preferred to sit in a chair. The chair was metal and had white plastic webbing. DeSantis had put a table next to it, one with a glass top, and on it there was a white vermouth on the rocks, untasted: he thought that his clothes, the chaise where Beverly Mason usually stretched out, the arrangement of the chairs, the clean Frank Lloyd Wright terrace on which he sat, the city below, spread out like a sequined dress dropped on the floor, the avenues glittering through the layer of smog, all revealed beauty productively mingled with treachery. He liked to sit up here. DeSantis figured that altitude worked in Los Angeles the same way speed did: it made you feel your own perspective was the really important one. He glanced down at his brown shoes; the color and shine were soothing. Yeah, well, it was a good shine. It was reassuring that shoes could look like that, especially now.

At first he hadn't known what to think. Beverly had been moody before, but this was different. For instance, she had nailed the windows shut. She'd done it when DeSantis wasn't around; he'd gone into the bathroom to find a nail driven into the frame. He had told her they were living in a Frank Lloyd Wright house, practically a museum, and she had just stared at him, nodding, saying only, "I've got my reasons."

Well, sure. Everybody's a got a reason to do something like nailing a window shut. But what the hell was it? At first DeSantis had thought that Beverly had taken to checking the doors in the house two or three times a day and sleeping with the light on because she had found out something about what DeSantis was doing those afternoons when he went to see the Chinese woman he supported in Chinatown.

So he had approached his wife with a mixture of treachery and sympathy, asking in a gentle voice whether she would like him to bring home some won ton soup, while at the same time he was quietly alert, prepared to go from a sweetly considerate companion to the victim of unscrupulous snooping in an instant.

"No," said Beverly. "I don't want any soup."

"You sure?"

"Look," she said. "I already told you. All right?"

She started crying, putting her face in her hands.

"Listen," he said. "I didn't mean anything about the soup. OK? Forget the soup."

She looked up at him and shook her head, her face wet.

"I won't mention soup again, OK?"

After not getting anywhere with the soup, he had asked her to come out to the terrace, but she just looked at the ridges on either side of the house. Then she said, "You know, someone with a high-powered rifle could shoot us right off the terrace, you know that?"

This morning Beverly had woken up and sat at the side of the bed. She was trembling. Then she started crying, blowing her nose into her nightgown. The first thing DeSantis said was, "Maybe we should call Dr. St. James," but she cried harder and shook her head, and then he sat and looked out the windows that had been nailed shut. The goddamned shrink wasn't going to do any good. What the hell was he charging all that money for, then?

DeSantis got up and shaved and took a shower, and when he came back, she was still there, crying, blowing her nose on the sheet.

"I think you'd better tell me what's going on," he said.

"I don't know," she said. "I just don't know."

"Well, I do," he said.

"Don't get that way," she said.

"What way?"

She went right on crying, as though she had to do it to breathe.

"I'll make something to eat," he said.

"I don't want anything."

"Maybe some orange juice," he said.

She looked at the windows that were nailed shut.

"You aren't going anyplace today, are you?" she asked.

"I got a little business," he said. "I got to go down to Chinatown."

"Can I come with you?" she said.

"It's business." He shrugged. "You know."

She picked up the sheet and wiped her face on it and then looked at him.

That goddamned shrink. Just look at this.

"I don't want to be left alone here," she said.

"Come on," he said. "There's nothing to bother you. No bogeys are going to get you."

"Don't say that," she said.

"Don't say what?" he said. "You know something? I'm losing my patience."

"Just don't go down to Chinatown. I'm asking you a favor."

He sat down next to her and took one of her hands. Her voice had a breathy quality, and from time to time she looked up from the damp sheet she held in her hands and faced him. He sat quietly, nodding, asking, "How much? Twenty thousand? Small bills?" But, at the same time, his alertness about the money was mixed with something else, and when she spoke about the times she had spent in the barn where she grew up, the heat there, her sweaty skin, and the man who had caught her, there was a frankness she had never shared with him before. He didn't know what surprised him more, the fact that he knew so little about her or that she had taken a package of money, which she had gotten from his account, too, and left it in a fucking mailbox in Laurel Canyon.

Then he cooked her breakfast, bacon and eggs and toast, setting a place for her in the bright kitchen, giving her a napkin, and then sitting opposite her, nodding, listening to her. She took a sleeping pill right after she finished her eggs, and DeSantis sat with her, holding her hand while she lay in bed, waiting for the drug to give her the sensation of falling into a dark, but strangely airy hole. He tucked her into bed, pulling back the sheets for her and then lifting her legs and sliding them in, doing so with a tender interest and thinking, too, about her voice as she had said, "Maybe he'd bring a cord, or he'd cut it down from the curtains . . . he'd tie a special knot . . ."

She fell asleep. He went out to the terrace to think things over. In the distance, above the grayish-red smoke, there was a smudge which DeSantis thought probably came from the airport. He thought about the atmosphere at the airport, the shriek of the airplanes, and that greasy air which always reminded him of the dump where fires consumed old tires and gas seeped up from the depths.

It was noon, and DeSantis could see all the way down to the beach, the avenues gridlike but all seeming to originate from one place in the distance down by San Pedro, and as he stared, he began to consider Thompson Street in New York City, where he had grown up. The smoky air of Los Angeles seemed a long way from his neighborhood in New York. In the East, things had been more orderly. There had been the yearly arrival of the San Gennaro festival, with its orgiastic odor of cooking sausages and frying dough which mixed with the incense of the church on the corner. At Christmas there had been the hint of snow in the air. There had been greengrocery and cheese shops, all with glass windows with gold lettering on them, and every store had a bell on a spiral spring. Even now DeSantis could remember the bell in the pork shops and bakeries, the women in them drying their hands on white linen aprons. There was a place on Houston Street that sold fresh pasta, which his mother made with a clam sauce, or sometimes with squid. There was freshly ground Parmesan cheese on the table, rank as a dirty sock. Sometimes, after dinner, DeSantis would go to Ferraro's for a cup of coffee and a sweet.

There were old women who wore black, and they gathered in the street in twos and threes, their axelike faces put together as they whispered, their fingers tightening on a black shawl. Even twenty years and three thousand miles away, DeSantis remembered them in the street, their hair in a bun beneath the shawl, each in a pair of heavy black shoes. They existed in a miasma that DeSantis still felt, an acrid fury unlike any other on earth, although now he wasn't so appalled by it anymore.

Once a young man named White or Brown or Green had been selling marijuana out of an apartment in DeSantis's neighborhood. DeSantis's mother was the first to suspect it, and when she had her suspicions confirmed (by making a joke with someone who came out of the apartment, smiling at him and laughing, as wise as a serpent, until he showed her what he had bought), she went up to the social club on the corner, where she sat down and asked for a moment of one of the members' attention.

DeSantis had stood in the street in front of the building where the young man had lived. It was a cold, late February evening, and the street was dark, marked here and there by a purple sheen from the street lamp. A few people walked by, trailing clouds of mist. DeSantis had looked up, feeling the cold and realizing the keen and complete emptiness of the apartment after the young man had disappeared. There was a hush in the street, and the silence seemed to flow not just from the empty apartment but from a presence which, while general, nevertheless was distilled into the air of the social clubs and made more palpable by the dark clothes those women wore when they stood in the street, seemingly indifferent to pedestrians but nevertheless not missing a thing.

Well, DeSantis had come to California ten years ago, when he was twenty-five. After all, while money didn't grow on trees in Los Angeles, it was about as close as you could get to it. Where else could you buy an unusable gully and fill it up with dirt and sell the lots made this way for five and six times what you paid to begin with, even figuring in the price of the dirt? Tires, body shops — you couldn't miss. DeSantis had started in the laundry business, organizing a fleet of trucks that picked up dirty sheets and towels from motels and hotels: he figured this was a good way to get a look at what was happening in the hotels and restaurants. It wouldn't be hard to get a foot in the door, since, with all the managers and the owners seeing gurus and swamis and God knew who else, it was easy to scare them. There were other possibilities, too, like landfills and private carting, but before long DeSantis knew he had to make a decision between picking up garbage and getting into the movie business.

He put some money into B movies. None of that highbrow stuff. Good, honest entertainment. DeSantis liked the atmosphere of these pictures, the barely masked viciousness of them seeming to him to be "more like the truth than that highfalutin stuff." But, after a while, he started putting some money into more legitimate features, although he could tell a lot of people didn't like to do business with him. He figured that would change. In fact, it had been one of the reasons he had married Beverly Mason, although maybe that hadn't worked out so well, what with her knack for getting into trouble. When DeSantis had told his mother he was getting married, she asked if the woman was Italian, and when DeSantis had said no, she replied, with tears in her eyes, "Why have you waited so long to disappointment me?"

*   *   *

It was hard to find a place to park in Beverly Hills, and DeSantis drove around for a while before discovering the lot behind the building in which Dr. August St. James had his office. It was one of those parking lots in Beverly Hills where there was a sickly looking hedge planted to hide a low chainlike fence. There wasn't an American or a Japanese car in the lot, as though there were some connection between driving cars made in Germany and England and the practice of psychotherapy. In a spot under a sign that read, "Dr. St. James," there was a new white Land Rover station wagon. Four-wheel drive. DeSantis looked at it, wondering why St. James needed four-wheel drive. Mostly the floods got bad in the valley. Beverly Hills was high ground. DeSantis stared at the Rover for a long time, and then he parked and went into the building, taking the elevator to St. James's office. The elevator went only two stories, but it ran with an oil-like smoothness. There was no Muzak in it, and DeSantis didn't think much of an elevator that didn't have Muzak. It was another thing he put down against St. James.

There was no receptionist, and DeSantis sat down on one of the cream-colored sofas. A middle-aged woman came out of St. James's inner office. She was wearing a blue dress with small white flowers on it, and she had a reddish, puffy expression that made DeSantis think of the label of a Beefeater gin bottle. She put on her dark glasses and stepped outside to wait for the cool, smooth glide of the elevator. Beverly had a pair of dark glasses just like that.

"Excuse me," said St. James, coming into the waiting room, "but I don't think you have an appointment, do you?"

"No," said De Santis.

St. James was balding, and he had blondish hair and blue eyes.

"You've got to call to make an appointment," said St. James.

"I don't think so," said DeSantis.

"What gives you that idea?" said St. James.

"Let's go inside," said DeSantis.

"Maybe you can tell me what it's about?"

"It's about Beverly Mason," said DeSantis.

"Oh, Mr. Mason . . . ," said St. James.

"No. Not Mason. That's her name. DeSantis is my name. Let's go inside."

DeSantis didn't think it was very warm in the room, but he noticed St. James had begun to sweat: a line of beads, the color of baby oil, had appeared almost as though by legerdemain across his upper lip.

"All right," said St. James. "Come in."

DeSantis had never seen a couch before, not one in an office like this, and as he came into the room, he hesitated, looking at the long leather thing with the leather buttons on it. The couch was black and had a wooden frame, and there was a sheen on the leather from the light on St. James's desk. The office had a bookshelf with heavy books on it, and two framed diplomas hung on the wall, one in Latin, which made DeSantis think of those masses of his youth and the deep, resonant voices of the priests as they intoned the old words.

"Is Beverly upset?" asked St. James.

"Nothing I can't handle," said DeSantis.

"Maybe you should let Beverly be the judge of that," said St. James.

"Uh-huh," said DeSantis, looking around. "Is it private here?"

"Certainly," said St. James.

"No one can overhear what we say?" said DeSantis.

Jesus, the guy was sweating again. DeSantis waited for a long time, saying nothing, watching him sweat.

"I asked you a question," said DeSantis.

"No one can hear us now," said St. James.

DeSantis made a small snorting sound, not of disbelief so much as growing impatience.

"Do you keep notes on your patients?"

"Yes," said St. James.

"Any other records?"

"Like what?" asked St. James.

"You tell me."

"I don't see how it could possibly matter," said St. James.

"No?" said DeSantis.

St. James licked his lips.

"There's always the tapes," he said, looking down now.

"Tapes," said DeSantis. He looked around. "Is this place wired for sound, is that it?"

St. James nodded.

"Do you tape Beverly?" asked DeSantis.

"I don't think . . . ," said St. James, but DeSantis was already shaking his head back and forth.

"Listen," said DeSantis. "I'm going to do you a favor. I'm going to ask you one more time."

He sat opposite St. James, looking at him.

"I tape Beverly," said St. James.

"Who can get to the tapes?" asked DeSantis.

"Well, other than me?"

"Yes," said DeSantis.

"No one," said St. James.

DeSantis looked around the office.

"Who cleans this place at night?"

"Someone from the maintenance service," said St. James. "I had to call them once to get in late at night when I was locked out. I've got their number. Do you want it?"

"Yes," said DeSantis.

"You don't mean to suggest that anyone is listening . . ."

"No," said DeSantis. "I was just asking."

In Watts, he talked to the manager of Southwest Maintenance. He found out that a new man, just out of Soledad, was cleaning the office. Victor Shaw. Then DeSantis drove to the airport. A friend of his from Thompson Street ran the trucking union local at the airport, and as DeSantis drove, seeing the long streaks of exhaust from the jets coming in to land, he thought it had been a long time since those days in New York.

DeSantis's friend was Umberto Patalano. When Umberto looked up and saw DeSantis in the doorway of his office, he said, "Hey, DeSantis. It's been a coon's age. What can I do for you?"

"A little something," said DeSantis. "Is there someplace we can talk?"

Patalano looked at DeSantis for a moment.

"Sure," he said. "Out in the parking lot. The noise from the jets makes everything private. Something wrong?"

"Yeah," said DeSantis.

Spike

TAYLOR HAYDEN woke at 7 A.M. to the sound of artificial bird sounds from his alarm clock. The high-pitched twittering always brought a kind of fatalism to mind: maybe, one day, there wouldn't be any birds left, and then they'd have to invent some artificial ones that went around and made noises in the springtime. He guessed it would be better that way. The little robot birds wouldn't make those spots on his car. He liked to keep the car clean. He had a small vacuum with a long extension cord, and twice a week he went over the car, sucking up the dust and stuff that got into it. The smell of the clean car always had a devotional quality for Taylor, a hint of triumph over disorder, the secret of which, Taylor knew, was in getting hold of the details.

He was thirty-six years old, tanned, the muscles in his arms and chest defined by the hours he spent in the gym. His bedroom had white walls, a modern nightstand made of cherry wood, a floor lamp, a matching cherry bureau, a shaggy white rug, and a closet in which the clothes hung in their plastic bags from the dry cleaner. Taylor put on a silk bathrobe and went into the kitchen, where he squeezed six oranges (six was a number that brought good luck) and drank the juice, enjoying the pulp in his mouth. He ate some organic oatmeal and an apple, all of which he laid out on a blue place mat with a blue napkin in a cherry ring. The vitamins he took sat in a special blue dish, and he washed them down, picking each capsule up and swallowing it, staring out the window. He lived in a small canyon off the Cahuenga Pass, and his kitchen window looked over a garden with flowers, ivy, and grass. There was a Buddha in the garden, too, and he stared into its face as he took his vitamin pills. Then he went out for a six-mile run, and after he bathed, he went down to the gym, where he worked with the weights for a while. After that, he read the out-of-town papers, stopping at a story about a body found in a trunk in Chicago or Boston or Miami. Yeah, things were really hopping in Miami these days. Well, you got to figure you're dealing with Cubans, and they learned some nasty stuff with Batista.

The phone rang as he was getting dressed. He took a pair of beige slacks from the thin plastic bag the dry cleaner put it in. Some cleaners were using plastic that had things printed on it, like, "Look Your Best," or "Make a Good Impression," but Taylor wanted his clothes to be in uniform bags, each as clear as a bubble, and he didn't want the tops of the hangers wired together, either: it gave him a small sense of claustrophobia he didn't like. He had laid out the pants, keeping the creases untroubled, and folded the bag six times, into a small, neat square, around which he put a rubber band, thinking, "That's a little good luck, right there. It all adds up." He thought he'd wear a light blue shirt. In fact, he saw the light blue shirt and the beige pants as being harmonious, like a brown landscape with a sky above the horizon. He thought of the horizon as being right at his waist. And as he reached for a shirt from a pile that had been laundered and folded with a strip of paper around it, just like a pack of hundred-dollar bills, Taylor reminded himself of his procedures: one was that right after using a pistol, he would take a rat-tail file and run it up and down, up and down in the barrel, so that even if it were found, the ballistics test would come to nothing. Use a belly gun, not an automatic. Break it into pieces when you're done. Get rid of it fast.

He wanted to let the phone ring six times, but instead he let it go three, half six and all right, really.

"Uh-huh. What time? Sure. I can make that. At the airport? Sure. I know the parking lot you mean. Have you ever known me to be late?"

He hung up and went back to dressing, checking the shine on his shoes and stopping from time to time to think about the future and those little mechanical birds. Well, they would probably be controlled by the government, right? But maybe there'd be a way to nominate which birds got made into robots, just the way you could nominate someone to be put on a postage stamp. He guessed he would nominate cardinals and robins, although he didn't know if they were good singers.

Then he thought about meeting Umberto at the airport. These union guys were always hard to figure. Taylor knew that you could get a big job from one of these guys and then when you'd done it, you'd turn around and find the guy who had hired you getting ready to kill you. It made sense, because that put everything one step farther away from the job. But still, it was a problem. Taylor thought about it as he shined his shoes, not too much sheen, just a deep, nice-looking brown. He sat down and tied his shoes, making sure the bows on each were the same length. That's two. Three times two was six. There were six holes in the shoes for laces, three on each side. Perfect. Taylor figured he'd do the job for Umberto only if it was someone small. That made everything a lot safer.

They met in the parking lot at the airport. It was a five-story lot, and to get up to the roof, you had to go around in long, lazy circles, which reminded Taylor of the path described by a hawk or a vulture as it coasted, trying to stay inside a thermal. Then he came out on the roof and parked at the end, next to Umberto's car. In the distance, beyond the terminal and the tower, with its bunch of aerials and high-tech dishes and revolving electronic equipment, Taylor saw the airplanes, the long silver bodies rushing down the runway and making a noise which he stood up to, as if it were a wind. Taylor glanced back at the tower. Maybe when they have a bunch of little mechanical birds flying around they will be controlled from a place like that. It might be nice, sitting in there, in front of a radar screen that showed where the birds were, flying around, making a little chirp like an electric alarm clock.

"Well, well," said Umberto. "Long time no see. What are you up to?"

"This and that," said Taylor.

"Like what?" said Umberto.

"There are some opportunities opening up."

"Tell me one," said Umberto.

"Russia is the thing of the future," said Taylor. "You're going to be amazed what comes out of there and what goes in, too. Going to be dynamite. So, I'm thinking about getting into import-export."

"Uh-huh," said Umberto.

Taylor swallowed and wiped his hands on a handkerchief he took from his pocket. The handkerchief had been ironed.

A plane started its takeoff, the silver fuselage at the end of the runway making a turn and coming along now under full throttle. The runway had a lot of tire marks on it, and the air over it was a little thick with the grayish-brown plumes of exhaust. The jet came along, getting louder, and as it lifted into the air, the wings wobbling a little from side to side, Umberto said, his voice penetrating the shriek of the engines, "I got a job for you. Guy in Hollywood."

"Does he know it's coming?" asked Taylor.

"Naw," said Umberto. "He's too dumb to know which end is up. Just got out of Soledad, the dumb bunny."

"Does he have any connections?" said Taylor.

"Naw," said Umberto, the jet still shrieking, its trail of exhaust stretched out in a long, slowly expanding plume. "He's a nobody. He's got nothing to do with anybody. Guy by the name of Victor Shaw. Take your time. Easy does it, right?"

Taylor looked at him.

"Yeah," he said. "I guess so."

They watched the jet trail away, and then another one started shrieking. Then they talked about money and shook hands, even though Taylor didn't like to.

Taylor got back into his car, which he thought he'd wax again that afternoon. Inside, on the ramps of the garage, there was the scent of damp cement mixed with the odor of kerosene from the jets, and Taylor circled down now, going around and around like a hawk or a vulture, thinking it was an OK deal.

There was a car wash near a *go* club in West L.A., and Taylor left the car there and walked up to the club's entrance. Hibiscus grew out front and some gardenias, too, the scent seeming very strong in the ashy stink of the smog. Inside on a table in the foyer there was an arrangement of flowers, lilies and a few delicate strands of tall grass, the lines like brush marks in a Japanese painting. Then Taylor sat down to play with a stranger, both of them very polite, carefully drinking tea and putting down their cups so that the click of the porcelain cup in its porcelain saucer blended into the slow, thoughtful cadence of stones being placed on the *go* board. Well, with a new player, a stranger, it was always best to feel him out.

Sharks

THE NIGHT WARREN HODGES met Marta he went to bed
late and alone. Before getting under the covers he sat on the
turned-back sheet, staring at a painting on the wall of his bedroom. It was a Monet, and it depicted a field, painted in late
summer, and in the brownish grass red flowers seemed to glow,
piercing the landscape like the tip of an electric soldering iron.
Warren looked at them, thinking about Marta.

She had sat in the car, the blanket over her shoulders. Her
hair had been wet, and corkscrew-shaped curls, shiny in the light
from the street lamp, hung around her face. She sat back in her
seat, her posture a combination of contradictory states, like ex-
haustion and a furious alertness. She had held the blanket together with one hand, and in the dark had let it go for a moment
as she stared out the windshield. The scent in the car, on the
warm air that came from the heater, had been of her skin and of
the ocean, too, and now, as Hodges looked at the painting, it
suggested the memory of that warm fragrance. Her wet hair had
been filled with the gleam of streetlights, her expression intent as
she reached up and pulled the edges of the blanket together.

Now, in the morning, he remembered her hands as they had
gone to her face, the sudden, intimate appearance of the blood
between her fingers, her figure as she emerged from the water,
the lacy foam running down her legs. She had reached out and
taken the blanket from him, their fingers touching, the tips flut-
tering against one another.

Well, why don't I drop everything?

He sat up and looked at the Monet, the colors at once bright and soothing, the paint itself seeming to convey a dusty Mediterranean afternoon in August in which the earth luxuriates in sunlight. Hodges imagined he could find out the name of the man who had brought her to his house. After all, hadn't someone actually bought a car from him once? A Mercedes or something like that? Warren sat there, looking at the Monet and thinking about who had bought a hot car with "full documentation." It must have been an actor. Only an actor would do something as stupid as that.

Warren sat up and put his feet on the floor. The room was large, with windows on one side that faced the Pacific. The walls were white, museumlike. Opposite him there was only the Monet. Through the window beyond the foot of the bed the ocean lay in the distance with a smoldering blue quality, like a gas that has turned to liquid at a hundred degrees below zero. Warren slept nude. He was tall and thick in the chest and arms, and his legs were long. He was narrow-waisted and the musculature showed in neat, defined sections.

He stood up, thinking about the party he had given the night before. In the living room there had been some cherry candies on small sticks . . . Warren couldn't remember where the housekeeper had got them. Marta had reached down and picked one up and put it into her mouth, sucking on it, making the tip of the candy pointed. Her lips had become red with the cinnamon-scented candy, and she had pursed them a second before sucking the pointed tip, the gesture at once abstracted and keen. The glossy sheen on the candy and her lips had been almost the same.

It was five o'clock in the morning now. In a couple of hours the phone would ring from New York, as it did every morning at 7 A.M. Well, there were people he had to keep in line. The stock analysts took some grooming . . . a rumor, a picture that was running over budget, a few bad reviews, bad box office, and the stock slid. Warren glanced at the Pacific and wondered what happened to the money when it disappeared that way. Where did it go? Was there a kind of antimoney, like antimatter, where the value of stock went when it took a tumble because something stupid appeared in the *Wall Street Journal?*

How hard would it be to find her, anyway?

He wanted to be exact about the impulse to do so. More than anything else he had the sensation of being locked out, of being surrounded by glass walls, and when he hit them, it was always at an angle, so that he felt as though his path was always curving away from the destination he was trying to reach. Then he glanced up at the Monet again: those points of color in the field were an expression of beauty so efficient as to be usually tucked away in strands of DNA, although here in the painting Warren could get a glimpse of it. And now, as he stared, he could smell the salt on Marta's skin as it had dried in the car, and he could see, in an almost hallucinatory image, the shape of her lips, stained by the cherry candy, and the tip of her tongue as she licked it.

Warren Hodges was curious, too, as to how he had come to this moment, waiting for New York to call while he sat on the side of the bed, his hands still trembling just as they had the night before.

He had to be careful. There were arrangements he was trying to make . . . certain things could be advantageous, such as access to capital, no questions asked. There were parts of the business he could streamline. Smoothness was everything. There were the details of International Pictures's financing. After all, it was risky, but he didn't think there would be any trouble with it, not really, not if all his ducks were in a row. He glanced at the phone. He'd have to be careful even about his tone of voice. Well, there it was again: how much of his life had been dedicated to illusion. That was the thing about the Monet. It was an illusion, but it hid nothing. Or better, it gave you that glimpse.

Warren glanced from the painting to the Pacific, which was delineated by the window's cherry wood frame. Hadn't Monet always liked cherry? The climate here was similar to that of southern France. Hodges wanted to have some flowers planted outside so he could see them when he looked at the Pacific. Bright red ones that would pierce the otherwise Mediterranean, dung-colored landscape.

He was determined to know what it was that had left him at the side of the bed, his head in his hands, trembling, thinking about that young woman. He was certain now who had bought that Mercedes. Jackie Carson. Sure. That's who it had been. The Mercedes had been yellow and had had a cream-colored top. He hadn't paid much for it . . . ten thousand, twenty. Couldn't have been more than twenty. Not even someone as stupid as Jackie Carson could have paid more than twenty for a car that had been stolen.

Well, are you afraid to really let go? Are you? Let's face it, you never have before, have you?

There were reasons not to.

Yeah, well, what reasons are there now?

It's going to cause trouble.

Well, maybe it's time to cause some trouble. How about that?

He put on a pair of swim trunks and sandals and a T-shirt, and then he went downstairs, where he got into the car. It was the same one he had driven the night before, and as he turned the keys in the ignition, he looked over at the pigskin seat where she had sat. On the edge, over the small stitching, there was a spot of blood, no bigger than the nail on his small finger. He concentrated now, trying to decide what it reminded him of. It took a minute, mainly because the spot was rust-colored now, but even so, it came to him: those flowers in the painting.

He drove down to the beach and parked where he usually did. The waves were smooth at this hour, glassy green like an old Coke bottle. There was the salty iodine scent of the air, and as Warren dropped his shirt and took off his sandals, he was still trying to be precise. The water was cold and salty.

You know, maybe I'm tired of being orderly. Good and tired.

Usually he swam a mile along the coast and then turned and came back. Many times he would start the swim with an idea, and if he could still remember the idea after the two miles, then he knew he didn't have an idea anymore. He had a belief. So he began, cutting a small V-shaped wake, reaching out into the green-brown Pacific, feeling the pressure of the sharks in the water: he knew they were there. They always were. The question was, how did he come to terms with them? Well, that was easy enough. He just kept swimming.

Then, how had he come to this particular morning?

He swam with long, smooth strokes (smoothness was everything, even in the water), and as he went, he thought of what he should say to New York, the colors in the painting, Marta's glistening skin as she came out of the water, the dark crash of the wave closing out onto the beach, her lips pursed as she languidly brought the candy to her mouth . . . candy the color of a bright, wet cherry.

He began searching, looking through the things he had. After all, if he was going to run off with her . . . then he stopped, having put some words to it.

Is that what he meant to do? And what made him so sure she would go along?

For a while he thought about the sharks, swimming in the depths, their bodies moving with a kind of spring-loaded strength, a gray blur of the tail, a bend in the body, those neatly aligned vents of the gills like something on a plane or a racing car, that jagged mouth, all seeming to make the water a little more alive and mysterious than otherwise. And as he swam, trying to feel the sharks, he had the notion they were like things out of his past, not always thought about but still there, just beneath the surface and waiting for a dangerous moment. Warren had been good at forgetting: there were certain things you had to give up when it was tough and you had to find your way out of the flat part of Hollywood. That's how he saw it, flat . . . down there around North Flores, Van Ness, Franklin. There wasn't too much to be gained by looking back, or so he had always thought. He had worked long hours for years. He had gotten up and faced those calls from New York, never showing a thing, not a flutter in his voice, nothing but that quiet, certain, unemphatic quality that implied not belief so much as absolute certainty. Well, he had given some things up. He had simply willed it to be so. It had been tough.

His parents had come to California in the early thirties, his father from a farm in Rutland, Vermont, by way of Boston. Warren's grandfather was a farmer who had taken another mortgage every year, slipping into debt as if buying baubles for a woman he couldn't possibly afford. Warren's grandfather had died nursing the illusion that he was going to make the farm pay, and even when Warren was young, he was told by his father that there was more money to be made in nursing illusions (as the bank had done) than in the thing the illusion was based on. Warren's father had tried to put this advice into practice by coming to California and opening a used car lot on Ventura Boulevard in the valley.

Warren's mother had met Warren's father when he sold her a lemon. They argued about the car so often that, while they thought they were doing business, they in fact had already begun a courtship. Warren's father got Warren's mother pregnant in the back seat of the lemon.

Warren's mother said she knew of a doctor in Providence, Rhode Island, a man who fixed up bullet wounds for gangsters and who did plastic surgery and changed fingerprints and who would be willing, for a price, to take care of pregnancies. The doctor fixed birth defects, club feet, and he had once made a woman who had been hit by a shotgun blast into someone more beautiful than before, although, when the woman smiled, you could see some small white lines around her mouth.

"No," Warren's father had said. "No gangster doctors."

"Well," said Warren's mother, "what do you expect me to do?"

"Marry me," he said.

So Warren grew up working with his father. His job was to write the prices on the windshields of the Fords, the Chevrolets, and the occasional lemon Pontiac or Buick. He did so with a mixture of starch and water, putting one price on and then, a week later, after hearing the disappointment in his father's voice, he scrubbed it off and painted on another, lower one. He learned that if you are selling a cheap illusion, the price had better be right.

Warren went to Hollywood High, where he played baseball, and even had a tryout with the Chicago Cubs, but it didn't come to anything. He was a member of a gang called the Mohicans, for which, as warlord, he negotiated a fight with a gang in China-town. Some Chinese gangsters stopped it. Warren's counterpart, a young Chinese man, said he was leaving town. It wasn't safe anymore. Warren thought this over. Then he caught the bus to Las Vegas, taking with him a hundred dollars ready money and a lot of knowledge about how to sell cars. Warren's Quality Cars was on a bare piece of sun-baked dirt in the desert outside of town, and he stayed at it for a couple of years, putting up, as a symbol of the place, a large foil-covered star.

He was in his early twenties when he came back to Los Angeles, bringing some cash with him, a bundle of hundred-dollar bills with a bright red rubber band around it. He rented a house in Hollywood, at the bottom of Laurel Canyon.

It was a small house, set back in a grove of eucalyptus trees. He would sit there, smelling the dusty, medicinal odor. From time to time he would go down to the beach, driving past the colony at Malibu, not impressed by it so much as feeling vaguely excluded from something that was rightfully his. He kept in touch with the Mohicans, which now was no longer a high school gang but a loose organization of young men inclined toward a mixture of money and trouble.

He wasn't in the movie business, not yet, but he was thinking about it. The one who was responsible for more than just thinking about it was a Gypsy, a woman by the name of Nicole. She had sold amulets and charms on Eighth Avenue in New York and had told fortunes in an office she rented by the day, but New York was a hard, dying place (or so it seemed to Nicole), and with a thorough dismissal and a lack of regret, she took the train west, getting off it with her one black suitcase and then staring at Los Angeles City Hall. It seemed white and clean against the gray-blue sky, colored by the smoke from the smudge pots that had been lighted the night before in the orange groves. She was twenty-one years old.

She got a ride into Hollywood and was let off on Sunset near Laurel Canyon, and after buying a newspaper, she rented a room in that flat section of Los Angeles. Then she strolled up Laurel Canyon, where she stopped on an impulse, in front of the small house surrounded by eucalyptus trees.

Nicole was a tall woman with reddish hair and blue eyes, and she had a few freckles over her nose which gave her an air of girlish innocence. She was wearing a black dress and stockings, dark shoes, and a blue scarf, which made her eyes seem very blue. She walked up to the porch, her hand trailing languidly over her skirt to touch the shape of the switchblade knife she wore in the top of her stocking. It was hot and she was sweating, a small mustache of beads forming on her upper lip.

Warren opened the door. It was ten thirty, and he was still wearing a silk polka dot robe and a pair of slippers, and he was smoking a strong French cigarette. He was tall, with blondish hair, and his eyes were the same color as hers. She felt moist and hot under her clothes. She waited in the yard, smelling the eucalyptus (and thinking that the next time she made an amulet for rheumatism she should put some eucalyptus leaves into it, for the scent, which was like the soul of medicine), and while she thought about it, and wanted, at the least, to get away with a handful of leaves, she looked not directly at Warren but at a point just above his head. This was an old Gypsy trick to make someone think you were looking right through them.

"It's hot," she said. "Could I have a drink of water?"

"Of course," said Warren. "Would you like to come in, out of the heat?"

She shrugged.

"OK," she said.

In the living room a bare light bulb was screwed into a socket in the ceiling above a card table where Warren had laid out a hand of solitaire. The cards weren't new, and the game hadn't been worked all the way out.

"Red queen on the king," she said. "You missed that."

Warren looked down at the cards.

"Yes," he said. "Well, doesn't that beat all?"

Warren went into the kitchen, where he stood and looked out the window at the hillside. It was shady and blotchy where the light came through the grove of eucalyptus trees, and in the long beams there were bits of dust, shiny as flecks of sequins. He faced Nicole, who sat in the dimness, her dark clothes, her eyes, her red hair, her long fingers giving her a sultry quality which seemed to overwhelm the house.

They began to meet once or twice a week, Nicole seemingly looking for a business partner. She said she had come to California to make money. Warren pointed out that she wasn't the only one who had made the trip for that reason. She listed the ways she had made money, such as the Murphy, or selling a machine that supposedly made money, pills to insure potency or multiple orgasms (vitamin C in a gelatin capsule), or starting a scheme that involved communicating, for a price, with God. In addition, she told fortunes and picked pockets. It seemed to her, just looking around, that there were a lot of people in California who had a slender grasp on reality.

"Well, yeah. What did you expect? It's California," said Warren.

"Listen," she said. "Maybe you could get a job working on houses. I could come with you and look around the houses and see what there is to steal. If I'd steal for you, it means I'm a good woman, don't you think?"

"Well," said Warren. "I don't know."

Nicole gave him that same Gypsy stare, focusing on a distant spot just above his forehead. Then she got up and went to the door of the bedroom, where she turned back, saying, "Come here. We might as well get this out of the way, too."

She moved in. In addition to her dark skirts and dresses and her one good black lace shawl, she brought a book (*Three Hundred and Twenty-Five Objects in Dreams Explained*), a sewing kit, a piece of cloth for her amulet bags, a hairbrush, a toothbrush, and a lemon, with which she washed her face and hands and which she believed would keep her skin smooth and young forever.

Now, after she finished her job as a taxi dispatcher, from which she got off at two or three in the morning, she would walk into the canyon where Warren's house was. In the middle of the night the insects flew around the streetlights in a chaotic frenzy, the swirling movement reminding her of those moments in the bedroom when she and Warren seemed to be only lightly attached to the world and when gravity itself seemed to be letting go, announcing its departure with a warm buzzing. When she came home late, the walk up to the door of the house and the drive were dappled with the shadows of eucalyptus leaves which lay as if they had been cut out of dark paper and scattered in the purplish light from the street lamp. Even the light seemed imbued with the fragrance of eucalyptus. Inside, she undressed in the dark and folded back the sheets, slipping into them and saying, "I've been thinking about it all day. Do you think I'm losing my mind?"

In the evenings, they went to a bar on Santa Monica called Barney's Beanery, where Nicole discovered baseball. Or, maybe it is better to say she discovered a baseball player. Nicole began by watching games on an enormous TV, the actions of the players and the things the announcer said leaving her almost mesmerized, and as she watched, the rules of the game beginning to be apparent, she said, "Tell me. What is a Slugfest in Bean Town?"

Warren looked across the table at her and said, "A lot of home runs hit in Boston."

Nicole discovered the Stars, a minor league team that played in a park in Hollywood, by seeing an advertisement in a throw-away paper she usually read for its astrology column. The place where the team played had a backstop made out of telephone poles and wire fencing; there was a loudspeaker, a scoreboard, and one man who sold hot dogs and hot peanuts out of an aluminum box he carried by a strap over his shoulder. Nicole was usually there early, watching the groundskeeper raking and watering and laying out the long, straight white lines on the field.

The first time she saw Josh Fulsome was on a Thursday afternoon. He arrived late, carrying his bag in one hand and two bats in the other. He walked with a straightforward, almost malicious gait, looking neither to the left nor right. He wore a leather jacket and a pair of jeans, and he was carrying over his shoulder a pair of well-worn cleats.

He was of medium height, broad in the shoulders, tanned, with clear, clean features. He changed and began to warm up, fielding balls that were hit by the coach, and Nicole watched, unsure why she felt a sudden unexplained loneliness when she looked away from him. Fulsome was an outfielder, and he stood on the green grass away from the white lines, waiting, then running for the ball, making throws that were on the money. He was twenty-six or so, two years out of the army.

Fulsome noticed her in the stands. Her hair was glossy, a dark reddish color, and her skin was pale and white. Fulsome came in from the field and glanced at her, and then sat down and picked up a bat, running a bone along it to make it harder. She stared at the bone, hearing the *slick slick slick* of it over the bat, the sound ominous and yet practical and suggesting Fulsome's empathy, too, with her own fierce belief in the uses of potions and charms. While she worked in the evenings, making an amulet, she wondered whether Fulsome had any Gypsy blood in him.

The next game Fulsome went four for four with a walk, picking up three runs batted in, and when he walked out of the dressing room, Nicole was waiting for him, already holding out the amulet.

"Here. This is for luck," she said, offering it.

He looked at her, thinking it over. Then he reached out and took it.

"It smells like eucalyptus," he said.

"Keep it under your pillow," she said. "Before a game, rub it along the bat."

Soon they were having dinner in the coffee shops and greasy spoons on Hollywood Boulevard, Fulsome sitting opposite her and providing more technical information about the game than she had dreamed possible.

In the evening she went to the Beanery, where, if a game wasn't televised, she listened to one on the radio that sat behind the bar next to the cash register. The radio was in a brown wood cabinet with dark brown knobs, and it always reminded Nicole of a fat man wearing a brown suit.

"How's the baseball going? Stars doing all right?" asked Warren.

"Yes," she said. "They're on a tear. Do you know some pitchers keep Vaseline on their uniforms?"

"No," said Warren. He looked at her. "Why do they do that?"

"They doctor the ball with it. You know, to throw a spitball," she said.

"Is that right?" said Warren.

"Yes," she said. "And some keep a little bit of emery board, too. To scuff up the ball."

"No kidding?" said Warren.

"No kidding."

"How did you find out?" he said.

"I just heard some people talking," she said.

"Oh," he said. "Maybe you'd like me to come to a game sometime."

"I don't know," she said. "I guess I've just gotten into the habit of going alone."

In those days Warren had taken to going to a bar across the street from Warner Brothers. Technical people, film editors and cameramen, makeup men and hair stylists, went there to drink in the afternoon or on a day off, and he had been trying to get them to tell him something, almost anything, about what he should know. He was going to UCLA, not having the money to register but hanging around the classes where lighting and sound were taught, getting kicked out from time to time but coming back anyway. He was also busy trying to make a little money, and these days that had more to do with the Mohicans than anything else. Right now one of them had a truckload of TV sets, Motorolas, still in the box, "Not hot, just warm," the Mohican said. Would Warren help? So he had his hands full, but even so, he stopped and looked at Nicole.

"Well, sure, if that's the way you feel about it."

The next day, around noon, Warren got into his car and drove away from the house in Laurel Canyon, and as he drove out Sunset Boulevard, hoping someone would tell him something he wanted to know about sound, he came up against the memory of that look in her eyes.

Nicole bathed and put on a dress with a pleated skirt, which she had ironed carefully, and then she started the long walk down Hollywood Boulevard, seeing here and there people standing in sandwich boards which had written on them in red letters, next to some childish bursts, like thick explosions, "Maps to the Stars' Homes." She kept walking until she came to the Palace Hotel, a place which young actors and actresses from Kansas and Oregon seemed to gravitate to as though by radar. They sat in the lobby and read copies of *Variety* and the *Hollywood Reporter*.

Nicole went to the desk and rented a room, took the key, and went upstairs, where she opened the door. There was a double bed, some white towels in the bathroom, a chair in the corner, and white, faintly yellowed curtains, and when she opened the window, they blew in the wind. She opened the door to the closet and looked at herself in the mirror; a woman in a white dress with smooth skin and blue eyes holding a hotel key on a little plastic paddle. A film of dust covered the nightstand and bureau, the white mist of it seeming like a condensation of dreams that rose steadily from the lobby downstairs and settled here like ash. She ran her finger through it, and then opened the closet door so that the mirror on the back reflected the white counterpane on the bed. Then she went out.

The groundskeeper was already at work, and the grass had just been mowed so that the outfield had a checkerboard pattern beneath the shimmer of the grass. The foul lines were so white and straight as to suggest a mathematical concept, and the outfield stretched away into an infinity of hope and possibility. Nicole sat with her hand in her bag, reaching in from time to time to touch the key and thinking about the room on Hollywood Boulevard.

After the game, she went with Fulsome to a coffee shop, and they sat opposite each other, Fulsome tanned and smooth-skinned, and Nicole sitting with her bag on the seat next to her, resting one hand on it, listening as Fulsome described, with a kind of fury, the problems he was having with the bat. He had struck out three times and flied out weakly, and now he sat with a plate full of corned beef hash with two eggs on it, shaking his head. Then he looked up and said, "Can you make me another amulet?"

"Maybe," she said.

"Have you got one in your bag?" he asked. "Is that what you have your hand on?"

She shrugged. "Something like that."

"Will it bring me good luck?"

"Maybe," she said. "But it's not all here. We have to take a walk to get the rest of it."

"I'm a little tired after the game," he said.

"Well," she said. "Do you want it or not? You decide."

"We're going to play a double-header in Fresno," he said. "The bus is going to leave in a couple of hours."

"Is it?" she said. "Well, like I said, you decide."

They walked in that blue-pink dusk of early summer, and as they strolled, their hands not even touching, they passed under the bright yellow lights, so much like a carnival, on the underside of the theater marquees. They came up to the hotel, and Nicole said, "In here."

Nicole removed the key from her bag. They went to the elevator, passing the actors who sat on the worn sofas, some with too much hope and others with too little. In the room, Nicole reached down and took off her shoes, and as Fulsome looked around the room and said, "This is pretty nice," she said, "Yes, I guess it is. Leave the closet door the way it is."

*   *   *

In the evenings Warren sat with some books and technical information about movie equipment, but now he didn't spend much time at it since he could tell that something had changed. It made him feel the hours he had spent with Nicole had simply been an illusion and that he had never been able to reach her, not really; instead, he was faced with a distance, the gulf seeming chaotic and incomprehensible. Nicole seemed to notice it and she struggled against it as well, as though it were evidence of something that had come unexpectedly into her life, too. When they lay in that bed where they could smell the eucalyptus, they both felt it was not the same, and to make up for it, they were more ardent, the falseness bringing a poison that was worse. Warren sat at the kitchen table in his polka dot bathrobe, a strong drink by his hand and the cards laid out for a game of solitaire. Then Nicole came into the room and sat down opposite him.

"Have you ever played double solitaire?" she asked.

"No," said Warren, without looking up at her. "Why don't you show me how?"

So she got out another deck and laid out another game opposite his, and the two of them sat there, playing onto each other's cards, neither saying a word in the silent kitchen. Warren went through his deck, slapping the cards down, as if he could make sense out of the change in his life this way. What he wanted was for things to be the same as they had been, and when he couldn't stand the kitchen one minute more, he stood up and said, "I'm going to the movies. Do you want to come?"

"No," she said, "I'm a little tired. I've had a long day."

Twice a week Nicole went to the Stars' games and then to a greasy spoon with Fulsome, where the waiter put down the "usual" with a comforting, even homelike regularity. Fulsome was now hitting .390. In their room in the Palace they could hear the crowds in the twilight on Hollywood Boulevard, the voices and the sound of the cars in the street rising to the room, where they were cut off by the scrape of the shade against the window frame. Nicole looked over at the mirror on the inside of the door.

"Here," she said. "Move over this way a little."

Nicole took a shower and got dressed, walking into the warm, California evenings, arriving at work a little later with each passing week. One day the man she worked for said, "Nicole, you're late."

She stood in the doorway, looking at him.

"I'd better quit," she said.

In July the winds began to blow, filling the streets with dusty shapes and making the air dry, and when Warren came into the Beanery a spark jumped from his finger to a metal stool. A friend of his from the Mohicans, a tall, blond man who had a habit of breathing through his mouth, sat in a booth. He talked very slowly, and this gave him time to think. There were three current investigations in the city of Los Angeles in which he was involved, any one of which could have caused him, at the right moment, to leave the state for good.

Warren sat down opposite him and said, "The wind makes me edgy."

"It's just air," said the Mohican, whose name was Jack.

Warren put a hand to his head and felt the static electricity in his hair. It made a snap. "Yeah?" he asked.

"You're too jumpy," said Jack.

Warren looked across the table.

"You're worried about Nicole," said Jack, "aren't you?"

"So what?" said Warren. "Is that a crime?"

"No," said Jack. "Do whatever you want. You want to worry, worry."

Jack shrugged.

Outside the wind blew across the roof, making the ventilator hum like on a ship. There was another sound, too, a high, lonely whistle that had an ebb and flow to it, sometimes stronger, sometimes weaker, but always there.

"She's got a baseball player," said Warren.

"How do you know?" said Jack.

"I went to a game," said Warren. "He plays for the Stars."

"Double A or triple?" asked Jack.

"What the hell difference does it make?"

"Maybe it makes some," said Jack.

"Like what?" said Warren. "What possible difference could it make if he was playing triple A rather than double A?"

"Triple A is closer to the majors," said Jack. "Don't sell possibility short."

"Possibility?" asked Warren.

"Possibility," said Jack. "Hope. Call it what you want."

The wind blew across the roof, the whistle getting a little louder. Warren listened to it, wincing a little, as if the sound came from a dentist's drill.

"Are you making any money these days?" Jack asked.

"No," said Warren. "But that's going to change."

"Good, good," said Jack. "Count me in, too. I got to look ahead."

"What for?" asked Warren.

"I think I might have some legal expenses," said Jack.

Jack shrugged. Then both of them sat there and listened to the wind.

*   *   *

Warren and Jack met the tire bootlegger outside Phoenix. They had rented a truck in Los Angeles, making an arrangement with the owner for a share of the profits, if any, Warren already showing an interest in how the profits were going to be determined, just like in the movie business. The tire bootlegger was six foot three and heavy, and he wore overalls. One eye was larger than the other, and he smoked Pall Mall cigarettes, which he carried in the rolled-up sleeve of his T-shirt, which he wore under the overalls. His face was almost purple, as though meanness of spirit had a complexion, and he had black stumps for teeth. On the way to meet him, when they were driving through the desert, Warren took a blue-black .38 caliber pistol from the glove box and shot it out the window at the moonlit dunes, which were rilled by the wind into undulating lines of black and white. The bullet hit with a little splash of sand, and Warren said, shouting over the ringing in his ears, "I think it will help to have the smell of gunpowder in the cab, don't you?"

"What?" said Jack. "I can't hear a thing."

The tire bootlegger bought tires in Mexico, ones that were supposed to be Pirellis and Firestones, and then brought them across the border, doing so through an intricate embrace of corruption and back yard organization. The tires did look good, on the outside anyway, but the inside, the cords and rubber, was another matter, the contents of which were probably not even known to the bootlegger humself, although there were some workers in Mexican factories who had a pretty good idea.

When the tire bootlegger came up to the cab of the truck, he sniffed the air and said, "What stinks?"

Warren and Jack bought some tires and drove back to Los Angeles, where they went from one tire warehouse and discount auto parts store to another, selling the Pirellis and Firestones, the tires having the color and the shine, too, of pieces of licorice. Then they made another trip, going through the All American Desert by moonlight again, the dunes casting shadows that looked like large pieces of black silk that had been laid over the sand. In the bluish sky the stars were silver as pinheads, their brightness having that particular sheen which the natural world has when things are uncertain and filled with unpleasant possibilities. A bundle of tens and twenties sat on the seat between them, the bills held together with rubber bands the color of nicotine stains, and as they went, Warren glanced down at the money, the edges of the bundle glowing softly in the moonlight.

This time the bootlegger met them on a back road outside of

town. In the distance they could see the lights of Phoenix, which was pushing into the desert. The bootlegger took the money.

"This is all right," he said. "So far as it goes. Only it doesn't go that far. If you want to make real money, you got to do better."

"We're pushing pretty hard now," said Warren.

"Are you?" asked the tire bootlegger. "OK. If that's what you got to say."

"I guess we can do better," said Warren.

"Sell them for less," said the bootlegger. "That way you can sell more."

Behind him the dawn began to come into the sky, the layers of pink, yellow, and blue like the colors of popsicles.

"So, next week," said the bootlegger, "bring a bigger truck."

They went back to Los Angeles, smelling the new rubber of the imitation Pirellis. Warren drove, and in the dark cab of the truck he said, "What's the best team in the majors?"

"The Yankees," said Jack.

"What team are the Stars associated with?"

"St. Louis," said Jack. "They're rebuilding."

"Nicole's pal is hitting .360," said Warren. "But I bet he can't hit a changeup."

Jack shrugged.

"Every now and then he reaches into his pocket and takes out a little bag. Just like the kind Nicole used to make."

Jack looked across the seat.

"I got other things on my mind than baseball," said Jack. "Jesus, these tires stink, don't they?"

The next time they rented two trucks, Warren driving one and Jack taking the other, and they met the bootlegger, his figure emerging from the dark shape of the tractor-trailer at the side of the road. The starry sky of the desert was behind him. He lit a cigarette, his face visible in the glow, his features thick and bloated, the skin almost blistered with excesses of one kind or another. He took the money, his face in the glow of the cigarette showing a contempt, as if each week's sum of money, while greater than the last, were somehow still insufficient. Warren stared at him, as though he were the physical embodiment of what had come into Warren's life and what, since he couldn't make it vanish, Warren so desperately wanted to ignore.

When they stopped at a diner to eat, Warren said to Jack, "He's still going good, isn't he? Three eighty. Three ninety."

"He went three for four last night," said Jack.

"Yeah?" said Warren. "Well, when you're going that good they start to throw at you, don't they?"

So, they went on doing business, meeting the tire bootlegger in the desert, the deals getting a little bigger each time. Jack went out and put a lawyer on retainer and seemed, as he drove a truck into the desert, like a man who has made a will and whose worldly affairs are in order. When they met the tire bootlegger, Jack watched him carefully, the man's face almost purple in the dim light of evening, his enlarged eye slick. The bootlegger spoke about bringing more money for more tires, although he seemed fatigued and a little sad. He showed up drunk sometimes.

"Warren," said Jack one day, "I got to tell you something. I think we should get out of the tire business."

"Why?" said Warren.

"That guy is getting ready to kill us both."

Warren looked up from a pile of brochures for new cars he had spread out on the table in front of him.

"I guess that's right, isn't it?" said Warren.

"Well," said Jack. "I'm glad you can see things clearly."

"Uh-huh," said Warren.

"What are you going to do now?" asked Jack.

"I'm going to buy one of these new cars," said Warren. "I bet Nicole would like one, don't you think?"

"Sure," said Jack. "Why wouldn't she like a new car?"

*   *   *

Warren picked out a convertible, a cream-colored Buick with cream-colored seats and a white top, at a dealership on Sunset. It had chrome along the sides, and it had skirts over the rear wheels. It was not quite white so much as a pale lemon, like yellow roses. Warren and Jack looked it over, sat on the leather seats, and carefully examined its Firestone tires. The car had wheels with chrome spokes, a radio, and a cream-colored steering wheel with a chrome band inside that worked the horn.

He paid cash for it, counting the bills out in the dealer's office, Warren's thumb coming down *thump thump thump* onto the top of a heavy oak desk. The dealer taped a temporary paper license plate to the car and passed over the keys, which were on a chain of small brass balls. Warren got behind the wheel and Jack sat in the passenger's seat and they drove into the traffic of Sunset Boulevard.

"How does it handle?" asked Jack.

"Like a dream," said Warren.

Warren drove up Laurel Canyon to Mulholland, and there, with the valley in the distance, he stopped, put the car in first gear, and then raced the engine and popped the clutch: the Buick took off in a stench and a black cloud of burning rubber, and with a shriek, too. Warren kept the accelerator down, speed-shifting through the gears, the tires chirping a little each time. At each shift, Warren said, "A ball player. A damn baseball player!" Then he slowed down and finally stopped and put his head on the steering wheel and said, "OK. It's broken in. Let's go."

Then Warren dropped Jack off and drove home, parking the car in the front yard.

* * *

The Stars were playing a night game, and even though Fulsome usually didn't like to spend time with Nicole before he played ("It might take the edge off, you know"), he still had spent the afternoon in that room above Hollywood Boulevard, where Nicole left him sleeping for an hour before he got up and went to the park. Nicole walked down Hollywood Boulevard, under the marquees, her languid gait a reflection of being a little dreamy, but through it all she could feel the first stirrings of . . . well, she didn't know what to call it, aside from the knowledge that things could not go on like this forever.

So, when she came up Laurel Canyon, her head down, still remembering the sight of her skin and Fulsome's in the mirror on the inside of the closet door, she was almost disoriented, or in that pleasant state of memory mixed with desire and apprehension, too, over how little time she and Fulsome had left. She was thinking about the dust in the room, the heat of the sheets, the taste of sweaty skin, and the occasional scratch of the shade against the window frame.

The Buick was in the yard. It was parked under the eucalyptus trees, the yellow machine streaked with chrome, its tires dark and shiny with a thin strip of whitewall, and in the exact center of each a chrome hub with chrome spokes. The convertible top was cream-colored, although now it was folded away so the leather seats could be seen. They were large and comfortable, the leather tucked into segments by fine stitching. The Buick sat in the yard, the chrome bright in the diffused sunlight that filtered through the trees.

Warren came out on the porch.

Nicole made a gesture over her shoulder, toward the car.

"What's that?" she asked.

She kept on looking into Warren's eyes, as though this moment could be made easier or better if she could just look deeply enough into the man who stood opposite her.

"It's yours," he said. "I hope you like it."

He walked over and opened the door.

Nicole got in behind the wheel. The leather seats were fragrant and comfortable, and the steering wheel seemed substantial. There was a large rear-view mirror, and the top of the windshield was heavy chrome with two handles that worked as levers to hold the top down. Nicole smelled the eucalyptus and thought of that room, of the image of bare skin pressed together and of her own compulsion to keep going back to it, the afternoons and evenings somehow not making her life fuller but instead bringing her an unbearable emptiness. So, now, she looked at Warren, and then she put her head down and burst into tears.

"What is it, Nicky?" said Warren. "Jesus Christ, what is it?"

She went on crying, smelling the eucalyptus. Warren came around and got in the other side, sliding across the seat and sitting next to her. He put his hand out and touched her back, feeling the heaving of it. Nicole said, "It's such a beautiful car.

It's just so beautiful." So she sat there, crying, not saying a word aside from, "It's a beautiful car."

Warren stood and gazed at the hillside, amazed that he could ever have been so stupid and convinced now, too, that the problem wasn't with the illusion but with the scale of it.

"I don't have to drive it now, do I?" asked Nicole.

Warren shook his head.

"No," he said. "Maybe some other time."

The Buick sat in the yard, getting dusty. After a couple of weeks Warren went out in the morning and hosed the car down, not using a bucket and soap and a chamois for the chrome but just standing out there, with the nozzle turned to a harsh, hard spray.

* * *

Fulsome received word about nine o'clock one morning that he was being sent up to the majors. He was still asleep in the room he rented in the house of a socialist couple who had decorated the walls, even around Fulsome's bed, with posters of Stalin and Lenin and of muscular men holding a hammer and a sickle. The socialists didn't eat meat, wore rubber shoes, and left pamphlets, which were written with phrases like "the jackboot of oppression," "the octopus of the ruling class," and "the lackey dogs" for Fulsome to read. One of the couple, the woman, knocked on his door and said, "Mr. Fulsome. There's a phone call for you."

Fulsome spoke for about sixty seconds and then came back into the room and took from the closet the bag he had brought to Los Angeles, and then he began to pack, putting into it the bone that he used to smooth down the surface of his bats, his baseball almanac, his one brown suit and bottle-green tie and wingtip shoes, his cleats, his glove, and the amulets Nicole had made for him, the whiff of the eucalyptus in them scenting his clothes so much that later, when he opened his suitcase on the train to St. Louis, he smelled it and thought about those afternoons in the Palace. But in the socialists' house in Hollywood, he sat on the bed and reached over to the nightstand, where there was the book Nicole had given him (*Three Hundred and*

Twenty-Five Objects in Dreams Explained). He sat at the edge, holding it, and realizing, too, that he was going to have to let Nicole know he was leaving. He took a piece of paper he had picked up in a hotel in Sacramento and a stub of pencil he used to keep score, and wrote, "Nicky, I guess I will be gone when you receive this . . . ," but then he stopped and looked at the note and threw it away, before picking up the book and walking down Santa Monica toward Barney's Beanery.

It was one of those late summer days in California which begin with fog that burns off about noon or so to reveal a sky the color of gray fox. But as he went, holding the book, the fog hadn't burned off yet, and he walked through it, the landscape around him revealed in shades of gray and pale white. Through the hazy light he saw the Beanery.

Warren and Nicole were inside, having lunch, Warren talking on the phone which was on a cord long enough so Warren and Nicole could sit in one of the booths opposite the bar. Warren was trying to talk his way into an editing room. The editor Warren was talking to said he wasn't going to go to work that day, and he described his symptoms, which seemed to be a combination of astrology and salmonella.

Nicole went into the bathroom.

Jack sat at the bar, reading a catalogue of electronic equipment. Every now and then he underlined a price that interested him.

Fulsome came in, carrying the book and walking directly up to the booth where Warren sat. Warren stared at the trim man, medium-sized and fit, who already from a distance seemed to be sizing him up.

"Well," said Warren into the mouthpiece. "I'm sorry you're under the weather. Capricorn is always tough. Talk to you later."

Warren hung up.

Fulsome stood in the cloud of cigarette smoke that hung in the air. Then he stepped back, obviously not wanting to break training. Jack went on reading.

Warren said to Fulsome, "What are you doing here?"

Fulsome looked down the bar, where a member of the Hell's

Angels was reading the *Racing Form* and writing notes in the margins in letters that looked as if they had been made with matchsticks.

"I got sent up," said Fulsome. "I came to tell Nicky."

"*Nicky*," said Warren. "You hear that, Jack? He says *Nicky*. He comes right in here and begins to talk that way."

"Listen," said Fulsome. "I didn't come here to make you feel bad. I came to say good-bye. Maybe that's best."

Warren looked back at Fulsome now.

"Jesus, what an asshole," he said.

Fulsome shrugged. "Where's Nicole?" he asked.

Warren got up and walked into the gray-green shadows at the end of the bar where there was a hall that led to the bathrooms. Warren knocked on one of the doors and said, "Nicole. There's someone here to see you."

Nicole came out. She was wearing a blue dress, and her hair had just been brushed so it was glossy. She walked right up to Fulsome and said, "So, you're going."

"That's right," he said. "On the two o'clock train. You want to see the ticket?"

Warren came up now, too. "Why don't you get out of here?" he said.

"I wanted to thank you for everything," Fulsome said to Nicole.

Nicole closed her eyes. "You want to thank me?" she said.

"Get out of here," said Warren.

Fulsome ignored him, keeping his eyes on Nicole.

"You didn't have to thank me," she said. "You could have said a lot of things, but you didn't have to say that."

She went on shaking her head. Then she looked up at Fulsome, her eyes focused in the center of his forehead, as though she were looking right through him.

"Tell me," she said, her voice trembling now, "what was it you wanted to thank me for?"

"You know," Fulsome said.

"The amulets?" she said. "Do you think they brought you luck?"

"It wasn't the amulets," he said.

"Well, then what was it?"

"You know," he said. "The room. It kept me calm."

"Did it?" she said. "And you want to thank me?"

"I knew you'd understand," said Fulsome.

"Oh, God," she said. She shook her head and swallowed. "Oh, God, oh, God."

"What did he say?" asked Jack.

"He thanked her," said Warren, swallowing now, putting a hand to his head. Then he sat down, his elbows on the bar, head down over a newspaper opened to the sports section. There were some box scores and a black and white photograph of a baseball player sliding into home plate, one foot tucked under the other knee, a hand in the air, a mist of dust trailing behind him. Warren glanced at it and then closed his eyes, and said to Nicole and Fulsome, "Go on. Go on. Go over to one of those booths so you can talk if you want. Go on."

Nicole and Fulsome walked over to a booth upholstered in red imitation leather. They sat down opposite each other, as though a careful, physical geometry would make everything clearer, easier. Fulsome glanced up at the clock to see how much time there was. Nicole said, "You didn't have to thank me."

Fulsome shrugged. Then he pushed the book, *Three Hundred and Twenty-Five Objects in Dreams Explained*, across the table. He had a magazine with him, too, a *Cosmopolitan,* and he pushed that across the table. There was an article in it entitled "How to Get Over Being Dumped."

"Maybe that will help," said Fulsome.

Nicole glanced from the magazine to him and said, "I think you should go now."

He looked around the room, his eyes lingering over the cigarette smoke.

"It's stuffy in here anyway," he said.

"Yes, I guess it is," she said.

"Well, I'll be seeing you."

He turned to go, but as he did, she said, "Wait."

"What do you want?" he asked.

"I want to ask you something."

"Sure," he said. "Shoot."

"Don't you remember the room, the noise from the street? Don't you remember any of that?"

"Not so much," he said. "I got other things on my mind."

Then he turned and walked out the door, into that almost white fog. His footsteps were loud in the room and on the sidewalk outside.

After a while Nicole put her hand out and touched the book, flipping from one end to the other as she looked up "Apple Trees," "Automobiles," "Green Snakes," "Laundry on a Line," "Moving Clouds," "Bathtubs Filling with Water," "Baseballs." She opened it now and read, "To dream of empty rooms, particularly hotel rooms, indicates problems in breathing and difficulty in the heart."

Warren got up from his stool and came over, not taking Fulsome's seat but sliding in next to her, where she made room. She went on looking at the book, although she said, "Tell me, Warren, what are you going to do?"

"I'm going to make a movie," he said.

"About what?"

"About baseball," he said.

"Well," she said, "I hope you have better luck than I did. I'll go up to the house and get my things."

"Wait a minute," he said.

"No," she said. "It's best."

She put a hand into her hair and fluffed it out.

"What have you been dreaming of recently, Warren?"

"Turtles," he said.

She reached out and flipped through the book and then read, "To dream of turtles, especially with black shells, means you are ready for anything." She closed the book. "Here. I guess you'd better keep this, too."

She shoved the book against him, making him get out so that she could go, walking out the door and into that same screen of white fog.

*   *   *

Years later Warren recognized the tire bootlegger (who had come up in the world) at a party for studio bankers and investors, the deep lines in the bootlegger's face, his overly tanned skin, looking, even though the man was in a tuxedo, just as they had in Phoenix, which is to say like evidence of murder and greed. They stared at each other and shook hands as only two people can who have come close to killing each other. The first movie, by the way, Warren ever made was *American Skyline*. It was a tremendous hit about a baseball player who made it to the big leagues. The baseball player leaves a woman behind and regrets it.

So Warren had worked hard. Everything had to do with having access to the right people, and Warren had a gift for guessing who was going to be able to do business or be in a position to help. It could be a little thing that tipped him off — the way someone dressed or spoke — just a small, seemingly unimportant thing that suggested an entire world of ambition, of unstoppable vitality. These details had to be separated from mere eccentricities, which, while seemingly important, were of no consequence whatsoever. He had heard once that James Dean rolled up his socks into tight little balls and put them under his mattress every night: this was the kind of thing not worth worrying about. He learned early that an independent producer was just someone who was out of a job. Even now Warren was amazed at the long hours, the worry, the sensation of forever being on a tightrope, a feeling that got worse or more pronounced as the stakes increased, such as the International Pictures's financing.

As he turned and swam back along the coast, imagining himself from up above, making that small V in the brown-green water, he wondered what had been behind those endless hours. An attraction to an illusion that had begun with the failure of a yellow Buick in a yard in Laurel Canyon? Whatever it was, it had begun almost innocently. What pleasures had he taken in producing visions of romance in which no one was stuck with that yellow Buick, that romantic lemon? He had been involved with many women, but it had all been . . . romantic. And when he came up to the moment when there was some greater risk, he had found himself simply working harder than before, the time required for his work leaving him almost solitary. He thought of the papers he had carted home, the piles of them everywhere, even in racks in the bathroom, the proposals, plans for studio organization, accountants' statements, the books . . . Well, he was convinced as he swam, still feeling the pressure of the sharks in the water, that the paper alone could fill a freight car. What had happened to it all? It was almost inconceivable to him the number of hours that had gone into the financial offerings, the negotiations, the access to capital, the changes brought about by the international nature of the business, the covering up of the occasional big mistake, the endless partial alignments with other people.

There was something else that seemed inconceivable to him as well. He had been busy. He had made money. There had been a number of women. The inconceivable thing was that in the hard work, in that pulling back from the brink of something more than the romantic, in his own secret belief that he wasn't quite good enough (like that Buick sitting in the yard), he had slipped into making a sacrifice. Only now was he beginning to understand the scale of it. And the substance, too. The sacrifice came in the hard work, in the desire to know exactly how far — and not one inch beyond this point — he could trust someone else. Well, wasn't love one of those things you had to discard when the pressure was way up there? He hadn't even made this decision; it seemed as though it had simply happened, or that matters had somehow taken their own course. He went on swimming, thinking about the smell of eucalyptus and that beautiful, worthless Buick.

Recently he had been dreaming of creatures with dark shells. He saw them swimming through the green depths, their eyes small, about as large as a grape, opaque yet certain. He had never felt so incomplete as when he woke after one of these dreams and sat at the side of his bed, raising a hand, gesturing. What, exactly, was he trying to say? Certainly he wanted to convey something deeper than just loneliness . . .

In recent months he had been looking for the critical, central thing that was simply abandoning him, that left him sitting at the side of the bed with his hands shaking. He invited those people from "flat" Hollywood to his house, since their desperation always seemed to contain some clue. What had been lost between then and now? The intimate promise of youth? So the cause of his exasperation had been right there, at the tips of his fingers. He had stood up to it, smiled, keeping his hands together or clasped behind his back so no one could see them. Or keeping his doubts out of his voice when he spoke to New York. What the hell did his doubts, his furious certainty that he had missed something, have to do with the price of stock anyway?

He had been standing on the balcony as the guests arrived at his party. Marta had walked out of the shadows, her head turning toward the house, glancing up at him. Even from a distance he could tell she was standing up to something, too. She trembled with it, her broad, slender shoulders square, her metal-colored hair taking the light, her eyes fixed on Warren's. He had stood there, realizing he had simply been waiting for the young woman who stood, half in the light, half in the shadows, at once defiant and seeming to hover over an abyss. So he had looked at her, only able to say, "Who's that?" And later, when she had sat in his car, her hand to her nose, the blood running between her fingers, he had been polite, not wanting to embarrass her.

Now, he came out of the ocean and stood, with the towel wrapped around his shoulders, the water running down his legs. He could see the horizon, the blue sky and the blue water meeting at an invisible point. Then he got into the car and drove home. The telephone was ringing, and he sat down on his bed and stared at it. He knew it was New York. It stopped and rang and stopped and rang, and when it had stopped for good, he picked up the receiver and dialed a number, and while he looked at the colors of the Monet, the flowers in the field so bright as to suggest secret delights and the intricacy of life at work, he spoke to a man who worked for him. "Hi, Jake, it's Warren. Say, what was the name of the guy who sold that Mercedes to Jackie Carson? Well, can you find out? No. I mean right away."

He stood and went to the bookshelf at the end of the room, and there he removed the copy of *Three Hundred and Twenty-Five Objects in Dreams Explained.*

The phone rang again, and after Warren answered it he said, "Nicky White. On Highland. Yeah. I got it. No, I'm not going to buy a car. Not exactly. I got an old one to sell."

BOOK
3

The Scandal Sheet

Scandal Sheet Classifieds. They get action.

CLASSIFIEDS

WANT NICE LEGS AND HIPS? PERFECT BREASTS? Try Zolar's Perfect Cream. It improves tone, slenderizes and firms, applicator included, cellulite reducer at no extra charge. Box 2897, Department Y, Reseda, CA 91337.

NAVAHO CLAIRVOYANT, romance, financial matters a specialty, including jewelry appraisal. Rings, bracelets not kept more than an hour! Confidential. The Great Spirit Wants You to Be Rich. 897-8791, Castiac, anytime. All major credit cards.

ORGASM POWER, secret formula from the ancients, Cleopatra, Jean Harlow, Marilyn Monroe . . . why not you? Twenty capsules, $39.99. Box 3198, Downey, CA 91346.

ENERGY TO GET THAT PART, proven formula, memory booster, skin with that youthful glow. Also, Diplomas from Eastern Schools, Harvard, Columbia, Yale in *Latin,* 3419 Reseda Blvd, Reseda, CA 91335.

COSSACK PSYCHIC, 349-3981, noontime, Silverlake.

HOW TO MAKE MONEY OUT OF THE BIG EARTHQUAKE, foolproof, easy, can be done at home in spare time, small capital investment, 569-0982, Burbank.

SECRETS OF THE STARS' BURIALS, lingerie, photographs, last requests, stuffed animals. Send $5.00 to No Secrets, Box 691,

North Hollywood Station, CA 90034. Maps to Graves, $5.00. Updated yearly.

UNHAPPY WITH PLASTIC SURGERY RESULTS? J. T. Appleman, Esq. Free consultation. Malpractice a specialty. 13478 Wilshire, L.A. 90087, 609-3425.

GOOD LUCK DOUCHES, all occasions, all flavors, Spirit Sprays, Intimate Imports, Box 4589, West L.A., CA 90045.

WRANGLER, steady, Canoga, evenings, 897-8790.

JACK HAWK'S AROUND TOWN, *Scandal a la Mode.*

At a party given in Malibu, **Sharon Dyer,** the most beautiful woman in the world, was seen murmuring sweet nothings into the ear of **Warren Hodges,** her host and the town's most eligible bachelor. Is this, as they say, the beginning of an item . . . ?

OBITUARIES

Kelly Petersen, child star in 30s, of accidental overdose of barbiturates, in Downey.

Douglas Carey, swashbuckler in pirate pictures, including *Captain Plank* and *Ghost of Red Beard,* of leukemia, in Las Vegas, where he had been working as a bartender.

Jack North, screenwriter, drowned, in Laguna.

The Rose Bushes

VICTOR SHAW SAT in his apartment, looking out the window. He used to look through the dusty glass because he was bored, although now he did so because he was alert. Yeah, well, there was a big difference between having possibilities and being just another dummy with a grudge. He had a cup of coffee which was cooling as he held it by the tips of his fingers. Outside, a woman rolled her shopping cart up the street.

Victor thought about the trip back to L.A. from the party at Malibu. Nicky had started talking business right off the bat. It was as though the guy could smell money or something. He looked over at Victor and said, "Listen, I can get you, like, a BMW, full air, leather seats (you ever smelled real leather . . . there's nothing like it, drives the ladies nuts), tinted glass, whitewalls, full documentation. Make me an offer."

Marta had sat in the back seat. She didn't say much. Victor had the money they had picked up in the pocket of his coat: he couldn't resist. It seemed as though he had been waiting for this moment for years, from the minute his mother had made him put back that first Twinkie. He took out the bills and showed them to Nicky.

"Well, well," said Nicky. "Well, well. Where did that come from?"

"The juice business," said Victor. "The first thing you do in the juice business is put the squeeze on."

"Of course," said Nicky. "That's right. You got to get vitamins. You don't want to get heart disease, do you?"

"No," said Victor.

"Well, let me tell you, one of the best ways to stay healthy is to drive the right car," said Nicky. "You simply got to have the right machinery. Now, you don't want just any old thing. What you're in the market for is a *vehicle*. You understand my meaning? Am I communicating? Maybe BMW isn't right. Maybe Jaguar is more the right style."

"Maybe," said Victor.

Goddamn it. He shouldn't have shown the money. How stupid could he get? Marta was still sitting in the back, just staring out the window. Jesus, he took her to a party, didn't he? Did she realize how many women in town would give anything, a tit, for Christ's sake, to meet Warren Hodges? And there he was, in the flesh, and interested, too. Victor knew about this kind of thing. He was sure. All he really wanted was to get back to town so he and Marta could have a talk. That was the important thing.

They pulled up in front of Nicky's apartment house. It was late, and everything was misty. There weren't many cars out, and all the lights seemed like spheres made of bits of mist. They looked beautiful tonight, although before, Victor had always shivered a little when he saw lights in the mist, as though someone had walked over his grave.

"When you're talking about a British car, what you are talking about is not simply an object."

"No?" said Victor. He wished Marta would say something instead of looking out the window like that.

"No," said Nicky. "What you are talking about is generations of craftsmanship. Now, you look at the steering wheel of a Jaguar. Put everything else aside. Forget the body work, the engine, the transmission. Let's talk just about the steering wheel. You see how it's made out of wood. Now what kind of wood is that?"

"I don't know," said Victor.

"Oak," said Marta.

"That's right," said Nicky. "And it's been fabricated. You hear the word? *Fabricated*."

Victor got out of the car and held back the seat for Marta to get out.

"This is it," he said. "Come on."

"I'm not done yet," said Nicky.

"Maybe tomorrow," said Victor. Marta and I have got to take a little drive up to her car."

"Well, sure," said Nicky. "You know where to find me."

* * *

Victor's car was parked at the curb. It was covered with moisture from the fog, and everything about it seemed a little irritating somehow, especially when Victor felt the money in his pocket. Well, maybe a Jaguar was the right thing after all. You know, you buy a nice green one and a tweedy coat and a pair of leather gloves to drive it. Makes you feel like you're listed in *Debrett's Peerage*. Well, maybe not. All the British aristocrats were epileptics or something, weren't they?

Marta got in and sat on the right side. Still not saying anything aside from that one word. How the hell did she know it was made out of oak? Maybe it was cherry or maple. Didn't maples grow in England?

Victor started the engine and made a U-turn in the middle of the street, thinking, Careful. What if you get stopped out here? How are you going to explain the damn money?

He looked across the seat.

"Looks like you and Hodges were doing OK," said Victor.

Marta shook her head.

"No," she said.

"What do you mean?" said Victor. "I've got eyes, don't I?"

Marta glanced across the seat. Only the windshield wiper on Victor's side of the car worked, and on the glass in front of her the rivulets of water cast shadows which lay across her face in the light from the yellow street lamps. It gave her the momentary appearance of a woman, behind a window covered with rain, who is waiting for someone. This mien didn't last long — just a mixture of anticipation or desire blended with fatigue, and then, as quickly as the car moved into a shadow, she seemed to have pushed a thought out of her mind as she faced Victor.

"I guess so," she said.

"Guess so?" said Victor, pointing a finger at his eyes. "What do you think these are?" He waited for a moment for this obvious proof to sink in. Then he said, "The guy's interested. I can tell."

She shrugged. "So what?"

Victor shook his head. They were going down Santa Monica now, the two shiny edges of the train tracks diminishing in the distance, where they finally disappeared into the damp red and golden-green clutter of stoplights and neon signs for liquor stores and dry cleaners.

"Do I have to lead you by the hand?" he asked.

"No," she said.

She looked over again, alert now.

"Well, looks like we're making progress," said Victor. "You could tell he was interested, too, couldn't you? I knew it. There's one thing about Victor Shaw. He knows what's in the wind."

"I don't think he was so interested," said Marta.

"He took you for a drive," said Victor. "You think he was doing that because he's such a nice guy? Well, let me tell you, when a guy does that, he's got only one thing on his mind."

"I just want to go home," said Marta. "I want to sleep."

Sleep. Jesus. Wouldn't it be nice to do that? But there were too many things to think about. Like just for instance there was the matter of dropping Marta off at her car. Had the guy in the kitchen been found yet, and if so, was anybody watching the street? So, what would be better, dropping Marta off and letting her walk up to her car, or would that attract attention, too? Sleep. Tell me another.

"We got to come to an understanding," said Victor.

"Do we?" said Marta.

"You better believe it," said Victor. "That is, unless you want to go walking around with, you know, handcuffs. You know they got the gas chamber back in business in this state? Good thing, too, if you ask me."

Marta looked out the window.

"I want to get back to my car," she said.

"Listen," said Victor. "Now, this Hodges guy is going to call you up. He's probably pretty good over the telephone." Victor thought of the phone in his own apartment, how the presence of the thing made the place seem all the more quiet, if only because it hardly ever rang, or when it did it was a wrong number. Well, maybe he was going to be able to change that. "So, when he calls, what are you going to do?"

"I don't know," she said. "Anyway, he's not going to call."

"I thought we had that settled," said Victor. "You know what? I am going to lose my patience with you."

Marta just looked across the seat.

"Now, when he calls, everything's going to be fine. You'll get along fine. Except after a while you're going to need money. You know, like you got problems. The rent's due and you spent the money. Happens all the time. For Christ's sake, don't let him *buy* anything for you. Not unless you can sell it easy. Cash is the best. You cut me in and everything will be fine."

She sat there, nodding.

"Well?" he asked. "Do you understand me?"

"Yes," she said. "Perfectly."

"If you play this right," he said, "there's real money in it."

"Real money," she said.

"You're not just tooting," he said, but then he glanced over and looked at her face.

"Remember," he said. "No presents like silk blouses or clothes or dresses."

She closed her eyes and sat there. They were moving up toward Ferndale, going out along Franklin. They passed the mouth of Beechwood Canyon, and from the intersection of Beechwood and Franklin she could almost, but not quite, see her mother's house.

"Listen," said Victor. "What were you doing up there anyway?"

"Where?" said Marta.

"At the house where you killed that guy," said Victor. "What were you doing up there?"

"Picking up something for my boss," she said.

"What?"

"Some film," she said.

Hot stuff, too, thought Victor. I'll bet it was. Sure would like to get a look. But then he thought of what it would be like to go into the house. Maybe he should send Marta, but that didn't seem too smart. He had another problem.

"What's your story?" he said.

She stared through the windshield.

"I mean, when your boss asks you what the hell happened you got to have something to say, right? Or you know what? They're going to be dropping gas pellets under your seat."

Victor put a finger inside his cheek and popped it out twice to make the sound of a pellet falling into some liquid. It made a *pwoop pwoop* that was very realistic.

"I don't think he's that interested," said Marta.

"Who? Your boss?"

"No," said Marta. "Warren."

"Warren," he said. "Listen to that. *Warren.*" The streets were wet and shiny, like a new tire. There was an odor of wet pavement, a sandy, almost acrid scent that always reminded Victor of those times when he came home late.

"Look, nature worked things out so that Warren's got, like, his own agenda," said Victor. "What you got to worry about is your boss. What do you tell him?"

Marta bit her lip now.

"I hope he doesn't come around," she said.

"Warren Hodges? What?" said Victor. "And miss a million-dollar deal? Grow up."

Victor stopped at a red light. There were apartment houses on either side of the car, the two- and three-story buildings simply stretching away into the distance delineated by those diminishing yellow globular streetlights: it was the loneliest landscape that Victor could possibly imagine. Not a light on anyplace. The best thing, he thought, is that maybe you could climb in through a window and go through everyone's junk while they were asleep. Find all kinds of things.

"Here's what you say to your boss," said Victor. "You tell him you went up there and knocked on the door and no one answered."

Marta sighed now and put her head in one hand.

"You got that?" said Victor. "No one answered."

"Oh, God," said Marta.

"Snap out of it," said Victor. "Then you went out to a party."

Marta swallowed and nodded.

"All right?" said Victor.

"All right," she said. "What was that money I picked up?"

"That?" said Victor. "Oh, that. Some guy owed me some money."

They stopped at the corner of Earl Graves's street.

"Your car's up there," said Victor. He pointed down the street, through the darkness that was marked at regular intervals by purplish street lamps. Victor wished the city of Los Angeles would get itself straightened out on the color of the streetlights. Yellowish some places. Purplish others. What the hell were you supposed to make of that? Street looked quiet, though. Victor was beginning to feel that he could sense things that had happened, as though they had left a whiff of some turmoil in the air, as distinct as a chalk mark on the sidewalk where a body had been. He stared up the street. No, the place didn't have the atmosphere that was left behind after a bunch of cop cars and an ambulance had been around. He couldn't see Earl Graves's house, but he was certain there was no yellow CRIME SCENE ribbon stretched across the front yard. Well, that was something.

Before Marta got out of the car, he reached over and took her by the forearm.

"Listen," he said. "I live right across the street from you."

Marta swallowed.

"I've been watching for a while. And you know something? I'm going to be right there, keeping an eye on you."

"I'm tired," she said. "I'm just real tired."

"Sure," he said. "Go home. Get your beauty sleep."

Marta got out and started walking, her figure disappearing into the shadow under a tree, the dark tracery of its limbs passing over her face and shoulders.

"Pssst. Hey," said Victor.

She stopped and looked back.

"Hey," said Victor. "Hey. How about a little peck good night?"

She shook her head.

"No," she said. She shook her head again. "No."

Better not push too hard. You got to keep everything cool.

"OK," said Victor. "No hard feelings."

Oh, yeah, sure, thought Victor. No hard feelings. Oh, sure. Maybe some other time.

Then he went down the street and turned around and started to drive back toward Western. After a while he saw lights in the rear-view mirror, and he knew Marta was coming home, too.

*   *   *

So now he sat and looked out the window of his apartment, the dust on the glass showing the pattern of the rivulets of rain that had been on the window. Well, there was a lot of dust in that Los Angeles air, and everyone knew it was unhealthy. Sometimes the air looked good, though, all golden and shimmering, like on a June morning after the fog burned off, or better yet, on those days in September when the air was clear even out in the valley. Victor remembered those times when he was just a kid, five or six years old, when he and his mother had gone out to the end of the valley and picked oranges, the things as big, or so it seemed in retrospect, as bowling balls. Victor could still remember the big juicy sacs breaking in his mouth. It was one of the few times Victor remembered being really full. On the way home his mother had bought him a Twinkie. He had started crying because he was so happy.

A dark blue car stopped in front of Victor's apartment house. If nothing else, Victor was sure the car had been made in Europe, the word "fabricated" coming into his mind with a kind of lightness, like a bubble rising from the bottom of a carbonated drink. The car was compact, low, and it pulled up to the curb with a murmur, not to mention that the door opened with the sudden cracking sound of an air lock being broken. Warren Hodges got out of the car and walked up the sidewalk, not glancing at the brown grass that grew on either side of it or at the row of dead rosebushes planted at the property line, with their tags from the nursery, the price marked down, still attached to the dead limbs.

It took a moment for Warren to find the right door, and when he knocked, Victor thought, Well, well. What is he doing here?

Then he thought, Sure. How could I have been so stupid. He's got to find out where she lives.

Victor hadn't shaved. He was wearing a pair of blue jeans and a T-shirt, and the remains of his breakfast, some scrambled eggs and a piece of toast and a glass of Tang, sat on the table in the living room. A cloud of smoke hung in an island about six feet off the floor, and the light from the windows came into the smoky room in slanting lines.

Warren knocked.

Let him wait a minute, thought Victor. Let him worry. Victor rubbed his hand across his face, hearing the *hush hush* of his hand against his beard. Warren knocked again, and then Victor got up and went to the door. He opened it and stood there opposite the tallish man.

"Are you selling something?" asked Victor. "Because if you are, you came to the wrong place."

"No," said Warren. "I'm not selling anything."

"Well?" said Victor. Jesus, look at the guy's jacket. I can tell you one thing, that jacket didn't come from the May Company. Victor kept his eyes on Warren, thinking, Should I make him pay for the address? Should I get him used to the idea that money is involved right from the beginning?

"Can I come in?" said Warren.

"Sure," Victor said. "If you're not selling anything. Because I want to keep that clear. I'm not interested in life insurance, burial stones, vitamins, any of that kind of stuff. I got all the subscriptions to magazines I need."

Warren came in and closed the door, giving it a firm shove.

"You're Victor, aren't you?" said Warren.

"Am I?" said Victor. ·

Warren looked him directly in the face.

"Yeah," he said. "You're Victor. You were at my house last night."

"Oh," said Victor. "Yeah. Sure. I remember. Is there something missing from your house? Jesus, there were some guys there last night . . . you know, they'd boost your stove if they could."

"No," said Warren. "My stove's still there."

"Glad to hear it," said Victor. "That's great."

Warren sighed now. Victor had the impression that Warren was taking the place in, not to mention that he seemed to be looking Victor over, too. Victor hadn't been sleeping too well and he'd had things on his mind, so he couldn't expect to be real quick, but even so he was certain he had seen that expression before. It took a minute, and bingo, yeah. It was like the look those tired guards at Soledad used to give him. Well, didn't that beat all.

"How did you find my address?" said Victor.

"Nicky White," said Warren.

"That goddamned Nicky," said Victor. "Always telling people where I am."

"Uh-huh," said Warren. "How much do you want for it?"

"For what?" said Victor.

"The address of the woman you brought to my house last night? Isn't it a matter of money?"

Victor nodded. And as he did, he stuck out his lower lip and his chin became pitted.

"Yeah," he said. He nodded again. "I guess that's right."

Warren looked back, not flinching, not even showing any expression at all, aside from one that seemed at the same time to be a little hard and a little friendly.

"A hundred?" asked Warren.

"Yeah," said Victor. "Sure. Make it a hundred."

Warren took a money clip out of his pants pocket and removed two new fifty-dollar bills, which he put down on the table. They were still folded, and each sat up on edge, like a matchbook.

"Across the street," said Victor. "Ground floor in the back. 1D."

Warren opened the door, letting a wedge of light into the room, which made the smoky island seem that much whiter. Warren said, "Thanks," and then went out, closing the door behind him and going up the sidewalk, which was cracked here and there as it ran between the brown grass and those dead rosebushes. That goddamned landlord, always looking for something cheap. Anyone could have told him those things were going to die.

Victor sat down and looked at the money. Then he picked it up and put it on the plate with the last yellow remains of his breakfast. You want to know what I think of your lousy hundred bucks? You want to know? There were some matches tucked under the cellophane of a cigarette box, and now he took them out and struck one, holding it to the edge of the bills, and as the yellow flame, shaped like a painter's brush, moved along the paper, a thread of smoke wavering into the air and rising into the smoke that was already in the room, Victor thought, It's going to cost you more'n a hunnert. More'n a hunnert, asshole.

After a few seconds nothing was left but a slender, darkened ash, the color almost like a negative of a photograph of a fifty-dollar bill, the surface having an almost discernible sheen and a fragility that suggested the wing of a butterfly. Then Victor thought, How did he know about the money part? I never mentioned it. And that look like a goddamned guard. Well, we'll settle that one up, too.

The refrigerator in the apartment was cheap, just like those dead rosebushes out front, and now it began to throb, the steady, insistent *uh uh uh* pressing into the room and meshing with the throb of Victor's headache. It seemed to him that the throb in his head was an echo of the throb of the icebox. Victor closed his eyes. He imagined the darkness he saw as like the depths of the earth, where the coal waited under hundreds of feet of rock. There were even little glints here and there, just little flashes in the dark pressure.

He started thinking about Frank. That goddamned kid. You could see he had an instinct for causing trouble. Victor sat there, thinking about Frank's mother, her legs in those fishnet stockings, her bleached hair, the red vest of her waitress's uniform, the scent of her cologne . . . or maybe it was an after-bath splash. Maybe Victor should go up to see her.

Victor looked out the window again, and as he did, a little

thrill of recognition ran through him. Maybe it's this way. Maybe the damn landlord wanted the rosebushes to die. Then everybody could see that the landlord had tried to do something. And he didn't have to look after the damn things, either, the dead bushes standing there like a monument to the landlord's good intentions.

Warren was inside for a long time, and then the two of them came out, Marta looking beautiful in the light, her skin pale. She was carrying a small suitcase. Then they got into his car. Just like clockwork.

Victor hadn't prayed in years, but he felt the impulse to do it now. He guessed what he'd pray for was the thing most people wanted: a little more time. He wondered what was the best way to put it. As he sat there, he could almost feel time, like some clear, slow-moving stuff, streaming through his hands. Then he got up and thought, Maybe that kid will come home.

Spike

TAYLOR HAYDEN sat in a rented car in the parking lot of a Travelodge on Ventura Boulevard, out by the Market Basket. He was wearing a pair of driving gloves, and his hands lay neatly folded in his lap. The creases in his pants ran from the exact center of his kneecaps and swung out, away from his shins, until the point of the end of the cuff was suspended exactly over the middle of his brown shoes. The shoes had a nice shine. Hayden was thinking that somebody had to do something about inflation. Everything was getting so expensive. He didn't like spending the kind of money he had to for a pistol, a belly gun, nothing fancy, nothing to jam. Walnut grips on it. He got his guns from a Hawaiian who worked in a gun factory. Each part smuggled out before it was ever stamped with an identifying number.

The Hawaiian had big plans. He was going to start a band, all Hawaiian — steel guitar, drums, maybe even a little brass. He was overweight, and Hayden didn't like to see him hitching up his blue jeans over the roll of fat at his waist. Didn't the guy know the link between high-fat diets and heart disease and cancer?

The Hawaiian pulled into the parking lot, too, and went up to a room at the end of the Travelodge. He was carrying an aluminum suitcase, like the kind you'd keep good camera equipment in. Overweight. Just like always.

Inside the room there was a smell, a particular odor Taylor thought came from the hundreds of times that air filled with cigarette smoke had been run through an air conditioner. It was the smell that Taylor most associated with what he did, as though killing could be distilled down to the rank odor of the Travelodge motel room. From Taylor's point of view the anonymous coupling of the people who rented a place like this for an hour, the cigarettes they smoked, the smell of the sheets, the bourbon on their breath, the small Jack Daniel's or Old Grand Dad bottles that were left behind, only half finished, all added to the atmosphere of buying a gun. The things lay there on the gray foam inside the case, three of them, all belly guns, all newly blued, like water seen on a moonlit night, the grips a little redolent of newly worked wood, and, of course, the barrels and the cylinders had the slightly intoxicating odor of milling oil.

Hayden still had his driving gloves on.

"You need to lose weight," he said.

The Hawaiian laughed.

"You always say that, Spike," said the Hawaiian.

Hayden looked down at the pistols.

"You should come out with me. I know a place on Sepulveda that marinates ribs for two weeks. They come with a side order of pineapple. Real pineapple," said the Hawaiian.

"Uh-huh," said Hayden. "Don't call me that."

"Don't call you what?"

"Spike," said Hayden.

Hayden passed over the money, the bills new and crisp. They weren't in an envelope or anything at all. Hayden was already thinking he'd burn the pants the money had been in, just in case anyone ever did some lab crap and tried to prove the money had been in his pocket. Then he picked up one of the pistols, broke it, sighted through the barrel, dry-fired it a couple of times with a dummy .38 in the chamber to protect the pin, and put it in a baggie. Then he put the baggie in his jacket pocket.

"You should lose some weight," he said.

Taylor got into his car and put the gun in the glove box, just like the rest of the armed population of L.A. He went through the Cahuenga Pass and down to Santa Monica. From there he went up to Western and turned right. The street he was looking for was on the right, and he turned into it, driving slowly, gliding by the building with the speed of the shadow of a bird, a hawk, say, that is working over a field. It was too bad about the apartment being in the front. He didn't like that so much. Then he shrugged and thought, Have to see what kind of hours the asshole keeps. That's the first thing. Bet he's overweight, too. Low IQ. Probably can't even add two and two.

A Small Town
on the Coast

A S THE CAR DROVE along the coast, Marta thought about
how much money Victor wanted. He hadn't come right out
and said ten thousand or twenty thousand or anything like that.
He had only said that he guessed Marta would be able to know
what she could get. She looked over at Warren.

She shook her head now.

What would it do to me to get money out of him? What
would it feel like the first time he gave me a check or some cash,
bundles, both of us avoiding each other's eyes but all the while
knowing that one of us or maybe even both of us were getting
ready to go right through the floor? What would I say, Thanks
for the wad?

The ocean was on the left-hand side of the car, the sea and
the sky appearing to meet in the distance as though the horizon
was a taut wire. Well, what would it do to us? Then she thought
about that house in Ferndale, and about the man who had fallen
toward her, and the sound that had filled that kitchen, the steady
tip tip tip as something dripped onto the linoleum floor. As she
stared at the horizon, she tried to think things over clearly.

Hasn't enough happened to me already without having to ask
for money? Didn't being in that kitchen with that man leave me
feeling that I had been at the center of some kind of explosion,
and that all the parts that had been me were now streaking
outward, just particles that seemed to be moving through dark
space, like shooting stars? Hasn't that been enough? I wish I
could reach out and grab one of those flecks, or find some way
of pulling myself back together. Then I'd know what was right

and what was wrong, just the way I used to. Maybe that's the trouble with having killed someone: maybe you don't know about right and wrong so much anymore.

She put her hand on the seat, moving it over toward Warren's about a quarter of an inch, somehow hoping he'd notice and put his hand on hers. He smiled. She wanted to grab the keys from the car, or make Warren pull over, and then they could walk up in the tall grass at the side of the road where no one could see, and then maybe that way she'd begin to find a way of reaching out for that first bit that was streaking away.

At first she thought Victor might want as much as twenty thousand . . . maybe even more than that. She wished that Victor had been more specific, since that way she could say, all right, the problem is just a twenty-five-thousand-dollar problem, but somehow she suspected it was more than something that had a number on it. But maybe it would be worth it just to buy time. That's all you can ever buy anyway, isn't it?

The car started to make a funny smell. For a moment the sensation of being uncertain of herself, the realization that a choice was coming, and the memory of that house in Ferndale all seemed to coalesce into the stink that came from the engine.

"What's that smell?" she asked.

"I don't know," said Warren.

They were on the coast highway, at least a hundred miles south of San Francisco. The car was new, and for a while Warren had thought that the burning smell was from something that had been sprayed onto the engine block to keep it from rusting when it was shipped across the Atlantic. There was nothing on the dashboard to tell him what was wrong: everything there, all the gauges, seemed about right, although he didn't really know. Even then he was thinking about her lips, the tip of her tongue as she had lifted that red, cinnamon-scented candy toward her mouth.

On the left-hand side of the road there was a cliff, a straight drop to the ocean: it seemed as though the tops of the trees on the lower part of the slope were at the base of those above. In the ocean, rocks stuck out of the water, the waves breaking around them into the lacy pattern of foam. Warren kept hoping the odor in the car was only some protective coating that was burning off.

"I wish we knew what that stink was," said Marta.

"Maybe it will go away," said Warren. "Do you mind?"

"No," she said. "Just so long as it doesn't . . . you know, mean anything."

"Maybe it will stop," said Warren. "Let's talk about something else."

"Have you ever made a movie about blackmail?" asked Marta.

"Offhand," he said, "I can't remember."

The coast now curved away to the right, and in the distance the brownish-green landscape combined with the air to suggest a haze. The fields at the side of the road were a combination of the sere and the fertile.

"*Midnight Passage,*" said Warren. "Yeah. That was a picture about blackmail. Greer McKinnon and Barry Ryan. An insurance investigator falls in love with a woman after he finds out she's been killing people. He starts embezzling for her. He gets blackmailed. He thinks that knowing she's a killer is proof against falling in love with her, but it isn't."

"What happens?" said Marta.

"He dies," said Warren. "But he takes a hell of a lot of people with him."

"Do you think things like that happen?" she asked.

"Sure," he said. "Half the business in Hollywood is blackmail, isn't it?"

"I wouldn't know," she said.

Warren shrugged.

"Well, maybe not half," he said. "Maybe it's three quarters."

"What's the other quarter?" said Marta.

"Usually the other quarter is a mistake. A lot of interesting pictures get made by mistake. You know, good movies get made while no one is keeping an eye out."

"I guess no one could blackmail you if you weren't afraid," said Marta.

"Well, in Hollywood a lot of people are afraid."

"I always thought you shouldn't be afraid," she said. "It

was dangerous to be afraid. If you were afraid, you did stupid things."

"Uh-huh," said Warren.

"But what happens if you get changed into something you don't want to be? Maybe that's worth being careful about," she said.

"Uh-huh," said Warren.

"Are you following me?" she asked.

"No," he said. "I'm worrying about that smell. I wish it would stop."

"Me too," said Marta.

"It's definitely something burning," said Warren.

Ten thousand. Maybe it would just be ten thousand.

Down below waves were washing up on small, impossibly isolated beaches.

"Tell me again, will you?" she said. "What's it like where we're going?"

"It's a lake," he said. "There's an island in the middle of it, and just the one cabin on the lake. No houses on the shore. I bought it a few years ago. You know, I kept thinking I'd get up there. But I haven't."

"Why?" she asked.

He shrugged and looked over at her.

"I got sidetracked," he said.

As they drove along the coast, Warren felt the cool moment when you have pushed that first yard into someplace that is unknown.

"No one in Hollywood ever gets what he really wants anyway," he said.

"No?"

"No," said Warren. "You know the story about George Bernard Shaw and Hollywood?"

Marta shook her head, still hoping about the ten thousand. She put her hand on the leather armrest of the door, feeling her palms sweat.

"There was a producer, a tough old guy who had made millions. At the end of his life he wanted to make a great movie. None of his usual stuff, but the real thing. So he says to an assistant, 'Who's the best playwright in the world?' The assistant scratches his head and says, 'Well, that's got to be George Bernard Shaw.' 'All right,' says the producer. 'Get me Shaw.' "

Marta let go of the armrest. Then she looked up the coast. "What happened?"

"Shaw comes to Hollywood," said Warren. "He gets together with the producer. His name was Nelson Barry. They talk every afternoon for about a month about this great movie they're going to make. At the end of the month, Shaw says, 'Mr. Barry, can I ask you a question?'

" 'Go ahead,' says Barry.

" 'Why is it that you always talk about art and I always talk about money?' "

"Did they ever make the movie?" asked Marta.

"No," said Warren. "It was just a dream."

The smell got worse.

"I wish I hadn't stopped smoking," she said.

"Why is that?" said Warren.

"I'd like a cigarette," she said. "I just feel like maybe I'd like one."

Warren looked at the gauges, and still there wasn't anything wrong. It was as though the car was running not with any noise, or with any discernible unevenness, but more with a lack of power that suggested pressure was being lost somewhere along the drive train, in the cylinders, the cam, the transmission or rear end.

"Maybe we should have stayed in Los Angeles," he said.

"No. That would have been the worst thing in the world."

"What's wrong with Los Angeles?" he asked.

"I don't know," she said. "The thing about L.A. is that it doesn't have enough time down there. You're there and you always feel it's running out on you."

Her hands were in her lap, but her fingers were shaking a little. He hadn't even touched her. When he had asked her to come, the two of them sitting in her apartment drinking the strong coffee she had made, she had thought it over for a couple of minutes.

"How long will we be gone?" she asked.

"I don't know," he said. "A week."

A week. Just one.

"That smell is getting worse," he said.

They came into Marston, a town of about five hundred people. In advance of it they saw a small sign, about two feet by one foot, that said, "Marston Pop. 549." At first there was nothing more to it than a few house trailers and isolated buildings, but then the town itself came into view. There was a gas station and a couple of stores, one for work clothes and the other for stationery, newspapers, and greeting cards. A beauty parlor and a coffee shop were across the street. There was a hardware store with some lawn mowers out front marked down as a special for the approach of fall. Beyond the gas station a road ran a hundred yards to a motel, which was not new and sat on the bluff that ran along the ocean.

So, at the end of the week, what will happen? Marta thought about going home to her apartment to wait for the slow, steady footsteps of Victor, who'd walk up to her door with the knowing smugness of a man who was certain he was finally onto a good thing. Well, maybe the thing to do is just to keep right on going without ever returning to Los Angeles. Marta thought about this for a moment, and as she did so, she imagined Victor going into the Hollywood police station and standing there at the desk, behind the glass, with a childlike seriousness, as though he were going to tattle on someone, the seriousness and sweet apprehension of revenge mixed with a fury she couldn't imagine, aside from her certainty that it was there. Oh, it was there all right.

Somehow she imagined that on the strength of Victor's expectations (not to mention the money she had picked up for him) he had gone out and bought some new clothes, a leather sport coat and a yellow tie and a blue shirt, the objects suggesting to Marta a kind of horror, as though she could see him dressed in the costume of malice made visible. She hoped he wouldn't be wearing anything new when he came up to her door, his shoes making that steady tapping on the sidewalk.

Warren pulled into a gas station and they sat in the car, the odor curling around them like some invisible feather boa. There was the slightest sound coming from under the hood, a moan and a little whir. Warren looked through the windshield at the place, which, even though there were a lot of parked cars around, nevertheless looked deserted. Then, inside the garage, he caught the movement of a man in a dark blue jump suit, his shape like that of a phantom.

"A yellow tie," said Marta.

"What?" said Warren.

"Pie in the sky," said Marta, blushing. "Maybe it's pie in the sky that this place can do anything for us."

"Well," said Warren. "You never can tell. I'll go take a look."

Warren got out and let the door swing shut, the *clump* of it reminding Marta of some domestic thing: she tried to think what it was, and after a moment it came to her. An icebox. The sound of an icebox door shutting.

Warren walked across the black macadam, disappearing into the shadows and the strange emptiness of the garage, the shapes in it, the toolbox, the long silver column beneath the lift showing as bright smears. After he went inside, a light came on, a bulb in a cage, the sudden brightness startling Marta and leaving her desperate to put a word on the thing that had frightened her. Oh, shit. Maybe Victor's already gone to the police. Isn't that possible? Maybe she could tell it had happened just by her fear.

Or what's to keep the police from finding out some other way? Maybe they're already looking for me. How will it happen if they catch me now? Will they stop the car and ask me to get out? Will they ask me if I'm carrying a weapon? Will we have to stand there by the side of the road, Warren on one side of the car and me on the other? Will he watch as they put those hand-cuffs on me?

A police car came by, a local one, metallic blue with a ten-pointed star painted on each of the front doors, and on the roof it had a bank of red, white, and blue lights. The tires were new and shiny, and as the car went by the driver, a man with a haircut so severe as to look almost stylish, turned and gazed at Marta. His gaze lingered on her. Then the sheriff's car went further up the highway and disappeared around the bend, leaving Marta to stare across the street and onto the promontory of land where the town's one motel, white and flat-roofed, sat overlooking the sea.

Well, she had called her boss, just the way Victor had told her to. Somehow she trusted Victor's instincts about this, as though his perspicacity in being there when she had killed the man in Ferndale had other implications as well. Maybe he had a kind of knack for dealing with trouble. And even as she realized she was angry with herself for believing this, or giving Victor any due at all, she nevertheless hoped it was true. She had called her boss and said she had gone up to see Earl Graves. She told him she had knocked on the door and no one had answered. Then she had gone to a party.

"Nothing went wrong up there, did it?" Bobby Salinas asked.

"No," said Marta. "He just wasn't there."

"Well," said Bobby Salinas. He swallowed. You could hear him through the phone. "If anybody should ask you if you were up there, why, you just weren't there."

"I told you," said Marta. "Nothing went wrong."

"I hear something in your voice I don't like."

"There's nothing in my voice," said Marta. "I'm just tired."

Salinas thought for a while, the dark silence seeming to hang between them like the black loop of a phone line between poles.

"I don't want you around here for a few days," he said. "Take a trip or something. Leave town."

Then Warren came out of the garage.

"They want to roll the thing inside and get it up on the lift," he said.

She got out of the car and looked up the street, trying to see if the sheriff's car had pulled over, or, worse, whether it had turned around. But all she saw was the empty clutter of the town, the buildings on the main street sweeping down to the road, their brown-gray architecture seeming at once nostalgic and oppressive. Marta glanced up the short road toward the motel, and for a moment she thought of having the key in her hand, just going up to the door and pushing it open.

She thought of what it would be like to be on the run by herself. She guessed her natural surroundings, if only because they would be safest for her, would be the strips on the outside of almost every town she could think of, streets filled with Burger Kings, McDonald's, Wendy's, Kentucky Fried Chickens, and Pizza Huts, the almost clinically clean gas stations with the whitish-blue glow of their lights. It seemed to her that this world of familiar logos held some contagion, some predisposition toward chaos, as though the rankly practical obliterated everything but the worst.

Marta walked along Main Street, stopping for a moment at the window of the beauty shop. Inside, on a yellowed wall, there were some black and white photographs of women which had been distributed by a cosmetics company. The models had a cool, insouciant gaze, as though they knew a secret you would die to know about. Then Marta turned away, thinking, Are they after me yet?

The salty air was cool. The temperature and the dampness seemed to be not just part of the weather but the claustrophobia of being looked for by the police, as though the air, the last of the fog, even the gray color of the distant sky were part of the miasma of unstoppable pursuit. And the coolness brought something else to mind, too: the fear of what had been done to her because she had killed that man. Was she still the same person she had been just a few days before? The damp, salty air seemed to go right through her clothes.

A week. At the end of it do I say to him, "Look . . . I need some money." Sure. Saying that is going to be like weaving things together, the desire to stay alive being perfectly blended with having no more reason to live.

Well, sure. Taking his hand and walking up to that motel with paint peeling along the wood of the flat roof, maybe that would take care of that feeling, make that terror disappear for a while. That wasn't much to ask for, not really. If you had something no one could take away from you, then you had lived hard enough, or been lucky enough to face up to almost anything.

She turned and started to walk back, feeling that cool and salty wind and seeing, along the precipice, the sea gulls hovering, just hanging there in the air, their wings white, their bills the color of a carrot. In the afternoon mist the buildings of the town were hard to discern, and their shapes, where the mist was thick-est, were vague and only partly visible, as though the entire town had been painted on a piece of canvas that had been half shred-ded in a storm. Sure, thought Marta. That's how you begin to go screwy in a place like this. You begin to wonder after a thou-sand days like this if the place is really here, and then you begin to wonder if you're really here. Then they probably call the county for an ambulance. Hardly any vitamins here. Everything comes in a can.

She began to imagine what the rooms in the motel were like. There's got to be some chairs with black metal legs and plastic seats and a dusty mirror, a bed with a white counterpane. Well, I'll make him watch as he sits there on that bed with the white counterpane, maybe he'll want to see what is worn under these jeans (not the delicate things his women wear, that expensive lingerie from Paris), maybe he'll see those pale white briefs as they're discarded. Well, the thing is to be frank. There, in the half shadows, he'll see me standing right in front of him.

It was getting a little misty, the air gray and cool. There was always that hour or so in those towns along the coast when it wasn't so much that the sun was setting as that something, some vital thing, was leaving the air. You've got to take a little of it with you, thought Marta, watching the sun begin to turn yellow-red as it got closer to the horizon. Got to keep it overnight, just a small, hot, bright kernel of it, almost too much to handle, a golden bit that you have to hold yet keep moving so as to make sure you get through the night all right.

She thought of running a finger across his beard, of the elec-tric quality and surprise of it, the smoothness of her own lips against it . . . each detail sinking down into that dark, crucial mystery which she now faced. What if, when you kill someone, you are no longer able to love anyone again, that your punish-ment is to be alive but no longer quite human?

At the gas station the door to the garage had been rolled up, and inside on the wall there was an array of stainless steel tools, all of them arranged by size. They almost appeared like shapes on an evolutionary chart, as though each century or each million years a tool got a little bigger than it had been before. Marta stood at the entrance, looking at the tools until Warren came out and said, "We're stuck here for a while."

"Oh?" said Marta.

"You don't mind?"

She looked at him. Then she reached into the back of the car and took out her small bag.

"There's a place to stay out here," she said, gesturing to the motel. "Doesn't look so bad."

*   *   *

The motel was almost empty. So, as they walked toward the white building, it was obvious they would have the place to themselves. The road from town rose a little along the narrow ridge of land, and as Marta felt the presence of the precipice, hearing from below the constant *slush* of the Pacific as it broke around the rocks, she kept her eyes on the motel, feeling a desire to speak so frankly as to be . . . almost inflammatory, and if she thought it would have done them any good, she would have begun, looking him full in the face as she did so, using vulgarity if that had been necessary. The sky stretched horizon in the parabola that describes anything that leaves the earth and then falls back under its own loss of velocity. She held his hand and kept her eyes on the white building.

Their room was on the side that faced the ocean. They had to walk down a hall to get to it, each of them still carrying a bag, Marta holding the key now, which swung back and forth. As she went, the key bright in the darkened hall, Marta felt as though she was going not just down a hall smelling of stale cigarette smoke and disinfectant, but through time or memory, which may also have had that concomitant rank odor.

The door swung open. The room had a double bed with a white counterpane. There was a bureau along one wall with a mirror over it. There was a door, too, a glass one that opened onto a small balcony over the ocean a hundred feet below. Marta went in and dropped her bag; she turned around and put one finger out and pushed the door closed.

Yeah, look at that white counterpane. You knew it was going to be there. Can't avoid it.

They sat down on the bed. Marta undid the laces on her shoes, which she took off and put neatly together on the floor.

"I don't care about this place being a motel in some half-deserted town. Do you?" she said.

He shook his head.

Well, she thought, I just want to go on calling myself Marta, so I can eat and sleep and be an ordinary human being, if only for a few days. Then she closed her eyes, imaging that first gold speck, the farthermost bit of herself, like a flake of something that had exploded, which now, out of the darkness, somehow reversed direction and, gathering with other bits, began their slow, unstoppable movement toward her, the sensation of them, as they got closer, making itself apparent as a chill.

*   *   *

The light left the room in a steady retreat, the sense of its departure like a blanket slowly being pulled off of them, the colors going from pink, like a rose petal, to yellow, to blue, and finally to gray. They listened to the sound outside, that slush and ebb, and the occasional splash around the rocks. They could see, further north, a little of the coast highway, and on it the occasional light, which seemed to hover along the coast and then disappear. There were lights on in town, too. Sure, thought Marta. Low wattage. In a town like this everyone starts with a hundred-watt bulb, but soon they've turned it down to seventy-five, and after a while everyone is squinting at the paper under a forty-watt bulb.

She stood and went over to the window, where she stretched, the gray light there making a sheen on her skin. The stars had come out, a few of them, just purple points with a shimmer to them. The room was quiet, and there was nothing more than the odd hush of the motel, the misty, oddly alive air around it on the promontory, the sibilance of the Pacific.

Outside, down below on the other side of the small bay, some gulls were perched on the rail of the pier. Earlier they had been working at crumbs or scraps that had been left from the fishing boats that had brought their catch in. Marta remembered them now, their heads going up and down, their waddle, their fierce pleasure in having got a scrap of fish. What a life, waiting for crumbs, out there in the wet. Well, it's a small thing that gives them pleasure. But at least they have the sense to know where to begin.

Then she looked at Warren and thought, What if he's just having an adventure? What if this is nothing more than a distraction?

She came back to the bed and moved her hand across the sheets, passing a wet spot, her fingers taut. The light was darker blue now, and there was the salty, keener scent as the tide rose, along with a louder noise from the water as it broke over the rocks and rubble on higher ground. If he is just being polite, if he is just amusing himself, if he is having an adventure, why, then, I'll . . . She stood there, thinking over the possibilities of what she could do.

She got up and went into the bathroom, the yellow light from the door cutting into the room, falling across his legs. Then she closed the door and looked at herself in the mirror, her lips moist, her skin a little roughed up, her hair in disarray. She splashed water onto her cheeks and forehead and dried herself with the thin towel.

If he says the wrong word, the wrong syllable, if there is the wrong look in his eye . . . if he does the least thing that suggests he's not in this with me . . . Then she ran the water some more, splashing some on her face, it seemed to her, in a kind of ritual of hope. But then she stood there, her face dripping, her hands shaking. All right. He'd better not say the wrong thing. Not even the wrong glance.

She came back into the room, walking slowly, glad of being naked, of moving through the warm air and over the carpet.

Didn't even have the sense to bring slippers. Not even a pair of slippers.

She sat down at the edge of the bed and spread her hand out on the sheet again. Her feet were flat on the floor, her torso turned toward him. He had one arm behind his head, his back propped up by the pillow. It was dark in the room, and she turned on the light.

"Are you ashamed of me?"

"No," he said. He shook his head.

"Are you having an adventure with me?"

"No," he said.

She reached over and took him by the hair, pulling his face closer to the light.

"Tell me," she said. "I want you to look right at me. I want to see your face when you say it."

"I just want to be with you," he said.

"Is that all it is?" she said. "This isn't just for fun?"

"No," he said.

She let go.

"I'm sorry," she said. "Maybe I'm just tired. That's all."

"Me too," he said. "Sometimes I think I'm going to fly into a million pieces. Sometimes I think I'll fly off into little bits, you know, like a sparkler."

"A sparkler," she said.

"Uh-huh."

She stretched out, staring at the ceiling. Then she jerked a pillow and put it near the edge of the bed, putting her face against it.

In the dark, with the sound outside of the pebbles clicking in the receding water, she tried to concentrate. She thought, It's just the opposite of those worn-out women in this town who first put in a hundred-watt bulb and then a seventy-five and then a forty, squinting at their crocheting or at their day-old papers. Becoming me again is like starting at that forty-watt fleck and then building to seventy-five and then a hundred and then more, the sensation like being in the dark and seeing in the distance a bunch of lights that lead you to a beacon, just like those that are in front of a movie theater on the night of a premiere, which, if you look into them, blind you with a brilliant, overwhelming light.

"Why are you crying?" he asked.

"I don't know," she said. "I'll get over it."

Cygnus, the Big Dipper, and Ursa Minor

WARREN WATCHED her sleep. She lay on her side, the sheet pulled across her ribs, which showed more distinctly as she took deep, almost frighteningly spaced breaths, as though sleep was at once both restful and somehow profoundly hard work. In the dim light he saw the line of small mounds made by her vertebrae, the shape of a shoulder blade, the down that ran along the nape of her neck, beginning as a whorl and trailing off into filaments of silvery gold.

Warren had seen enough frightened people to know one when he saw one. So, if nothing else, he was certain that she was scared. He got up from the bed and stood there, running a hand through his hair. Then he went over to the desk which was attached to the wall and turned the chair away from it so he could sit down. The silence of the room was relieved only by the distant sound of a car and the shriek of a bird. He sat, thinking it over. She was scared. What was he going to do about it?

Warren had been good at taking care of things. In fact, he liked to think of himself as someone whose greatest gift was the way in which he could make difficulties either disappear or become irrelevant. But as he sat there, apprehending the silence of the room as a kind of hint, as a suggestion of her worst moments, he wanted to be careful.

He could just ask what was scaring her, but this was going to produce nothing but lies. It's like a guy who really needs money. The last thing in the world he's ever going to do is ask for it. He's too ashamed. It's always the people who have money who can ask for it without batting an eye. If you ask the guy who needs it, he'll say everything's fine. Just fine.

He stood up now and looked out the window, remembering her voice, the heat of her skin or the slippery warmth of her mouth, the glance in her eyes, at once abandoned or furious, charming or exhausted, the accumulation of details permeating the atmosphere of the room like an essence. It was like a cloud or chiaroscuro from those moments when he had been cut loose from almost everything, anchored to this room by her murmur and the salty taste of her skin. Outside, the last of the afternoon light turned the fog from gray to blue. As he listened to that almost inaudible breathing, the delicacy of it made him consider, in the face of vagueness, just how careful he wanted to be. What was he going to do about her being so scared?

Well, that's the first problem. He nodded, putting his hand into his hair. Yes, that's right. Are there any other problems? After all, this is no time for lies, for half truths, for any kind of euphemism. So, as he looked out the window, he admitted he was afraid, too.

Then he dressed slowly, picking up his pants and pulling them on. All right. What was there to be afraid of?

He sat down and tied his shoes, pulling the laces taut, jerking them a little. Well, there was something in the suddenness of . . . finding himself here.

He admitted he had been in an odd mood recently. Well, so what? Everybody's got a right to be in an odd mood, especially if you're trying to raise money, serious money, and you don't want every two-bit guy who thinks he knows what sells a ticket to a movie theater looking over your shoulder. But then he shook his head with a kind of shame, as if he had caught himself in a lie. No. That's not it at all. It was more the fact that the impulse to be in this room was a symptom — that was the word he stopped at. Did it mean that some peril was approaching, a breakdown, a moment when everything he had worked for could simply evaporate into some flaw, some weakness, some personal spiraling down, some private suction that had been getting stronger for years now and had finally made itself apparent in the form of this young woman who had simply walked into his house?

He left a note on the nightstand, almost directly in front of her face. It would be the first thing she would see when she opened her eyes: "Gone to check car."

When he put down the paper it made a slight *click,* and as he heard it, he turned away from where she lay, half covered by the sheet, one arm thrown upward, the stubble of her underarm reminding him of the electric touch of it against the tip of his tongue. Then he stood still, looking at the door of the room, trying to stay alert in the face of this new thing that had seemed to come into the room at the sound of that gentle *click.* Well, all right. As he took a step, feeling a little tremor in his shoulders and upper arms, in the tips of his fingers, he resisted anything ambiguous or equivocal.

He had worked hard. He had been careful about letting go. And now it seemed, as he stood in this room, hearing this woman breathe, that his hard work, the entanglements of his life, had been a kind of barrier, which, without warning, he was crashing through. He could even imagine this barrier as a piece of glass, breaking up in shards around him as if he were a stuntman in some Western where a cowboy gets thrown through the plate glass window of a saloon. In slow motion, too.

So what if you break through it? What if you do that in a room like this, with this young woman, and what if, when you peel the layers away, one after another, abandoning restraint as you go, simply handing it over as you begin to trust someone else, what if, when you get to the bottom, you find something that you don't like? Let's put a word on it. A murderer. A pervert. A bully. What had he been hiding?

Would he begin to live for the infinitely pleasurable moment of laying his hand against hers and feeling that there was no difference between them? In the sensation that ran back and forth between their skin, he had begun to think it was impossible to exist as he had been before. So he stood there, feeling as if he were poised on a high wire, not quite falling but certainly aware of the space below, or the terrors of simply abandoning one's idea of who or what one had always been.

He began to consider Marta's fear again. What was he going to do? Well, he could . . . but then he stopped. What could he do after all? He thought of all those times when he had interfered or taken charge of something only to find that after he had been successful, he was left somehow confined by the things he had always thought he wanted.

He went out the door, shutting it behind him, feeling the puff of air around the edges of it, which brought to mind the slight touch of her breath when she had looked at him, holding his hair, jerking him a little bit, saying, "I want to see your eyes . . . now . . . when I'm about to . . . when I . . ."

He wanted a cigarette, too. There had been a connection between smoking and the movie business: people always had an almost cinematic idea of themselves when they lighted a cigarette and dropped a match or clicked a lighter shut. Bogart died of lung cancer. There were others. A lot of deaths.

He went up the street, turning on to the sidewalk and approaching the gas station where the car was sitting. The gas station had a small island beneath some lights, and the building itself was square with two double doors. A few other cars were parked there, too, mostly with a spider web of cracks in the windshield where someone had had a bad moment on the road that ran along the coast. Then Warren stopped in front of his car.

He looked at it, suddenly finding that the sight of it alone gave him a moment's pause. For a little while he wasn't sure why this was so, although, as he stood there, it became more obvious. The thing was, after all, beautiful . . . or at least, even now, he still could see how people would imagine it as having a kind of beauty.

The car was long and blue, discreetly streaked with chrome, without one emblem or word anywhere on it to betray the manufacturer's name, as though vagueness, at this level of financial commitment, was a kind of distinction. The car had about it an aura of promise. Warren opened the door and looked at the cream-colored leather seats, the steering wheel, the gauges with their crypto-scientific quality. Then he closed the door and looked at the top of the car as it sat collecting dust, in spite of its promise. And as Warren looked at it, he felt it was like something that had been trusted (like a dog, a shepherd, say) suddenly revealing a previously hidden, vicious side. The car appeared, in a moment of transformation, like the ugly residue of delusion: it was what he had in place of what he needed. It had come into his life by his assumption of a thousand disguises, each one cunningly designed to keep moments like this one at arm's length. After all, who is better at trapping yourself than you? His realization made the car look cheap.

He had been waking up late at night, the house ringing with the suddenness of his waking, the shadows seeming to stream toward him with all the obvious menace of things about to go irrevocably wrong. He had always assumed he was in control of his illusions, like the things this car implied (safety, control, distance from the mundane), and now, to his horror, it seemed the opposite was true.

Just look at the cars he had bought, each one forever promising something, each having all the guile of short-term perfection, but yet, when push came to shove, when the illusion was about to be tested, it came to nothing more than another promise, another need endlessly delayed, the style of things continually without substance.

Well, maybe it had happened just because of where he lived and what he did. The real secret was that Hollywood was such a dull place. Or, maybe the work that went into making illusions left everyone tired. The stockbrokers filled in those places where the romance failed. If anything, the place was like a mining town, the men standing in front of the gate, the long line of them gray and serious, knowing they were about to descend into the depths. The sound stages, the sets, the back lots all had a weight, a kind of deadliness, that came from the effort to get chaos under control but never quite succeeding. Well, it had come back to haunt him late at night, his ears ringing, as he tried to guess what was loose in the shadows of his house, the darkness seeming almost to sparkle with maliciousness.

Now as he turned and faced the coast, which gradually emerged as the fog disappeared, it seemed that all along, in every illusion, in every comfort, he had always been promising himself something, but yet the promises had only led to other ones, always delayed, deferred, lost. No wonder he had been waiting for her to come into his house, her eyes filled with a mixture of fear and vitality, her expression betraying a knowledge of what was behind the ordinary appearances of things.

So, all right. Marta had been fierce about stripping everything away, of just existing for a moment when the two of them seemed to hover over the depths. He thought about the prospect of peeling away the layers, discarding the endless checks he had always invoked from habit (using half truths and half lies): now there would be none of that. She would have the freedom to do with both of them what she wanted. He glanced up at the white building, isolated on its promontory, remembering her voice as she had said, "I wonder . . . how much living can you get into a week?"

She had looked down when she said this, running a finger through the perspiration on her breast, seemingly distracted by the sheen of it. Then she stopped and just looked out the window, toward the ocean.

Well, all right. Let's find out.

There was a telephone at the side of the gas station, and Warren went up to it and made a call. He spoke for a while and ended up by saying, "Yes, there's a dock here. There's no problem about that."

Then he hung up and walked up to the motel. As he went, he thought maybe he could find the right opening, the place where he could begin to address what was bothering her.

In the room, Warren stood at the side of the bed, her stillness, her lack of movement somehow making him feel awkward, as though he had come into the room as an intruder. Her skin was pale, her brows a metallic blond, her lashes lying on her cheek; she seemed not so much to be resting as contracted, waiting.

Then she woke up. For a moment she just stared at him, seemingly confused or disoriented, and as she did so, he looked directly down into her eyes. She seemed to be gathering herself together, or perhaps, as she stared up, she was not really anyone at all yet, and in that instant, transfixed, he watched her being summoned from the recesses that seemed deeper than just sleep.

He had the sensation of some glassy surface toward which she rose, and as she did, she seemed to be thinking of the things they had done together in this room.

"I don't mean to stare," he said, looking away.

"It's all right," she said. "I don't mind. I was sound asleep." She blushed.

"Listen," he said. "I think we'd better pack."

She blinked. "Why? Are we leaving already?"

"Yes," he said.

"They fixed the car so fast?"

"No," he said. "An airplane — you know, a seaplane — is coming to pick us up."

"Can we afford something like that?" she said.

"Yes," he said. "We can afford it. Money isn't the problem." He sat down next to her.

"Let's get out of this town. What do you say?"

She glanced at him, and there was a reminder in her expression of what he had seen when she had first woken up.

"All right," she said.

*   *   *

Out the window, in the distance, a dark, almost black shape against the gray-blue sky resolved itself into a float plane. It came straight in from the ocean and then made a long circle over the harbor, the town, the motel, the pilot checking to see which way the wind was blowing or if there was anything half-submerged, floating in the water. The airplane was gray, with a blue stripe on it. It had a wing above the passenger compartment, smooth cowling, a propeller which appeared a mere circular blur. It came in and landed, the spray flying away from the floats. Then it started taxiing slowly, coming up to the dock.

Warren picked up their bags, and they went out along the precipice, beneath which, on the thin beach, a line of white foam washed over the stones. A few gulls tottered on the breeze, their beaks orange.

Fishing boats were moored at the dock, each of which had a functional-looking deck, a glassed-in wheelhouse, and a roof bristling with antennas and radar. There were a couple of sailboats, too, their hulls streaked with dirt and the tarp over the boom covered with bird droppings.

The pilot of the airplane waited for them at the end of the dock, holding onto the airplane by a nylon rope that hung down from the strut of the wing. He took their bags and put them into the airplane while Warren held the rope, and then they climbed in, Marta getting into the back where there was a newspaper with a picture of Earl Graves on the front page. He looked a little younger, and he had a mustache, but there was something in his eyes that was the same as what she had seen the evening she had gone to his house. The caption read, "Hollywood mobster found murdered."

The pilot looked over his shoulder and said, "Looks like a cheap mobster got what he deserved, doesn't it?"

"Yes," said Marta. "I guess so."

The plane taxied into the wind, and as the pilot opened the throttle, she could feel a growing pressure in her back from the acceleration.

* * *

The lake was high up, at five thousand feet at least, and around it were soft woods, tall, pointed trees, which, when the water was still, revealed themselves not only against the sky but in a reflected shimmer as well. The cabin, made of logs, had a front porch and a chimney of cobbles chinked together with white mortar. The shingles on the roof, the logs, the boards of the porch had all weathered to a dark brown. There was no electricity, but there was light from gas lamps. Copper tubes ran across the inside walls, the copper bright and reassuring, and the lamps that were attached to the tubes were small, covered with a shade, and inside there was a mantle of ash so delicate as to seem almost like a memory.

The airplane had let them off at a dock below the cabin. A metal bedstead that had been painted white stood upstairs in the loft under the cathedral ceiling. It had bars at the head of the bed, and when Marta stretched out, she reached up to them, taking them in both hands, feeling the coolness of them.

The pond seemed to change between dawn and dusk, and

Marta watched it, glancing up from the bed. At dawn the small lake was a gray, still piece of mirror around which she could see only the dark masses of trees, their silhouettes black against the sky and in the water, and as the last few stars faded, as the pond turned yellow, there came a moment of keen expectation in which it seemed all possibilities approached, danger among them. Marta waited then, sometimes with her fingers on Warren's side so as to feel him breathe. The first bird began to chirp, and with it everything changed, the atmosphere turning with this one, minute sound from the ominous to the orgiastic. The sun rose and the pond became blue, the shade deepening until at noon it was lost in a silver glare, which receded back into that same blue as Marta said, Look at me, look, please, look at me now . . . Outside the colors changed, turning a deeper blue, and finally that roseate color, the hue of it warm and almost dusty. The surface of the pond became still in the evening, just before dusk, its glassy calmness bringing a hint of the ominous, and then the darkness began to flow around every object, the trees turning black and spear-shaped as they formed a wall, and in front of them the pond had a gold liquidity in which one star appeared, as if a countless number of flecks from a Fourth of July sparkler had been collected there.

A green canoe lay overturned against a tree by the dock. In the evenings, after having spent the day in that loft room, Warren and Marta put it in the water. There was a wicker seat with a back that opened up, and Marta sat in it while Warren paddled, the canoe cutting an almost oily V through the flat surface of the lake. From time to time a ring appeared in the water where a mayfly emerged, its wings white as moonlight, and occasionally a trout rose to take an insect on the surface, leaving a small boil where it had been. Warren and Marta stayed out until after dark and then returned to the cabin, paddling toward the yellow gas lamp they had lighted before leaving, the canoe gliding over the constellations reflected in the water, its dark bow moving with a liquid shove and glide through Cygnus, the Big Dipper, Ursa Minor.

It was cold when they came in. As Marta stood in the living room, hugging her shoulders, Warren brought in some wood and kindling and newspaper. Marta knelt in front of the fireplace, saying, "Here. Build it slowly. Don't let it go out."

"I know how to build a fire," said Warren.

"Here. Be careful. Let me do it."

Upstairs the sheets were cold, and Marta shivered under the covers. Warren's footsteps were loud on the wooden stairs as he came up, and as she listened to them, she thought of a hotel in San Francisco where she had gone to dinner when she had been a student. A small dining room had been on the top floor of the building, and cut flowers in a small vase were sitting on each linen-covered table. The waiters had been in black tie, their movements around the room quiet and pleasant. As Warren pulled back the covers, letting the air rush along her skin, she reached out, pulling him against her. She glanced out at the pond, its surface dark as black paper. Then she waited for the cold to leave the bed, thinking of that dining room, trying to recall the light hitting the silver, the glasses, and the ice in them, the sheen of it on the bubbles that rose in a chain from the bottom of a glass of champagne, the tingle almost palpable now: she imagined it spreading, sweeping over her skin and into the warmth under the covers.

At the end of the week, Marta woke at dawn. Warren was awake, too. She could tell by his breathing. She looked at the pond, the surface of it emerald green in the shadows, and as she heard Warren's breathing, she thought of Victor, coming up to the door of her apartment in his new clothes (she was convinced he would be wearing some gaudy leather jacket). She could even hear his voice as he said, "Well, how did you make out?"

"Are we going back soon?" she asked.

"What did you say?"

"I wanted to know how much time we've got left," she said.

He listened to her voice, part whisper, the words having a breathy sibilance, and as he did, it seemed that whatever was there, whether fear or turmoil, was stronger than ever, so palpable now as to be like the boil a trout makes on the surface of the water as it turns and vanishes into the depths. So, there it was. That was the tone he had been waiting for. It was so obvious that she couldn't deny it.

"The plane's coming for us today," he said.

"Today."

"I don't want to pry . . ." he said.

"Then don't," she said.

"You could just talk to me," he said. "We could find something I might do . . . you'd be surprised."

"Yes," she said. "I would be surprised."

"Give me a chance to fail," he said. "I'm just asking for a chance to help you out. It's no secret something's eating at you."

She turned and looked at him.

"No," she said.

"Listen," he said. "There are things . . ."

She shook her head. "No. Why don't we enjoy the time we've got. Don't you think that's wise?"

He waited, feeling that sense of claustrophobia as on other occasions when he had made an effort and had been left with that same feeling of confinement. He'd never been able to arrange things just right, not really. There had always been some failure, some brutality that made itself necessary. She looked at him as if to say, Well, are you going to let go or not?

"I'll bet you're good at controlling things," she said.

"I don't know anymore," he said.

She shrugged.

"I'm asking you to trust me," she said.

"You mean that I just take things on faith?"

"Yes," she said. "On faith."

He swallowed. "All right. We'll just take it as it comes."

She looked out at the lake.

"The plane will be here soon," he said.

"OK. Maybe we can take a swim before it comes."

"Sure," he said. "That'll be nice."

"Yes," she said. "Won't it?"

Homecoming

M ARTA CAME INTO HER APARTMENT and sat down, finding that even the stuffiness of the room was a little reassuring, as though it evoked her life before she had made the mistake
of running an errand to Ferndale.

She opened a window and then went into the bathroom to
take a shower. When she came out, she stood by the window
again, letting the cool breeze wash over her skin, its refreshing
touch strangely at odds with what she saw in the distance: the
conglomeration of houses on the hills, the observatory with the
green roof, the red-gray layer of mist that lay over the city like a
figment of some malicious imagination. The breeze felt wonderful on her skin.

She made some coffee, and as the water dripped through the
cone-shaped filter into the pitcher below, filling the room with a
bitter scent, she thought she was just imagining the sound of
footsteps outside. They came with exactly the same cadence of
the water. The steps had about them the light, maddening approach of anything that appears to be one thing but really is
something else altogether. Then she stood up and turned her
head. Sure. That's him all right. You can hear him walking along
just like someone counting nickels, holding a hand beneath a
table and dropping them into his palm two at a time, two at a
time.

Victor knocked, then opened the door and said, "Hiya."

He closed the door behind him.

"How are you doing?" he said.

Victor was wearing a new suede coat. It had a reddish cast to it and was cut with wide lapels. It smells, too, Marta thought. There are some things you just can't avoid.

"Say, what's the matter?" said Victor. "Don't you like my coat? Don't you like suede?"

"It's OK," she said.

"I was waiting for you."

"Were you?" said Marta.

"I can see the front of your building from my apartment. Say, that coffee smells good."

He went over and poured himself a cup, the brown stream reflecting a streak of silver from the light overhead. He looked up and smiled as he held the cup, saying, "You got anything to put in it? A little bourbon maybe?"

Marta took a bottle from a cabinet and pushed it toward him, sliding it across the Formica counter that separated the kitchen from the living room.

"Thanks," he said. "You're a sweetheart. How did you do?"

"All right."

"Did you?" he said. "Well, that's good. I knew I could depend on you. That's what I said to myself the first time I saw you. There, I said, is a woman I can trust. These days, you know, women have got some screwy ideas."

"Do they?"

"Sure," said Victor. "They've dumped morality. Everything is ambition now. It's everything you can get."

He shrugged.

"What are we talking about in terms of dollars?" he said.

He took a drink from the coffee cup, holding the fluid in his mouth, washing it back and forth.

"What were you expecting?" she asked.

"Well," he said, "I think you got to start pretty small. Five, ten thousand. Then you work up for a while. Most people will take a lot of little bites before, you know, they balance the checkbook and see what the hell they got in for."

"Uh-huh," she said.

"Time is a consideration, though," said Victor. "I'm going to take a trip, you know that? South America. Argentina. Down there you can make a dollar last, you know that?"

She nodded.

"This is a one-time-only transaction," he said. "Do you believe me?"

She stared at him. Out on the street someone honked a horn. From another apartment she heard a slight *snap,* which made her think of a mouse getting caught in a trap.

"Yes," she said.

"Well, that's good," he said.

He took another drink. Just look at that coat, would you? Maybe it was possible she could just get him some money and that would be it, but then she looked at the coat again. No. How can you trust anyone with taste like that? Money wasn't going to do it, not for long. She wondered what kind of funeral Victor would choose if he had the chance. Then she thought of the odor of churches and funeral homes and of those times when her mother had let go and started to cry along with the rest of the mourners.

"Well?" said Victor.

"I'll have something for you tomorrow," she said.

"Where?"

"At Warren's house in Malibu," said Marta.

"*Warren's house,*" said Victor. "Jesus, you have been getting it on, haven't you?"

"Tomorrow afternoon. Five o'clock," she said. "You come out there. There's an orange grove. You meet me at the end of it, the side away from the house, all right?"

"Sure, sure," he said. "But listen, how much are we talking about? I'm not driving all the way to Malibu for a lousy five hundred dollars. Jesus, I'll have the rush hour traffic, too. Have you noticed how bad the traffic is getting these days? Nothing holds a candle to the Ventura Freeway, right there at Sepulveda."

"Plenty," she said.

"Well, that's good," said Victor. "That's the best news I've had all day." He finished the coffee and poured out a little more bourbon, which he took in sips, holding each one in his mouth before he swallowed it. "Yeah, that's terrific. Tomorrow, then. I'm going to go up to the travel agency and begin to make plans. You ever heard of the Plaza Hotel in Buenos Aires?"

"No," said Marta.

"Well, it's one of the best in the world," he said. "It's just a terrific place. I've seen brochures like you wouldn't believe."

He put down the cup.

"You can trust me," he said. "You know that? You really can. I've made a few mistakes. But I've paid my debts. There were nights at Soledad, you know, in July —"

"You were in Soledad?" she said.

"Did I say that? I must be talking too much. Well, I'm going to turn over a new leaf. That's all I really want. I'll get down to Buenos Aires and play some chess in one of those plazas they have. Get some good vitamins. Vitamin C, you know. Live forever."

*   *   *

Marta stood in the doorway of the *Romance Advertiser*'s building. Slanting away from her, going upward into the shadows of the second story, was the stairway with the rubber-covered tread. It was brown rubber, the color of semisweet chocolate. Someone had gotten into the building again the night before, and there was a smell of urine behind the door, and a bottle in a paper bag had been left there, too. Marta could see the potted palm at the landing opposite the *Advertiser*'s office. The palm was dying, its leaves yellowing, and before long her boss, Bobby Salinas, would have the thing thrown out and replaced with another, the carcass of the first one carried out like a vision of romance after a bad night. Marta guessed this palm was about a week from being put out on the street. Once she had got something called Miracle-Gro and mixed some of it up in a bucket in the bathroom and poured the stuff into one of the pots. It had helped a little, but the palm had still been dragged out and left on the sidewalk for the trash man. Marta made the long climb up to the *Advertiser*'s office, where she opened the door and took the plastic cover off her typewriter. She guessed there were some things that needed to be cleaned up here anyway, and, as far as she could see, it was best to do them now, while she still had the chance.

Spike

TAYLOR HAYDEN WOKE to the sound of a fly in the room. He opened his eyes, not moving his head or showing any other sign that he was alert. Then, when he was certain the noise was a fly, he sat up and watched it. The path of the insect had an erratic but not mindless pattern. Taylor followed it with his eyes, giving the fly a grudging respect if only for its reflexes or the speed with which it could change course. Then he got up, neatly folding back the sheets.

The bedroom was composed in planes and triangles — the white triangle where the sheet was turned back, the rectangle of the carpet on the floor, the walls themselves, which were painted a cream color. Then Taylor picked up a newspaper, a gossip sheet he had been reading, which he now folded. Three times. Good luck as always. The fly landed on the wall, but he didn't kill it there. That always left a mark, and he knew he'd see it and think that leaving a mark like that was just stupid. He didn't like leaving marks.

Taylor closed his eyes and listened only for that thin buzzing, and when it stopped, he went right to the place where the fly had stopped on the window, the papery *whack* cutting into the otherwise silent room. Then he took a piece of Kleenex, which he pulled from the box with a dry *hush,* and wiped up the mess. There was a bottle of Windex in the kitchen cabinet, the bottles lined up in groups of three, and Taylor cleaned the window, the ammonia bringing him fully awake and sure. That smell of ammonia. That's what things should smell like. Cold as moonlight. Or the smell in a freezer when you just crack open the door.

He looked at the calendar in the kitchen. It was the third.

Taylor had nothing against working in broad daylight. In fact, he thought it was the best time of the day for certain kinds of setups. Take this poor dummy Victor Shaw. Now there is a guy you couldn't really figure. He looked gray, as though he wasn't getting enough sunshine, but then the reason for that was pretty obvious: it hadn't taken long for Taylor to discover Victor worked at night. But the grayness came from something worse than just the lack of sun. For a while Taylor thought it was a matter of diet. The guy wasn't only working at night, he probably was eating a lot of meat. Greasy stuff from McDonald's or Burger King. Taylor believed there was an entire science to complexion, and that certain people showed their bad luck in their gray skin. Like a leprosy of luck. You didn't see too many guys with a tan looking like they had made a private pact with doom.

Victor's clothes didn't make sense, either, like the guy wore some old blue jeans and a blue work shirt and a jacket that must have cost a thousand dollars at least. Looked like it came from Paris. Continental cut. But above everything else, Taylor kept coming back to Victor's complexion. He had thought about it a lot as he had sat in his car, watching Victor's apartment or the building where Victor went to work. Maybe there was some chemical in the stuff Victor used to clean, a solvent or something like that. Solvents were hard on people. But even a solvent wouldn't do that. Victor's skin had a color like dirty socks or ice on which some fish scales have been left behind. Jesus, what Victor needed was a couple hours under the sun lamps. They had some you could climb into, just like a big coffin.

Yeah. Today's the day. What Taylor liked were those moments when everything fell into place, the patterns of three, the neat disposal of a pistol, the bags from the dry cleaner, all lined up in the closet, the packages of oat bran lined up in the refrigerator, the sheets, clean from the laundry, smelling in the closet like a whiff of paradise.

Still, a lot of things didn't make sense about Victor. How could a gray dummy who cleaned an office at night have pissed off a union guy at the airport? Maybe it was some kind of psychological kink. The things that were going on in the bars these days . . . all kinds of weirdos getting sideways with each other. Look normal as hell, too, five days a week. Then the weekend rolls around and the vampires come out, looking for . . . God knows what. Especially down around Venice. Jesus, what a place. Not as bad as Torrance, though. Or those nights when the ghouls went up to party at Trancas.

Taylor made the bed and took a shower and shaved, looking at his face in the mirror. He had warm, gray-blue eyes. He liked them to be very clear, and as he used some eyewash, he could feel the coolness of it sweep from his eyes all the way into his brain. Then he made breakfast, setting the table as always, making coffee and juice, taking his herbs for energy, making sure he was getting the necessary trace elements. Most people didn't know they were deficient in potassium.

There were some occasions when the daytime was all right or even better than at night. Like a nice, ordinary neighborhood where everybody goes to work. It's never more empty than at two thirty in the afternoon, before the kids start coming home from school. One little whack, well, who's around to hear it, and who really cares anyway? Or the morning is good, too. Right around ten thirty. Everyone's gone and the neighborhood is sleepy, the occasional dry cleaning truck passing through, the atmosphere made up of the first smog mixed with the tired odor of the morning's coffee. The cars putter by. Maybe the steady *twit twit twit* of a sprinkler, the mist of it filling the air with a suggestion of wet fertility made all the more keen by an occasional, sudden rainbow. It was amazing how deserted most Los Angeles neighborhoods usually were.

Taylor liked to go right up to the door. He had a badge, a real one he had bought a few years before from the Hawaiian who sold guns. The Hawaiian had a friend who had stolen it off a uniform that was being dry-cleaned in West Hollywood. That Hawaiian. Always thinking about that steel guitar band. He never wanted you to say, "Ha-why-ee." It always had to be "Ha-vi-ee." Anyway, Taylor liked to go right up to the door, where he showed the badge in its little leather holder and identified himself as a detective from Santa Monica or some other beach town. It always sounded a little sexy. Then he asked to come in.

Never failed. Taylor would come in and close the door, being careful to do it with his elbow.

Taylor laid out his pants, the seat of them on his bed, the legs hanging down: the effect was that of a shadow across a big step. Then he put a blue shirt above the waistband of the pants and his shoes on the floor underneath the legs. He looked at the clothes, which now appeared as though someone had simply evaporated out of them. The idea of disappearing left him thinking about the most important moment of all. Taylor liked to think of it as closing the door. Time was up. He was going to close the door on Victor. In the midst of someone's dying, in the shock and the suddenness, as everything became real, Taylor always stood right next to a mystery, the scale of which was so large as to leave him certain he could almost feel something, like the caress of a piece of silk being dragged across his face. There was an essence, at once sacrificial and cleansing. It was this essence that Taylor tried to honor, lining things up in threes, being neat and precise, keeping himself fit, reading Seneca and Tacitus and Livy and the lives of the samurai. Yeah, maybe he would learn how to perform the tea ceremony. Maybe that would help.

He looked at his clothes laid out on the bed, like an image of himself, their inanimate appearance a kind of totem against disaster. Then he dressed, carefully tucking his shirt in, buckling his belt into the third hole, each piece of apparel seeming as cool as armor.

It was noon when he walked out of his apartment, carrying a thin leather briefcase in which there was the pistol, loaded now but still in a baggie. He took the bus down Pico to a wrecking service which also sold cars that had been stolen for no more than twenty-four hours. Taylor liked to have a nice fresh one that he could use and then get rid of, along with the pistol.

The man he met there was short and a little hard of hearing. He had dark skin, and could have come from the Mediterranean, but Taylor figured he was from just across the border. His name was Bernal.

"Hiya, Spike," said Bernal.

"Don't call me that," said Taylor. "How many times do I have to tell you?"

Bernal shrugged.

"I don't hear so well, you know?" said Bernal. "A guy comes in and says he wants a Montero. I get him a Camaro and he's pissed."

"Get a hearing aid," said Taylor.

"I don't like the way they feel," he said. "Everything sounds tinny."

"Well, have you got the Chevy?" said Taylor.

"Sure," said Bernal. " 'Chevy' doesn't sound like anything else. Sure I got it. Gray. Low mileage."

"Good rubber?"

"Great rubber," said Bernal. "Firestones."

"They aren't recaps, are they?" asked Taylor.

"Would I sell you recaps? Look at me and say, 'You sell me recaps.' "

Taylor looked at him for a minute.

"Christ, you're —," said Taylor, but then he stopped. He was about to say, *Christ, you're nothing but a thief. How can you be upset about some tires?*

"What?" said Bernal. "Chrysler? I never sold you a Chrysler. I always gave you GM products."

"I just asked if the rubber was good," said Taylor. "That's all. Give me the keys and I'll get out of here. Is there any gas in it?"

"I always give you a full tank," Bernal said. "Always. I check the oil. The power steering fluid. The water. It's ready to roll."

"Good," said Taylor. "Fine. Glad to hear it."

"You shouldn't say I sold you recaps," said Bernal.

"Let's drop it," said Taylor.

"It's a sore point with me," said Bernal. "All right?"

"Give me the keys," said Taylor. "Forget I ever mentioned it."

Zimba

O N   A   B A C K   R O A D in Malibu there appeared in the heat, partially obscured by a long smokelike plume of dust, a fast-moving truck pulling an elephant in a trailer. It was afternoon, and the sun fell with an almost fluid quality, seeming to gather into bright pools where the ruts in the road were filled with whitish dust. The truck came down a road that branched off from the main highway and then drove along the foot of the grassy hills. Even from a distance there could be heard the occasional sound of trumpeting, which seemed to be both a challenge and a warning.

The trailer was a cream color on the sides, and it had a green cover which looked like an awning over a California patio. The canvas had been a dark, dignified green, but now it was faded and marked by a straight line of bird droppings. The elephant was inside, swaying from side to side in the half light of the trailer, sometimes sticking its trunk into the air by slipping it through the space between the slats and the roof, the pink end slobbering in the breeze. On the side of the trailer a sign read, "Zimba, the King of Elephants." It was printed in the reds and yellows and in the type usually seen on a circus poster.

The truck moved with a rocking, bouncing locomotion, at times barely touching the ground, the entire collection — the machine, the trailer, the elephant — all appearing to have been shot out of a cannon. The speed, the squeaking springs, the popping of the engine through the last shreds of metal that had once been a muffler all added to the contradictory cheer of a circus.

"We're late," said the driver of the truck to his companion. The driver's name was John Blaine, and he was wearing a pair of loose white cotton pants with billowing legs, the kind usually known as sultans' pants. He also wore a white T-shirt with "Zimba" across the front in letters that had been made with glue and then sprinkled with glitter. He was about thirty, with a good tan and blue eyes. He wore a turban on his head with the indifferent air of a man who has worn a costume many times.

"Then give it some gas," said the other man. He was about twenty-three and sick with a hangover. His name was Will ("Just plain Will. That's what people call me.").

Blaine gave the engine some more gas, and the truck seemed to lift a little from the ground, as though, with this much speed, it was finally becoming nothing more than a streamer of metal, noise, dust, and that constant, almost hysterical trumpeting.

"I guess we're going to make some kid pretty happy," said Will. "You know, having Zimba at his birthday party."

Blaine looked at him, his turban turning under the headliner of the truck. He had very blue, vacuous eyes, and he just stared at Will for a while. He began to laugh, steadily, unemphatically, without mirth. Then Will laughed too, although he didn't know why. The truck began to go uphill, the grass streaking by and the trailer rocking a little more than before. There was a piece of ruby-colored glass about the size of a pocket watch which Blaine wore on a chain in the front of his headdress, and it jumped and swung as the truck went along the road.

After a moment Blaine said, "I wish he'd stop that rocking from side to side back there. He's going to break a spring."

"I thought elephants were, you know, placid," said Will.

"Not always," said Blaine.

"He's giving me a headache," said Will. "That shrieking is pretty loud, don't you think?"

"He's been louder."

"Come on," said Will. "You're kidding."

"I don't ever kid," said Blaine.

Blaine pulled the truck over to the side of the road. The field on the right was spotted here and there with clumps of eucalyptus. Blaine got out and stood in the blowing dust in which the truck, the trailer, the elephant, and the bright circuslike sign existed as nothing more than gray-red outlines. The trailer rocked from side to side, almost tipping over. The elephant trumpeted in the obscurity, the half-musical shrieks seeming all the more ominous, like anything that is threatening yet only partially seen.

The dust blew by. The elephant's trunk moved back and forth, waving in the air, although there was something in the curve of it, in its tactile caress as he ran it along the stakes of the truck, that suggested he was just looking for a good hold. Blaine peered through the slats. One of the elephant's eyes showed white around the edges.

Will swallowed and said, "I'm pretty thirsty right now. Can't you get him to shut up a little?"

He raised his voice as he spoke across the seat and through the open window so Blaine could hear him.

"You know," said Blaine. "Raj always sweet-talks the elephant. Zimba isn't going to get any of that from me. I've just about had it. There's a cattle prod behind the seat."

Blaine leaned closer to the shadows, putting his face between the slats and looking up into the animal's eye.

"Too bad Raj is sick," said Blaine. "He went to the hospital for some test or other."

"Uh-huh," said the younger man. He spoke while looking straight down, like a man on a carnival ride who is just waiting for it to be over.

"I guess Raj is pretty worried," said Blaine.

"Well, everyone's got to go sometime," said the younger man.

Blaine came back from the side of the truck and looked in the window.

"Wait until you're a little older. You might feel different about it," said Blaine.

"I don't know," said Will. "Considering the way I feel this morning."

Blaine went on staring at him for a moment and then climbed back into the truck.

"Yeah," said Blaine. "Raj can get this elephant to tap-dance. Walk a tightrope. Any damn thing you want. But there's more than one way to skin a cat."

Blaine stared through the pitted windshield, beyond which the road was defined by pools of glare where the dust was heavy. Otherwise it was just a quiet lane, filled with the sunlight. Up ahead about a hundred yards the road forked, and on a post driven into the dry ground was a sign, the black letters wavering like smoke in the glare of the sign's white background. Blaine went on staring at it until he said, "It says Hodges. The place we're going is beyond Hodges's."

"Maybe Zimba's getting his *must*," said Will.

"We've got the cattle prod," said Blaine.

"Well, yeah. I guess that will hold him," said Will.

Blaine put the truck into gear and started again, the low gears moaning, trailer and machine bumping back onto the road and gathering speed. Blaine changed gears. As the truck began to move faster, Blaine seemed to relax a little, finally becoming almost cheerful, while the truck moved along the sun-heated road, the trailer rocking from side to side, the dust coming off the wheels in gray-white curdles, the elephant trumpeting as before. The truck and trailer, which appeared to touch the road only as part of a continual bounding, had about them all the momentum of something not so much delivered by express as simply launched. Zimba's trunk waved from under the canopy, and the colors of the circus sign brought a hint of disaster, as though the colors were an advertisement for a fire.

The birthday party was being held in a gray house with a flat roof which sat, at once modern and stodgy, on a grassy hillside. It was long and low and was built in a U shape around a patio. There was a swimming pool and a cabana, a garage, and some Chinese elm trees which had been brought on a truck and planted with the help of a small crane, although now the leaves were a little yellow. The house had large glass windows and cement floors which were heated by electric coils. In front of the door there was a small cactus garden, the spiny plants looking healthy. From the back yard, beyond the tops of the Chinese elm trees, the Pacific could be seen. It was only about three quarters of a mile away, just close enough to offer the promise of escape.

There were other houses here, thirty or so altogether, the group of them seeming vulnerable to canyon fires and earthquakes, too. The architecture suggested a cemetery in which each monument is put up without concern for what the ones around it look like.

A bunch of balloons, bright as a handful of jelly beans, were tied to the front door. The air was still and the balloons pulled against their strings, but they were absolutely motionless. The truck stopped in front of the house, the trailer still covered with dust and appearing like some rented thing that, in new surroundings, suddenly looks tawdry.

"Jesus," said Blaine. "How much do you think it would cost to buy that house?"

"I'm not really too concerned about material possessions," said Will.

Blaine stared at him for a moment. Then he said, "Everyone in California is into real estate, even swamis."

Will shrugged.

"I just want a drink," he said.

The door of the house opened, and they could see all the way through the house into the back yard, to a bright blue shape like a pennant, which was a section of the pool.

A woman stepped out onto the porch and then into the sunlight, putting her forearm over her eyes. She was tall and thin, in her mid-thirties, and she was wearing a pair of white shorts and a blue man's shirt, the tails of which she had tied together. Her hair was frosted and cut short, and she had large white teeth. Her hair, her eyes, and her skin, too, seemed to have a sheen to them, a silver or almost whitish cast which suggested the glitter of snow after a cold night. She had a glass of fruit juice and ice in her hand, and when she took a step, she wobbled a little bit, not much, but enough to leave Blaine looking at her and saying to Will, "The thing about birthday parties is the kids never forget what happens."

Will looked at the glass the woman carried.

"I don't know," he said. "It might work out."

Zimba rocked from side to side and trumpeted, the noise lingering in the yard and over the other houses, insistent, demanding, and with an edge of desperation, too, which seemed to be just this side of despair.

A boy came out from behind the house, running with a furious locomotion along the side, racing up the drive and then turning toward the front door. He kept right on running until he stopped and stood by his mother and looked at the sign that said, "Zimba, the King of Elephants."

"Goddamn it, Mike," said the woman to the boy, "Your hair isn't combed. It's all messed up. Bend over."

"What are you going to do?" said the boy. As he asked the question, he kept his eyes on the elephant, which trumpeted again, a harsh, dry keening sound.

"Bend over," said the woman.

She poured half of her grapefruit juice and vodka into his sandy hair, the sticky fluid breaking over his head like water being poured onto a rock. His hair was very dry and it took a moment for the vodka and juice to sink in, and then he stood up, his eyes set on Zimba's. The woman had a comb in her back pocket and she used it now to comb the boy's hair, pushing it back in stylish, heavy strands. "There. You look nice."

The boy broke away, running straight to the truck, where he looked up at Blaine and said, "Are you really Raj?"

"No," said the driver. "Raj is sick."

"I saw Raj in an advertisement once," said Mike. "For Oscar Mayer franks."

"Zimba was in it, too," said Blaine. "They don't pay like what you'd think."

"Maybe you should tell the other kids the elephant is here," said Will.

Mike blinked in the sunlight, his hair smelling of grapefruit juice. He had an open, guileless expression. After a while he said, "I don't know any of them."

"Why not?" said Blaine.

His mother had a sip of her drink, rattling the cubes as she turned the bottom up.

"They're hired," said Mike. "We're new here and I don't know anybody yet."

"Well, the elephant's here," the woman said. "Everything will be fine now."

"Help me get him out," said Blaine to Will.

The elephant began to rock back and forth, the springs of the truck making a steady, repeated *squeak squeak squeak squeak*. In the greenish darkness underneath the canvas an eye could be seen as the animal swung its head up and down and tossed its trunk against the side of the trailer. The elephant had a scent, too, an acrid odor. In the shadows, the eye was dark and impenetrable. Blaine and Will got out of the truck.

Behind the house by the swimming pool there were eight or so boys, each sitting in a lawn chair and dangling his legs, each wearing a party hat. A record player had been set up, and the sound of early Beatles was reflected off the still swimming pool. None of the boys swung his legs in time to the music. There was a cabana in the back yard, a table with a cake and some soft drinks on it, and next to it a man was cooking hamburgers and hot dogs on a barbecue. In a diminutive way, the boys had the air of men waiting in an unemployment office. Mike told them the elephant had arrived, and they all stared at him. Then they went back to swinging their legs and waiting for the hamburgers to be cooked. Finally, Zimba made a very loud noise, and a couple of the boys raised their shoulders, which made each of them look like a turtle pulling in its head.

The tailgate was too heavy to put down gently, and the metal edge of it hit the ground with a *klang* in a sudden cloud of dust from the gutter. The elephant trumpeted and backed out, emerging from the shade inside, its hindquarters shifting this way and that, its feet, which were as big around as telephone poles, moving onto the ramp with a steady, surprisingly quick gait. Then Zimba emerged into the sunlight.

The elephant shook its head, the motion reminiscent of a dog that has gotten wet and is drying off, and as it did so, its ears sounded like a canvas sail luffing in a breeze. Then it stood on the grass and trumpeted, the sound clear and defiant. The grass had been sunburned to a yellowish green.

"Zimba. Zimba," said Blaine.

The animal didn't respond. It stood on the dry grass, throwing its trunk into the air.

"It's got its *must*," said Blaine. "Get the cattle prod."

"The elephant has its *must*," said Mike to his mother.

"Does that cost extra?" she asked.

Zimba charged. He seemed to be already running in the first two or three strides, the previously floppy, even silly gait transformed by its speed into something else entirely, the motion of his hips and shoulders, his legs, not only fast but somehow inspired: the movement was like that of some ponderous thing, like a wrecking ball, which, while slow to start, is nevertheless committed to one clear, direct course.

The elephant trumpeted and went past the corner of the house, its feet, like gray trash cans, tearing divots in the lawn the size of platters, its eyes rolling, its trunk swinging from side to side; the flanks, which worked in gray heaves as the elephant ran, the ears, the trunk, the blocklike compactness of the creature all combined into one onrushing and yet massive blur.

Will and Blaine simply turned and stared.

"I wish Raj was here," said Blaine.

The boys in the yard stood in an erratic line, all of them watching the elephant, each motionless, as though captured in one single frame from a film of the party.

The elephant charged down the drive, its gray shape somehow blending with the gray garage at the end, and for a moment there was a confused disorder, of both sound and motion, as the animal collided with the edge of the building; it seemed as though the siding had suddenly come alive, and then, there appeared in the air a number of small gray bits, which spun around the animal's head like insects in summer, but which in fact were pieces of wooden siding, thrown up in the first moment of impact. Then the elephant grunted and continued, leaving in its wake bits and pieces of wood and a yellow gash where the unpainted wood of the building could be seen. Then it passed between the pool and the garage, but it still hit the cabana, which was flimsy and burst into splinters, the pieces settling in front of the boys, who now turned to stare in the direction in which the elephant had gone.

"You get the truck," said Blaine. "See if you can keep parallel to him. I'll take the cattle prod."

*   *   *

Victor woke late and sat in bed, smoking cigarettes, watching as the threadlike strand of smoke rose into the cloud above him. He had a paint can on the floor which he used for an ashtray, and from time to time he put his hand out, letting his arm flop at the side of the bed, the ashes falling into the can. As Victor moved his arm, he thought, yeah. That's Zen. I can get the ashes in there without even looking.

The sun came in through the crack at the side of the shade, and the light cut into the smoke, making a kind of whitish sheet that stretched from the top of the window to the middle of the floor. It angled down like a rope holding up a circus tent. Then Victor began to think of Argentina. He figured that by the time he got there he'd have a suit, a good one like he saw in the *Esquire* dressing guide. He'd stay at the Plaza Hotel in Buenos Aires. Victor could almost see himself in the lobby, walking between the overstuffed chairs and the planters with the gigantic ferns growing in them. Yeah, sure. A bunch of greasers around to bring drinks.

He took a shower and dressed, taking a shirt from a pile of new ones, removing the pins and making an arrangement of them, and then pulling out the plastic strip from under the collar. He put on a pair of new gray slacks with pleats. The shirt was yellow, and he didn't think it went so well with the slacks and the suede jacket he had bought, and as he stood in front of the mirror, he thought the effect wasn't quite what he had wanted. Well, he'd buy another pair of pants and some wingtip shoes. That ought to take care of it.

He got into his car and drove out Sunset to North Flores Drive. It was just after two o'clock, and he was pretty sure that Frank's mother would be coming home soon from working the lunch shift. Victor pulled over and sat there, looking at the house. The flowers were the same as the last time he had been here, and for a while he thought of getting out and actually touching the flowers so he could tell, once and for all, if they were real or not. The house seemed quiet, but it also had a kind of sultry and only half-realized domestic quality, which Victor figured was a reflection of the fact of divorce: it left you with the anxiety of youth, but not with so many of the possibilities. After a while an older man who needed a shave walked by, pulling a shopping cart full of dirty laundry up to the corner. Must be a laundromat up there on Sunset. Probably charges a couple dollars a load.

Victor was glancing at his watch when Maggie emerged at the top of the block, walking in her high-heeled shoes and her fishnet stockings and that short skirt. She had on a red vest, too, over her blouse. She came along, passing the steps of the other houses, and as she walked she smoked a cigarette, swinging it back and forth next to her legs as she came. She stopped in front of her house and waited, looking at it with a kind of incomplete relief. Then she went up and pulled open the door.

Victor got out of the car and walked up the steps, glancing once at the flowers. Well, lookit that, will you? The things are real. Hell, you can grow anything in California. Just throw some seeds in the ground and you get anything you want. Smog doesn't seem to bother the plants at all. Not really.

He stood on the front porch. It was cool under the roof, and there was the scent of damp concrete, a slightly musty odor Victor associated with stifled desire. He could hear Maggie walking back and forth inside, the sound of her feet muffled, since she had kicked off her high-heeled shoes. Then Victor tapped on the frame and called through the screen, "Maggie."

She stopped now and came back, coming up close. Victor could smell the tobacco on her clothes, a kind of cologne or bath splash and a sweet fragrance of alcohol on her breath.

"Oh," she said. "It's you."

"Yeah," he said. "Can I come in?"

"Oh, sure," she said, unlatching the door. "Sure. I'd be glad of some company."

"No news of Frank is there?" said Victor.

"No," said Maggie. "Come in. You want something to drink?"

"Maybe just something to hold in my hand," he said.

"Sure," she said. "I know just what you mean."

The living room had a large, green sofa with a fuzzy material on it, a coffee table with some magazines, *Sports Afield* and *Cosmo*, and a rug on which some stains were visible. There was a TV set in a blond wood cabinet, and on top of it stood a planter with some ivy in it. The stuff looked real, too. Unbelievable. As Maggie went out to the kitchen, Victor watched the seams of her net stockings, which ran right down to the darker material of the heel. Then she came back and put a drink on the coffee table, moving over a copy of *Sports Afield* to put the drink on.

"Frank's taken off before," she said. "Everyone knows that."

"Uh-huh," said Victor.

He took a little sip. Old Grand Dad. Just like home.

"He'll turn up," she said.

"I guess it's a worry," said Victor.

"You don't know the half of it," she said.

She had been sitting with her knees together, elbows on them, but now she sat back.

"I guess that's right," he said. "But I've been thinking about him."

"He's a hard kid," she said. "Like his father. Look, I got these outdoors magazines, but he never looked at them. Except for the gun ads."

"Uh-huh," said Victor.

He took a sip of his drink now, wishing he hadn't. Got to be clear-headed in Malibu in a little while. Don't forget it.

"The worst is when I come home and the house is lonely," she said. "You hear the refrigerator going *uh uh uh* like I don't know what."

"It's the compressor," said Victor.

"Well, that's what I hear all the time," she said.

"Look," he said, "I'm sorry about Frank running off. That's all."

She leaned forward now, putting one hand on his sleeve.

"I know you are," she said. "I'm sorry he went."

Victor reached out and put his fingers on hers, which were warm. They sat that way for a moment, the house silent, that musty smell from the porch almost overwhelmed by her perfume and the smell of her cigarette. She smiled and then looked down.

Didn't take her hand away. Victor thought, I've forgotten how nice that is. Just to hold hands.

Got to get out to Malibu. Haven't got too much time.

"That's a new jacket, isn't it?" she asked.

"Yeah," he said. "Cost a thousand bucks."

"Did it?" She removed her hand and sat back.

"I was thinking of going on a little trip," he said. "Down to South America. Look around."

She nodded.

"You ever heard of the Plaza Hotel?" he asked.

"No," she said. "I haven't."

"It's real nice," he said. "In Buenos Aires. They call it B.A. You know, like L.A."

It was quiet now, but then the refrigerator came on, the sound throbbing, constant. A little breeze blew up, and the swing on the front porch began to make a slight creaking sound as it swayed back and forth. Maggie leaned forward, her hand on the sofa not far from his. Victor had another sip. Goddamn. No more to drink. Got to be sharp. Then he had another sip.

"I guess it's bad at night," he said.

"You don't know," she said.

"Don't be too sure," he said.

She looked right at him, leaning forward, and as Victor put down his drink, the telephone rang. Maggie turned and sighed and then got up and answered it.

"Yes," she said. "Speaking. Yes? When? Oh, God."

She covered the phone.

"They found Frank," she said. "He was in San Diego. Can you believe it?"

Then she put the phone back to her ear and listened, saying, "Uh-huh, uh-huh. When? Tomorrow? I'll be there. I'll write down the address. Sure. OK. Tomorrow afternoon."

She hung up and said, "Oh, God, isn't that wonderful?"

"It's a load off my mind, I can tell you that," said Victor.

He took another sip.

"Isn't that just wonderful?" Maggie said. "Oh, I just feel great."

"Yeah," said Victor.

"Maybe everything will be all right," she said. "Sometimes I get to the point where I think it's all going to cave in and then, you know, the phone rings."

Victor nodded. She sat down now on the sofa, Indian-style, the pattern of the net stockings becoming a little elongated on the inside of the thighs. The compressor in the refrigerator started its long, steady throb. Victor put his hand out on the sofa between them.

"I've been a little lonely," she said.

"Sure," said Victor. "It's no crime."

"Sometimes it feels like it is," she said.

Victor shrugged and felt stupid.

"Then they'd have to arrest me, I guess," he said.

"You?" she said. "With your thousand-dollar coat? Come on."

"I can't seem to find the right pants to go with it," said Victor.

"What you've got on is fine," said Maggie.

"Are you sure?"

She nodded.

"Well, I'm glad about Frank," said Victor. "I was worried."

"I know," she said.

She put her hand on his.

"Maybe I'll call in sick," she said.

In the bedroom, she undressed quickly, taking off the net stockings and the short skirt and getting under the covers. The room had the scent of perfume and cigarettes and that odor of damp concrete, but under the covers the touch of her skin was very warm, and even the whiff of the bourbon on her breath had a kind of magic to it, the scent of it simply leaving Victor with the impression that he was somehow pulled along by it, the warmth of it running through his eyes and mouth, through his arms and along his spine. She said, "That's wonderful. Just wonderful," and closed her eyes. Sure. Some things just work out after all. They sat side by side, both of them smoking, and when Victor flopped an arm to the side of the bed and let the ash go, he saw that it had fallen into an ashtray, right there. Yeah. Some things are just fine. Might be nice to spend a little time here, not long, just a couple of nights. He sat there, a little surprised by the sudden ache. She'd be there in the middle of the night. He'd be able to hear her breathing.

"I've got to go soon," he said.

"Where?"

"Out to Malibu." He reached down for one of his socks. "I'll call you later."

"Promise?" she said.

"Sure." He picked up the other sock. "Maybe we can go out and celebrate."

"I'd like that," she said.

"Well, OK," he said. "It's a date."

The sound from the compressor came on again, and Maggie listened to it, closing her eyes as she did so.

"We're going to have a lot to celebrate," said Victor. "You just wait."

"Are you really coming back?" she asked.

"Well, sure," he said. "I give you my word."

She looked at him, trying to decide what it was worth.

"Just show up," she said. "You don't have to make a federal case out of it."

Then he got up and started dressing, listening to the sound of the refrigerator. Maybe he could buy her a new one so she wouldn't have to listen to that sound. Brand name, too. Norge. G.E. Whirlpool.

*   *   *

Taylor Hayden thought the Chevrolet ran just fine, although there was a smell in it he didn't like, a rank, penetrating odor he thought might be cigar smoke that had been run through the air conditioner a couple of times, but as he drove the car, he became convinced it was something else. Maybe someone had been doing ether or something in the car, because there was, underneath the lingering stink of the cigar, a medical quality, the two odors intermingling. Taylor drove the car with only a little bit of his fingers touching the steering wheel, and when he changed gears, thanking God that the thing was an automatic, he took the lever with just the tips of his fingers. Then he was sure what the stink was. Some guy probably was getting chemotherapy for cancer somewhere and on the way home he got sick in the car. That's what the stink is. And then the guy leaves his car for a while and comes back to find the goddamn thing stolen.

Taylor drove at the speed limit going up Pico, and then he pulled over and stopped, getting out and going into a cut-rate drug store, where he bought a can of Lysol which he sprayed around inside to cover up the smell. Then he sat and thought that now, after the Lysol, the car smelled just like the room in the Travelodge out there on Ventura where he had bought the gun.

He dropped the nearly full can of Lysol in a trash can and then drove over to Western. There wasn't much traffic, and he drove slowly, handling the car with a subdued air. He made a smooth turn into Victor's street, pulled over, and waited, smelling the reassuring odor of the Lysol but still not liking the stink that had been underneath it. Sometimes he was convinced there was an odor to bad luck or stupidity, and he imagined that if there was one, it was like what was in the car. Then he counted to thirty by threes and said, Yeah, sure. It's the third. Time to close the door.

He had parked on the north side of the street, which was where Victor's apartment house was. That way when Taylor came out, he wouldn't have to cross the street. People can always get a better look at a man standing in the open, like in the middle of a road, than when he is surrounded by clutter, the dead bushes on the walk, say, or maybe some garbage cans on the street, or the interior of a stinking car. That goddamn hard-of-hearing car thief. Next time he was going to have to get a car that didn't stink like cancer treatment.

Taylor had the badge in his pants pocket and the pistol in the side pocket of his sport coat. A cheap one from J. C. Penney's, just like some cop on a half-assed salary could afford. The baggie was in the glove box. Badge, bag, and piece, that made three. Everything fine.

Victor emerged from the apartment door. He was wearing a yellow shirt, a pair of gray pants, and that suede jacket. Usually Victor stayed in his apartment all afternoon, doing nothing until he was ready to get something to eat at the chicken takeout place up on Western. Sometimes he went down to see a hooker who hung around in bars on Melrose and Western. Taylor had gone in once and asked for change, just to see what was going on. The woman Victor sat with was short, with blond hair and thin legs. Taylor bet he didn't even use a condom. Jesus. Taylor liked the idea of condoms. Keep everything neat and clean. No mess. All the bodily fluids under wraps. If you looked at it the right way, it had a kind of beauty. He drew the line at colored ones, though, the pink and red kind. If he wanted to look at a flower, then he'd go to a florist. You don't have to make your pecker look like a chrysanthemum, for Christ's sake. But then again maybe there was a possibility of putting a message on the things, advertisements maybe, like "Shop at Ralph's." Taylor would have to think it over.

Now, though, Victor came out of his apartment. Taylor knew what the drill was here. If the schedule wasn't right, if somebody is doing the wrong thing, then go home and come back the next day. Or come back and wait until later, then do it the way it had been planned, just walking up to the door. That way you kept control of everything, no chances, no stupidity, everything as clean as a dry cleaner's plastic bag. So he sat there, watching Victor, thinking it over. Taylor figured Victor wasn't dependable.

Taylor had the impulse to go up to the walk that led from the apartment house and do it right by those dead rosebushes, just *bang* and then turn and walk away, the entire thing not taking more than five or ten seconds. Impulses were a sign of boredom or maybe impatience, but in either case they were a warning. Definitely. Taylor waited, the urge to do something stupid ebbing now, leaving him a little tired and faintly nauseated.

Victor got into his car and started the engine. It burned oil, and a black column of smoke rose in discrete pulses from the exhaust pipe. The odor, like the smell of a burning tire, drifted toward Taylor's car, penetrating even through the cracks around the rolled-up windows. Well, he's going to get a ticket. Taylor hoped it wasn't going to happen while he was following the car.

Taylor thought about a friend of his, a doctor he had met at the health club who had told a story about medical school. Taylor's friend had been in an anatomy class where everyone had been assigned a cadaver, and the instructor had said, "There is one rule here. You must never, and I mean never, try to find out who these people were." Taylor had understood this immediately: he had a rule, too, which was to keep what you knew to a minimum. It was the best way. But even so, Taylor thought, didn't a medical student ever get a little curious? Or want to know one small, definite thing, like what kind of ice cream the poor bastard liked, or what he wore to get married, or what made him cry?

Taylor knew the smart thing was to turn around and go home, or to drive over to the *go* club and find somebody who would give him a real game, maybe one of those Japanese guys who work for the electronic companies out there in Little Tokyo. Some of them were so gentle they looked like a newly uncurling leaf. So, it came as a surprise to Taylor that he had started the engine and begun to follow Victor, thinking, There's a lot about this whole thing that doesn't add up. Like where did that hick get the money to buy a coat like that?

Victor drove to North Flores and stopped in front of a house. A woman came down the street. Victor went in. The street was pretty quiet, the air smelling of the reassuring scent of stale cooking and grass that had been cut the day before. Taylor thought maybe he could go into the house right here, but then he didn't know what he would be getting into this way, and so he went on waiting, thinking about the woman in those fishnet stockings. He bet that Victor wasn't using a condom here, either. Let's face it, the guy's a one-man epidemic. Sometimes Taylor was amazed at how dangerously people lived. They didn't think about the future. Taylor had a stock portfolio in which there was a nice mixture of stocks and bonds, and he had a little venture capital, too. The right amount of cash. He particularly liked some of those high-yield municipals. He had it all worked out, right down to the amount of risk and exposure he could take even in a bad market. There were some tricks of the trade. What he really needed was enough money to get into selling pornography in Russia. The Russians were just bleeding meat.

Victor came out of the house and stood in the shadows of the front porch, looking first one way and then the other, running a hand through his hair. Maybe he's thinking he should have used a condom. Maybe that's it. But Taylor wasn't so sure. Victor walked out into the street, his shadow sweeping along the ground around his feet in a round gray blob. Then Victor got into his car and drove up to Highland, and then, in front of the Hollywood Bowl, he turned onto the Hollywood Freeway, outbound.

Taylor followed Victor to the Ventura Freeway and then out through Malibu Canyon. It was late afternoon now, and the edge of those smooth, reassuring hills cast bluish shadows. The afternoons were always the nicest time of the day in California, especially out toward the beach. Taylor thought, The guy's going to Malibu. Probably going to bring some disease out there. But then Taylor thought about it some more and decided that, if anything, Victor was going to do some business. Taylor kept on following the car, shrugging as though there were some things that couldn't be avoided. Finally, Victor turned onto a dirt road in Malibu.

Taylor waited for a minute and then made the turn too, figuring he could stay back and still keep track of where Victor went by the dust that hung in the road. The dust mixed with the blue-gray smoke from Victor's car in such a way as to remind Taylor of something final, like ashes and the scent of a newly polished urn.

*   *   *

In the afternoon the light hit the front of Warren Hodges's house, bringing out the mica in the stone. The filaments of it were large, and from a distance their shimmer had an ethereal quality, as though there were thousands of insects with transparent wings clinging to the front of the house.

Marta drove through the orange grove. In the yellow light the leaves seemed muted and soft, and the hazy globes of fruit suggested warmth, like lips covered with a bright orange lipstick. In the center of each tree, tatters of green light hung in the darker, more emerald shade.

Marta pulled up in front of the house and switched off the

engine. Above her she could see the filamentlike shimmer of the stones of the house, and as she looked at it, she wondered what it was that made the difference between things turning out the way you wanted and their collapsing into disaster. She concentrated on the mica in the stone. The flakes had a magical quality, if only because of the days they had been seen when the house had been on the coast of France. It seemed to her that the shimmer must have been more beautiful in France than here.

Warren answered her knock, pulling the door open and letting her in, saying, "Hello." He was wearing a pair of cotton pants and a blue shirt and brown shoes, and his hair was slicked back, wet from the shower. He was about to speak again, but he hesitated and then shut the door behind her. The door was heavy, and it made a small, dry sucking noise as it swung into the frame, and as Marta heard the sound, she thought about his hesitation. Maybe he's had time to think it over. Maybe he's realized he met me at one of those parties he gives for hustlers and dreamers. I guess he thinks he's made a mistake. So she waited, angry about the time he had spent away from her, as though those hours had pulled him back into a life in which there was no place for her. Just like that.

Then she thought, Maybe he will offer me money.

"Let's sit here," he said, moving into the living room. There were two sofas, set together at right angles, cream-colored ones in front of which there was a large, low table. There was a bowl of fruit on it now, the green orbs of the grapes, bunched together in clusters, the delicious apples with a sheen like lipstick, and bananas, each curved into a shape like a jumping trout. Through the clean glass of the window, beyond the bowl of fruit, the Pacific was visible, the horizon appearing like a piece of light blue paper laid across the middle of another piece which was a darker blue. A knife with a wooden handle and a sharp blade sat on the table next to the fruit.

She didn't look at him. Marta wanted to have no illusions about what was happening here and what was waiting for her, too, at the end of the grove. It was difficult to keep them separate, and for a moment it seemed to her the atmosphere Victor carried with him was somehow loose in this room.

He picked up the knife and a pear and said, "Would you like a slice?"

"No thanks," she said.

"Are you sure? They're very good."

"I said I didn't want any," she said.

He glanced up at her. Then he put the knife and the pear down.

"You seem on edge," he said.

"A little. Not much."

"What's the trouble?" he asked.

"You speak as though you could fix it," she said.

"Maybe I can," he said.

She looked out the window. The sky was a high gray-blue, marked here and there by a trail left by a jet airplane, the smoke flowing in a long, straight curdle.

"You can speak frankly," he said.

"I don't know," she said. She shook her head. "I just want to spend a nice afternoon with you. That's all."

"Is it money?" he said. "Do you want to ask me for money?"

She closed her eyes.

"Is that it?" he said.

"You think that of me?" she said. "That I'm just someone you met at the parties you give here and that now I'm going to put the bite on you. Is that what you think?"

"It's happened before," he said. "Sometimes more gently than others. But, yeah. It's happened."

"And you'd give me money?" she said.

"I guess so."

She stared at him and thought, See. Just like that. How easy.

She glanced out the window, the one in the front of the house, beyond which there stood the orange grove. It seemed that she could see a faint line of dust rising from it, going into the air like smoke, or maybe a pesticide that had been sprayed there. Is that him? she thought. Is Victor out there waiting?

"How much would you give me if I asked?" she said. "How about twenty thousand dollars?"

"In cash?" he said.

"Yes."

"I could probably get it," he said. "The bank down by the sheriff's station would probably give me the cash if I called."

They sat opposite each other, both of them trembling a little. He picked up the knife and then put it down again with a hard, final click.

"Well, is that it?" he said.

She stared out at the horizon where that line divided the sea from the sky.

"Is that the way you think of me?" she said.

She reached over and picked up the knife.

"Well," she said, "Tell me. Do you think I just want money?"

Her fingers were trembling as she picked up a pear and cut a slice from it, which she put into her mouth, chewing it, tasting the juice, the sweetness of it seeming to coalesce with her anger, as though fury could be a cloying, sugary liquid.

He looked directly back at her and said, "I love you." He looked down. "Let's stop talking about money. I don't think that's what you're interested in."

Marta glanced out now at the grove. The dust at the end seemed to be a little thicker, as though a car had pulled up out there.

"I'm having a little trouble with some people in New York. Everyone seems to want money," he said. He looked out the window. "I'll take care of New York. I know what they want. It's nothing that can't be fixed." He looked back now. "I'm a little tired, I guess. Maybe we could sleep for a little. Maybe that would help us both."

She was sure now. It was dust all right, the stuff billowing up into the air.

"Maybe for a little while," she said.

"It would be nice," he said.

She looked at him and nodded.

"Yes," she said. "Sure."

She glanced out the window.

"If I can't sleep, maybe I'll take a walk," she said. "Maybe I'll just go out into the grove."

They walked upstairs, around the broad staircase and then down the hall, into which wedges of light shone from the windows. From the bedroom windows Marta could see the dusty leaves of the eucalyptus trees on the hillside and the fawn-colored bark, which had peeled away to reveal pinkish wood. Warren lay down and was almost instantly asleep, saying once with his eyes closed, "I offered New York everything I could. You know that? Well, let them wait for a while." Marta curled up next to him and looked at the painting in which there were those piercingly bright colors. The flowers in the field the painting depicted looked like hot coals. So hot as to be sticky.

In the distance she heard a high, almost musical sound, and even though she couldn't distinguish it clearly, she still had the unmistakable sensation of a junglelike shriek, not monkeys exactly, or birds, although that was a possibility, but something else. Then she guessed her nerves were getting the better of her.

In the bathroom she splashed some water on her face, staring at her expression in the mirror, which gave her a moment's pause: she didn't look resigned, as she had imagined, but almost serene. Well, it figures, doesn't it? You make a decision and that brings something right away. Then she sat down on the edge of the tub, her head in her hands, realizing there was no way of avoiding the grove any longer. And as she sat there, she heard again that distant, wild sound, part shriek, part deep and vibrant trumpeting.

Downstairs she stood in the living room, feeling around her the silence of the house. The silence had a softness, almost a powdery quality which seemed, above everything else, dry and clean. There was no dust in the air, and there was the slight, reassuring odor of furniture polish, which, as nearly as she could make out, had a little lemon in it. Everything about the furniture and the clean windows seemed to her evidence of all the promise she had somehow been denied. She could have waited there for hours, taking from this comfortable, clean room filled with sunlight an idea of how she would like to live, as though that warm caress of the air in the room, almost like the touch of powder against her skin, contained the essence of her most secret, most cherished desires. Then she reached down and picked up the knife that lay on the table next to the bowl of fruit. The blade was about five inches long and made of the best steel. She hid it in the sleeve of her jacket, an expensive one she had bought through the mail.

She opened the heavy door downstairs, noticing how little effort it took to move it on its hinges, and the smoothness and the weight suggested to her the ease with which her anger now seemed to move through her: it seemed to have an almost silky quality, as it worked its way out of the repository where it was usually confined. She started walking away from the house toward the end of the grove, where she had seen the dust but where the air was now clear and still.

A hawk sat on top of one of the telephone poles that ran along the drive, its feathers dappled, brown and dark brown and a little white, its beak hooked, its head turned over one of its shoulders as it looked at the grass beyond the grove.

The dust made puffs around Marta's feet, its whiteness trailing away in slow-moving clouds. It reminded her of smoke, and she liked the idea, which came and went very quickly, that she was scorching the earth just by walking across it. From the groves came the acrid odor of citrus trees and the scent of the oranges, which hung symmetrically, like balls on a Christmas tree. And as Marta went, she noticed, too, the smell of a cigarette: Victor was there.

The trees were laid out in ten rows, each about thirty trees long, and she walked between them, stopping from time to time to see if she could hear any movement, any shuffling, anything at all. The odor of cigarette smoke was stronger now.

A howl came from the ridge behind the grove, a long shriek, not trumpeting so much as something like the rising protest a saw in a lumber mill makes the instant it cuts into a log. Marta stopped to listen, momentarily distracted not by the sound so much as by something else altogether: she recalled that moment when she had sat in the house in Ferndale, when she had felt reduced to nothing more than bits and pieces, and now, as she anticipated letting go, the sensation came back again, checked by one thought now: how would she go on loving someone if she had simply turned into a chaotic impulse, if she had ceased to exist?

She realized that she was standing in the shadow of a large

tree, trembling. Then she started walking again, toward that scent.

"Hiya," said Victor.

Marta stood before him.

"You got it?" asked Victor.

"Yeah," she said. "Right here."

"How much?" he said.

"Oh," she said. "I'll let you count it."

"Good," said Victor. "Give it here."

She looked him full in the face.

"You're shaking like a leaf," he said.

"Am I?"

"You got a cold or something?" he said. "If you got a fever you should be in bed. Best thing. Take something like Tylenol."

The blade of the knife was up her sleeve and her fingers were around the handle of the knife, which she squeezed, clinging to it as though it were the one hard thing that kept her anchored to this spot. She glanced at Victor's coat. Jesus, just look at it. It's got gold buttons, doesn't it? And it smells like a new football.

"Well," said Victor. "What are you waiting for? Give it here."

He held out his hand.

"Hey, cat got your tongue?" said Victor.

"No," she said. "No. I came out here to tell you something."

"No you didn't," said Victor. "You came out here to give me money. Remember?"

She shook her head.

"I'm not giving you any money," she said.

"Well, well," said Victor. "And I'm going to have to drive through the rush hour traffic for this?"

"I'm not giving you any money."

"Well, well," said Victor. "If that's the way you want it, I guess I'll just go down to the Hollywood station. I guess that's what I'll do."

Marta shrugged. "I'm going to take my chances."

"Lady," said Victor, "you haven't got a chance. See ya."

The elephant appeared now, coming over the top of the ridge. It stood in profile, like an immense gray cutout, dusty, seeming to materialize there. Its ears hung at the side of its head, and its trunk hung straight down, although it was clear that it was taking huge breaths. It looked back, the way it had come, and then raised its head, swung its trunk up, and trumpeted. The elephant's back was dusty, and for a moment Marta stared at it, blinking until she was able to think, That's not flour. That's plaster.

A green piece of cloth, scalloped along the edge and lined with white piping, hung from the animal's head. It gave the elephant a riotous quality, as though it wore what was left of an awning as a costume.

"That looks like part of an awning," said Marta.

Victor just stared, as though the elephant's arrival was more unexpected luck he just couldn't make sense of.

Warren now came up through the orchard, looking toward the elephant, which stood on the ridge. He called out once, and as he did, Victor stepped back into the shadows, simply vanishing into the edge of the grove, where he waited.

Hodges was buttoning his shirt as he came up, saying, "Look. Look at it."

Marta put the knife into the pocket of her coat. The animal trumpeted and then eased its weight from one foot to another. Finally, it stood absolutely still, the triangular slash of its mouth red, one of its eyes large and glassy, its tongue rounded and dry-looking.

Marta turned to Warren and said, "I couldn't kill him."

Warren glanced up at the elephant and then back again, his eyes sweeping down to Marta. Her hair was bright in the sunshine as she bit her lips, her entire aspect one of coming to terms with something, and as she waited, mystified by the appearance of the animal and the possibilities she now faced, Warren concentrated. He didn't know who she meant, but as she stood in the sunlight, her expression a mixture of defiance and relief, he realized she was giving him something. Then he thought, Whatever you do, don't ask any questions. Not now. She'll tell you. Just keep your mouth shut.

So he stood there, waiting, glancing from time to time at the elephant, which began to shift its weight again from one foot to another. Then Warren turned back and said, "Well, thank God you didn't kill him."

"I've got some trouble now," she said.

"Who doesn't?" said Warren.

The elephant turned its head once toward the cluster of houses below. Then it started moving downhill, back the way it had come, going through the grass, the awning streaming along its sides. The animal left a wake through the grass about as wide as the path of a bulldozer. Down below there were the houses, some of which, even from a distance, showed traces of that same schematic path, although it wasn't just a matter of flattened grass but of walls destroyed, fences smashed, and a kind of wake of lawn chairs, awnings, wire, uprooted trees, and at least one over-turned automobile. Two police cars from the sheriff's station and two uniformed officers were down below, the men obviously hoping the animal wouldn't come toward them. One of them reached into his car and picked up the microphone of the radio. Even from a distance it was clear that he was shouting into it.

"Why don't they leave the damn thing alone?" said Warren. Then he and Marta started following it.

Victor waited for a few minutes and then walked back into the sunlight. He climbed the ridge and looked at the houses, some of which showed the sad disorder of broken walls through which furniture was visible. Debris was spread through the yards and across swimming pools, the prospect of damage appearing like an aerial photograph of a town after a windstorm. Victor looked at it until Taylor Hayden stepped out of the shadows and said, "Psst. Hey. Over here."

"What?" said Victor. "Jesus. Look at all those houses. All broken up. Who knows what kind of stuff there is lying around down there. It's a real opportunity."

"Down here," said Taylor. He held out the badge. "Stand down here below me. In the shade."

"Are you a cop?" asked Victor.

"Yes," said Taylor. "From Santa Monica."

There were shots from the other side of the ridge. The elephant trumpeted.

"Right here," said Taylor.

"They're shooting at the elephant down there," said Victor.

"I guess I have to tell you three times," said Taylor. "Get down here."

*   *   *

The elephant stood in the back yard of a house not far from the beach. The ground here was sandy, and the elephant pawed at it a little, looking one way and then another. The piece of awning had been lost along the way, although someone, a resident with a pistol probably, or maybe someone with a deer rifle, had taken a shot, and on the gray skin a wet and ruby-colored streak ran from a hole in the elephant's shoulder. Across the back of the yard stood a group of people, all of them sweating in the heat. A man in a business suit, his hair powdered with plaster dust, watched the animal with constant, if not profound disbelief. One of the policemen had a rifle, which he now pointed at the elephant. He started shooting, once and then again, emptying the clip. The elephant flapped his ears each time he was hit and then looked around at the hillside and the pale darkening sky above it. The dusk had come with a purple quality in the east, although lighter colors, yellows and a deep red, were higher in the sky. When a bullet hit the elephant's side, it made a sound like someone beating a carpet with a broom. The policeman with the rifle stood, too, looking at the elephant. He held the empty rifle and waited.

"I guess they don't go down like in the movies," he said.

"No," said the other policeman. "I guess not. What are we going to do now?"

"I don't know," said the first policeman. "Wait."

"Look at this place," said the other policeman. He gestured toward the houses on the hillside, their walls broken, cries of disbelief falling into the back yard as gently as snow.

"Well, there's nothing left to do but wait," said the first policeman. "That's arterial blood, isn't it?"

"Maybe," said the other policeman.

Warren and Marta came up to the yard, emerging from the dry grass, and stood at the back of the group of fifteen or so people who were watching the elephant. Marta was breathing hard, and as she looked at the elephant, it seemed to be the physical locus around which everything that was unpredictable coalesced. Then she put a hand to her face and said to Warren, "You have no idea how close I came to doing it."

"I understand," said Warren.

Marta now turned and stared at the elephant, which swung its trunk back and forth like a pendulum. Then the elephant started running, pushing past the people who had followed it, its motion somehow making the animal seem a little more compact and unstoppable, like some usually stationary thing, a refrigerator, say, that has been pushed down a ramp. The people were accustomed to this now, and they didn't shriek or make any sound at all; they just got out of the way, although one of them, rather than yelling or shouting, began a steady, unemphatic swearing. Then Warren went after the animal, with one seamless impulse, as if by going after it he could find out what he should say. Well, it had better be the right thing.

The ground rumbled, and there was an ominous cracking as a fence gave way, the weathered gray planks breaking and revealing the white wood underneath, the splinters seeming to fly into the air as if the elephant trailed bits of itself. And even before there was any cessation of the sound of the fence breaking, even while there was still debris in the air, bits and pieces of wood and leaves making a kind of cloud, the people drew in behind the elephant and followed. Blood now trailed over the gray skin in rivulets as thick as a finger.

"I wish they wouldn't shoot it," said Warren.

The elephant turned over a car, a small Japanese one, which made a crumpling noise as it came to rest on its side. Then the animal walked more slowly, its eyes turned toward the ocean.

The brownish landscape dropped off abruptly into the narrow coastal plain. There was a road that went between two humped-up hills and then down to the highway, but the road curved, and the elephant now chose to walk in a straight line, its eyes set on the horizon.

On the flat land between the hills and the ocean there was a greenhouse, a long one, the panes of glass filled with light and appearing like square pieces of foil. It was impossible to see inside, but there were rows of flowers, and the collection of petals, red and green and bright blue, made for an unexpected moment as the elephant went through the glass, knocking pieces of it into the air like a mastodon running through an ice-encrusted forest at the beginning of the Ice Age. The glass rose in triangular sections, each catching the light, and around the flashing pieces in the yellow and silver sections, there was that sudden appearance of bright red and yellow and orange petals, which then mixed with the splinters and hung there with them, all turning in a slow and appalling levitation before simply collapsing into a pile of junk as the elephant departed and began to make its way to the beach. And as the glass and flower petals hung in the air, Warren stopped, reached out and took Marta's arm, stopping her. He was panting now, and he said to her, the words coming in bunches, "I'll take my chances with you. All right?"

The elephant crossed the highway and passed between two houses down to the sand. Its footprints were the size of a trash can lid and the trail it left behind suggested the path of some large piece of machinery. It crossed the sand and went down to the water, where it stopped and looked into the distance before wading out. The surf was calm, and the animal went through the three-foot waves, the foam splashing around it in a V-shaped wake. In the west the sun was almost gone, and the sky appeared in neat layers, red, then yellow and gray-blue. The water around the animal took on a pinkish cast, and washed along the coast, drawn by the currents. The foam had a reddish tint. There were probably twenty-five or thirty people who stood on the beach watching, many of them covered with plaster dust, all of them looking tired. The animal stared at the horizon, where it seemed to be attracted to some infinite distance, as though the elephant could be unmolested there. It waded out until its shoulders were covered, its head up, and then it began to wash itself.

The elephant trumpeted again, more urgently than ever. Then it went back to washing itself in the pink foam until it seemed to kneel, its legs collapsing, the water closing over its head and back. Birds turned in a downward spiral over the turmoil the elephant had left behind on the surface of the water.

Two men walked down to the beach from the truck that had the circuslike sign on its side, the reds and yellows and the legend "Zimba, the King of Elephants." Blaine still wore his sultan's pants, although he had lost his turban someplace and his face was scratched, the congealed blood at the end of each scratch as bright as a cherry. He stood and stared at the ocean and said, "What are we going to say to Raj?"

Spike

T AYLOR HAYDEN SAT at table in a *go* club in Little Tokyo
opposite a man who wore a dark suit, a white shirt, and a
blue tie. In the room there was an arrangement of flowers, the
chrysanthemums and ferns and a couple of orchids startling
against the gray background of the wall behind them. The *go*
club had good, heavy stones to play with, and you could get a
cup of tea, too. There was almost no noise of traffic from the
street, and the only sound in the room was the occasional movement of someone walking quietly out to the bathroom, the gentle
touch of a porcelain teacup on the table, and the final click as
someone in the club made a decision and put down a stone.

Taylor had done everything right: he had put a rat-tail file in
the pistol and had roughed up the inside so the ballistics were
changed forever. Then he had broken it down and thrown the
pieces in the ocean at different places. He had burned the clothes
he had worn in the fireplace in his apartment, which had a gas
starter underneath the rack that held logs. In fact, the fireplace
was the reason Taylor had rented the place. And when the
clothes had been reduced to nothing more than ashes, he had
spread them along Mulholland Drive, out there on that part
toward the radar station. He pretended he was looking at his tire
when he had done it. He could see Los Angeles clearly from
there, the blue mountains in the distance, the clutter in the valley,
the island of smog which hung above the houses. He guessed
he'd like to live some other place. Maybe he'd take a trip up to
Seattle. That was the hot place these days, wasn't it?

Taylor held a stone in his hand and thought about making his play, but as he did, he kept thinking, There are some things you just can't figure. He had leaned down, close to Victor, who was trying to say something, just whispering into the dust at the back of the grove, his lips moving slowly, like a tired fish that's been out of water just a little too long. So Taylor bent down and listened, and Victor said one word, over and over, just one: "Twinkie." Then Taylor pushed it out of his mind and made his play. Yeah, Seattle might be the place. California was winding down.

The Scandal Sheet

CLASSIFIEDS

ZEN SHOES FOR TIRED FEET. Buena Vista. Ask for Sam. Evenings. 768-4578.

FREE CASH, anytime. Big Bucks. Call the Money Man. Visa Card Required. Redondo, mornings. Ask for Mickey. 879-8976.

BIGGER BREASTS. Easy, no-staining cream. Stars swear by it. Burbank, Box 3458, Department E-1457.

DIPLOMAS, Harvard, Yale, Dartmouth, Medical and Law Schools in *Latin*. Don't be held back by lack of an education. International Certification, North Hollywood, Box 4451.

CURE CANCER, Tibetan recipes, rice and herbs, proven formulas. Box 369 Redondo, Flower-patterned condoms, other novelties.

ANTI-AGING CREAM, secret of the Aztecs, six scents. The straight dope. Call Marylee, Van Nuys, 349-1098.

JACK HAWK'S AROUND TOWN, *Scandal a la Mode*

Thrill Seeker Killed in Malibu Mayhem. Things in Malibu took a turn for the worse the other night when Zimba the Elephant (herein advertised) went wild at a birthday party. Local citizens, including International Pictures' own **Warren Hodges,** took pains to remove the offending animal. Three quarters of the residents of Malibu are armed, and in the random shooting a thrill seeker,

Victor Shaw, was apparently killed in a freak accident. Hodges, by the way, is going to tie the knot, girls, with a townie, **Marta Brooks.** Marta's mother, Blanche Brooks, was quoted as saying the couple is going to have a wedding with "all the trimmings."

OBITUARIES

Jack Nelson, cowboy who worked with Crash Corgon and Gabby Hayes.
Miguel Serrano, one-time hairdresser for Troy McGill.
Zimba.